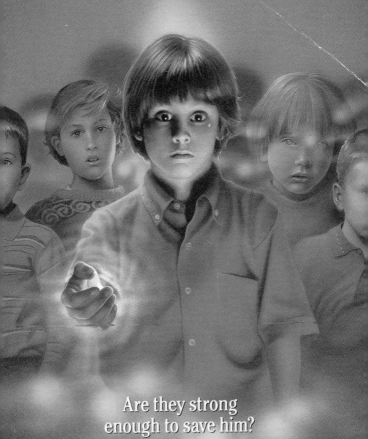

Are they strong
enough to save him?

BY THE SAME AUTHOR

Xenocide
Maps in a Mirror: The Short Fiction of Orson Scott Card
The Folk of the Fringe
The Abyss
Treason
Seventh Son
Red Prophet
Prentice Alvin
Wyrms
Ender's Game
Speaker for the Dead
Saints
Songmaster

LOST BOYS

ORSON SCOTT CARD

HarperPaperbacks
*A Division of HarperCollins*Publishers

HarperPaperbacks *A Division of* HarperCollins*Publishers*
10 East 53rd Street, New York, N.Y. 10022

To Erin and Phillip Absher
for sharing your lives with us
and for your love and care
for Charlie Ben

Acknowledgments

My thanks to:

The students of Watauga College at Appalachian State University, who heard the first impromptu telling of this tale on Halloween;

Ed Ferman, for believing in the original short story;

The people who wrote heartfelt letters responding to the short story, which helped me keep this tale alive;

Eamon Dolan, my editor, for insightful suggestions and patience beyond belief;

Wayne Williams, for an extra week at the beach, where the first half of this novel was written;

Clark and Kathy Kidd, for the second half (among so many things);

Scott Jones Allen, for downloading reams of text and a thousand other helps;

Clark L. Kidd, for the third word of Chapter 8;

Dave Dollahite, for a parallax view;

Jay Wentworth, for filling in and making the show go on;

Erin, Phillip, Jones, Kathy, Geoff, and Emily, for reading and responding to chapters as they came;

Kristine, for keeping the children alive, the cars running, the floors dry, and both story and storyteller in balance;

and Charlie Ben, for the heart of the tale.

Contents

Boy   1

1. Junk Man   4
2. Maggots   17
3. Gallowglass   32
4. Yucky Holes   52
5. Hacker Snack   89
6. Inspiration   139
7. Crickets   172
8. Shrink   246
9. June Bugs   289
10. Independence Day   331
11. Zap   365
12. Friends   415
13. God   452
14. Christmas Eve   491
15. New Year   524

Contents

• B O Y •

This is what his father always called him whenever he'd done something bad: "Where were *you* when this happened, *Boy?* What did you think you were doing, *Boy?*"

He took that word inside himself and it became the name for all his bad desires. It was Boy who made him play pranks that weren't funny to anybody, Boy who made him cheat on tests when he felt like it in school, even though he always knew the answers and didn't have to cheat. It was Boy who made him stand and watch from the closet when his parents thought he was in bed and he saw them do the dog thing, Father's belly so loose and jiggly, Mother so white and weak and dead while it happened, her breasts flopped out flat to either side like fish.

1

It was the worst thing Boy had ever made him do, to watch that, and to his surprise Boy didn't like it, no, Boy hated it even worse than *he* did, to see Father be so bad.

I will never do that, said Boy inside him. It's ugly to kill a woman like that and then make her still be alive afterward so you can do it all again.

From then on when he looked at big women with their breasts and their secrets and their faces that could turn dead looking at a man, Boy went away. Boy didn't want to be part of *that* game.

But that didn't mean that Boy was gone, no, nor silent neither. Boy was still there, and he got his way sometimes, yes; and he found new things to want. Only Boy wasn't careful. Boy only wanted what he wanted until he got it and then he went back into hiding and left *him* to take care of everything, to take all the blame for what Boy had done even though *he* hadn't wanted to do it in the first place.

Now none of his people would let him near their children because of the things Boy had decided he had to do. Damn you Boy! Die and damn you!

But they promised not to tell, says Boy. The children said they wouldn't tell but then they did.

What do you expect, you stupid ugly Boy? What do you expect, you evil Boy? Didn't you ever think maybe there's another Boy inside *them* that makes them lie to you and promise not to tell but then they break their word because *their* Boy made them? And now here you are, and that'll show you, Boy, because nobody will let you near their children anymore so you'll just have to chew on yourself when you get hungry and drink yourself when you get dry.

No I won't, says Boy. I'll make a place and I'll take them there and I won't ever believe them when they promise not to tell. I'll take them there and nobody will know where they are and they'll never come back and so they'll never tell.

You won't do anything like that, Boy, because I won't let you.

And Boy just laughed and laughed inside him, and he knew that he *would* do it all, he would prepare the hiding place and then he would go and find them for Boy and bring them back, and Boy would do what he wanted. Boy would not be afraid. Boy would do everything he thought of doing, because he knew that they would never leave and they would never tell.

That was why those little boys in Steuben started disappearing, and why not one of them was found till Christmas Eve in 1983.

1

·JUNK MAN·

This is the car they drove from Vigor, Indiana, to Steuben, North Carolina: a silvery-gray Renault 18i deluxe wagon, an '81 model with about forty thousand miles on it, twenty-five thousand of which they had put on it themselves. The paint was just beginning to get tiny rust-colored pockmarks in it, but the wiring had blown about fifteen fuses and they'd had to put three new drive axles in it because it was designed so that when a ball bearing wore out you had to replace the whole assembly. It couldn't climb a hill at fifty-five, but it could seat two adults in the leather bucket seats and three kids across the back. Step Fletcher was driving, had been driving since they finally got away from the house well after noon. Empty house. He was still hearing echoes all the way to Indianapolis. Somewhere along the way he must have passed the moving van, but he didn't notice it or didn't recognize it or maybe the driver had pulled into a McDonald's somewhere or a gas station as they drove on by.

The others all fell asleep soon after they crossed the Ohio River. After Step had talked so much about flatboats and Indian wars, the kids were disappointed in it. It was the bridge that impressed them. And then they fell asleep. DeAnne stayed awake a little longer, but then she squeezed his hand and nestled down into the pillow she had jammed into the corner between the seat back and the window.

Just how it always goes, thought Step. She stays awake the whole time I'm wide awake and then, just as I get sleepy and maybe need to have her spell me for a while at the wheel, she goes to sleep.

He pushed the tape the rest of the way into the player. It was the sweet junky sound of "The E Street Shuffle." He hadn't listened to that in a while. DeAnne must have had it playing while she ran the last-minute errands in Vigor. Step had played that album on their second date. It was kind of a test. DeAnne was so serious about religion, he had to know if she could put up with his slightly wild taste in music. A lot of Mormon girls would have missed the sexual innuendos entirely, of course, but DeAnne was probably smarter than Step was, and so she not only noticed the bit about girls promising to unsnap their jeans and the fairies in a real bitch fight, she also got the part about hooking onto the midnight train, but she didn't get upset, she just laughed, and he knew it was going to be OK, she was religious but not a prig and that meant that he wouldn't have to pretend to be perfect in order to be with her. Ten years ago, 1973. Now they had three kids in the back of the Renault 18i wagon, probably the worst car ever sold in America, and they were heading for Steuben, North Carolina, where Step had a job.

A *good* job. Thirty thousand a year, which wasn't bad for a brand new history Ph.D. in a recession year. Except that he wasn't teaching history, he wasn't *writing* history, the job was putting together manuals for a computer software company. Not even programming—he couldn't even get hired for *that*, even though Hacker Snack was the best-selling game for the Atari back in '81. For a while there it had looked like his career was made as a game designer. They had so much money they figured they could afford for him to go back to school and finish his doctorate. Then the recession came, and the lousy Commodore 64 was killing the Atari in the stores, and suddenly his game was out of print and nobody wanted him except as a manual writer.

So Springsteen played along to his semi-depressed mood as Step wound the car up into the mountains, the sun setting in the west as the road angled them mostly east into the darkness. I should be happy, he told himself. I got the degree, I got a good job, and nothing says I can't do another game in my spare time, even if I have to do it on the stupid 64. It could be worse. I could have got a job programming Apples.

Despite what he said to encourage himself, the words still tasted like failure in his mouth. Thirty-two years old, three kids, and I'm on the downhill slope. Used to work for myself, and now I have to work for somebody else. Just like my dad with his sign company that went bust. At least he had the scar on his back from the operation that took out a vertebra. Me, I got no visible wounds. I was riding high one day, and then the next day we found out that our royalties would be only $7,000 instead of $40,000 like the last time, and we scrambled around looking for work and we've got debts coming out of our ears and I'm going to be just as broke as my folks for the rest of my life and it's my own damned fault. Wage slave like my dad.

Just so I don't have the shame of my wife *having* to

take some lousy swingshift job like Mom did. Fine if she *wants* to get a job, that's fine, but not if she *has* to.

Yet he knew even as he thought of it that that was what would happen next—they wouldn't be able to sell the house in Vigor and she'd have to get a job just to keep up the payments on it. We were fools to buy a house, but we thought it would be a good investment. There wasn't a recession when we moved there, and I had a good royalty income. Fools, thinking it could just go on forever. Nothing lasts.

Feeling sorry for himself kept him awake enough to keep driving for an hour. The tape was on its second time through when he started down the steep descent toward Frankfort. Good thing. Bound to be a motel in the state capital. I can make it that far, and DeAnne won't have to wake up till we get there.

"Dad," said Stevie from the back seat.

"Yes?" said Step—softly, so he'd know not to talk loudly enough to waken the others.

"Betsy threw up," said Stevie.

"Just a little bit, or is it serious?"

"Just a little," said Stevie.

Then a vast, deep urping sound came from the back seat.

"Now it's serious," said Stevie.

Damn damn damn, said Step silently. "Thanks for telling me, Steve."

The sound came again, even as he pulled off the road, and now he could smell the bitter tang of gastric juices. One of the kids almost always threw up on every long trip they took, but usually they did it in the first hour.

"Why are we stopping?" DeAnne, just waking up, had a hint of panic in her voice. She didn't like it when something unexpected happened, and always feared the worst.

Springsteen had just sung about the fish lady and

the junk man, so for the first time in a long time, Step remembered where his pet name for DeAnne had come from. "Hey, Fish Lady, take a sniff and see."

"Oh, no, which one of them?"

"Betsy Wetsy," said Stevie from the back. Another old joke—DeAnne used to get impatient with him for the irreverent nicknames he gave the kids. She hated the nickname Betsy, but because of the joke, the name had stuck and now that was what Betsy called herself.

"More like Betsy Pukesy," said Step. Stevie laughed.

Stevie had a good laugh. It made Step smile, and suddenly it was no big deal that he was about to be up to his elbows in toddler vomit.

Step had parked on the shoulder, well off, so that he could open Betsy's door without putting his butt out into traffic. Even so, he didn't like feeling the wind of the cars as they whooshed past. What a way to die— smeared like pâté on the back door of the car, a sort of roadkill canapé. For a moment he thought of what it would mean for the kids, if he died on the road right in front of their eyes. The little ones would probably not remember him, or how he died. But Stevie would see, Stevie would remember. It was the first time Step had really thought of it that way—Stevie was now old enough that he would remember everything that happened. Almost eight years old, and his life was now real, because he would remember it.

He would remember how Dad reacted when Betsy threw up, how Dad didn't swear or get mad or anything, how Dad helped clean up the mess instead of standing there helplessly while Mom took care of it. That was a sort of vow he made before he got married, that there would be no job in their family that was so disgusting or difficult that DeAnne could do it and he couldn't. He had matched her, diaper for diaper, with all three kids, and a little vomit in the car would never faze him.

Actually, a lot of vomit. Betsy, white-faced and wan, managed a smile.

By now DeAnne was outside and around the car, pulling baby wipes out of the plastic jar. "Here," she said. "Hand her out to me and I'll change her clothes while you clean up the car."

In a moment DeAnne was holding a dripping Betsy out in front of her, taking her around the car to her seat, where she had already spread a cloth diaper to protect the leather.

Robbie, the four-year-old, was awake now, too, holding out his arm. He had been sitting in the middle, right next to Betsy, and there was a streak of vomit on his sleeve. "Wasn't that sweet of your sister, to share with you," said Step. He wiped down Robbie's sleeve. "There you go, Road Bug."

"It stinks."

"I'm not surprised," said Step. "Bear it proudly, like a wound acquired in battle."

"Was that a joke, Daddy?" said Robbie.

"It was wit," said Step. Robbie was trying to learn how to tell jokes. Step had given him the funny-once lecture recently, so Robbie wasn't telling the same joke over and over again, but the different kinds of humor still baffled him and he was trying to sort them out. If Stevie's experience was a fair sample, it would take years.

DeAnne spoke to Robbie from the front seat. "We'll change your shirt as soon as your father has finished wiping up Betsy's booster seat."

Step wasn't having much success cleaning down inside the buckle of Betsy's seat belt. "The only way our seat belts will ever match again," he said, "is if Betsy contrives to throw up on all the rest of them."

"Move her around in the car and maybe she'll have it all covered by the time we get to North Carolina," said Stevie.

"She doesn't throw up *that* often," said DeAnne.

"It was a joke, Mom," said Stevie.

"No, it was wit," said Robbie.

So he *was* getting it.

The baby wipes were no match for Betsy's prodigious output. They ran out long before the seat was clean enough for occupancy.

"When they hear you're pregnant for the fourth time," said Step, "I think Johnson and Johnson's stock will go up ten points."

"There's more wipes in the big gray bag in the back," said DeAnne. "Make sure you buy the stock *before* you announce it."

Step walked around to the back of what the Renault people called a "deluxe wagon," unlocked the swing-up door, and swung it up. Even with the bag zipped open he couldn't find the baby wipes. "Hey, Fish Lady, where'd you pack the wipes?"

"In the bag somewhere, probably deep," she called. "While you're in there, I need a Huggie for Betsy. She's wet and as long as I've got her undressed I might as well do the whole job."

He gave the diaper to Stevie to pass forward, and then finally found the baby wipes. He was just stepping back so he could close the wagon when he realized that there was somebody standing behind and to the left of him. A man, with big boots. A cop. Somehow a patrol car had managed to pull up behind them and Step hadn't heard it, hadn't even noticed it was there.

"What's the trouble here?" asked the patrolman.

"My two-year-old threw up all over the back seat," said Step.

"You know the shoulder of the freeway is only to be used for emergencies," said the cop.

For a moment it didn't register on Step what the cop's remark implied. "You mean that you don't think that a child throwing up in the back seat is an emergency?"

The patrolman fixed him with a steady gaze for a moment. Step knew the look. It meant, Ain't you cute, and he had seen it often back when he used to get speeding tickets before his license was suspended back in '74 and DeAnne had to drive them everywhere. Step knew that he shouldn't say anything, because no matter what he said to policemen, it always made things worse.

DeAnne came to his rescue. She came around the car carrying Betsy's soaked and stinking clothes. "Officer, I think if you had these in your car for about thirty seconds *you'd* pull off the road, too."

The cop looked at her, surprised, and then grinned. "Ma'am, I guess you got a point. Just hurry it up. It's not safe to be stopped here. People come down this road too fast sometimes, and they take this curve wide."

"Thanks for your concern, Officer," said Step.

The patrolman narrowed his eyes. "Just doing my job," he said, rather nastily, and walked back to his car.

Step turned to DeAnne. "What did I say?"

"Get me a Ziploc bag out of there, please," she said. "If I have to smell these any longer I'm going to faint."

He handed her the plastic bag and she stuffed the messy clothes into it. "All I said to him was 'Thanks for your concern,' and he acted like I told him his mother had never been married."

She leaned close to him and said softly, affection-ately, "Step, when you say 'Thank you for your concern' it always sounds like you're just accidently leaving off the word *butthead*."

"I wasn't being sarcastic," said Step. "Everybody always thinks I'm being sarcastic when I'm not."

"I wouldn't know," said DeAnne. "I've never been there when you weren't being sarcastic."

"You think you know too much, Fish Lady."

"You don't know anywhere near enough, Junk Man."

He kissed her. "Give me a minute and I'll be ready to put our Betsy Wetsy doll back in her place."

He heard her muttering as she went back to her door: "Her name is Elizabeth." He grinned.

Step got back to wiping down Betsy's seat.

"I didn't even hear that cop come up," said Stevie.

"Cop?" asked Robbie.

"Go back to sleep, Road Bug," said Step.

"Did we get a ticket, Daddy?" asked Robbie.

"He just wanted to make sure we were all right," said Step.

"He wanted us to move our butts out of here," said Stevie.

"Step!" said DeAnne.

"It was Stevie who said it, not me," said Step.

"He wouldn't talk that way if he didn't learn it from you," said DeAnne.

"Is he still there?" asked Step.

Stevie half-stood in order to see over the junk on the back deck. "Yep," he said.

"I didn't hear him either," said Step. "I just turned around and there he was."

"What if it wasn't a cop and you just turned around and it was a bad guy?" asked Stevie.

"He gets his morbid imagination from you," said DeAnne.

"Nobody would do anything to us out on the open highway like this where anybody passing by could see."

"It's dark," said Stevie. "People drive by so fast."

"Well, nothing happened," said DeAnne, rather testily. "I don't like talking about things like that."

"If it was a bad guy Daddy would've popped him one in the nose!" said Robbie.

"Yeah, right," said Step.

"Daddy wouldn't let anything bad happen," said Robbie.

"That's right," said DeAnne. "Neither would Mommy."

"The seat's clean," said Step. "And the belt's as clean as it's going to get in this lifetime."

"I'll bring her around."

"Climb over!" cried Betsy merrily, and before DeAnne could grab her, she had clambered through the gap between the bucket seats. She buckled her own seat belt, looked up at Step, and grinned.

"Well done, my little Wetsy doll." He leaned in and kissed her forehead, then closed the door and got back in to the driver's seat. The cop was still behind them, which made him paranoid about making sure he didn't do anything wrong. He signaled. He drove just under the speed limit. The last thing they needed was a court date in some out-of-the-way Kentucky town.

"How much farther to Frankfort?" asked DeAnne.

"Maybe half an hour, probably less," said Step.

"Oh, I must have slept a long way."

"An hour maybe."

"You're such a hero to drive the whole way," she said.

"Give me a medal later," he said.

"I will."

He turned the stereo back up a little. Everybody might have been asleep again, it was so quiet in the car. Then Stevie spoke up.

"Daddy, if it *was* a bad guy, *would* you pop him one?"

What was he supposed to say, Yessiree, my boy, I'd pop him so hard he'd be wearing his nose on the back of his head for the rest of his life? Was that what was needed, to make Stevie feel safe? To make him proud of his father? Or should he tell the truth—that he had never hit anyone in anger in his life, that he had never hit a living soul with a doubled-up fist.

No, my son, my approach to fighting has always been to make a joke and walk away, and if they wouldn't let me go, then I ran like hell.

"It depends," said Step.

"On what?"

"On whether I thought that popping him would make things better or worse."

"Oh."

"I mean, if he's a foot taller than me and weighs three hundred pounds and has a tire iron, I think popping him wouldn't be a good idea. I think in a case like that I'd be inclined to offer him my wallet so he'd go away."

"But what if he wanted to murder us all?"

DeAnne spoke up without turning her head out of her pillow. "Then your father would kill him, and if he didn't, I would," she said mildly.

"What if he killed both of you first?" asked Stevie. "And then came and wanted to kill Robbie and Betsy?"

"Stevie," said DeAnne, "Heavenly Father won't let anything like that happen to you."

That was more than Step could stand. "God doesn't work that way," he said. "He doesn't stop evil people from committing their crimes."

"He's asking us if he's safe," said DeAnne.

"Yes, Stevie, you're safe, as safe as anybody ever is who's alive in this world. But you were asking about what if somebody really terrible wanted to do something vicious to our whole family, and the truth is that if somebody is truly, deeply evil, then sometimes good people can't stop him until he's done a lot of bad things. That's just the way it happens sometimes."

"Okay," said Stevie. "But God would get him for it, right?"

"In the long run, yes," said Step. "And I'll tell you this—the only way anybody will ever get to you or the other kids or to your mother, for that matter, is if I'm already dead. I promise you that."

"Okay," said Stevie.

"There aren't that many really evil people in the world," said Step. "I don't think you need to worry about this."

"Okay," said Stevie.

"I mean, why did you ask about this stuff?"

"He had a gun."

"Of course he had a gun, dear," said DeAnne. "He's a policeman. He has a gun so he can protect people like us from those bad people."

"I wish we could always have a policeman with us," said Stevie.

"Yeah, that'd be nice, wouldn't it?" said Step. Right, nice like a hemorrhoid. I'd have to drive fifty-five *all the time*.

Stevie had apparently exhausted his questions.

A few moments later, Step felt DeAnne's hand on his thigh, patting him. He glanced over at her. "Sorry," he whispered. "I didn't mean to contradict you."

"You were right," she said softly.

He smiled at her and held her hand for a moment, until he needed both hands on the wheel for a turn.

Still, all the rest of the way into Frankfort he couldn't get Stevie's questions out of his mind. Nor could he forget his own answers. He had stopped DeAnne from teaching Stevie that God would always protect him from bad people, but then he had gone on and promised that he would give his life before any harm ever came to the children. But was that true? Did he have that kind of courage? He thought of parents in concentration camps who watched their children get killed before their eyes, and yet they could do nothing. And even if he tried, what good would Step be able to do against somebody bent on violence? Step had no skill in fighting, and he was pretty sure it wasn't one of those things that you just know how to do. Any half-assed hoodlum would make short work of Step, and here he had kids who were looking to him for protection. I should study karate or something. Kung fu. Or buy a gun so that when Stevie is fourteen he can find it where it's hidden and play around with it and end up killing himself or Robbie or some friend of his or something.

No, thought Step. None of the above. I won't do any of those things, because I'm a civilized man living in a civilized society, and if the barbarians ever knock on my door I'll be helpless.

They pulled into Frankfort and there was a Holiday Inn with a vacancy sign. Step took it as a good omen. Officially he didn't believe in omens. But what the heck, it made him feel better to take it that way, and so he did.

2

▪ MAGGOTS ▪

This is the house they moved into: The only cheap wood siding in a neighborhood of red brick. No basement, no garage, not even a roof over the carport. Brown latticework around the base of the house like the skirting around a mobile home. Blue carpet in the living room, which wasn't going to look too good with their furniture, an old-fashioned green velvet love seat and overstuffed chair Step had bought from Deseret Industries when he was in college back at BYU. But it had four bedrooms, which meant one for Step and DeAnne, one for the boys, one for Betsy and the new baby when it came in July, and one for Step's office, because they still hoped he could do some programming on the side and then they could go back to living the way they wanted to, and in a better place than this.

In the meantime, the movers had piled the living room six feet high with more boxes than they could ever unpack and put away in a place this size, and they had a single weekend to get settled before work started for Step and school started for Stevie. Monday, the deadline, the drop-dead day. Nobody was looking forward to it with much joy, least of all Stevie.

DeAnne was aware of Stevie's anxiety all through the weekend of moving in and unpacking. Stevie mostly tended Robbie and Elizabeth, except when Step or DeAnne called for him to run some errand from one end of the house to the other. As always, Stevie was quiet and helpful—he took his responsibilities as the eldest child very seriously.

Or maybe he just seemed serious, because he kept his feelings to himself until he had sorted them out, or until they had built up to a point where he couldn't contain them. So DeAnne knew that it was a real worry for him when he came into the kitchen and stood there silently for a long time until she said, "Want to tell me something or am I just too pretty for words?" which was what she always said, only he didn't smile, he just stood there a moment more and then he said, "Mom, can't I just stay home for another couple of days?"

"Stevie, I know it's scary, but you just need to plunge right in. You'll make friends right away and everything'll be fine."

"I didn't make friends right away at my old school."

That was true enough—DeAnne remembered the consultations with Stevie's kindergarten teacher. Stevie didn't really play *with* anybody until November of that year, and he didn't have any actual friends until first grade. If it weren't for his friends at church, DeAnne would have worried that Stevie was too socially immature for school. But with the kids at church he was almost wild sometimes, running around the meeting-house like a movie-western Indian until Step intervened and gathered him up and brought him to the car. No, Stevie knew how to play, and he knew how to make friends. He just didn't make friends *easily*. He wasn't like Robbie, who would walk up and talk to anybody, kid or adult. Of course Stevie was worried about school. DeAnne was worried for him, too.

"But that was your first school ever," she said. "You know the routine now."

"When Barry Wimmer moved in after Thanksgiving," he said, "everybody was really rotten to him."

"Were you?"

"No."

"So not everybody."

"They made fun of everything he did," said Stevie.

"Kids can be like that sometimes."

"They're going to do that to me now," said Stevie.

This was excruciating. She wanted to say, You're right, they're going to be a bunch of little jerks, because that's the way kids are at that age, except you, because you were born not knowing how to hurt anybody else, you were born with compassion, only that also means that when people are cruel to you it cuts you deep. You won't understand that you have to walk right up to the ones who are being hateful and laugh in their faces and earn their respect. Instead you'll try to figure out what you did to make them mad at you.

For a moment she toyed with putting it to him in exactly those terms. But it would hardly help him if she confirmed all his worst fears. He'd never get to sleep if she did *that*.

"What if they were unkind to you, Stevie? What would you do?"

He thought about that for a while. "Barry cried," he said.

"Did that make it better?"

"No," said Stevie. "They made fun of him crying. Ricky followed him around saying 'boo hoo hoo' all the time from then on. He was still doing it on my last day there."

"So," said DeAnne, partly to get him to talk, partly because she had no idea what to say.

"I don't think I'll cry," said Stevie.

"I'm glad," said DeAnne.

"I'll just make them go away."

"I don't think that'll work, Stevie. The more you try to make them leave, the more they'll stick around."

"No, I don't mean make *them* go away. I mean make them go *away*."

"Do you want to hand me that roll of paper towels?" He did.

"I'm not sure I'm clear on the difference between making *them* go away and making them go *away*."

"You know. Like when Dad's programming. He makes everything go away."

So he understood that about his father, and thought it might be useful. "You'll just concentrate on your schoolwork?"

"Or whatever," said Stevie. "It's hard to concentrate on schoolwork because it's so dumb."

"Maybe it won't be so dumb at this school."

"Maybe."

"I wish I could promise you that everything will be perfect, but I really don't think they'll treat you the way that Barry Wimmer got treated." DeAnne thought back to the couple of times she'd seen the boy when she brought treats or some project or a forgotten lunch to school. "Barry's the kind of kid who . . . how can I put it? He's a walking victim."

"Am *I* a victim?" asked Stevie.

"Not a chance," said DeAnne. "You're too strong."

"Not really," he said, looking at his hands.

"I don't mean your body, Stevie. I mean your spirit

is too strong. You know what you're doing. You know what you're *about*. You aren't looking to these kids to tell you who you are. You *know* who you are."

"I guess."

"Come on, who are you?" It was an old game, but he still enjoyed playing along, even though the original purpose of it—preparing him to identify himself in case he got lost—was long since accomplished.

"Stephen Bolivar Fletcher."

"And who is that?"

"Firstborn child and first son of the Junk Man and the Fish Lady."

Of all his regular answers, that was her favorite, partly because the first time he ever said that, he had this sly little smile as if he knew he was intruding into grownup territory, as if he knew that his parents' pet names for each other were older than he was and in some sense had caused him to exist. As if he had some unconscious awareness that *those* names, even spoken in jest, had sexual undertones that he couldn't possibly understand but nevertheless knew all about.

"And don't you forget it," she said cheerfully.

"I won't," he said.

"Mom," he said.

"Yes?"

"Please can't I stay home just a couple more days?"

She sighed. "I really don't think so, Stevie. But I'll talk to your dad."

"He'll just say the same thing."

"Probably. We parents are like that."

The worst moment was at breakfast on Monday. The kids were eating their hot cereal while Step was downing his Rice Krispies, looking over the newspaper as he ate. "This is almost as bad a newspaper as the one in Vigor," he said.

"You aren't going to get the *Washington Post* unless you live in Washington," said DeAnne.

"I don't want the *Washington Post*. I'd settle for the *Salt Lake Tribune*. Salt Lake is still a two-newspaper town, and here Steuben can't even support a paper that puts the international news on the front page."

"Does it have Cathy? Does it have Miss Manners? Does it have Ann Landers?"

"OK, so it has everything we need to make us happy."

There was a honk outside.

"They're early," said Step. "Do you think I have time to brush my teeth?"

"Do you think you could stand to get through the day if you didn't?"

He rushed from the table.

"*Who's* early?" asked Stevie.

"Your dad's car pool. For the first week or so one of the men from work is picking him up in the morning and bringing him home at night so we'll have the car to run errands and stuff."

Stevie looked horrified. "Mom," he said. "What about school?"

"That's the point. You'll be riding the bus after today, but your dad's carpooling so I'll have the car to take you to school."

"Isn't *Dad* taking me for my first day?"

Too late she remembered that when Stevie started kindergarten, she had still been recovering from Elizabeth's birth, and it was Step who took Stevie to his first day of school.

"Does it really matter which one of us takes you?"

The look of panic in his eyes was more of an answer than his whispered "No."

Step came back into the kitchen, carrying his attaché case—his jail-in-a-box, he called it.

"Step," said DeAnne, "I think Stevie was expecting you to take him to school this morning."

"Oh, man," he said, "I didn't think." His face got that look of inward anger that DeAnne knew all too well. "Isn't it great that I've got this *job* so I can't even take my kid to school on his first day."

"It's *your* first day, too."

He knelt down beside Stevie's chair. Stevie was looking down into his mush. "Stevie, I should've planned it better. But I didn't, and now I've got this guy outside waiting for me and . . ."

The doorbell rang.

"Geez louise," said Step.

"You've got to go," said DeAnne. "Stevie'll be all right, you'll see. Right, Stevie?"

"Right," said Stevie softly.

Step kissed Stevie on the cheek and then Betsy was saying "Me too me too" and he kissed both the other kids and then grabbed his case and headed for the front door.

DeAnne tried to reassure Stevie. "I'm sorry, but this is how your dad is earning the money we live on now, and he can't very well . . ."

"I know, Mom," said Stevie.

"We'll head for school and you'll meet the principal and . . ."

Step strode back into the kitchen. "I explained to him that we had a crisis and tomorrow he'll find me waiting on the curb for him, but today I'm going to be late. Got to take my son to second grade."

DeAnne was half delighted, half appalled. She knew perfectly well that in his own way, Step dreaded going back to an eight-to-five job as much as Stevie dreaded starting a new school. "This'll really impress 'em, Junk Man," she said, smiling grimly. "Missing your car pool and showing up late on your first day."

"Might as well get used to the idea that I'm a father first and a computer manual writer eighth."

"What comes between first and eighth?" asked Stevie, who was obviously delighted.

"Everything else," said Step.

"You'd better call," said DeAnne.

Step got on the phone and she knew at once that it wasn't working the way he had so glibly assumed it would.

"Bad," he said when he was done. "They have a staff meeting at eight-thirty and they were planning to introduce me there and everybody has sort of scheduled everything around my being there on time this morning."

"But now your ride is gone," DeAnne pointed out, trying not to be mean about it.

Step was kneeling by Stevie's chair again. "I can't help it, Door Man."

"I know," said Stevie.

"I tried," said Step. "But the family really needs me to keep this job, especially since we moved all the way to North Carolina so I could get it."

Stevie nodded, trying to look game about the whole thing.

"I do *my* job for the family," said Step, "and you do yours."

"What's mine?" asked Stevie. He looked hopeful.

"Toughing it out and going to school," said Step.

Apparently he had been hoping for an alternate assignment. But he swallowed hard and nodded again. Then he thought of something. "How will you get there now that your ride is gone?"

"He'll fly," offered Robbie.

"No," said DeAnne, "that's your mother the witch who knows how to fly."

"I guess we'll all pile into the car together and you'll *take* me to work on the way to taking you to school."

"Couldn't you take me to *school* on the way to taking you to *work*?" asked Stevie.

"Sorry, Door Man," said Step. "That would be backtracking. Geography is against it. The clock is against it. All of time and space are against it. *Einstein* is against it."

When they got to Eight Bits Inc., Step leaned into the back seat and kissed Stevie good-bye, and even though Stevie was well into the age where parents' kisses aren't welcome, this time he made no fuss. While Step was giving Robbie and Elizabeth the traditional noisy smack, DeAnne looked over the one-story red-brick building where Step was going to be spending his time.

It was one of those ugly flat-roofed things that businesses build when they have only so much money and they need walls and a roof. That was actually a good sign, because it suggested that the owner of the company had no delusions of being in the "big time," spending all the company's cash from the first hit programs on gewgaws that would mean nothing at all when slack times came. If only we'd been so careful, thought DeAnne, when the money from Hacker Snack started flowing in. Not that we spent it on nothing. A Ph.D. in history, that was something. And helping out family here and there. And a beta-format VCR for which they could not find rental tapes in Steuben, North Carolina.

"Bye, Fish Lady," said Step.

"Good luck, Junk Man," said DeAnne.

She watched him go into the building. He was striding boldly, almost jauntily. She liked the look of him, always had. He exuded confidence without ever looking as if he wanted to make sure everyone *else* knew how confident he was, like a salesman who had memorized a book on power walking. But this time she knew that, for once, his confidence was a lie. Just walking into this building spoke of failure in Step's heart, despite the fact that the top people at Eight Bits had been so impressed that Step Fletcher *himself* had actually applied for a job with them. The very fact that they were so impressed was really a symbol to Step of how far he had fallen—he was now working for the kind of company that would never have imagined they could get someone as accomplished in the field as he was.

"Am I going to be late, Mom?" asked Stevie.

Step was inside the building now, and there was no reason to wait. DeAnne put the car in gear and pulled off the shoulder, onto Palladium Road. "You were going to be late getting into class no matter what," she said. "We have to go by the principal's office and sign you in."

"So I've got to walk in right in front of everybody," he said.

"Maybe the door will be in the back of the room," said DeAnne. "Then you'll be behind everybody."

"I'm not joking, Mom."

"It's scary, I know," she said. "But the principal is really nice, and I'm sure she's picked out a wonderful teacher for you."

"Can't I just meet the principal today and then come to school tomorrow at the regular time?"

"Stevie, the other kids are going to notice that you're new, no matter what. And if you just showed up tomorrow, how would you know where to sit? You'd end up standing there feeling like an idiot. By going in today, you'll get a seat assigned to you right away and people will explain to you the things you need to know."

"Still."

"Stevie, there's a law that says we have to have you in school."

"Wow," said Robbie. "You could go to *jail* for letting Stevie stay home?"

"Not really. But we abide by the law in our family."

"Daddy doesn't," said Robbie. "He drives too fast all the time."

"Your father thinks the speed limits all mean 'give or take ten miles per hour.'"

"Will they put Daddy in jail?" asked Robbie.

"No. But they might take his license away."

"They almost did once before, didn't they?" asked Stevie.

"Your father had a year of probation once," said DeAnne. "But it was before any of you kids were born. He really is an excellent driver, and he always drives safely." Not for the first time, DeAnne wondered whether Step would change his driving habits if he could actually *hear* how the kids noticed his speeding. It was hard enough teaching children right from wrong without having to include ambiguities, like laws that Daddy felt he didn't have to obey because he didn't speed fast enough to get *tickets*. She could see herself explaining to her kids when they got to be teenagers and started dating, Now, you're supposed to be chaste, which means that you can do whatever you want as long as you don't do anything that will get somebody *pregnant*. But Step couldn't—or wouldn't—see the relationship between traffic laws and the commandments. "Laws of men and laws of God are two different things," Step always said, "and our kids are all smart enough to know the difference."

Ah well. Marriage meant that you had to live with the fact that your spouse's foibles would rub off on the kids. She knew how it annoyed Step that the kids had inherited her attitude toward shoes—they just couldn't keep them on their feet. Step was always walking into a room and either stepping on somebody's shoes, tripping over them, or—when he noticed them soon enough—placekicking them into the hall or putting them under the offender's pillow. "The difference between civilized people and barbarians," he would say, "is that civilized people wear shoes." Step had to live with barefoot barbarians, and DeAnne had to answer questions about why Daddy broke the law all the time. Not exactly a fair trade—she couldn't see that there were any moral implications to bare feet—but she lived with it, grumbling now and then, and so did he.

To get to Western Allemania Primary School you

had to drive past the high school, also called Western Allemania. Yellow buses had been herded into a large parking lot, waiting for the end of the school day. What she liked least about sending Stevie to this school was that the little kids had to ride the same buses as the high-schoolers—and the drivers were high school students, as well. The idea of a seventeen-year-old having the responsibility for not only keeping all the children on the bus alive, but also maintaining discipline—well, what could she do? The principal had looked at her oddly and said, "Mrs. Fletcher, that's the way we do things in North Carolina."

She drove down the hill into the turnaround in front of the school. Before and after school the turnaround was reserved for buses—parents who were picking up their kids had to drive on a completely different road to a small parking lot at the top of a hill about two hundred yards from the school and wait for their kids. She pointed out the hill to Stevie as she was getting Elizabeth out of her booster seat. "Whenever I pick you up, you go up that stairway leading to the top of that hill. I'll be there for you."

"OK," said Stevie.

"And if something ever happened, like the car breaking down, and I'm *not* there, then you head right back down to the school and go straight to the principal's office and wait *there* until I come in and get you."

"Why can't I just wait up there?" asked Stevie.

"Because this isn't a safe world," said DeAnne. "And what if somebody comes to you and says, 'Your mother asked me to pick you up and take you home'?"

"I don't go with them."

"There's more to it than that, Stevie."

"I get away from that person right away and head straight for the nearest person in authority."

"At school that means Dr. Mariner. And if you're not at school?"

"If the person is following me then I don't hide, I run right out into the open, where there are the most people, and if he comes near me I scream at the top of my voice, 'He's not my father!' Or 'She's not my mother! Help me!'"

"Very good."

"I know all that, too," said Robbie.

"I know I know," said Betsy.

"I wish I didn't have to teach you things like this," said DeAnne. "But there are bad people in the world. Not many of them, but we have to be careful. Now, what if I really *did* send somebody to pick you up, because maybe there was an accident and I had one of the other kids at the hospital or something?"

"The password," said Stevie.

"And what is it?"

"Maggots," said Stevie.

"Little oozy baby fly worms!" yelled Robbie. Step had thought up the password, of course.

"Quiet, Road Bug, this is serious," said DeAnne. "And do you ask them about the password?"

"No. I don't even tell them that there *is* a password. But I never go with anybody unless he says, 'Your parents told me to tell you *Maggots*.'"

"Right," said DeAnne.

"If they don't say that, then they're a liar and I refuse to go and I scream and scream if they try to take me anyway."

"Right," said DeAnne.

"Mom," said Stevie.

"What?"

"What if nobody hears me scream?"

"You should never be in a place where nobody can hear you yell for help, Stevie," she said. "But *please* don't worry too much about this. If you do all that you're supposed to, I'll do all that *I'm* supposed to, and so nothing will go wrong. OK?"

"Mom, I'm scared to go in."

Great, thought DeAnne. And I just went through a kidnapping-prevention catechism, to add a whole new layer of terror to the day. "Come on, Stevie. Dr. Mariner is a wonderful kind lady and you'll like her."

Dr. Mariner did have a knack for putting kids at ease, and within a few moments Stevie was smiling at her and then laughing when she told a joke. But the fear returned when, after only a few minutes in the office, Dr. Mariner took Stevie by the hand and said, "Let's go to class now."

Stevie withdrew his hand and immediately rushed to stand by DeAnne. "Can't Mom walk me to class?"

"Certainly she can, if she wants," said Dr. Mariner. "Your teacher's name is Mrs. Jones. *That's* an easy name, right?"

"Mrs. Jones," said Stevie. He repeated the name several times, under his breath. Mrs. Jones. Mrs. Jones.

DeAnne let Dr. Mariner lead the parade through the corridors, for all the world like a tour guide. She pointed out where the kindergarten and first-grade classes were, and then brought Stevie along to the vestibule that Mrs. Jones's classroom shared with another. It was time for Stevie to go into the class. He clung tighter to DeAnne's hand.

"Do you really want your mother and brother and sister coming into class with you on the first day?" asked DeAnne.

Stevie shook his head violently.

DeAnne shifted Elizabeth's weight on her hip and squatted down beside him. "Sometimes you just have to drink the cup," she said.

He nodded, remembering. It was when he was only three and had a bad stomach flu, and didn't want to drink the prescription Tylenol syrup that she had to give him to help bring the fever down. Step had knelt beside his bed and told him the story of Christ praying in

Gethsemane. Sometimes you just have to drink the cup, Step had said then, and Stevie had drunk it without another murmur.

It worked the same way now. He tightened his face and nodded to show that he understood. Then he turned and walked through the door that Dr. Mariner was holding open for him. His stride was so like Step's had been earlier today, trying to be brave. DeAnne felt a lump in her throat for both of them.

Inside the classroom, there were immediate cries of "New boy! New boy!" She caught a glimpse of the teacher, Mrs. Jones, who was turning without enthusiasm to look in Stevie's direction. Then Dr. Mariner swung the door shut.

3

· GALLOWGLASS ·

This is the company where Step worked: Ray Keene had been the computer systems guy at UNC-Steuben when the Commodore 64 started showing up in Kmarts. Ray saw right away that it was the 64 that was going to put computers in every home in America, if somebody had the brains to come up with cheap software so people could *do* something with the machine. Commodore sure wasn't coming up with the right combinations—in Ray's opinion all the software *they* offered was second-rate and way too expensive. So he came up with Scribe 64 and sold it for twenty-nine bucks, discounted to nineteen bucks including postage if you ordered it direct from Eight Bits Inc.

There were a couple of bad times early on. Right at

first, Ray's lack of business experience nearly killed the company—he was paying so much for packaging that in fact he was actually *losing* 22¢ with each unit sold. So when he ran out of that first run of a thousand boxes, he began shipping in a much smaller box with *no* printing on the outside, just a sticker that said "The only word processor you'll ever need—$29" and began making four dollars a unit. It sold even faster, and the profit per unit got even better, and one day his wife said, "Ray, I got no house left, it's all Eight Bits Inc. Either me and the kids move out or the company does."

That's when Ray Keene bought the ugly building on Palladium. It had originally been a climate-controlled clean shop for the assembly of calculators in the mid-70s, but it had been standing empty for a couple of years and the owner sold it to Ray at a price that said he was just glad to get it off his hands. Ray had the whole thing rewired and half the big factory space cut up into offices. There weren't any windows and the place was ugly but everybody in the company, which was up to ten employees by then, was so happy to have enough room to turn around that they loved it like a mama loves an ugly baby.

When Step came down for interviews six weeks before, all he got from everybody was that sense of exuberance and excitement. But this first day at work there was something else. Ray Keene had remodeled his office since Step was there before, and it showed signs that Ray had apparently read that book about power that was on the lists the year before. Ray now sat behind a massive desk in a rock-back chair while all the chairs that visitors had to sit on were hard and too low and didn't have enough space from front to back, so that you always felt like you were sitting on the edge of the seat because, in fact, you *were*.

"You won't report to me," said Ray. "I've made Dicky Northanger the vice-president in charge of the creative end of things, and you'll report to *him*, but send me memos from time to time. We'll be hiring an assistant for you as soon as we can, but for now all the manuals for all our software will come through you, but pass it all by Dicky for final approval."

Dicky Northanger was the guy who used to do all the manuals. He was the first person Ray Keene had hired, and he and Ray were now great buddies, going every Sunday afternoon to pick up the *New York Times* at the Magazine Rack bookstore. He was genial, heavy-set, and middle-aged, probably the oldest man in the company, and Step didn't see any problem with report-ing to him. But he felt a vague sense of disappointment, since the job had been represented to him as one that would report directly to Ray. Of course Ray couldn't have *everybody* report to him, but the company only had twenty-five employees right now, and it seemed weird in a company that size that Step was already being told that he was *not* to contact Ray except by memo.

After Step met with Ray alone for that half hour of physical discomfort, they went straight on in to a staff meeting, where the new health plan was explained to everybody and, as an incidental at the end, Step and a new guy in the art department were introduced around. Dicky introduced him, and Step was a little embar-rassed when Dicky made a great point of talking about what a genius Step was for having programmed Hacker Snack—and then, even more embarrassing, he pointed out to everyone in excruciating detail that Step would report only to him, and that while Step must have access to every programmer at every stage of development of all software, he had no authority over anyone and no one was to ask him for advice about anything to do with programming. Step was here *solely* to write manuals.

Why don't you just cut off my balls and hold them up for everyone to admire? thought Step.

Then he went straight in to a meeting with Bob, the

"vice-president in charge of finance"—he had been the
bookkeeper until job inflation struck Eight Bits, apparently within the past six weeks. He was a lean, weathered-
looking man in cowboy boots who had more of a Texas
twang than a southern drawl, and the first thing he did
was slide a two-page contract across the desk for Step to
sign.

"What is this?" Step asked, for he had already
signed the employment contract.

"A confidentiality agreement," said the cowboy
accountant. "Industry standard."

Step read it anyway, though Cowboy Bob kept
shuffling papers to show his impatience with Step's taking so much of his time. And sure enough, it turned out
to be a lot more than a confidentiality agreement. "This
contract buys all rights to anything I do in programming
for the rest of my natural life," said Step.

"Well, not exactly," said Cowboy Bob.

"I just came from a meeting where I was specifically and totally excluded from *all* programming here at
Eight Bits."

"Eight Bits *Inc.*"

"So why should I sign a contract giving Eight Bits
Inc. all rights to any programming I come up with during my time here? I won't *do* any programming, right?"

"Oh, that was just Dicky," said Cowboy Bob. "He
got jealous because even though you were coming in to
write the manuals, everybody knew you were the most
successful programmer ever to set foot on the premises,
so he's just making sure everybody knows that he's your
boss. In fact Ray and I expect that you'll sort of do quality control over all the software, because Dicky isn't that
good a programmer and he kind of makes changes in all
the programs and then they end up getting released with
bugs. Sometimes. Just between you and me, of course."

"Dicky just forbade anyone to ask my advice about
programming," said Step.

"Yeah, well, just don't rub his nose in it, that's all me and Ray expect from you."

"So you're telling me that in fact, besides manual writing, I'm to be the quality control officer, only I can't tell my direct supervisor that that's what I'm doing and I have to carry on all such activities behind his back?"

"That's why we're paying you thirty thou a year, my friend."

"And in the meantime, I'm supposed to sign over every idea I ever have to Eight Bits . . . Inc.? Why not just everything I come up with related to software being developed in-house?"

"This agreement is a condition of employment, Step," said Cowboy Bob. He still seemed friendly and genial, but if this had been a saloon in a western, the tone of his voice would have sent half the customers out into the street to avoid getting hit over the head with a breakaway chair.

"This agreement makes me promise that if I leave here I'll *never* enter into competition with Eight Bits Inc."

"Our lawyer said that was a real good idea."

"Well, try this. I came here to write manuals, not to develop software. I'll help out with quality control if Ray wants me to, but I want it to be out in the open so I don't have to skulk around like a spy. And I won't sign this agreement until it's rewritten to limit the non-competition clause to one year, to protect my rights in all software I wrote *prior* to coming here, and to protect my rights in all software I might write *after* leaving here."

"No way," said Cowboy Bob.

Step stood up. His knees were trembling and he felt a little faint, but he also knew that there was no way he could sign that agreement. "I just moved my family to Steuben on the strength of a contract with Eight Bits that said nothing about *this*. As far as I'm concerned, this paper means that you are in material breach of our contract. So if your lawyer won't revise this agreement, he'll be talking to *my* lawyer about getting from Eight Bits the costs of moving here, the costs of moving *back,* and, if we can get the court to agree to it, and I think we can, a year's salary. You have my phone number."

Step could not believe that he was already quitting and it was only eleven in the morning, but in a way it was almost a relief. The scene in Ray's office and Dicky's display in the staff meeting had already made Step so wary of the future here that having an excuse to leave sounded just fine to him. But his bold talk about what a lawyer could get for him was just talk—even if it worked out that way, litigation would drag on until they were long past financial inconvenience. It wasn't just the mortgage on the house in Vigor and the cost of moving here. It was the fact that they had expected to pay last year's taxes out of the royalty check this past fall, and so now they were deeply in debt to the IRS, and even bankruptcy couldn't get them out of *that.* Quitting this job would be such a devastating blow that they'd probably end up slithering back to Orem, Utah, to live in DeAnne's parents' basement while the IRS auctioned off everything they owned.

And still it felt pretty good to be walking toward the door in Cowboy Bob's office.

"Wait a minute, Step," said Cowboy Bob.

Step turned around. The vice-president of finance was reaching into a drawer of his desk and pulling out another paper. "Since you didn't like that first one, try this one before you walk out on us and we have to sue *you* for breach."

Step came back and took the paper out of his hand. He read it without sitting down. To his disbelief, it was a version of the agreement that could only have been written for him—it excluded prior software, it excluded programming on computers for which Eight Bits Inc. was not publishing software, and the noncompetition clause was for exactly one year.

"You already had this written," said Step.

"Yep," said Cowboy Bob.

"So why did you show me that other?"

"Because you might've signed it." Cowboy Bob grinned. "This is business, Step."

Step stood there looking at him, debating inside himself whether he wanted even to live on the same planet with this guy, let alone work with him.

"We've met every one of your objections, Step," Cowboy Bob prodded him.

"I'm just wondering whether there's another paper in that drawer."

"There is. It has our lawyer's phone number on it. How do I put this kindly, Step? Sign or be sued."

"Gee, Bob, is this the way you talk to all the boys?"

"Look at it this way, Step. You won't be working with me. The only thing you'll know about me is that I sign your paycheck, and after you get a few of those you'll like me just fine. You're pissed off now, but that'll pass, and in six months maybe we'll have a couple of beers together and laugh about how mad you were this first day."

"I don't drink," said Step.

"Yeah, I forgot, you're a Mormon," said Cowboy Bob. "Well, then, that's out. Because looking at you, I'd say you could *never* forgive me without a couple of beers in you."

He said it with such a twinkle in his eye that Step couldn't help but smile. So Cowboy Bob knew he was a son-of-a-bitch, and didn't particularly mind. Well, Bob, *I* know you're a son-of-a-bitch, and I guess I don't mind that much either.

Step laid the paper down on the desk, signed it, and walked out.

It was nearly noon, and even though he was probably supposed to go find Dicky and ask where his office was, Step needed to stand outside this building for a minute and decide whether to scream or cry or laugh.

On the way to the staff meeting he had seen a back corridor that led to a door on the north side of the building—Dicky had told him in passing that everybody in the staff used that door, since that's where the parking lot was. That's where Step headed now.

The scenery wasn't all that pretty outside—just a narrow parking lot, a high chainlink fence with barbed wire on the top, and then an overgrown pasture where the only things still grazing were old tires and a rusting refrigerator with the door off. Ray's Mercedes was in the only assigned parking place in the lot, directly across from the north door. Step felt a sudden urge to go pee on the tires like a dog, but he was satisfied just to imagine doing it.

I've been a free man for the past five years, he said to himself, not working for anybody. Living on student loans, I taught myself programming on the Atari just to get history out of my mind, and I ended up creating a program that gave some pleasure to a lot of people and it made me about a hundred thousand dollars in a year and a half. All that money is gone, I owe taxes on it that I can't pay, and I've just signed a contract to work for a company with byzantine internal politics, an owner on a power trip, a vice-president of finance who thinks that being in business means screwing anybody who'll let you screw him, and a supervisor who's so incompetent that they want me to clean up after him without letting him know I'm doing it. All for thirty thousand dollars a year. Twenty-five hundred a month. That's the price of my soul.

But it was no worse than what his dad had gone through, over the years. A sign company that went belly-up when Dad broke his back, and yet Dad refused to declare bankruptcy and paid it all off, slowly, over the space of ten years, during which time he went back to school, got his B.A., taught at San Jose State for a while, and ended up working at Lockheed designing training programs for missile operators. If Dad had ever had half as much money as I made last year, he would have made sure he was set up as a free man forever. He would have had money in the bank against a rainy day. I spent it like it was going to last forever, and now I'm right where my dad was, all those years at Lockheed, saying yessir to assholes and moonlighting weekends at a camera store in the Hillsdale Mall. Never heard him complain, except that he apologized to Mom when she had to go back to work as a secretary in the public schools.

That's why I signed that paper, Step realized. So I don't have to make that same apology to DeAnne.

And if I don't find a way to make some extra money in the next year or so, the IRS is going to put us in that situation anyhow.

The anxiety, the desperation, the memory of his father's defeats—it all surged through him and burned in his throat and he thought, If I let myself get emotional about all this, it'll show on my face when I go back inside. He swallowed hard and breathed deeply, slowly, forcing himself to calm down.

Somebody opened the door behind him and came outside. Step didn't turn around at first, half afraid and half hoping that it was Cowboy Bob or even Ray Keene himself, worried about him, wanting to smooth things over with him.

It was just a kid, looked to be still in high school, who wandered a few yards away from him and lit up a cigarette. He took a deep drag, let the smoke out slow, and puffed it into rings.

"How long did it take you to learn how to do *that*?" asked Step.

The kid turned to face him. He had black-frame coke-bottle glasses so his eyes looked like they were swimming around in a specimen jar. "I been blowing rings since my mom taught me how when I was ten."

"Your mom taught you how to blow *smoke rings?* When you were *ten?*"

The kid laughed. "This is tobacco country, Mr. Fletcher, and my people are all tobacco people. My mama used to blow smoke in my face when I was a baby, so I'd grow up knowing the difference between the cheap weed in Reynolds cigarettes and the good stuff in E&Es."

Step hoped that his shudder didn't show. When he and DeAnne were house-hunting, they had had to rule out the whole eastern edge of town, where the Eldredge & Emerson Tobacco Company kept the air filled with the pungence of tar and nicotine, like being trapped forever on an elevator with someone who put out his cigarette *just* before stepping on.

What business did Mormons have moving into tobacco country? Especially since DeAnne was so allergic to tobacco smoke that it made her throw up even when she *wasn't* pregnant. The idea of somebody blowing smoke in a baby's face made Step angry. There's things you just don't do to children, if you have any decency. And teaching a ten-year-old to blow smoke rings . . .

"I don't want to sound like some kind of dumb fan or nothing, Mr. Fletcher, but I thought Hacker Snack was the best game anybody ever did on the Atari."

"Thanks," said Step.

"Of course, your A.I. routines really sucked."

It hit Step like a blow, that forced change from shyly, genially accepting a compliment to suddenly having to take criticism.

"A.I.?" he asked.

"You know—artificial intelligence."

"I know what A.I. stands for," said Step. "I just don't recall ever trying to incorporate any of it into my game."

"I mean, you know, the way the bad guys home in on the player," he said. "The machine intelligence routines.

Way too predictable. It stayed too easy to dodge them until you finally beat the player down with sheer speed. Like bludgeoning them to death."

"Hey, thanks," said Step.

"No, really, I loved the game, I just wished you had kept the bad guys moving in a kind of semi-random way, so the player wouldn't catch on that they were homing in. So you couldn't *quite* be sure where they were going to go. Then the game would have stayed fun into much higher levels, and you would never have had to include that killer speed level where you *can't* outrun the bad guys."

"There *is* no killer speed level," said Step.

"Really?"

"Not if you find all the back doors out of the different rooms."

It was the kid's turn to look embarrassed. "Back doors?"

"Hacker Snack isn't an arcade game, it's a puzzle game," said Step. "Don't tell me you were trying to outrun those little suckers at every level."

"I got up to half a million points doing it that way," said the kid.

"That is the most incredible thing I ever heard. You should've been creamed before you got twenty thousand points. You must have the reflexes of a bat."

The kid grinned. "I'm the best damn video wizard you'll ever meet," he said. "You got to show me those back doors."

"And you got to show me what you mean about randomizing."

"Come on inside, I've got your game up on one of my machines, just in case you came by."

"You got an Atari here?"

"Hey, there's not a soul here who doesn't know the Atari is ten times the computer the 64 is. The only reason we're all writing 64 software is that millions of them are getting bought and the Atari is still going for like a thousand dollars which means nobody buys it."

Step followed him into the building. "How come you came outside to smoke?" he asked. "I notice people smoking in most of the offices."

"Not in mine," said the kid. "I don't let anybody smoke around the machines. Fouls them up. Like pouring Cokes on them."

The kid didn't *let* anybody smoke around any of the machines?

"What's your name?" Step asked.

"My parents call me Bubba, I was baptized Roland McIntyre, but I kind of think of myself as Saladin Gallowglass." He glanced back over his shoulder at Step and grinned. "You ever play D&D?"

"My brother tried to teach me Dungeons and Dragons one time, but after five hours the game itself hadn't actually started."

"Then he's a piss-poor dungeonmaster, if you ask me, no offense of course since he's your brother. A good dungeonmaster can get you into the game in half an hour and make it move along like you were watching a movie. Almost. Here's *your* office, by the way."

It was an empty room. They had known he was coming, and there wasn't even a desk inside.

"They had a desk in here but I made them move it out," said Bubba Roland Saladin Gallowglass. "I told them you weren't here to write prissy little maiden-aunt letters to your nieces and nephews, you were here to write manuals and for that you needed a full computer setup, complete with a word processor and at least one of every computer we do software for. So they're coming in this afternoon to put up a computer counter like the one I've got here. This is *my* office. You'll be sharing with me till yours is ready, if you don't mind."

Step walked into hacker heaven. Two desk-height counters ran along both the long walls of the room, with a couple of shelves above them. The lower shelf held monitors for a half-dozen computers, and the upper shelf held books and papers and stacks of disks. And the counter itself was crowded with 64s, a couple of VICs, a TI, a Radio Shack Color Computer, even one of those crummy little Timex computers. Also an old monochrome Pet, which was apparently used as a word processor. And an Atari, with Hacker Snack up and running in demonstration mode. Except that the demonstration mode was supposed to have the game at level one, and this one was running at level twenty.

"You broke into the code," said Step.

"I like to use the game as a screen saver, because everything shifts on it. But level twenty has the prettiest colors."

"That was copy-protected six ways from Tuesday."

"Yeah, well, it was a ten-minute job to break the scheme and another hour or so to disassemble the code." Bubba Roland Saladin Gallowglass looked proud of himself, and Step couldn't disagree with him. Step was a pretty good programmer, but this kid was a true hacker, a boy genius of code. And somehow this same kid had the authority to make Eight Bits Inc. remodel Step's office.

"What's your job here, anyway?" asked Step.

"Oh, I just hang around and do some programming. I'm really supposed to be a student at UNC-S, but I'm sort of between semesters right now."

"Spring break?"

"Yeah, for about a year now. I tried taking computer classes but they wanted to teach me COBOL, if you can believe it. Had to have FORTRAN or I couldn't graduate. Like making you study dinosaur anatomy in med school. A bunch of us are going to Richmond for the David Bowie concert this weekend. Want to come?"

Flattered at the invitation, Step had to decline. "We're still unpacking, and I'm more into good old-fashioned American rock and roll. Bowie's too disco for me."

"Oh, he's past disco now. He's past glitter, too. He's sort of in punk mode."

"Yeah, well . . ."

"I think of my D&D character, you know, Saladin Gallowglass, I think of him as looking like David Bowie. Or like Sting."

"Sting?" asked Step.

"With the Police," said the kid. When Step still showed no sign of comprehension, the kid shook his head and went on. "I understand you're going to be doing kind of quality control for us."

"From what Dicky said this morning," said Step, "I have to get him to unzip my fly when I pee."

The kid giggled. "That's Dickhead for you. No, Ray told me that you're a precious resource. The only way he could get Dickhead to accept the idea of hiring you was to promise that you'd have nothing to do with programming, but in fact he wants your fingers in everything. He thinks of you as the computer wizard of the universe."

"Well, I'm not," said Step. "I'm a historian who taught myself programming in my spare time."

"All good programmers are self-taught, at least in the home computer business," said the kid.

"Look, what do I actually *call* you?"

"Around here they call me Roland and you probably should, too," said the kid.

"But what would you prefer?"

He grinned. "Like I said, I think of myself as Saladin Gallowglass."

"So is Gallowglass all right, or is that too formal?"

"Gallowglass is great, *Mr.* Fletcher."

"Call me Step."

"Hey, Step."

"Mind if I ask, how old *are* you?"

"Twenty-two."

"And if you're just a common ordinary programmer,

how come Ray Keene tells you stuff that he doesn't tell Dicky?"

"Oh, I suppose because he's known me longer. I used to hang around his house and I learned programming on his Commodore Pet when I was, like, sixteen."

It dawned on Step: In all his interviews and meetings, no one had ever mentioned the existence of this wunderkind, and no one had ever told him who it was who actually coded the original software that had earned Ray Keene a Mercedes and a power office.

"You wrote Scribe 64, didn't you?"

Gallowglass smiled shyly. "Every line of it," he said.

"And I'll bet you're the one who keeps doing the upgrades."

"I'm working on a sixty-character screen right now," he said. "I have to use a sort of virtual screen memory and background character mapping, but it's going pretty well. I have this idea of using character memory as the virtual screen memory, since that means that I'm not actually using up RAM for the mapping."

"I don't know enough about 64 architecture yet to know what you're talking about," said Step. "But I hope I'm not too nosy if I ask you, since you *are* the person who actually *created* Scribe 64, how come you aren't vice-president of something?"

"Ray takes care of me," said Gallowglass. "I kind of make more money than God. And I'm not exactly management material."

"I'd be interested to know how much God makes, someday," said Step.

"And someday maybe I'll tell you." Gallowglass grinned. "What about you? Got any kids?"

"Three, with a fourth on the way."

"How old are they?"

"Stephen's almost eight, Robert is nearly five, Elizabeth is two, and the new one is negative five months now."

"I'll tell you, I really get along great with kids," said

Gallowglass. "If you want me to tend the kids for you sometime, let me know."

"Yeah, right. A programmer who makes more money than God, and I'm going to call him up to babysit for me."

"I mean it, I really like kids, and I get kind of lonely sometimes."

"You don't live with your folks?"

"Dad hates me," said Gallowglass. "I live by myself."

"*Hates* you? Come on."

"No, I mean it, he says it whenever I go home. I walk in the door, he says, 'Damn but I hate you, do you have to keep coming back here?' Mom's OK though. Hey, we're just a good old southern family."

"Sorry. I wasn't trying to pry or anything," said Step.

Gallowglass laughed. "I haven't seen a grown man blush in a long time," he said.

This poor kid, thought Step. A sweet, brilliant, *nice* kid, and not only does his dad hate him, not only did his mom blow smoke in his face as a baby, but also he's getting seriously ripped off by the very people that he trusts most in all the world. None of my business, I know, but this kid ought to at least know that something else is possible. "Let me tell you something," said Step. "The difference between royalties and bonuses is that a royalty is yours by right, by *law,* even after you leave the company, while a bonus is a gift and if Ray ever feels like not giving it to you, then that's just too bad for you."

Gallowglass looked at him steadily through those bottle-bottom lenses.

"I just thought you ought to know that," said Step. "In case you ever want to write another piece of software. Maybe on the next one, they'll mention your name somewhere in the manual. It's something we programmers don't get much of—credit for what we do."

"You had your name on Hacker Snack," observed Gallowglass.

"I turned down two software publishers because they wouldn't write that into the contract," said Step. "That's why you folks here at Eight Bits knew my name. But until this very moment, no one here *ever* mentioned *your* name. In fact, I kind of got the impression that Ray wrote Scribe 64 himself."

"You did?" asked Gallowglass.

"Not that he ever said so," said Step.

"Ray can't program a computer to print his name on the screen," said Gallowglass.

"Yeah, well, I didn't know that," said Step. "He never told me. Hey, not his fault if I got the wrong impression. The main thing is that I think it's important for programmers to get credit for what we do. Like an author getting his name on his own book."

"You weren't the first to get your name above the title, you know," said Gallowglass. "Doug Duncan got his name on Russian Front even before you."

"Yeah," said Step. "I already had my contract signed before Russian Front came out, but he *was* the first to get his game out that way."

"I met him at CES last year," said Gallowglass.

"Yeah?"

"I did him like I did you—told him it was a great game but then I laid into one of the flaws in the game."

"Oh, is this something you do to everybody?" asked Step.

"Sure."

"Where'd you learn *that* technique, from *How to Win Friends and Influence People?*"

Gallowglass giggled. "I just like to see how people react to it. You took it just fine. In fact, best ever. You actually *listened* to a kid with glasses and a pocket protector and you didn't know me from shit on the sidewalk."

"What did Duncan do?"

"Well, let's just say that Doug Duncan is the kind of guy who never, *ever* forgives anybody who dares to suggest that anything he ever did was somewhat less than perfect. He actually got me kicked off a panel at a conference six months later. Said he'd leave and not do his thing there if I was given a microphone at the conference. He never forgives and he never forgets."

"Maybe that would have taught you not to criticize strangers."

"Hey, it's my flaming-asshole test, and Duncan leaves a trail of ashes wherever he goes."

Step had to laugh. He liked this kid. Maybe a lot. Though if Dicky had overheard their conversation about royalties and credit for programmers, both of them would probably be in trouble. "Hey, uh, how sound-proof is this office?" asked Step.

"How the hell should I know?" asked Gallowglass. "But with all these games on, who do you think can hear us?"

Step thought, but did not say, that the games *in* the room made them talk *louder*, while the noise they made wouldn't interfere half as much with someone *outside* the room who wanted to listen in.

Someone knocked on the door.

"Come in!" yelled Gallowglass.

It was Dicky, and for a moment Step felt that rush of guilt that comes when you've just been caught. Dicky *had* been listening.

"So there you are," said Dicky. "I've been looking all over for you."

"Me?" said Step.

"I wondered if you wanted to go for lunch with me."

"He can't," said Gallowglass immediately. "He's going to lunch with *me,* so I can get him up to speed on the new features in Scribe 64."

"And I have to get him up to speed on everything else," said Dicky, looking a bit stern.

"Hey, leave me out of this," said Step. "This is my first day, I'll go wherever I'm told."

But Dicky and Gallowglass gazed at each other for a few long moments more, until at last Dicky said, "Come see me after lunch."

"Sure," said Step. "But you're my supervisor, Mr. Northanger, so my schedule is yours to command."

"Call me Dicky," said Dicky.

"Not Richard?" asked Step.

"Is there something wrong with Dicky?" asked Dicky.

"No," said Step. "I just thought—"

"Dicky is not a nickname for Richard," said Dicky. "It's the name I was christened with."

"I'm sorry," said Step.

"And meeting with you after lunch is what I *prefer*." Dicky closed the door behind him.

"Man, you're a champion suck-up," said Gallowglass.

Step turned on him. "What are you trying to do, get my supervisor permanently pissed off at me on my first day on the job?"

"Don't take Dicky so seriously," said Gallowglass. "He can't touch a program without introducing a bug into it. The guy's worthless."

Apparently Gallowglass had no concept of the kind of trouble that Dicky could make for a man in Step's position. This kid's relationship was with the owner, and he was the programmer of the bread-and-butter program that was paying everybody's salaries, so he really *could* treat Dicky however he liked. But that didn't mean Dicky liked it. In fact, if this had gone on very long, by now Dicky probably seethed at anything Gallowglass did or said. And he'd take it out on whoever was closest to Gallowglass who actually needed his job.

Step.

"Do me a favor," said Step. "Don't do anything to get Dicky any more ticked off at me than he is."

"Sure," said Gallowglass. "Don't get mad. It's really OK, I promise you. You're in like Flynn around here, everybody's really excited you're actually here. You'll see, it'll be great."

"No sweat then," said Step, though Gallowglass was probably wrong.

"And I really would be glad to tend your kids for you."

"Thanks," said Step.

"I'm really good at it. And I'm not afraid to change diapers."

"Sure," said Step. "I'll talk to DeAnne about it."

"OK. Squeet."

"What?"

"Squeet. It's just a word we use around here. It means Let's go eat, only the way you say it when you say it real fast. Squeet."

"Sure, fine," said Step. "Squeet."

4

▪YUCKY HOLES▪

This is why DeAnne, a westerner all her life, was unpacking boxes in the family room of a house in Steuben, North Carolina: Her earliest memories were of growing up in Los Angeles, in a poorer part of town back in the fifties, when gangs did not yet rule and blacks were still colored people who were just starting to march and had not yet rioted. Her neighborhood and school friends were of an array of races and nationalities. She barely noticed this until she left.

Her father got his doctorate and went to teach at Brigham Young University—the "Y." She was eight years old when she first went to school in Orem, Utah. All the children in her class were white, all of them were Mormon, and many of them were the same children she saw at church on Sunday. This was the fall of 1962, and the conversation among the children turned, eventually, to civil rights and Martin Luther King. Deeny was stunned to hear some of the other children speak of "niggers," a word she had thought was like any other word written on walls—one knew it existed but never said it where God could hear.

When they saw how upset Deeny was, they laughed, and some said things that were even nastier— that all colored people stank and were stupid, that they all stole and carried razor blades. She furiously told them that it wasn't true, that her best friend Debbie in Los Angeles was colored and she was as smart as anybody and she didn't stink and the only kid who ever stole anything from them was a white boy. This made them angry. They said terrible things to her and shoved her and poked her and pinched her, and she came home from school in tears. Her parents reassured her that she was right, but she never forgot the ugly face of bigotry, and how angry the other children got when someone stood up against them.

It was no accident that when Step decided to go on for a doctorate in history, they didn't even apply to a school west of the Mississippi. DeAnne was determined that her children would not grow up in Utah, where everyone they knew would be Mormon and white, and where children could come to believe terrible lies about anyone who wasn't just like them. Step agreed with her—as he put it, they didn't want to raise their kids where Mormons were too thick on the ground.

That was fine in theory, but the reality was this depressingly dark family room in this shabby house in Steuben, North Carolina. And Stevie had to walk into class today as a complete stranger, with no sense of connection.

In Utah, Stevie would have known all these children already, from the neighborhood, from church. He would share in the same pattern of life, would know what to expect from them. We've given our children a wonderful variety of strangeness, just as we planned, thought DeAnne, but at the same time we've deprived them of a sense of belonging where they live. They're foreigners here. *We* are foreigners here.

I am a stranger, and this is a strange, strange land.

Robbie and Elizabeth were down for their naps. For Elizabeth that meant serious hard sleeping; for Robbie, it meant lying in bed reading the jokes and puzzles in his favorite volume of *Childcraft*. Enough that they were pinned down and quiet. It gave her a chance to be alone, to empty the boxes, one by one . . . to brood about her life and whether she was a good mother and a good wife and a good Mormon and even a good person, which she secretly knew she was not and never could be, no matter how she seemed to others, because none of them, not even Step, knew what she was really like inside. How weak she was, how frightened, how uncertain of everything in her life except the Church—that was the thing that did not change, the foundation of her life. Everything else was changeable. Even Step—she knew that she didn't really know him, that always there was the chance that someday he would surprise her, that she would turn to face her husband and find a stranger in his place, a stranger who didn't approve of her and didn't want her in his life anymore. DeAnne knew that to hold on to any good thing in her life—her husband, her children—she had to do the right thing, every time. It was the selvage of the fabric of her life. If only she could be sure, from day to day, from hour to hour, what the right thing was.

The doorbell rang.

It was a thirtyish woman, slender as Jane Fonda, a bit shorter than DeAnne. She had three kids in tow, the oldest a boy about Robbie's age, and somehow—perhaps because of the kids, perhaps because of her practical cover-everything clothing, perhaps just because of her confident, cheerful face with hardly a speck of makeup on it—DeAnne knew that this woman was a Mormon. Or, if she wasn't, should be.

"Sister Fletcher?" said the woman.

She *was* Mormon. "Yes," said DeAnne.

"I'm Jenny Cooper, spelled with a *w* as if it was *cow*-per, only it isn't."

"Like the poet," said DeAnne.

Jenny grinned. "I knew it! I've lived here six years, and now when I've only got three-and-a-half months left before we move to Arizona, *now* somebody finally moves in who's actually heard of William Cowper."

Wouldn't you know it, thought DeAnne. I'm already starting to like her, and she's moving away. "Come in, please. My kids are napping, but as long as we stay in the family room—"

"Your kids *nap?* Let's trade," said Jenny as she strode in. She gave no sign of noticing or caring whether her kids followed her inside or not. "I know you're busy moving in but I brought a razor knife and I fed and watered my herd before we came, so show me where the boxes are."

"I'm doing books today," said DeAnne, leading her into the family room. "But you don't really have to help."

"Alphabetical order?"

"Eventually," said DeAnne. "But it's enough if you sort of group them together. Jenny, how in the world did you know my name? We didn't even go to church on Sunday."

"I noticed that," said Jenny. "A few weeks ago the bishop says that he got a call from Brother Something-or-other from Vigor, Indiana, who was going to move into a house in the ward on the first weekend in March. I figure, they'll need help moving in, so I waited for you to show up at Church, only you didn't come. So, this is what I thought: If they were inactive, Brother Something wouldn't have called. So either they didn't actually move on schedule, or they're the kind of *proud, stubborn, self-willed, stuck-up* people who wouldn't dream of asking for help and so they skipped their first Sunday and plan to show up *next* week, with everything all unpacked and put away, and when people offer to help, they'll say, 'Already done, thanks just the same.'"

DeAnne laughed. "You got us pegged, all right."

"So, I had the Sunday school hour—I don't go to gospel doctrine class, the teacher and I don't see eye to eye—and I ducked into the clerk's office, looked up the Vigor Ward in the Church directory, and made a long distance call to your home ward. Talked to *your* ward clerk, and asked him if they had any ward members who had just moved to Steuben, North Carolina, and he said, Yes, of *course*, the *Fletchers*, and they were the most wonderful people, Sister Fletcher had been the education counselor in Relief Society and Brother Fletcher was the elders quorum president and conducted the choir, they had three kids and a fourth due in July, and they were great speakers, we ought to get them both to talk in sacrament meeting as often as possible—"

"Oh, that was Brother Hyde, he was just being sweet." DeAnne could not believe that Brother Hyde had actually remembered when their baby was due, or that he had given that information to a stranger. But then, they were all in the Church, weren't they? And that meant that they were "no more strangers, but fellow citizens of the saints," or however it went in Paul's epistle to—to some bunch of Greeks. Or Romans or Hebrews.

"Yes, well, I'm sure," said Jenny. "He also gave me your address, and *then* I remembered that I had driven right by your moving van last Friday or whenever it was that you moved in and it never occurred to me that a *Mormon* family would move in only around the block from me. I mean, to have a Mormon *neighbor*. That just doesn't *happen* in Steuben."

Even if Jenny hadn't been meticulous about shelving the books alphabetically by author and in the right groupings, DeAnne would have enjoyed having her there, just to have relief from her own brooding. Somehow, with a completely different upbringing, Jenny had managed to acquire a similar attitude toward the Church. The difference was that Jenny was willing to say right out things that DeAnne would never have dared to admit to anyone but Step.

"I had to get here first," said Jenny, "or your introduction to the Steuben First Ward would have been Dolores LeSueur, our ward prophetess."

"Your *what*?"

"She's in the vision business. She has revelations for everybody. She's been dying of cancer for fifteen years only she keeps getting healed, but with death breathing down her neck she has become *so* much closer to God than ever before—and I'm sure that she was so close to God *before* that they probably shared a toothbrush. She can't say hello without telling you that the Spirit told her to greet you. You'll just love her."

"I will? I don't think so, if she's the way you describe her."

"Oh, you *will*, because if you don't that'll prove you're a tool of Satan and an evil influence on the ward. Don't worry, as long as she gets her way about everything she's harmless."

"Are you serious?"

"Absolutely. If she's in charge of a ward activity, everything will go her way. If she decides how you ought to run your ward organization, then your organization will run that way."

"You mean she claims inspiration?"

"Oh, she claims inspiration every time she has to use the john. No, if you don't agree with her, she just gets all her disciples to nag the bishop until he makes you do it her way just so they'll leave him alone. And if the bishop doesn't give in to her, she goes to the stake president, and if *he* doesn't give her what she wants, she calls Salt Lake until somebody there says something she can use to bludgeon you into submission. But don't let me bias you against her."

DeAnne said what she always said, because she knew it was right to reject malice. "I'd rather form my own opinions."

Jenny cocked her head and studied DeAnne for a moment, as if to see *just* how judgmental DeAnne might be. "Oh, I know this sounds like gossip. It *is* gossip. But I promise you, that's all I'll ever say about Dolores until you mention her again yourself. I just happen to know from experience that about six weeks from now, you'll be really glad to know that somebody else in the ward sees through her act. Nuff said. I'm probably too blunt, I know, but I grew up on a ranch in Santaquin where *manure* was a word we only used at church on Sunday, so I just speak my mind. For instance, I've noticed that you keep watching my kids and shooing them away from things and that means that *your* kids must be well-behaved and trained not to break stuff. *Our* strategy was to make sure we didn't own anything that we cared if it got broke. But I'll tell you what, we've about done with the books so let me finish this box and I'll get my monsters out of here so they can go back to tearing up *my* house."

"I really wasn't thinking . . ."

"We're careful of our children about the things that count," said Jenny. "A friend of one of the secretaries where my husband works had a cousin here in town who lost her little boy. Only she didn't even realize he was missing for ten hours. Can you believe that? I may not know what my children are doing every second, but I know where they *are*."

"Jenny, I *like* your kids, they're not a problem."

"Good. So do I. This evening you bring your family on down to my house for supper. We're two blocks up Chinqua Penn that way, turn right on Wally—that's a street, not a bum in the road—and we're five doors down on the right."

"I really couldn't put you out for supper—my kitchen is put together now, so—"

"I'm sure you're really looking forward to thinking up some kind of supper and stopping your unpacking long enough to prepare it," said Jenny.

DeAnne couldn't pretend that Jenny wasn't right, and besides, her mind was still back on what Jenny had said before. "That woman whose little boy was missing. Did they find him?"

"I don't know," said Jenny. "I never heard. By the way, in case you're wondering, I don't cook southern, I cook western. That means that there won't be nothin' deep-fried or even pan-fried. And I cook western *ranch*, not western *Mormon*, which means you won't be getting some tuna casserole and a Jell-O salad, it'll be an oven roast and baked potatoes and gravy, and I already bought enough for your whole crew so don't make it go to waste, just say yes and show up at six."

That was that. Jenny finished the box, called her kids, plunged out the door, and the kids straggled along behind her. DeAnne felt invigorated by Jenny's visit. Even better, she felt *at home*, because she knew somebody now, she had a friend.

She looked at her watch. It was two-thirteen. She was supposed to be at school to pick Stevie up in two minutes.

She bustled into the bedroom and dragged the kids out of bed—Robbie was actually *asleep*, today of all days—made them carry their shoes and socks out to the car and managed to get to that parking lot on the top of the bluff overlooking the school by twenty after. There were still a billion cars and parents there, or anyway more than the parking lot was designed to handle, and tons of children around—but no Stevie. He must have come up the hill and looked around and then, following her instructions, headed back down to wait for her in the principal's office.

She managed to get both of Elizabeth's shoes on her at the same time, and Robbie got his own on with the velcro straps fastened down—thank heaven for velcro. It was almost two-thirty when she finally herded the children into the front of the school. The last of the buses was just pulling away. Stevie was sitting in Dr. Mariner's office. The second he saw her, he was on his feet and heading out the door.

"Just a moment, Mrs. Fletcher," said the secretary.

DeAnne turned back to face her.

"If you aren't able to pick up your child on time, may I suggest that you have him ride the bus? Or arrange for the after-school program?"

"I'll be on time from now on," said DeAnne. "Or we'll set him up for the bus."

"Because this room is not a holding area for children, it's a working office," said the secretary.

"Yes, I'm sorry," said DeAnne. "It won't happen again."

"We like children very much here," said the secretary, "but we must reserve this area for adult business, and we appreciate it when our parents are *thoughtful* enough not to—"

"Yes," said DeAnne, "I can promise you that the only way I'll be late to pick him up again is if I'm dead. Thank you very much." Seething inside, she left the office, Elizabeth on her hip and Robbie in tow. Stevie was waiting at the front door of the school.

"I wasn't *very* late," said DeAnne. "But I thought that maybe your class hadn't gotten out yet, so I waited at the top of the hill."

Stevie nodded, saying nothing. As soon as she caught up with him he walked briskly on ahead, leading the way to the stairs up the hill.

Robbie broke free of DeAnne's grip and caught up with Stevie, but his relentless conversation couldn't penetrate Stevie's silence. He must be really angry with me, thought DeAnne. Usually Robbie could pull him out of a sulk in thirty seconds flat.

When they got to the car, DeAnne apologized again for being late, but Stevie said nothing, just got into the front passenger seat while she was belting the kids into their seats in back. "Is Stevie mad at me?" whispered Robbie at the top of his voice.

"I think he's mad at *me*," said DeAnne. "Don't worry."

She got into the car and backed out of the parking place, navigated a narrow road among a small stand of trees, and finally pulled out on a main road. Only then could she glance down at Stevie. "Please don't be mad at me, Stevie. It'll never happen again."

He shook his head and a silver tear flew from his eye, catching a glint of sunlight before it disappeared onto the floor. He wasn't sulking, he was crying.

She reached out and caught his left hand, held it. "Oh, Stevie, what's wrong, honey? Was it really so bad?"

Again he shook his head; he didn't want to talk about it yet. But he didn't take his hand away, either. So he didn't hate her for being late, and when he was able to he'd tell her what happened and he'd accept whatever comfort she could give. She held his hand all the way home.

He didn't want a snack—he headed straight for his room. She kept Robbie out, though it took practically nailing his feet to the kitchen floor to do it. She ended up giving Robbie and Elizabeth their snacks, and then decided that they needed a walk outside. They'd been cooped up in the house all day, and even though it was the first week of March it had been a warm winter, not a flake of snow even in Indiana, and almost balmy ever since they got to Steuben. They could walk down and make sure they knew which house was the Cowpers' while it was still daylight.

She leaned into Stevie's room. He was lying on his bed, facing away from the door. "Stevie, honey, we're going to take a walk. Want to come?"

He mumbled no.

"I'm going to lock the doors. I'll only be gone a few minutes, OK? But if there's a problem, we'll be out in front somewhere, we won't go out of sight, OK?"

He nodded.

Out on the street, she realized for the first time that there weren't any sidewalks. They couldn't even walk on the grass—people planted hedges right down to the street. How completely stupid, how unsafe! Where do children rollerskate? Where do you teach children to walk so they'll be safe? Maybe people in Steuben haven't noticed yet that cars sometimes run over children in the road.

It made her feel trapped again, as if she had found out that they would have to live in a house with no hot water or no indoor toilets. I had no business bringing my children to this uncivilized place. In Utah I could have kept them on the sidewalk and they would have been fine.

In Utah.

Is that what I am? One of those Mormons who think that anything that is different from Utah is wrong? She mentally shook herself and began giving the kids a revised version of the sidewalk lecture. "Stay close to the curb and walk on the lawns wherever you can."

Robbie was bouncing his red ball in the gutter as they walked. It was one of those hollow rubber ones about four inches across, small enough for a small child to handle it but big enough that it wasn't always getting lost. "I wish you hadn't brought that, Robbie," said DeAnne.

"You told me it was an outside toy, and we're outside."

"Well, if it bounces into the street, you *can't* chase it, you have to wait for it to roll to one side or the other, all right?"

Robbie nodded hugely—and then kept on nodding, not so much to annoy his mother as because nodding with such exaggerated movement was fun. "Look, Mom, the whole world is going up and down!"

Of course, he had not stopped bouncing the ball, and at this point the inevitable happened—it bounced off his toe and careened down the gutter away from them, rolling into the road and then drifting back to the curb, where it disappeared.

"My ball!" cried Robbie. "It went down that hole!"

Sure enough, the ball had, with unerring aim, found a storm drain and rolled right in. This was the first time DeAnne had really noticed what the drains were like, and again she was appalled. They were huge gaps in the curb, and the gutter sloped sharply down to guide the flow of water into them. The effect was that *any* object that came anywhere near them would inevitably be sucked inside. And the gap was large enough that a small child could easily fit into the drain. Naturally the people who designed roads without sidewalks would think nothing of creating storm drains that children could fit into.

"Mom, get it out!"

DeAnne sighed and set Elizabeth down on the neighbor's lawn. "Stay right by your sister and don't let her go anywhere, Robbie."

Of course, this meant that Robbie grabbed hold of Elizabeth's arm and Elizabeth began to scream. "I didn't mean tackle her and pin her to the grass, Robbie."

"She was going to go into the street," said Robbie. "She's really stupid, Mom."

"She isn't stupid, Robbie, she's two."

"Did I go in the street when I was two?"

Elizabeth had stopped screaming and was tearing grass out of the neighbor's lawn.

"No, Robbie. You were too scared that a motorcycle might come by. You had this thing about motorcycles. You used to dream that they were coming to get you and eat you. So you never went into the street because that's where the Motorman was."

In the meantime, DeAnne was down on her hands and knees, trying to see anything at all in the storm drain. It was too dark.

"I can't see anything," DeAnne said. "I'm sorry, Robbie. I wish you hadn't brought the ball on this walk."

"You mean you aren't going to reach in and hunt for it?"

"Robbie, no, I'm not," said DeAnne. "I can't *see* in there. *Anything* could be down in that hole."

Suddenly he looked terrified. "Like what?"

"I meant that I just don't know what's in there and I'm not going to go reaching around for it. For all we know it's eight feet down, or the ball might have already rolled halfway to Hickey's Chapel Road." She gathered up Elizabeth and took Robbie's hand and they walked on toward the street where the Cowpers lived.

"Stevie *said* this was a bad place."

"Stevie said what?"

"A bad *place*," said Robbie, enunciating clearly, as if his mother were deaf.

What could Stevie have meant by saying such a thing to Robbie? Did he mean the house? The neighborhood? School? Steuben?

Robbie looked over his shoulder again toward the drain. "Do you think that someday they'll find my ball down there?"

"Since the ball isn't biodegradable, it will probably still be there for the Second Coming."

Robbie was still trying to extract meaning from that

last statement when they got to the second corner. DeAnne stopped there and counted down five houses on the right. The Cowpers' was a one-story brick house with a station wagon in the driveway, with two kids climbing all over the top of it. DeAnne would never let her kids climb on the car. They could fall off. They could damage something. The hood of the wagon was up, and as she watched, she saw Jenny emerge from the hood, where apparently she had been fixing something in the car. Jenny stretched her back, looked around, and saw DeAnne. She waved the gray doughnut-shaped thing she was holding. DeAnne waved back.

Jenny yelled something, but DeAnne couldn't hear her, and it embarrassed her to have somebody yelling to her on the street. So she waved again, as if to say yes to whatever Jenny said—which was probably something like, See you at six, or, Nice weather we're having—and then turned and herded her little flock back toward home.

"Kitty!" shouted Elizabeth right in DeAnne's ear. "Kitty! Kitty!"

A jet-black kitten scurried across the road just as a car came speeding by. The cat dodged out of the way; the car made no effort to slow down or stop. DeAnne's fears about the dangers of the street in front of their house were all confirmed.

"Wow," said Robbie. "We almost had a kitty pizza."

Another Step-ism.

The cat headed straight for the storm drain and disappeared.

"Mom!" screamed Robbie. "The yucky hole got him!"

Robbie ran a few dozen steps toward the hole. Then he realized that he was not in the protection of his mother and started to run back. But he could not bring himself to leave the kitty, and so he stood there beating his fists against his hips, demanding that his mother hurry, *hurry!*

"Honey, the kitty probably goes down into that hole all the time and plays there."

But Robbie wasn't hearing anything she had to say. "The snake got him, Mom! You got to save him, you got to!"

Of course Robbie would imagine a snake down there. Step had taken them to a science museum and they had watched a snake eating a mouse. Robbie couldn't let go of the memory. Snakes had replaced the Motorman.

She knelt by him and put her arm around him to calm him. "Robbie, I promise you, there is *no* snake down there. Whenever it rains here, the water all rushes down into that drain, and if there were any snakes living down there they would have been washed out to the ocean years ago."

"The yucky hole hooks up to the *ocean?*" asked Robbie.

"Everything does," said DeAnne.

"Wow, cool."

Robbie took a wide berth around the drain, and as DeAnne stood at the front door, fumbling in her purse to find her keys, he stayed at the curb, looking back toward the yucky hole.

"What if it rains while the kitty's down there, Mom?" he asked.

"It isn't going to rain for days, and the cat will get hungry and go home long before then," said DeAnne. She got the door open. "Come on inside, Robbie."

"Do you think the kitty's playing with my ball down there?" he asked as he came through the door.

"Kitty," said Elizabeth. "Yucky hole, all gone."

"That's the story," said DeAnne. "Looks like we can't keep anything from *you*, Elizabeth."

"Drink," said Elizabeth.

Robbie had already rushed ahead to the room he shared with Stevie, shouting out the story about the ball and the kitty and the yucky hole long before he got to the room. DeAnne smiled as she took Elizabeth into the kitchen to get a drink. If anybody could get Stevie out of his blue funk, it was Robbie.

A moment later, Robbie was in the kitchen, looking mournful. "Mommy," he said. "Stevie told me to shut up and die."

"What?" asked DeAnne.

"He doesn't want a little brother anymore, Mommy," said Robbie.

DeAnne set Elizabeth down on the kitchen floor. "Stay with your sister for a minute, would you?"

"Can I turn on the TV?"

"The cable isn't hooked up yet so there's hardly anything to watch," she said, "but suit yourself."

She found Stevie lying right where she had left him before going on the walk. "Son," she said.

"Yeah?" he mumbled.

"Son, sit up and look at me, please," she said.

He sat up and looked at her.

"Please don't ever say anything so terrible to your brother again."

"I'm sorry," said Stevie.

"Did you really tell him to shut up and die?"

Stevie shook his head. "Not exactly."

"What did you say, then?"

"I told him to shut up, and when he just kept yelling about a snake eating a kitty I just told him to drop dead."

"Where did you ever hear an expression like that?"

"Everybody said it back at my old school, Mom. It doesn't really mean that I want him to die."

"Well, Robbie doesn't understand that, Stevie. You can't say things like that, even joking. Not to your own brother."

"I'm sorry."

He looked so miserable. And DeAnne could understand how, after years of sharing a room with Robbie, the dedicated extrovert, Stevie could have moments of complete exasperation, for once Robbie thought of something he wanted to say, he *would* say it, even if you begged him for silence. He simply could not leave a thought unspoken. The miracle was that Stevie was usually so patient with his brother.

"I'm sorry, too," said DeAnne. "I shouldn't have told you off like that." She sat down beside him on the edge of his bed and put her arm around him. "You've had a tough day, and here I am, no help at all."

"I'm fine, Mom."

"Can't you tell me what happened?"

"Nothing happened," said Stevie.

"Did you make any friends?"

"No!" he said, so vehemently that she knew there was far more to the story than he was telling.

"Were they mean to you?"

"No," he said.

"Is Mrs. Jones a nice teacher?"

He nodded, then shrugged.

"Did you have any homework?"

He shook his head.

"Do you just want me to leave you alone for a while longer?"

He nodded.

She felt so useless. "I love you, Stevie," she said.

He murmured something that might have been "love you too" and then, as she got up, he rolled back over, curled up on his bed.

She left his room, feeling deeply depressed. As she walked down the hall she could hear the television in the other room. Robbie was switching from channel to channel, so it alternated between loud hissing and very fuzzy reception on the local channels. For just a moment she couldn't bring herself to go into the same room with her children. She was supposed to know what they needed and provide it for them, and she was going to let them down because she didn't have a clue.

She went to the front door, opened it, and stepped out onto the porch. Then, in spite of the scoffing of her rational mind, she had to leave the porch and walk across the lawn and stand at the curb and look at the storm drain up the street. The yucky hole. Just to see if the kitten had come out.

Of course it had probably come out while she was in the house and so it was absurd to stand here, watching. She would go back inside. Right now. This was foolish.

A movement in the corner of her eye caught her attention. She turned toward the house, and there in the side yard between the house and the neighbors' fence was a gray rabbit. Robbie had told her he had seen one, but she hadn't believed that a wild rabbit could really be living in their neighborhood. It looked at her steadily for a moment, then loped off into the back yard.

She followed it, hoping to see where it went. Rabbits might be cute and furry, but they were rodents, like rats and mice, and they could carry diseases. She had to get some idea where it lived or at least where it came from. But when she got to the back yard it was gone.

She walked the wood-slat fence, to see where it might have gone under, but she couldn't see any rabbit-sized gaps. She also examined the latticework skirting around the base of the house, though the thought that the rabbit might live under her own house made her shudder. She *hated* the way that southerners built their houses up off the ground instead of putting in a massive concrete basement the way houses were supposed to be built. Anything could get in under the house—it must be filled with spiderwebs and beetles and who knows what other disgusting creatures, right there where all the waterpipes and wiring and heating ducts were. It made her feel naked, to know that her house was completely exposed on its soft underbelly.

But it didn't look as though there were any place where the rabbit might have slipped through or under the skirting. It was just gone. Probably went across to the driveway and back out into the front yard while I was walking around the other way, she thought.

DeAnne walked back around the house and was horrified to realize that she had left the front door standing wide open. She had never done that—she was an inveterate door locker. But this time she had forgotten. I was just stepping onto the porch, she remembered. I didn't plan to go into the back yard chasing a rabbit.

That was no excuse.

As she hurried toward the door, a *man* stepped through it. A *man* had been in her house! A stranger! With her children! She screamed.

He looked at her, startled and abashed. An old man, white hair sticking out like tiny feathers under a baseball cap. "Ma'am, I'm so sorry—"

"What were you doing in my house!" Somehow she had covered the gap between them and now shoved past him, to stand in the doorway between him and the children.

"Ma'am, the door was open and I called and called—"

She yelled over her shoulder. "Robbie! Robbie, are you all right?"

"Ma'am, please, you got to understand—"

"Get away from here before I call the police," she said. "If you have harmed my children in any way, I—"

"Ma'am," he said, "I used to live here. I just haven't shook the habit yet of walking in. I shouldn't have done it, I know, and I am *so* ashamed of myself, giving you a scare like that, I was plain wrong and I apologize, sometimes I think I still live out in the country I guess where a open door means come on in, folks is to home."

Robbie came up behind her. "Did you call me, Mom?"

"Is your sister all right?"

"We got a fuzzy channel on the TV and she's watching this guy who hits people in the head."

"Thanks, Robbie."

"Can I go back now, Mom?"

"Yes, please, thank you."

The old man resumed his explanations. "My boy Jamie owns this house."

"That doesn't give you the right," said DeAnne.

"I know it, like I said, I was plain wrong and I'm sorry, I won't ever do it again. But ma'am, you ought to be careful and not leave your front door open like that. Folks don't do that in the city. So when I saw it open, I did like country people and didn't even think twice. If it was closed I would've knocked and waited."

"I shouldn't have left it open," said DeAnne. "That was careless of me. Stupid of me."

"Well, now, not stupid. I'd say it was *trusting* of you and kind of sweet. Though I guess I hope I'm never on the wrong side of you again, cause you got a scream like to wake the dead."

DeAnne looked around, embarrassed. But apparently nobody had heard—at least, nobody was charging out of their houses to see why a woman had screamed at this hour.

"Ma'am, all I came by to do was to tell you that I been looking after this house for fifteen years now, ever since my boy built it for me and my missus, only she's dead now and my boy's wife sort of left him and he was lonely in *his* place and he wanted me for company and he needed the rental money on this place to help pay the child support and you know how it is. I moved. Spent the loneliest Christmas of my life here this winter, and so I suppose I'm glad to be moved out of it and I *know* I'm glad to think of a family here. Why, next Christmas Santa Claus will come to this house, will you think of that!"

Now that the fear was wearing off, she could see that there was no harm in this old fellow.

"My name's Bappy Waters," said the old man.

"Pappy?" asked DeAnne.

"Bappy, with a B. Short for my real name, which is Baptize."

"Not really," said DeAnne.

"Oh, yes. My papa was a Holiness preacher and he believed in baptism the way other folks believe in air. It was the cure for whatever ailed you. Other folks might hold with doctors or even with laying on hands, but Papa, he just pushed you down in the water and held you there till the devil come out of you. He was a deep baptizer, my papa was, and I was the firstborn in his family. And what with our last name being Waters, my name was sort of bound to happen, if you think of it. In fact he was set to name me Baptize All God's Children in the Holy, but Mama put her foot down on that and said that if he named a child that he'd deserve it if the boy grew up and shot him dead, and not a jury but would call it justice. Not that I was there to hear the conversation, mind you, but I heard reports of it, you may be sure."

DeAnne couldn't help but laugh. He was a charmer, this old man. And she could see how a country boy, a preacher's son, might act differently around an open door than a city man. How his stepping in like that meant nothing at all. In fact, it was kind of nice to imagine living in simpler times, when you *could* just leave your door open and a passing visitor would poke his head in and find you maybe in the kitchen baking bread or scrubbing the floor and you get up and serve lemonade and chat awhile. In the days before television and telephones and urgent errands. Bappy Waters was a visitor from a simpler time.

"What was it brought you by?" asked DeAnne.

"Well, I know this house inside out, you see. I done

all the handiwork here for fifteen years. So if anything goes bad, like a pipe gets bust in the winter or your cable needs hooking up or whatever, why, I'm equipped and qualified and I know where everything is. Why have some stranger go crawling up in the attic or under the house looking for what I know right where to find it, and besides, when you call me it's free."

"Oh, I couldn't ask you to—"

"Just protecting my son's investment in the property, ma'am."

"Call me DeAnne, please."

"Why, so I will. I knew a DeAnne when I was a boy, she was the prettiest little thing in the county. Died when she was just a slip of a girl, though, got herself drowned when her boyfriend was driving drunk and took them off into the Dan River in spring flood. There was only a half dozen cars in the county in those days, it being the Depression and all. Though truth to tell in Gary County the Depression started about halfway through the War between the States and it hasn't let up since." He laughed, and DeAnne laughed with him.

"For instance, ma'am, your kids are watching television, and I wonder if you know that I can just hook you right up to cable."

"We haven't paid for cable."

"Well, you just go down to the cable office and give them your money and you'll be just fine. They give you your box, then, if you want any of the extra channels. But the house is all wired, is what I'm telling you, and you just connect up to the wall, and it was their decision to leave it connected when I turned my box in at the end of December, so you won't be stealing a thing."

"Well, then, I'll have my husband connect the TV to the wall," she said. "When he gets home, which is any second now."

Bappy nodded and touched the brim of his baseball cap. "I understand, ma'am. After seeing me in your house like that, of course you aren't about to let me inside, and I don't blame you a bit. Tell you what, here's my number. I wrote it on this card for you already. Anything goes wrong with the house, anything at all, you give me a call. That's the home I share with Jamie now, and I'm always there, and when I'm not a machine picks up, if you can imagine. If it's something I can't fix myself, I'll call whoever can."

"Thank you," she said, taking the card.

"Times are tight, ma'am, and rent's high enough without y'all having to worry about paying for repairs and such. Think of me as a sort of free discount on your rent." He grinned again, touched the brim of his cap again, and then walked to the driveway and went left, around the house. That put another little scare into her—where was he going?

But by the time she got to where the front walk joined the driveway at the corner of the house, he was already backing down the drive in a little pickup with garden tools and a couple of big metal tool chests in the back. He was leaning out the window to see where he was backing, and of course he saw her as he slipped by. He stopped the pickup near the foot of the driveway. "Nice to meet you, ma'am," he said.

"Nice to meet you, too," she said, though it had not been nice. Or, well, in fact, it *had* been nice, once she got over the first scare, only it still bothered her, even though she understood the whole thing now, it still had her heart beating so hard that she could feel her own pulse in her head.

"Um, I don't know how to say this, ma'am, but it looks like you got yourself a habit needs breaking just like I do." He pointed behind her.

She turned. She had left the front door open again.

She turned back around, furious with herself, intending to explain—she'd just been walking to the driveway to see what he was *doing.* But he was already backing out into the road, laughing a little, it looked like. And then he waved a jaunty little wave and drove off.

As soon as she got inside she had to lock the door, then go through the whole house, looking behind all the furniture, checking all the closets, the bathrooms, the cupboards to see if he might have taken something or moved something or left something behind or just—just *touched* something. She wanted to take everything out of the cupboards and wash it all. And in the back of her mind there was also the question—what if someone *else* went through that door besides old Bappy, maybe *before* he did, and was now hiding somewhere in the house, waiting for them to go to sleep tonight?

Even as she moved through the house, she knew it was irrational of her to check everything like that, but this was exactly the way her mother had always checked over the house when they got home from a trip, and besides, once DeAnne *thought* of the possibility of someone sneaking into the house, she had to know. She could not just put it out of her mind. Her mind didn't work that way.

I screamed, right out in the front yard, and it was loud, and not one neighbor came out to see why.

Step called at 5:30 to say he was going to be late, but one of the guys he was working with would take him home. Don't wait dinner for him. When she told him about supper at the Cowpers', he said, "Take a picture of me and tell them I'm a miserable rotten husband who has never made it home in time for dinner in the whole time he's worked for Eight Bits Inc."

"Very funny," said DeAnne.

"And it's *true*."

"Please get home before eight, will you? Stevie had a terrible time at school today and he isn't talking to me about it."

"Ah, a father-and-son moment."

"I've never seen him like this, Step."

"I'll be home."

She took the kids to the Cowpers' and it was a circus. The Cowper kids were so undisciplined, running around and screaming, that Robbie soon joined in, and Elizabeth only refrained because DeAnne kept a firm grip on her. Stevie, however, sat at his place and quietly, dutifully ate whatever was put before him. He answered questions in a low voice and volunteered nothing. DeAnne had a sneaking suspicion that whatever had made Stevie upset at school was no longer the reason for his behavior. That what she was seeing now was sullenness, spite. Anger, passively expressed. Stevie was hurt at school somehow, but now he was just mad.

The Cowpers, however, had no notion that anything was wrong. Because they seemed not to care at all what their kids did, they were able to stay at the table and converse for a while after supper. But DeAnne could not bring herself to adopt their attitude toward child care. She felt an unceasing need to know what Robbie was doing and whether he was safe. Who knew what kind of insane games the Cowper children might decide to play? Hadn't she seen them climbing on the car this afternoon? All through the after-supper visiting she got more and more anxious until finally, using Elizabeth's bedtime and the possibility that Step had come home as an excuse, she headed home at seven-thirty.

It was dark outside, and all the way home Robbie told Stevie about the adventures of the walk earlier that day. Robbie took a wide berth around the yucky hole and begged the others to be just as careful. But Stevie just plowed straight ahead, walking as close to the hole as he could, which drove Robbie to fits of anxiety.

"Stevie," said DeAnne. "You may be angry at me, but Robbie hasn't done anything to you."

After a moment, Stevie said, "I'm sorry, Robbie. I'll be more careful next time."

It mollified Robbie—in truth, Stevie could do no wrong, as far as Robbie was concerned. Robbie seemed to have been born with the gift—or perhaps the curse— of empathy. If Stevie or Elizabeth or Step or DeAnne was hurt, Robbie got almost frantic in his sense of urgent helplessness. He had to *do* something to help, and yet at the age of four had no notion of what that might be. His life was almost entirely focused on others. And it made DeAnne wonder if a compassionate, Christlike character might be something you were born with, rather than something you acquired. Maybe all of Christianity was devoted to making normal people believe that they *should* live and feel and think the way that a few, special people just naturally did. In which case most believers would end up either frustrated at their failure to measure up, or frustrated because they *did* measure up but got no joy from suppressing all their natural instincts.

Nonsense, she decided. We are what we choose to be. Robbie is so profoundly compassionate because his *spirit* is that way, and always was that way, long before he was born. And if I'm not as good a person as he is, that doesn't mean that I can't learn to be. To believe anything else would be to despair.

To believe anything else would mean rejecting every other choice she had made in her life.

Step didn't get home by eight o'clock. DeAnne put Elizabeth and Robbie to bed, but she let Stevie stay up a little while longer, waiting for Step. "Here, sit and read a book to me."

He sat next to her, but then he said, "I don't feel like reading."

"Then let's see what's on TV."

But with the cable not yet hooked up, there wasn't anything watchable—too much fuzz, and only three

VHF channels, with a maybe on a fourth one. And two channels on UHF, one with a dingy-looking old western, and one with a screaming used-car salesman. She should have let the old man hook up the cable. Baptize. Bappy. What a name. Of course she would have to tell Step about what she did today. Leaving the door open like that. Or maybe she shouldn't, so he wouldn't worry. But no, she *had* to tell him, because they didn't hide things from each other, especially things that made them look stupid. Only this wasn't about whether DeAnne looked stupid, this was about whether the children would be safe. Step couldn't be worrying all the time about whether she was keeping them safe, he had to concentrate on work. Besides, if she told him he wouldn't blame her, he'd blame himself for not being home, for not having been a good enough provider so that now he had to go away all day and leave her alone to take care of everything. No, that would not be a good story to tell him. But she couldn't leave it unconfessed, either. She would write it in the family journal, and tell him later, much later, when she had gone for several weeks—no, months—without leaving the door open like that.

"I want to play Kaboom," said Stevie.

She sighed inwardly. He'd rather play a videogame than sit with her. A game that he could not win, a game that always made him so frustrated that he used to hit the computer or throw down the joystick until Step had to ban him from the computer several times, to help him learn to control his anger.

Anger was the mode he preferred tonight, apparently. "Go ahead," she said. "I don't know where the cartridges are."

"Right here," he said, going straight to a cardboard box and pulling out a plastic case with slots for all the Atari cartridges. Step had set up the computers the moment all the beds were together, and of course Stevie knew right where everything was.

It was nearly nine and DeAnne was about to send Stevie to bed when Step finally got home. He knew he had let them down and felt terrible about it. "I'm so sorry. Is he still up?"

"Playing Kaboom," she said.

He went to the family room and knelt down beside Stevie. "Son, I'm so sorry I was late. It wasn't my car, and we kept finding new bugs in the program, and I kept saying I had to get home, but he'd say, 'Let's just fix this one thing and try it,' over and over again, and it was *his* car, what can I say? Even as it is he's mad at me for leaving the thing unfinished."

Stevie said nothing, just kept swinging the paddle left and right to catch the little bombs as they dropped from various points along the top of the screen. Then he missed one, and all the bombs on the screen at that moment exploded.

"Stevie, your mom said you were upset when you came home from school today. Do you want to tell me what happened?"

Stevie just stared at the screen, until finally he said, "I don't want to talk to *you* about it."

That slapped Step hard, DeAnne could see it. "Well, then, who are you going to talk to?"

"Mom," said Stevie.

DeAnne could not believe what she was hearing.

Step stood up. "He's punishing me for not getting home soon enough," he said. "And probably for not taking him to school this morning." Step did that—stating out loud how he interpreted the kids' actions, so that they would see that he wasn't fooled, or correct him if he was wrong.

Stevie didn't correct him, so Step went on. "As long as you'll talk to one of us, that's all right. And if you were trying to hurt my feelings, then you've succeeded. I really am sorry that I wasn't here when you needed me, but we explained to you that this is the way it's got to be for a while. Most fathers have to go to work, and when you go to work, you can't always be home when your kids need you. That's the way it is, if we're going to have food on the table and a roof over our heads."

Stevie said nothing. DeAnne had never seen him so unforgiving. In fact, she had never seen him act unforgiving at all. Maybe what happened at school today really *was* awful, so awful that Stevie couldn't forgive his father for not being there to protect him.

Well, she'd find out soon enough now. "Come on, Stevie," she said. "Let's go to your room and you can tell me what happened."

"Not in front of Robbie," he said.

"OK, we'll go to my room," she said. "Step, if you can't wait for supper, fix yourself something, but if you wait I'll poach some eggs or something."

Step nodded, leaning against the bookshelves. As she followed Stevie out of the room, she thought she had never seen Step look so bent, so *broken*, in all the years she'd known him. It made her want to go to him and hold him and comfort him . . . but she knew that Step would understand, would agree that it was more important for her to be with Stevie. The child's needs always took precedence over the adult's. That was the way it had to be, when you had children. That was the contract you made with the kids when you chose to call their spirits from heaven into the world, that as long as they were young and needed you, you did whatever you could to meet their needs before you did anything else for anybody else.

They sat next to each other on her side of the queen-sized bed that Step's parents had given them as a wedding present. "What happened today, Stevie," said DeAnne.

Almost immediately, his face twisted up and the pent-up tears flowed again as they had flowed in the car. "I couldn't understand them, Mom!"

"What do you mean?"

"I couldn't understand what they *said!* To me, I mean. I could understand them mostly in class, when they were talking to the teacher, but when they talked to *me* I didn't understand hardly anything and so I just stood there and finally I said, I can't understand you, and they called me *stupid* and *retarded.*"

"Honey, you know you're not stupid. You know you're a straight A student."

"But I couldn't *understand* anything." He sounded fierce now; much of his anger, she realized, must have been from the frustration he had felt, being unable to communicate with the other kids. "I asked them what language they were speaking, and they said 'American,' and then they started making fun of the way *I* talk, like I talked wrong or something. But I didn't say anything wrong!"

"Honey, you've got to understand, this is a school in a fairly rural part of Steuben. A *country* school. They just have thick southern accents."

"Well they understood everything *I* said."

"Because you talk normal American English. Like on television. They all watch TV, so they're used to understanding the way you talk."

"Then why don't *they* talk that way?"

"Maybe in a couple of generations they will. But right now they talk in a southern accent. And besides, you *did* understand some of what they said, or you wouldn't have known they were calling you retarded and stupid."

He began to cry harder. "I made this one girl write it down for me. That's how I knew. And then they all wrote it down. Retarded and stupid. They wrote it on papers and gave it to me. All day. I didn't read them, though. I mean after the first couple."

"That was very wise of you," said DeAnne. "And very cruel of them."

"But when I was leaving at the end of school I left all those notes on the table and Mrs. Jones made me go back and pick them all up and take them with me." The humiliation of it made him shudder. "So I picked them up and threw them in the trash and then she yelled at me."

"She *yelled* at you?"

"She said that I had an unfriendly attitude and a chip on my shoulder and I'd better learn some manners or I'd never get along."

She put her arm around him. "Oh, son, I'm so sorry. She should never have said anything like that."

"They're all against me there, Mom," he said. "Even the teacher."

"Stevie, I know it seems that way —"

"It doesn't just *seem*, it *is!*"

"Mrs. Jones just didn't understand what those papers were, or what the other kids had been saying."

"She talks just like they do, Mom," he said. "They just hate me because I'm from Utah!"

"Kids are cruel," said DeAnne. "You knew that—the way they treated Barry Wimmer." She remembered back to her own childhood, to her parents' words to her. "Not *all* the kids were making fun of you, were they? Weren't most of them just standing around watching?"

"They didn't stick up for me, either," said Stevie.

"No, they just watched. They just watched, and that made you feel like they all agreed with the mean ones. But they don't, not really, Stevie. They just—they just hadn't decided anything at all. So if they see you tomorrow standing tall and—"

"Don't make me go back, Mom!" cried Stevie. He was trembling. "Don't make me go back to class! Not Mrs. Jones's class! Don't make me!"

"Son! Calm down, please, calm down." She had no idea what to do about this. Every natural instinct told her to say, Yes, Stevie, you're right, that class is the last place in the world I'll *ever* send you, and you can stay home with me and be safe for the rest of your life. But she knew that, however much she might *want* to say that, she couldn't. It wouldn't be right. "These things aren't under my control—I can't keep you out of school, and I can't get you into another class unless Dr. Mariner agrees."

"Don't make me go back," he whispered.

"Son, you'll see—tomorrow they'll probably still be mean, but it won't be *new* anymore and so they'll get bored and do something else. And in a few days the nicer kids will start being friends with you. Plus you'll get used to the way they talk and you'll understand them and things will be *fine.*"

"They'll never be *fine,*" he said, and he got up and stalked out of the room. It was sadly funny, his furious walk, the way he tried to be forceful as he opened the door, but ended up fumbling with the door handle because he was still small enough that door handles weren't easy. One thing was certain, though. She could not let this go without talking to Dr. Mariner.

The Steuben phone book was by the kitchen phone. Step was at the table, eating a tuna sandwich. With mustard on it, which always made her cringe a little, but he wouldn't have it any other way.

"What was it?" asked Step.

"The kids made fun of his accent and the fact that he couldn't understand *their* accent, and then Mrs. Jones actually told *him* off because he wasn't being polite enough to her or to them!"

"Adults can be so stupid with children sometimes," he said.

"He begged me not to send him back to school tomorrow."

"So keep him home," said Step.

"Are you serious?" She could not believe he was saying that.

"The teacher's unsympathetic and the kids are all little shits," he said. "Keep him home."

She hated it when he used words like that, even though he apparently thought it was cute—it was so juvenile of him to use shock words, as if she were his parent instead of his wife. But she had long since learned that it was better to pretend she hadn't noticed than to make a big deal about it.

"We can't do that," said DeAnne. "There are truancy laws, you know."

"Just for a day. And tomorrow you call Dr. Mariner and ask for him to be reassigned to another second-grade class."

"I was going to call her tonight."

"Tomorrow is business hours. Tonight is home time."

"This is a real problem, Step, and she will understand my calling her tonight. I can't let him miss tomorrow or he'll think that he can get out of school whenever he wants to avoid something unpleasant there."

"My mother let us stay home," he said. "One day. One day a year, she said, any one of her kids could stay home just because they couldn't stand to go. They could only do it once, but they got that one day. Most years I didn't even use it. But things were better because I knew I could. And when I went on those days that I didn't *want* to go, when I had almost decided not to, then I was there because of my own choice, and not because anybody made me. I think it was a good plan."

"But this is only his second day at a new school," said DeAnne. "And what if Dr. Mariner won't let him change classes? Do you think that on Wednesday it will be any easier for him to go?"

"It might," he said.

"And it might not," she said. "I can't see that it will help him if he clings to his mother's apron strings just because things were hard for him."

Step sat there, looking at his sandwich. "Do what you want," he said.

"Oh, Step, don't be that way. I thought we were having a discussion."

"No, you're right. He needs to go. I guess I was just thinking that if *I* didn't have to go back to work tomorrow, that would be the best thing in the world. Only if I stayed home tomorrow, then I'd never go back. So you're right." He looked up and grinned. "You got to send your little boys back into the cold cruel world."

"Was it that bad today?"

"Not bad, just weird," he said. "Don't worry about it. There were a couple of minutes that I just felt like quitting, but what can you expect? I haven't worked for anybody but myself in so long now, of *course* I felt rebellious and frustrated." He took a bite, but she didn't say anything. "And then coming home and having Stevie so mad at me—and I thought, He's right. I should have been home. I should never have taken this job, we should pack up whatever we can fit in the car and drive back to Indiana or back to your parents' place and I should sit down in the basement and teach myself to program the stupid Commodore 64 and somewhere between here and bankruptcy maybe I'll come up with a hot game and we'll be rolling in undeserved money again, like we were a year ago."

"That wasn't undeserved money," she said.

"Oh, you know what I mean," he said.

"If you want to quit, then do it," she said. "If we have to move, then we'll move."

"No," he said. "You think I haven't thought it through? We can't afford another moving van, we don't even have enough cash to get through the month, let alone get to another state. All of our credit cards are to the hilt. We've got no choice unless we want to go be street people or something. I go back to work tomorrow, and Stevie goes back to school, and if he hates me for not being there, then that's just one more part of being a father." He laughed bitterly. "Sons are *supposed* to hate their fathers. It just isn't supposed to start so young."

"He doesn't hate you," said DeAnne. "He was just—frustrated."

"Call Dr. Mariner before it gets any later."

She looked up the number and called. It was well after nine o'clock, and she might have gotten the principal out of bed, but Dr. Mariner *was* a southern lady, so she denied that she had been inconvenienced at all, and as DeAnne told her of Stevie's problems that day at school, Dr. Mariner clucked in sympathy. "I'll tell you what," she said. "Tomorrow I'll keep Stevie in my office, to take some tests that we need him to take anyway. Placement tests, to see if he should be in our gifted program—his records from that school in Indiana were quite impressive, you know. And while he's taking those tests, I'll talk with Mrs. Jones. And either we'll change his assignment, or Mrs. Jones will make sure that things go more smoothly in the old class. How will that be?"

"You're *wonderful*, Dr. Mariner," DeAnne said, trying not to gush in her gratitude. "Thank you."

"All in a day's work, Mrs. Fletcher. Thank you for calling. Good night."

"Good night."

DeAnne hung up the telephone and slumped into a chair.

"Good news, I take it," said Step.

"She's going to keep him out of class, taking placement tests," said DeAnne. "And then either reassign him or work things out so it'll go better in Mrs. Jones's class."

"Well, see? You were right. Calling her tonight was exactly the right thing. That's why I chose you to be the mother of my kids, because you're a thousand times smarter than I'd ever be."

"It's not that I wanted to send him to school tomorrow, Step."

"I know."

"I *wanted* to keep him home."

"I know, Fish Lady. You have a heart so soft that you'd die of terminal compassion if you ever let it get out of control."

"Now you're making fun of me."

"You're a wonderful wife and a wonderful mother and now you better go tell Stevie the good news so he won't get an ulcer before morning."

"Come with me," said DeAnne.

"He doesn't want to see me."

"Step, don't be as petulant as he was."

"What about my sandwich?"

"Let it dry out. I'll poach you those eggs."

"I ate two candy bars at work, it's not like I need dinner," he said as he followed her down the hall to the boys' room. "I'm going to get fat working there. There's a candy machine right around the corner from my office. Twenty steps and I have a Three Musketeers in my mouth."

"Well, don't do it," said DeAnne. "You worked too hard to get down to this weight."

Stevie was still awake, of course. DeAnne explained what Dr. Mariner had suggested. "Isn't that wonderful?"

Stevie nodded.

"She really *is* a good principal, Stevie. So you remember, you *do* have at least one friend at school already."

He nodded again. Then, glancing at his father, he reached out and put his hand behind her neck, to draw her close, so he could whisper in her ear. "You didn't tell Dad that I cried, did you?"

She almost told him that Step had wanted to keep him home from school; but they had decided years ago that they would never hint at disagreement between them on decisions dealing with the children, so that they'd never get the idea that they could play one parent off against the other. So instead she just shook her head. "But even if he guessed it," she whispered, "that's nothing to be ashamed of."

"I know," he said softly. "But don't tell." He lay back down and she tucked him in again and turned off the light.

"Leave the hall light *on!*" said Robbie loudly.

"Are *you* still awake, Road Bug?" asked Step.

"Don't nobody go to school tomorrow," said Robbie. "Not Stevie and not you either, Dad!"

"Don't I wish," said Step. He left the hall light on.

5

·HACKER SNACK·

Here is how Step's days were spent: Most days he drove to work, leaving the car for DeAnne only when she knew she was going to need it for shopping. He would rather have left it all the time, but he was never sure when he'd be coming home, and it was hard to carpool with such an uncertain schedule.

He always began the workday by drifting into the programmers' pit, a large room with even more computers than Gallowglass's office. Most of the machines were already up and running, usually with lines and lines of assembly language on the screen, though sometimes there was a screen filled with the faded-looking colors of the 64. As he moved from machine to machine, the programmers would point out what they were doing, and sometimes they'd have a problem and Step would pull up a chair beside them and help spot the flaw in the code or find some simple, elegant solution. Step usually felt inadequate at this, because all the programmers knew the workings of the 64 better than he did and quite often he had to ask, What are you getting from this register? Or, What does it mean to store that value in that location? And they'd kind of laugh and say, That's the current location of the character set, or, That's the wave-form for the sound, and the tone of their voices always suggested that *everybody* knew that.

But the truth is that while they knew the 64, Step had a gift for code and he knew it and they knew it. He could look at a routine for a few minutes and then rewrite it to cut the amount of memory it used in half, or make it run twice as fast, or make it smoother and more responsive on the screen. Back when he'd been working alone on programming, he thought of himself as a clumsy amateur, and he was always vaguely ashamed of his code. But now he realized that he was pretty good after all, or at least good enough to be better than the caliber of programmer that Eight Bits Inc. was able to attract.

Still, it wasn't too smart for him to keep thinking of himself as a programmer. Because whenever Dicky poked his head into the pit, Step had to drop back into manual-writer mode, asking questions of the programmer he was with about how the game worked. As often as not, he was asking about the very things he had just shown the programmer how to do, and as soon as Dicky left, the others in the room would erupt in silent laughter. But Step didn't think it was funny. It made Step feel dirty and cheap, to be playing a continuous trick on Dicky like that. And so many people knew about it he could not believe it was possible that Dicky would never find out. In fact, he suspected that Dicky already knew.

Yet he dared not test the hypothesis, because what if he was wrong? So Step kept up the charade.

Usually this took till noon, and he would go to lunch with a group of programmers and that was the good time during the day, because he wasn't lying to anybody then, he wasn't hiding anything, he was just himself, talking about stuff with these guys. It dawned on him during one of those lunches, as they sat there bantering with each other or swapping stories across the table at Swensen's or Pizza Inn or Libby Hill, that this was really the first time in his life that he had been part of a group of guys like this. He had never been an athlete, part of the team or even part of a pickup game at school or in the neighborhood. His friends during his school years had always been girls. He liked the way they talked, he had things to *say* to them. And they didn't despise him for being smart and getting good grades, they weren't ashamed of being smart themselves, and so they could talk about ideas in a way that he never heard guys talking about anything, as if they mattered, as if they cared. His only male friends during high school and on into college had been the few who were like him, who hung out with the smart girls.

But these programmers were all male, and it was definitely a male kind of conversation, and yet there was none of that hierarchical one-upmanship that had made Step so uncomfortable with "the guys" in school. Or rather, there *was*, but it was centered around programming rather than athletics or cars, and on that playing field Step was a star—with Gallowglass, he shared the preeminent position in the hierarchy, and since he and Glass got along so well themselves there was no rivalry at all. Step *belonged*, and it felt good.

Lunch ended, though—supposedly after half an hour, but they always took an hour or more—and then back they went to Eight Bits Inc., where now Step usually went to his own office and actually worked on manuals, often for games that weren't even finished yet. In fact, in the process of writing the manual he would really be designing the game, describing rules and features of the game that the programmer hadn't yet thought of. Or if he was writing about a game that was nearly done, he'd play the game over and over again to find bugs in the code or annoyances in the play of the game. Then he'd make notes and pass them on to the programmers. Because every game had to pass through his hands in order to get its documentation written, Step had his finger on the pulse of every project in the company. He knew, he *knew* what was going on. And since Dicky did *not*, it meant that in a way Step was the real head of the creative division of Eight Bits Inc. Dicky had the title and the salary and the Sunday afternoon visits with Ray Keene at the Magazine Rack, but Step had the respect and the influence and—most important to him—the results, the *games* with his fingerprints all over them.

The only program he never fiddled with was Scribe 64. That was Glass's bailiwick, and Step had no intention of intruding. He was writing the documentation for the new update, which was adding right-and-left justification and Glass's new 60-character screen, and while he still tested it and found bugs and passed them on to Glass, Step never, never touched the code. Because he didn't need to—Glass knew what he was doing. And because that was the unspoken basis of their alliance, that Step would do nothing to weaken Glass's position at Eight Bits Inc. So even when Step found a bug, he would pass the information to Glass in private, never giving a clue to anybody else that there had been the slightest flaw in the kid's original code.

Five o'clock came and went every day, but it had nothing to do with Step's schedule. He was always in the middle of something. There was always a section of code that he had to finish fiddling with before he went home, so he could leave it for the programmer to look at in the morning. Or a game that he had to finish play-testing at the highest levels, while the programmer hung around and kibitzed with him. Suppertime meant going around the corner to the candy machine and dropping in quarters. After a few candy bars there'd be a bag of potato chips because there was once a potato involved, which made it health food. And then a can of pop or even tomato juice, when Step was feeling really unrighteous about what he was doing to his body.

He was gaining weight, he could feel it. Some of his shirts were beginning to show a gap between the buttons when he sat down. His belt was getting less comfortable; he let it out a notch. Six weeks, and he was going to seed. But when during the day could he get any exercise? Back in Indiana he had ridden his bike fifty miles a week during the warm months and kept up on the exercise bike in the winter, but he could do that because he was keeping an academic schedule, which gave him plenty of free daylight hours.

Seven, eight, nine o'clock at night, depending on how stubborn the bug was or how fascinating the game, and Step would at last go outside into the darkness and find the Renault, pop the locks, and climb in. Then he'd head for home, saying to himself, I should have gotten away sooner, I should have been home for dinner. Most nights the kids were already in bed, or going to bed, before he got there; he could kiss them goodnight and hear a little bit about their day, but that was it, that was all.

It took him hours to unwind after the intensity of the day. He and DeAnne would talk, and now and then he'd help her fold the laundry or do up the dishes from a dinner that he hadn't eaten, and sometimes she would have saved him something from dinner and then he'd eat it while they talked, even though he wasn't hungry. She always looked so tired, and it made him feel terrible. She was pregnant, after all, and even though this pregnancy hadn't had anything like the horrible morning sickness of the first three, he knew that it always left her feeling wrung out. When the other kids were on the way, Step had been home to take up the slack. He was no help now. In fact, he suspected that he was another drain on her energy, like the kids. She'd just be getting them down to bed, about to have a few moments to herself after having been *on* all day, and here came hubby, home from work and ready to be entertained.

So he tried to break away from her fairly early, to let her get to bed and get the sleep she needed while he wound himself down from the tension of the day. He watched TV, or went to bed and read a book. DeAnne would watch TV with him sometimes, but she didn't really engage with most shows—she had enjoyed "M°A°S°H," but they'd had the final episode of that, and Step hadn't even been home to watch it with her. And when they lay in bed together, reading, she was so *tired* that he just didn't have the heart to make her stay awake just to make love, not unless she actually initiated it herself, which wasn't often. Even when she tried to stay awake to read something—he had bought her the new Anne Tyler novel, *Dinner at the Homesick Restaurant*, as soon as it came out in paperback—she'd end up asleep in moments, the book fallen over on her chest; he'd get up, slide her glasses off and lay them on top of the book on her nightstand, turn off her light, and then come back around to his side of the bed. Sacrificing his own sexual hunger for her sake made him feel both righteous and frustrated, a terrible combination because whatever satisfaction he got from knowing he had let her have the sleep she needed so badly did nothing to assuage his longing for sexual release. I could sleep myself, he thought, if only she could *see* how much I need her; and then he felt guilty even for thinking that, because *he* didn't have to get up and feed the kids in the morning and get Stevie off to school, *he* didn't have to go through a day of constant housework and tending kids while carrying around this *growth* inside his belly that was sucking the energy out of him, so how could he dare to feel resentful that she was so tired, that she didn't reach out to him? Why couldn't he just be satisfied that he had let her sleep? Why couldn't he be satisfied?

Consumed by guilt and desire, he would lie awake reading, or get up again and go in and watch the TV in the family room. Carson's parade of guests touting movies and TV shows. Letterman dropping things off buildings and putting on fake bus company ads by Larry "Bud" Melman and sometimes still the guy who lived under the seats. Then flipping around the cable channels, watching two or three bad movies at once, back and forth whenever he couldn't stand how boring or stupid one of them got. And then it was three in the morning and he knew he had to get up and finally, finally he was sleepy, maybe a little sleepy, and then he realized that he had been very sleepy for quite a while, that he had even dozed off in front of the set and now he knew that he hadn't been watching TV because he couldn't sleep, he had been watching TV because he didn't *want* to sleep, because he was *afraid* to sleep, and he'd go in to the kids' rooms where they slept with the lights on because they were so scared of the dark and he watched them lying there, Betsy alone in her room with the crib set up across from her, waiting for the new baby, her blond hair spilling across the pillow; Robbie in the bottom bunk in the boys' room, his covers always in knots because he flailed around so in his sleep; Stevie, quiet in the top bunk, his face so beautiful in repose; and Step would stand there at three in the morning, barely awake, feeling like he was in a walking dream, and he'd look at the kids and his heart would break.

Then he'd go to bed, getting in gently so that DeAnne wouldn't wake up; she usually stirred, but rarely did she wake—did she even know how late he stayed up at night? Three o'clock, three-thirty sometimes, sometimes four, and then he'd wake up with his alarm at seven-thirty or eight or eight-thirty and stagger into the shower and get ready for another day, thinking, It's all right if I'm late, it's all right if I take a long lunch, because I have to put in so much overtime at night.

DeAnne asked him once: If you got up and went to work on time, couldn't you get your work done and come home at five? If I packed a lunch, couldn't you take shorter lunch hours and come home when it's still daylight and you can maybe take a walk with the kids while I fix dinner? And he'd say, I'll try, and maybe the next day he *would* get up earlier and get to work on time, but then he'd be so tired that he'd drag around all day and hardly get anything done and the deadlines were still looming, weren't they? And most of the programmers were working past five, so they needed him to stay late to fix this or look at that, and so even after getting up early he'd still not get home till seven and dinner was already over and DeAnne would say, "I need the car tomorrow," and he'd say, "Fine, take me to work and I'll catch a ride home with one of the guys," and that would be the end of another experiment in trying to turn himself into an eight-to-five kind of guy.

Those were the days of Step Fletcher, and he hated his life and his job even though he loved his family and his work.

In April they were launching three new games and the Scribe 64 update at the Computer Faire in San Francisco

at the Cow Palace, and Ray and Dicky and the market
ing people decided they wanted to bring along Step and
Glass so that there'd be somebody there who actually
knew how the programs worked.

The flight was at two-thirty Friday afternoon, so
Step went home at lunch to pack and say good-bye to
Robbie and Betsy and DeAnne. Even though Step had
authored a top computer game, nobody had ever flown
him to one of these computer shows before, and he was
nervous and excited. DeAnne wasn't all that excited—it
meant a Sunday without him there, getting the kids
ready for church on time and then handling them
through sacrament meeting. And, as she said to him, "I
get lonely when you're not here."

"I'm not here even when I'm here," he said.

"But you *are* here," she said. "I mean, I know you're
coming home. And I sleep better when you're in the
house with me."

"I'll be back Sunday night."

"I know," she said. "Knowing that is what will keep
me alive over the weekend."

He was horrified. "What are you saying?"

She looked baffled. "What do you mean?"

"You're not feeling suicidal or something, are you?"

"No," she said, outraged at the suggestion. And
then: "Oh, Step, I didn't mean that I was thinking of
killing myself, for heaven's sake. I was trying to be
romantic. I was trying to say that I *live* for you."

He felt stupid. "Of course. I don't know what I was
thinking of."

"Probably *wishing* you could get a new wife who
didn't have this big belly."

"You ain't got nothin' in your belly that I didn't put
there," he said. "Besides, *I'm* the one who's getting fat.
And after nine months of putting on weight, I don't get
a prize at the end."

"July 28th," she said. "The hottest part of summer. I

can't wait to be carrying around ninety pounds of baby in the summer."

"I'll miss you," he said.

"I'll miss you, too, Junk Man." She wrapped herself around him, melted into him the way she did when she wanted to make love, only he had to go and catch the damn *plane*, why did she suddenly get romantic *now*, when there was no time, no *way* to do anything about it?

"What are you trying to do, make me late?"

"Yes," she said.

"Come on out to the car, Fish Lady, and take me to the airport. We'll take care of unfinished business when I get back."

"You are no fun," she said.

"Yeah, well."

"Our best times were always during the day," she said.

He remembered now that it was true. When he worked at home he also slept a weird schedule, different from hers, with a lot of all-nighters at the computer, either programming or writing on his dissertation. Then he'd get up in the morning, go to class or go out riding, and when he got home and showered there she'd be, waiting for him as he came naked into the bedroom.

That was how this new one got conceived, only that day she hadn't even been waiting for him, she'd been sitting on the edge of the bed, talking on the phone. It took only a moment of hearing her say "Mm-hm" and "Of course" and "You poor thing" for Step to realize that she was talking to Sister Boompjes, who was always good for an hour of misery. Not *serious* misery, not anything that anyone could *do* anything about; she just needed to make sure that someone knew she was alive, and since her arthritis and her lack of mail and the nasty neighbor children were the only events in her life, that was what she talked about. As DeAnne had said more than once before, for Sister Boompjes's rosary of woes to have a therapeutic effect, someone had to be on the other end of the phone, but it didn't take her full *attention*.

So while DeAnne was murmuring encouragement to Sister Boompjes, Step methodically removed her clothing. DeAnne's only protest was to roll her eyes— she appreciates the distraction, Step concluded, and so he went ahead. DeAnne never ceased in her sweet reassurances to this lonely sister, even as her husband eased her back on the bed and gave her a slow, thorough workout. DeAnne was usually a little noisy when things went well for her, but she managed to get all the way through without making a sound except for breathing very, very heavily, and of course she had covered the mouthpiece of the phone to conceal *that* from dear Sister Boompjes, so that the woman got the audience she wanted while DeAnne got laid.

The only real consequence was that DeAnne, having been on the phone, had not prepared herself with contraceptive foam, and sure enough, within a week she was nauseated and two weeks later she *didn't* have her clockwork period. The joke between them was that *every* time they had unprotected sex they got a pregnancy, and once again it held true. This would be either baby number four or miscarriage number three, all because he got randy while DeAnne was on the phone. They thought of naming the child after Sister Boompjes if it was a girl, but then they decided that no American child named Wilhelmina could live a normal life.

Daytime was their best time for sex, that was true. That had never occurred to either of them when they decided he needed to take a job, that having him gone every day would really foul up their sex life.

Out in the car, Robbie was busy trying to make Betsy's life miserable, which wasn't hard because she could be brought to furious tears with a funny look. Only when they were on 421 heading west to the airport did he remember. "I left *Name of the Rose* back in the office," he said.

"What's that?"

"A book. I was going to read it at nights during the convention. While the others are all out getting drunk at parties."

"Don't you have anything else to read?"

"I'll buy a magazine."

"No, we have time," said DeAnne. "Your luggage is all carry-on, isn't it?"

It was. She pulled into a 7-Eleven parking lot and then swung back out onto 421 heading east, and in a few minutes turned right on Palladium and there he was at Eight Bits Inc. at two o'clock on a day when he was supposed to catch a two-thirty flight. Oh, well, he thought, this is as close as a Mormon can get to living on the edge.

The Name of the Rose wasn't in his office. Where had he last been reading it?

He burst into the pit, practically flying, saying, "Hi, can you believe I'm so stupid I'm probably going to miss my flight for a *book*?" And there it was on the counter. He picked it up, turned to leave—and realized that they were all looking at him strangely. "What, my pants aren't zipped?" he asked.

Then he noticed that three of the screens showed views that were obviously from Hacker Snack.

"Is that what I think it is?" he asked.

"It was sort of a secret project," said one of the guys. "Kind of a surprise."

"Yeah," said Step. "I'm surprised."

They said nothing, and Step said "Bye," and then he was out the door, down the corridor, out the front door to where DeAnne was waiting in the car.

"What took so long?" she said. "I don't know if we can make it in fifteen minutes."

"Speed," he said.

"That's *your* talent," she said.

"Guess what I'm going to do in San Francisco," said Step.

"What?"

"Quit this damn job."

"What?"

"And when I get home I'm going to find me a lawyer and I'm going to sue their asses off."

DeAnne looked horrified. "Step, I know the kids are going to learn language like that but I'd rather they didn't learn it from you."

"Aren't you the teensiest bit curious as to *why* I'm going to sue their elbows off?"

"Thank you. And yes, I'm more than a little curious, yes."

"Because those sons-of-bitches have been adapting Hacker Snack for the 64 behind my back."

She winced.

"Pardon me. Not sons-of-bitches, kids, *bastards.*"

She looked angry. "Give it a rest, Step."

"They *never* asked permission, they *never* offered to buy it, there's no contract, no agreement to a royalty, and they never *once* breathed a single word, and I thought these guys were my *friends.*"

"That's no reason to take it out on me and the kids, Step."

"I'm not taking it out on you!"

"You're yelling and you're using language that I don't want to have to explain to the children."

Step leaned over and looked at the kids in the back seat. "I'm not mad at you kids. Some people at work have been doing something really sneaky and bad to me and so I'm angry at them. And as for the words I used, those are words that you shouldn't ever use except when somebody you trusted has stabbed you in the back, and on those occasions you have my permission to use those words but not in front of your mother."

"Thanks so much," said DeAnne.

"Like I'm sure they'll remember this conversation ten years from now."

"Somebody *stabbed* you?"

"It's a figure of speech, Robbie," said DeAnne. "Nobody stabbed your father. Though I might, in another minute."

"I'm sorry," said Step. "I was out of line. But I'm so . . ." He hunted for the word.

"Mad."

"*Mad.*" It wasn't the word he had wanted, but then the word he wanted probably didn't exist.

"So you're going to quit."

"Absolutely. I'm going to sue them for so much money I end up owning the company and then I'll *fire* them."

"Just a suggestion, Step," she said.

"Yes."

"Don't quit in San Francisco. They might cancel your ticket and we don't have enough on the Visa to let you charge a return fare."

"Yes, well," he said. "I suppose I'll wait till I get home."

"And maybe it was all a misunderstanding, did you think of that? Maybe somebody didn't realize that you had signed an agreement that excluded Hacker Snack. Maybe Mr. Keene didn't know that they were working on this."

"Maybe pigs have wings."

"Flying pigs!" cried Robbie. Flying pigs were a standing joke in the family—DeAnne even had two ceramic flying pigs and one stuffed one, which she kept on a shelf beside the mirror in the bathroom. "Watch out below!" The idea of flying pigs defecating on pedestrians had been Step's contribution to the family's flying-pig lore, and of course that was the part that Robbie loved best.

"Step, don't do anything rash."

In other words, thought Step, even when they're stealing from me, I have to stay at this lousy job with these weasels.

"It's not as if it should surprise you," said DeAnne.

"I mean, if they have you sneaking around behind Dicky's back, why shouldn't Dicky be sneaking around behind *yours?*"

"Well maybe I don't want to be where anybody sneaks around anybody's back at all."

"Exactly," said DeAnne. "You think I don't want you to quit? But think about it—the fact that they're trying to adapt Hacker Snack for the 64 means that it's probably a very good idea, commercially speaking. And there you'll be at the Computer Faire, with the heads of every major software company. Maybe it's time for you to sell the rights to Hacker Snack yourself."

"You know," said Step, "you really are good at this."

"Yes, I am," she said.

"What I want to know is, how did you learn corporate politics? When you were a secretary in the CDFR Department at BYU?"

"Nope," she said. "Everything I know about conniving I learned as a counselor in the Relief Society presidency, as we figured out how to get the bishopric to let us do what we needed to do even when they thought we didn't need to do it."

"So the plan is, I make nice in San Francisco, and come home with a deal to sell the program myself."

"And then you get to work first thing Monday morning, before anybody has a chance to tell anybody that you know what they're up to, and you get a copy of that agreement you signed that excludes Hacker Snack from your deal with Eight Bits."

"Right. I'll need that. Because they could just lose it, couldn't they—and claim that I'd signed the same agreement as everybody else but they lost it but look, here's the standard agreement and there's never been another . . ."

"Here we are," said DeAnne. "Have a wonderful flight. Now go. You have four minutes to get to the plane and you still have to get through the security gate!"

"I love you! Love you kids! Tell Stevie he still has a father."

"Kiss!" cried Betsy.

"There's no time, honey," said DeAnne.

But Step flung open the back door, gave both of the kids big loud smacks, then closed the door and ran for the plane. They were just closing the door when he got there, but they let him on. Compressed into his seat with his knees around his chin, he allowed himself to daydream a little about what might happen in San Francisco. All he needed to do was sell the rights to Hacker Snack to somebody who would pay him enough of an advance against earnings that he could afford to quit. He wasn't sure whether this was the kind of thing he ought to pray about, especially because his mood was so angry and vindictive, but he still had to say it, silently: God, make this go, please. Make this work. Set me free. Send me home.

Although Step had lived in the Bay area during much of his childhood, he had never been inside the Cow Palace before. Now, entering it for the first time, Step saw that it lived up to its name—a great barn of a building filled with rows of display booths like milking stalls. And every booth seemed to be making as much noise as possible. This was survival time, as well as strutting time—the computer business had been booming, but there were rumors that IBM's new PC was already threatening to take over the whole microcomputer market, driving developers of software and systems built to run with CP/M on the old Z80 chip to adapt or die, and everyone knew that IBM's half-secret Peanut project was going to blow out the home computers like the Commodore 64, just as surely as the 64 had swept away the Atari. So all that noise had a purpose—to grab reviewers and journalists and computer store buyers by the ears and drag them over to have a look at the new computer or the new joystick or the new game or the new word processor or the new computer dust cover that was going to revolutionize the world and make its developers as rich as Jobs and Wozniak. Or, failing that, at least as rich as Ray Keene.

And the people were there, in droves, eager to be dragged. It was hard getting through the aisles, and the noise of the computers *had* to be loud, to be heard over the monumental soughing of the crowd. Just when it seemed that human speech could not be made audible in this place, there came a voice, male but fairly high-pitched, with a harsh midwestern edge to it that threatened to shatter the bones of Step's inner ear:

"What the hell am I supposed to be impressed with about *this*?"

Step searched—against his will—for the source of this voice from hell. It was a tall, lanky man whose red face attested to the potency of the free cocktails in the SuperCalc suite. Step knew him at once—Neddy Cranes, a onetime Washington columnist who had occupied that broad range of the political spectrum between Benito Mussolini and Genghis Khan, and who now was best known for his long-winded, fascinating, and devastatingly influential monthly column in *Code* magazine.

"Mine," said Dicky immediately.

"No," said Ray Keene quietly.

Step watched how Dicky immediately stepped back to let Ray Keene go and face the tiger. But Dicky's outward compliance was not from the heart. Step could see how Dicky's jaw was clenched. How he held his pose of nonchalance a bit too long, with a bit too much effort. He hates Ray Keene, Step realized. And why shouldn't he? Ray undercuts him at every stage of his work. Ray undercuts *everybody* at every stage. But Dicky is determined to hang on. Dicky is determined to bear it, without showing Ray the slightest sign of resentment. But Dicky is also going to take it out on somebody.

Me.

Well, I won't be around when the ax falls, thought Step, unless of course the stupid, illegal attempt to steal Hacker Snack *was* the ax, in which case it's a dull blade indeed, since I never signed over the rights. No, the Hacker Snack project was almost certainly done with Ray's knowledge, so Dicky's nastiness toward me, when it comes, will take some other form. Some slyer, pettier form that will have no profit in it for anybody except for the nasty satisfaction it would give Dicky Northanger.

"*You're* not supposed to be impressed at all," Ray was saying to Neddy Cranes. "This is only something for the common people, not for computer experts with big expensive systems."

Ah, Ray was deft indeed, for Cranes could hardly let himself be painted as a computer elitist. His pose was that of the populist, looking out for the little guy. So the bandsaw voice came back again at top volume: "Don't tell me about common people! I can see you've got those little Commodore boxes here—paperweights, that's all they are, because you can't do a damn thing with 'em! Stealing money from the little guy, that's what Commodore's doing, stealing money while Kmart drives the getaway car!"

"We're making sure that when people get this paperweight home, Mr. Cranes, they can run a full-fledged word processor on it, a word processor for which they paid no more than thirty bucks, and if they buy it direct from us, twenty bucks."

"What, is the manual an additional fee of fifty dollars?" demanded Cranes. "Or do people have to pay a hundred bucks to get the extra module that allows them to print things out?"

"It's all in the same package," said Ray. "Not a

pretty package, of course. But that's part of why we can sell it cheap. Try it out."

Step watched in awe as Ray got Neddy Cranes to set his fingers on the keys of a Commodore in order to write something using Scribe 64.

"Come on, let's get out of here," said Glass.

"Don't you want to see what Cranes thinks of Scribe?" asked Step.

"Come *on!*"

Glass was really agitated. Clearly he had *no* desire to stick around for Neddy's verdict. "I'm hungry."

"I'm not," said Step, but he followed Glass away from the booth, and when Glass found a line of people waiting for a hot dog that looked like it had been made in the 1950s from the hooves and noses of diseased warthogs, Step stood in it with him and got a hot dog with mustard and onions.

"If you put this mustard on your car it'd take three paint jobs to cover it up," said Glass.

"That's OK. The onions are the secret ingredient in Ex-Lax."

They ate every bit of the hot dogs.

"Did you check us into our room?" asked Glass.

"What?" asked Step.

"Our room," said Glass. "When I got here I had to come straight to the booth, so my bag is under the table."

"We're sharing a room?" asked Step, horrified.

"Dicky said he told you," said Glass. "Ray says Eight Bits Inc. isn't big enough to fly first class or have private hotel rooms."

"Bet your little butt *he's* got a private room."

"No, his wife's with him," said Glass. "Hey, I knew you'd hate sharing, so I made sure they assigned you with *me*. See, I'm not addicted to cigarettes, so I won't smoke in the room with you."

"Thanks," said Step. But it wasn't just the issue of

smoking—it was the fact that Step loathed the idea of having no privacy. Undressing and dressing in front of someone else was unthinkable. He had hated it in high school even before he was old enough to go through the temple, and now that he wore the underclothes that symbolized the covenants he had made there, Step never put himself in a position to arouse questions or ridicule toward something that he took so seriously. If he had been warned that he was going to share a room, he would at least have brought pajamas, so he could change in the bathroom and leave Glass thinking that he was simply shy. As it was, Step had no idea *what* he was going to do. Pay for his own private room? Right—with nothing left on the Visa, that was likely!

"Man, it really bothers you, doesn't it," said Glass.

"Yes," said Step. "Not rooming with *you*, just sharing a room at all. I mean, they didn't tell me, not a hint. I don't *share* hotel rooms. I can't believe a company as cheap as this."

"I'd rather have my thousand-dollar bonus than a private room, I'll tell you that," said Glass.

Step looked at him oddly. "A thousand dollars?"

"I wasn't supposed to tell," said Glass. "Oops."

"How often do you get this?" asked Step.

"At the first of the year," said Glass. "Please, don't tell anybody else. Dicky told me that people would quit if they realized how big a bonus I was getting."

"Glass, a thousand dollars is nothing," said Step. "A thousand dollars is like peeing in your hand."

Glass looked at him—his turn to be stunned.

"Do you know what my royalties on Hacker Snack were, at its peak, every six months?"

Glass shook his head.

"Forty thousand," said Step. "And Scribe 64 has sold far more than Hacker Snack ever did."

Glass muttered something that might have been a

prayer, because it was addressed to God, but Step didn't think the tone was reverent enough for that.

"By the way," said Step, "I told *you* what my royalties were in strict confidence, too."

"Right, no talkee, no tellee, no catchee hellee," said Glass.

Step hadn't heard that since the days when *Reader's Digest* still published ethnic humor. "Where'd you pick *that* up?"

"My dad," said Glass. "Whenever I'm not paying attention, I turn into my dad."

That hot dog turned out to be supper. Contrary to any reasonable expectations, Ray didn't allow his people to have a supper break from duty in the booth. *He*, of course, with Dicky in tow, went to a fancy restaurant dinner for several of Eight Bits Inc.'s distributors, but that was business, as Ray patiently explained to Step— the eating part of it was merely incidental. And there'd be plenty of time to have supper at the hotel coffee shop after the show closed down for the night.

By the time they were through at the booth they were both too tired to hang out at the coffee shop long enough for a meal, and besides, the meals were *not* charged to the room—Step would have to pay cash and then turn in his receipts back in Steuben for a reimbursement. It seemed like a churlish limitation, but he was getting a pretty good idea by now of how Ray Keene was able to live so high off the earnings of, really, one bestselling program. Glass didn't mind skipping supper, either. He had apparently cleaned all the salted nut rolls out of the candy machine at work, so he had plenty to eat in the room. Step decided that he didn't like salted nut rolls, and said so, and thus could not eat any without shaming himself. It was a way of keeping himself from gaining any more weight than he had to on this trip.

When Glass went into the bathroom, Step got on

the phone and called home—collect, since Eight Bits
Inc. had arranged for all the phones to be blocked
against long-distance calls charged to the room. DeAnne
sounded tired—it was well after midnight in North
Carolina, but Step knew she wouldn't sleep, or at least
wouldn't sleep *well,* until he called. "Sorry I didn't call
before," he said. "They didn't exactly give me time."

"That's OK," she said. "I wanted to hear your voice
tonight anyway. I miss you."

"I've only been gone twelve hours," he said. "I work
longer days than that half the time."

"I know," she said. "Why d'you think I miss you?"
Then she seemed to force herself to wake up a little
more. "Talk to any other companies today?"

"They have me sharing a room with Glass here."

"Glass? Oh, the wizard kid."

"Actually, he's a combination knight and thief."

"What?"

"Nothing, he's just into Dungeons and Dragons and
that's his character, a knight who's also a thief."

"Real Round Table material," she said.

"And he's—what was it?—chaotic but good."

"Ah, to be young again," she said. "Still, even if you
can't talk out loud, you can answer my questions. Did
you talk to any other companies about Hacker Snack?"

"Nope," he said.

"Too busy?"

"Yep," he said.

"What about tomorrow?"

"Same thing, probably."

"Oh no!"

"It'll happen somehow or other," he said. Though
he was not at all sure he could bring it off. "How are
things with the kids?"

"Fine," she said. "Call me tomorrow, OK? And I'm
sorry you have to share a room. I know how you hate
having a roommate."

"There's one exception," he said.

"Yes, but you hated having *me* for a roommate at first."

"Not after you finally stopped leaving shoes out in the middle of every room in the house."

"Now that you're away, I've taken every pair I own and spread them all over, just to celebrate."

"Ah, the cat's away."

"This mouse does all her best playing when you're here," she said, in a cuddly voice that made him both horny and resentful at the same time. If she could act sexy after midnight when he was away, why couldn't she ever bring it off when he was home? He quelled the thought at once.

"How's the baby?" he asked.

"No kicks since that first one, but he sloshes a little now and then."

"Come on, you can't really feel that."

"Can so."

"So he's a swimmer?"

"I can wait awhile for the kicking, to tell the truth. Elizabeth nearly broke my ribs from the inside."

"Well, get your sleep now," he said.

"I know, it's long distance, but I miss you," she said.

"Love you, Fish Lady," said Step.

"Love you, Junk Man," said DeAnne.

"You hang up first," he said.

"No, you," she said.

When they were younger, just courting, that game could go on for a long time—a hundred and fifty dollars worth, in fact, the summer that she went to San Francisco to work while he was still getting his master's at the Y. Wiped out what little he had saved from the fellowship job, writing papers that went out under a full professor's name with not a single improvement from the old coot and not a speck of credit for Step, since he wasn't even a doctoral candidate yet. But even with no money, Step cadged twenty bucks from his folks and drove out and picked her up from the friend's house where she'd been staying in Orinda, and took her to meet his aunt and uncle in San Mateo, and then drove her home. It was on that drive home to Utah that he had proposed to her. And she had said thank you, let me think about it. Four and a half months of thinking—it was two days before New Year's when she said yes. A miracle they ever got married. But his mom was sure it was a marriage planned by God. "God never said he'd make life *easy*," Mom always said.

But they weren't kids anymore, and the game couldn't go on. He would have to hang up first, even though he knew that it hurt her feelings a little bit that he was always the one who could hang up first. I wouldn't be, he told her once, if *you'd* just hang up for once. But she couldn't do that either, apparently.

He hung up.

"Fish Lady?" asked Glass.

Step could not believe he would be rude enough to admit so openly that he had been listening.

"Oh," said Step, "was I talking that loud? I hoped I'd be quiet enough that you wouldn't be forced to hear what I was saying."

"Naw," said Glass, oblivious to the implied rebuke. So much for the Miss Manners method.

"Give me a salted nut roll," said Step.

"I thought you hated them," said Glass.

Oh, yes, thought Step. I'm not eating them. "Yeah, I didn't want to eat it, I wanted to break it into pieces and jam them into every aperture of your body."

"Kinky," said Glass.

"If you don't listen in to *my* phone calls, I won't listen in to yours."

"But that's hardly fair," said Glass. "I don't have anybody to call."

"Not your mom?"

"Dad would never let her accept the charges."

"I thought you made more money than God."

"But God doesn't own the credit card companies," said Glass. "No sweat, Mom knows I'm OK. How are the kids?"

"Fine," said Step.

"Must be tough on the two of you, having three kids and all that."

"Sometimes," said Step.

"You need some time together," said Glass.

"Marriage counseling now?"

"Everybody does."

"Your mom and dad?"

"Sure. She needs to have a chance to cry over his grave for an hour on Sundays." Glass grinned at Step's look of embarrassment. "A *joke*, son, a joke."

"*Son?*"

"OK, then, *Dad.* I really meant my offer to tend for you so you two can have some time together."

"I know you did."

"Yeah, but you blew it off," said Glass. "I know you did, and I want you to know I *mean* it. I love kids, I get along great with kids. I never had any younger brothers or sisters, and so I really like to take care of them now. Never had a baby in the house—but don't get me wrong, I'm real good with babies. I've tended a lot. There was this neighbor family, I watched their kids all the time when I was a kid myself—not that I'm, like, grown up or anything now. But you know what I mean."

"Yeah," said Step. What he was thinking was, Am I going to sleep in my clothes on the top of the bed? Or try to undress real fast and hope Glass doesn't notice my underwear. That wasn't too likely—Glass was apparently in a mood to notice everything. And he'd ask, and there'd be a long conversation, and it made Step tired to think about it. Besides, Glass must have known what they were doing with Hacker Snack. He must have provided the other programmers with a copy of his commented disassembly of Step's Atari code for the program, as a basis for their work. So it wasn't as if Step could *trust* him.

"I used to do everything for those kids. They had a little girl in diapers—Lulu, I called her, but I can't remember why, her name was something like Gladys or something, a stinker name for a little girl, anyway, so I called her Lulu—and she'd be dragging her pants around her ankles, you know how diapers get so heavy when they're wet, so she'd be running around in just her shirt and those wet diapers mopping every speck of dust off the floor."

"You're making me gag here," said Step. "Urine everywhere, my favorite nighty-night vision."

"Come on, little girls don't wet their panties with urine, they wet it with angel rain."

"Now I *will* puke," said Step.

Glass laughed in delight. "I thought that was funny, too, but that's what Mrs. Greenwood said, angel rain, I swear it."

"I got to tell you, Glass, I need my sleep. It's almost one Eastern time."

"But you aren't even undressed," said Glass, "and we don't have to be over at the show till nine, so we've got plenty of time."

"I have a mild sleep disorder," said Step, making it up as he went along but trying to come somewhere near the truth. "I have a hard time *getting* to sleep, which means I have to start calming down and stuff fairly early in order to get to sleep fairly late."

"And then, just as you're dozing off, you get up and change your clothes."

This was all too complicated and too infuriating. Step could handle being involved with people and paying attention to them and being polite and all for hours and hours at a stretch, but then he needed time to himself, time where nobody was making demands on him, and right at this moment he wanted Glass to get up and go to the window and jump out and die. Nothing personal, Step just wanted to be alone.

"Glass, is everything I do or don't do so fascinating to you?"

"I was just telling you why I'd be a good babysitter for your kids."

"I'm sure you would."

"I can change the diapers, that's what I was telling you. Wipe their little bottomses. I know that's not a man's job, but I can do it anyway."

"It's a man's job all right," said Step, surrendering to Glass's conversation. "I pity any man who doesn't have the sense to help with the diaper changing. That's how you bond with the baby—that's how you come to *love* the kid, for pete's sake—doing intimate personal service like that, doing something disgusting but necessary, and the kid knows it. I mean, a man can't *nurse* the baby, can he? He needs some point of contact."

"That's a pretty good sermon."

"Yeah, I gave the same speech to my older brother and he said, What, is she turning you gay or something?"

Glass hooted and laughed and slapped his thigh. Too much reaction, too much laughter, not at all appropriate. What's going on here, wondered Step. Why is he so keyed up?

"That's just it," said Glass. "The kid loves you for it, you're doing a service, cleaning up her little privates for her, she loves it."

Now it really *did* sound disgusting. Not the idea, but the way he said it, the words, the coy way he said "her little privates." This was making Step faintly ill. The boy simply didn't know how to talk about this, that was all. In his eagerness to be of service, he didn't realize that this wasn't exactly the way a father wanted to hear a would-be babysitter talking about changing his little girl's diapers.

"I even gave her a bath once," said Glass.

"Mm?"

"Lulu. Gladys. You know. She got herself all covered with honey. Not that I wasn't watching her, you know, but I'd had to do something with the boys, I can't remember what, and she just got into the honey, it was out on the table, and she poured it all over in her hair, and I couldn't think of anything to do except take off her little dollclothes and splash her into the tub. And there she was in the tub and I washed her hair and everything and then she gives me the washcloth and she says, 'Better wash down there, Rolly.' Like her mom must have taught her you always wash your little privates."

In that moment Step realized that never, never would Glass be left alone with any of his children, even for a moment, and most especially not Betsy. No, if Step had his way Glass would never even *see* Betsy, with her beautiful blond hair and her sweet smile and her perfect, perfect innocence.

"Rolly," said Step quietly. "Let's drop the subject, OK?"

"Sure," said Glass. "I didn't mean anything by it, you know. Just that I'm willing to tend, and I know how to take care of little kids, don't you see."

"Right, Glass. Look, here's five bucks, go to the coffee shop and have something on me so I can get to sleep."

Step was reaching for his wallet.

"Why not just slap my face?" said Glass.

"What do you mean?"

"Here's five dollars," said Glass. "Like I'm some beggar who's been panhandling you on the street or something. I've *got* money, you know."

"Sorry, I'm sorry," said Step. "But I told you, I need

to sleep. I'm *desperate* to sleep. This is why I didn't want to share a room. I have to have time to myself, time *alone,* deeply and completely alone, or I can't sleep."

"Must be great for your wife," said Glass nastily.

"Don't be my enemy over this," said Step. "I make a lousy roommate, I'm a complete son-of-a-bitch, I know it. But I'm begging you, go down to the coffee shop or go smoke in the lounge or something but please, please, let me be alone here for thirty minutes, that's all I ask."

"Right," said Glass.

"Don't be mad at me, I didn't mean any offense, I'm just tired."

"Right," said Glass. He walked to the door. Then he stopped and turned to face Step, waiting, obviously ready to say something.

"What," said Step.

"Don't *ever* call me Rolly," said Glass.

"What? I don't call you Rolly, I call you Glass."

"You called me Rolly a minute ago. *Nobody* calls me Rolly."

"Did I? Why would I call you Rolly? I didn't even know that was your nickname."

"It's *not* my nickname. It's my *father's* goddam nickname."

Then Step remembered. "You used the name yourself. You said that's what the little girl called you. I must have used the name because you said it, that's all."

"I did?"

Step remembered now exactly the sentence in which Glass had used the name Rolly. Better wash down there, Rolly. He was not going to repeat it. "Why else would I have called you that?"

"Nobody ever called me Rolly," said Glass, sounding very annoyed. "My nickname as a kid was Bubba. Rolly is my dad and nobody calls me that, ever."

"I never have before," said Step, "and I never will

again. Sorry I've been so tense, I told you I'm not good at sharing a room. But better you than anybody else, right?"

Glass grinned. "Like, better to eat the cockroach than the scorpions, right?"

"Right," said Step.

Glass was gone.

Cockroach. That was exactly right. Being with Glass now was like eating a cockroach. Better wash down there, Rolly.

Step got up and took his clothes off, all his clothes, carefully folding away his underwear and putting it back in his suitcase, under the clean clothes. And then, standing there naked, he couldn't bear the idea of getting into his sheets. Why? He couldn't. They were so clean. He had to wash first.

So he got in the shower and soaped himself twice and then he felt clean enough to go to bed. Glass was still gone, and an hour later when Step looked at the clock Glass was still gone, and then Step must have fallen asleep because he never heard Glass come in at all. In the morning Glass was in the shower when Step woke up, and his sheets were open and swirled and wrinkled on the bed, so he must have come in sometime during the night. And when he came out of the bathroom Glass was back to his old cheerful self and Step could almost, almost put out of his mind the things that Glass had talked about last night.

In the morning everybody was trapped at the booth, just as they had been the day before. It had never occurred to Step that Ray would bring his people out to San Francisco and then never let them go see the rest of the show, but then a lot of things about Ray Keene had never occurred to Step until too late. It looked like the only chance he'd have to scout around would be at lunchtime, and that would be only a half hour. And he'd have the half hour only if he didn't eat, since the lines at the snack counters were even longer than the lines at the women's restrooms. It almost wasn't worth trying to meet anybody, since it would take *that* long just to spot where the software companies were. And then he'd have to find one that knew his name and thought Hacker Snack was hot stuff, which might take a lot of looking, since that game was last year's news. No, two years ago, and it was all played out. No point, none at all, Step was permanently trapped in Eight Bits Inc., a chicken outfit where he'd be surrounded by sneaks and cheats and thieves and skinflints and guys who dreamed of washing little girls.

He felt sick. He toyed with the idea of pretending to be *really* sick in order to get out of the booth, but then there'd be hell to pay if he were caught visiting around at other booths when he was supposed to be sick in his room. Besides, just because *they* were liars didn't mean *he* had to be. At least, no more than he already was, skulking around running the creative end of Eight Bits Inc. while pretending to Dicky that *he* still ran it.

In fact, that was one of the hardest things about working the booth. People would come up and want to talk about the games, especially the demos, and Step would show them stuff and tell them about features to come, and then he'd realize that Dicky was listening— Dicky always seemed to be listening, drifting silently from place to place within the booth like a ghost that never quite touched the earth—and that Step was talking about features in the games that only he and the programmers knew were going to be there, features that had never been in any version that Dicky had seen. And once he thought of a rule that a game ought to have and was talking about it to a buyer from Service Merchandise, even though *nobody* at Eight Bits Inc.

had ever thought of having the game work that way, which would have been fine because Step pretty much got his way on these things, except that there was Dicky, staring off into space, maybe listening to him or maybe to somebody else or maybe to nobody at all. The Spy, thought Step. He recalled the old Authors cards from his childhood, the picture on the James Fenimore Cooper cards, the hatchet-faced weasely picture that always summed up the essence of spy-ness in Step's mind. From now on Dicky would replace Cooper as Step's image of a spy. Dicky stood there looking lost in thought, his eyes heavy-lidded, his thick sensuous lips making vague movements, pursing and unpursing, as if he were drinking from an imaginary straw or kissing an imaginary aunt.

I've got to get out of here, thought Step. Not just out of this booth, but out of Eight Bits Inc.

He finished with the buyer from Service Merchandise, who didn't buy games anyway, he just wanted to know about them so he'd know which machines would have the hot software, and then Step walked straight to Dicky and planted himself in front of him, not sure until he started to speak what it was he planned to say.

"I've got to get out of the booth, Dicky," he said.

"Oh? We're all here to work this booth, Step." Dicky looked detached, uninterested. This subject was not even going to be an argument, because Dicky would never bend.

Step raised his voice a notch, to make sure the others in the booth heard him. "I have to see the other packages, Dicky. I have to see what the competition is doing."

"We don't do packaging," said Dicky. "That *is* our packaging. And besides, that's the art department, not the *manuals*."

"I have to see the level of documentation," said Step. "I have to see the style. I have to see how much personality they're putting into their packages."

"If you want to try something new with our manuals, write it up and bring it to me and Ray and I will decide whether you can do it."

Step raised his voice yet another notch. "So what you're telling me is that Eight Bits Inc. went to the expense of flying me out to San Francisco and now you won't let me go around and see what ideas I can come up with to help us make our documentation keep up with the competition?"

"Nobody opens the packages to see what the documentation is like when they're deciding whether to buy a game," said Dicky. "The documentation is irrelevant to competitiveness. And documentation is all you are responsible for."

"Word of mouth is what sells our products," said Step, "and word of mouth comes from the whole package. If our manuals are just right, then that's part of what the customers tell their friends about."

"The answer is no," said Dicky. "You came to work, not play, and that's final."

Step should have given it up long ago, if he cared about antagonizing Dicky. But he did not care, he intended to go on and on until—until what? Until he was fired? "I'm not proposing to play, Dicky, I'm proposing to work—effectively. Every other software house here is sending their people around to look at the competition, and we sit here locked in this booth, learning nothing. It's a recipe for turning Eight Bits Inc. into a dinosaur preserve."

Finally, *finally* Ray Keene walked over and stood silently with them for a moment, his eyes focused somewhere between them, at chest level. Then he looked Step in the eye and said, "Go ahead."

Dicky showed no sign of minding that he had just been contradicted after taking a stand.

"How long?" asked Step.

"A couple of hours," said Ray. "And then we'll send

everybody else out, one at a time." He looked at Dicky now. "New policy."

Dicky nodded. "Excellent idea."

Step turned to Dicky, and keeping all hint of triumph out of his voice, said, "I'll take my lunch during the time I'm gone, so I'll be back at one-thirty."

Dicky nodded graciously. Step could see his jaw clenching. I'd better find something, thought Step. I'd better meet somebody and make a connection because my days at Eight Bits Inc. are numbered now, and whatever days I have left are not going to be fun, because I have faced up to Dicky and won and he doesn't like being humbled, he's not good at that. He knows enough to suck up to Ray about it, but he'll make me pay.

Still, it felt sweet to have joined battle with Dicky and carried the field. And as he left the booth, Glass and a couple of the marketing guys glanced over him and surreptitiously pantomimed applause.

As he pressed through the crowds, passing booth after booth, he began to realize the problem he was going to face. He didn't know anybody. He had worked solo, had never been to one of these conventions, though of course he had heard all about them—had read about them in Neddy Cranes's column, for one thing. He couldn't just walk up to a booth and ask who the president of the company was, and if he was there, and could he speak to him. But maybe he'd have to, whether he thought he could do it or not. Besides, he wasn't asking for a *job*, he needed to talk about licensing an adaptation of Hacker Snack for another machine. Who do you talk to about *that*? Without telling every flunky manning the booth, so that word spread that Step Fletcher was out trying to make a deal?

So there he stood at the Agamemnon booth, looking at their games—so smooth, they were a great outfit, the best—when suddenly that squealing-balloon voice came out of nowhere. "The PC may be the worst computer ever foisted on the American public that wasn't made by Commodore," Neddy Cranes was saying, "but that doesn't mean that it won't be the new standard. Sixteen bits is sixteen bits, and now that programmers can design software for more than 64K of RAM at a time, they're going to be able to pile features onto their software and it's going to kill CP/M and all these little so-called home machines, too. Stick with Commodore and Atari and you'll go down with them, mark my words!"

Step had to listen. They had an IBM PC at Eight Bits Inc., and Ray Keene was still waiting to decide whether or not they were going to port their software over to it. Step was pretty sure they would not, because Glass hated the PC so much. Step himself hated the PC, with its screwy display memory and pathetic four-color graphics when you weren't stuck with monochrome. It was like taking every annoying aspect of the Apple II, making it all a little more complicated and pathetic, and then selling it for five times as much. But Neddy Cranes wasn't a fool, even if he sounded like an obnoxious blowhard. And Cranes wasn't in anybody's pocket. He didn't care about making enemies. He wasn't a flack for IBM. If he was saying IBM was the future, then probably IBM was the future, sad as that might be.

Whoever it was that Cranes was talking to, they weren't *arguing* with him. Probably they were trying to convince him that they were just as visionary as he was and they agreed with him *completely* and now look at this great software, we'll send it to you, give it a try, you'll see how great it is. And since it was Agamemnon, it probably really *was* great.

"Lord in heaven above, it's Step Fletcher himself!"

The blast of Neddy Cranes's voice at such close range almost made Step cringe, but he managed to control himself, because that was hardly the way you responded when Neddy Cranes recognized you right in front of the Agamemnon booth.

"Hi," said Step.

Cranes turned to some guy inside the Agamemnon booth. "What you need is to put somebody like Step Fletcher here onto software for the PC. Get him to adapt that game of his—Hacker Snack—great game, played it for longer than I'll ever admit—get that game of his onto the PC, and it'll look shitty because everything looks shitty on the PC, but those poor bastards who have to *use* that machine every day are gonna be so grateful to have something on there that's actually not hellish to use that they'll make a line five miles long just to lick your butt."

Step wondered if his own forays into crudeness made DeAnne feel as uncomfortable as Cranes's even cruder talk was making *him* feel. Not for the first time he resolved to stop tormenting her by using language that Mormons weren't supposed to use.

The guy from Agamemnon finally got a word in. "Nice to meet you, Mr. Fletcher."

"Step," said Step.

"Oh, haven't you met each other?" said Cranes.

"I actually haven't met anybody," said Step. "Not even you, Mr. Cranes."

Cranes threw his head back and laughed—a sound that attracted attention like the sudden cawing of a crow. Step could feel the general movement of the surrounding crowd as they turned to look, for a moment, to find the source of that incredible sound. And for that moment, inside the circle of space immediately surrounding Cranes, Step felt how all that attention had a kind of energy in it. It made Step feel shy, burdened by it, but Cranes seemed to draw strength from it. "Well it's nice to meet you, Step! I spent so much time with your goddam game that I felt like you were my ugly brother-in-law!" And to Step's astonishment, Cranes threw an arm around

him and hugged him. It was an impossible moment—
what was Step supposed to do, hug him back?

He didn't have to do anything. Cranes still gripped
him around the shoulders as he turned back to the guy
from Agamemnon. Step read the name tag. It was Dan
Arkasian. Arkasian himself, Agamemnon's founder and
president. And a nice guy, it seemed, handling this invasion from Neddy Cranes with grace and patience. This
was exactly the man he wanted to meet, the man who
could get his games published with the best distribution
in America, in the best packaging, and it had to be with
Neddy Cranes *hugging* him.

As Cranes rattled on, Arkasian was looking Step in
the eye—no, looking him *over*—and all Step could do
was smile wanly.

"You've hitched yourself to all these toy computers
with no more than 48K of usable RAM, and it's gonna
kill you," said Cranes. "But you get somebody like Step
Fletcher to design you some real software—I mean, this
guy isn't just a computer nerd, he's got a Ph.D. in history!
He *knows* something!"

Step couldn't believe that Cranes knew *that* about
him. And then he remembered—Eight Bits Inc. had
put out a press release about hiring him, and that
included the fact that he had just got doctorate. Step
had assumed that nobody read that stuff.

"I'll bet that standing right here, Step has more
ideas about what you can do with the PC than just about
anybody here. Come on, Fletcher, tell him one, he
needs a new idea, all that Arkasian has going for him is
that his product is slick, he needs a new idea!"

This was awful, this was impossible. He had to
come up with *something* or he'd look like a fool. Something
that would work with the pathetic graphics of the IBM
PC. Something that needed more RAM. And all that
popped into his mind was that wonderful old atlas he
had spent two days practically memorizing at the Salt

Lake City library, the one that had maps showing the electoral and popular votes in every U.S. election since 1788.

"An atlas," said Step.

"We've thought of that," said Arkasian. "They can buy the *book* for less than the software would cost, and we can't match the graphics."

"No, you do what only the computer can do with it. Like . . . elections. Next year Reagan's up for reelection and what with the recession it might be a tight race."

"Recession's over," scoffed Cranes. "Reagan's in with a landslide."

The recession isn't over for *me*, thought Step bitterly. But what he said was, "Why not an atlas that shows every election since 1788, the states colored in by party? You can animate it by screen flipping, move through Democratic Party electoral votes through history, backward or forward, or flip through all the third-party candidacies that actually got electoral votes. People love maps, they love maps that *change*. The computer can do it, and the book can't."

Arkasian shrugged and nodded. "OK, that's something."

"And Congress," said Step, warming to it. "A map showing every congressional district in every state. You can do a closeup on the state and show how the districts have changed with every census, and what party held the district. Animate an entire state's history and watch it change over time. Same thing with population, county by county."

"You'd need a hard disk for all *that* information," said Arkasian.

"Not if you use vectors and fills. Like you said, if they want a road atlas they'll buy the triple-A and put it in the car. So we don't have to get the borders exactly right, we can store everything as coordinates and numbers and draw it in realtime."

"But who'd buy it?" asked Arkasian.

"Every parent who wants his kids to succeed in school. Everybody who's interested in politics during an election year. And you could even sell it as a tool for business planners—you include projected population growth, maybe include a media-markets map with all the TV stations marked."

Arkasian laughed. "This is a program that'll need 512K just to run."

"And so what about *that!*" demanded Cranes. "I tell you that in five years they won't dare offer a PC for sale that doesn't have a *megabyte* of RAM in it!"

"Neddy, you're off your rocker and you know it," said Arkasian.

"I'm off my rocker but that doesn't mean I'm not right! You'll see! And when your company is in receivership because you kept on doing games for the Commodore 64 and ignored the PC, you'll remember that I told you back in 1983!"

Finally Cranes let go of Step and moved on, not even saying good-bye. The man gave off self-importance in great crashing waves, and Step had been caught in the undertow. He watched Cranes go for a moment, then turned back to Arkasian and smiled ruefully, offering his hand. "It *was* nice to meet you, Mr. Arkasian."

"My pleasure," said Arkasian. "Why do I feel like I'm just coming up for air?"

Step laughed. "He's got a lot of . . . presence."

"I actually liked your idea for that atlas program," said Arkasian.

"Oh, really?"

"You were winging it, weren't you?"

Step shrugged. "He kind of put me on the spot."

"That's what Neddy does. But you performed, Mr. Fletcher."

"Please call me Step, Mr. Arkasian."

"Step. Everybody calls me Arkasian. Without the mister. Of course, even if Neddy's right, it'll still be a couple of years before it'll be practical to do that atlas program."

"Yeah, well, it would actually take that long just to do the research for it, if you're going to do it right."

"That was really something, you know," said Arkasian. "Coming up with all that right out of your head, out of the air, complete with the marketing strategy. No wonder Eight Bits Inc. hired you!"

And there it was. Arkasian thought that Eight Bits Inc. owned him, and if Step just said outright, I want to quit them and I'm looking for something better, he'd be tagged in Arkasian's eyes as disloyal. Any offer that was going to be worthwhile had to come from Arkasian, without Step asking.

"They just have me writing manuals," said Step.

"Are you kidding?" asked Arkasian.

"I'm not there as a programmer."

"What were they *thinking* of?"

"Internal politics, I think," said Step. "Doesn't matter, I enjoy the work."

"So you're *through* with programming?"

Here was the moment.

"I still have the rights to Hacker Snack," said Step. "And I can write programs on any machine that Eight Bits Inc. isn't developing for."

"They aren't developing for the PC?"

"Ray hasn't decided."

"Come here," said Arkasian. He beckoned Step to come around inside the Agamemnon booth.

Unlike the Eight Bits Inc. display, the Agamemnon area—which was twice as large to begin with, an end-of-the-row double—had something like a private room in it, a three-sided vertical display unit with a lockable door. Arkasian led him inside, into a small roofless space cluttered with empty boxes and packing materials. Arkasian closed the door behind them, and then said, firmly, "Ray Keene is the worst lying son-of-a-bitch in this business."

Now was not the time for Step to badmouth his boss, not to someone who might later want to be able to rely on Step's loyalty. "I've only been at Eight Bits Inc. since the first of March, and I don't see much of Ray."

"Why didn't you talk to *me* before you went to work as a manual writer for Ray Keene?"

"I sent my résumé to Agamemnon, but I got a form letter back saying you weren't hiring."

"Damn," said Arkasian cheerfully. "We're so big now that we've got a personnel director. Of course we weren't hiring, but we would have hired *you*."

This was the chance Step had been hoping for—it would never get better than this. Might as well ask for the moon. "I don't want to work for anybody, Arkasian. Not even Agamemnon. If I leave Eight Bits Inc., it'll be because I have a development deal with somebody, and I can work on my own, at home, with an advance large enough to live on while I write code. And I have a one-year noncompetition clause with Eight Bits Inc. Hacker Snack is excluded, though, and also programs for machines that Eight Bits isn't developing for."

"And how much would you need?"

"Depends on how long the program would take to develop," said Step. "That atlas would take a long time."

"What about Hacker Snack for the 64?"

"Two months," said Step.

"And what about Hacker Snack for the PC?"

"I don't know 8088 machine code."

"So include the learning curve."

"Six months at the outside," said Step. "But it won't look as good in IBM's lousy three-color graphic screen."

"I want it monochrome first, anyway."

"Why not do both versions and put them in the same package? That way if they upgrade their machine, they already have the game."

"Why not sell it to them twice?"

"Because they'll feel robbed," said Step, "and if they're *thinking* about upgrading you don't want them to put off buying Hacker Snack until after they've decided about the upgrade. Heck, they might upgrade just *because* they already own the color version of the game."

"Let me think about this," said Arkasian. "I can tell you right now, I want Hacker Snack for the 64. But different. Upgraded. So we can say, Better than the Atari version. New improved, all that bullshit."

"I'll think of stuff," said Step.

"We haven't decided about the PC, either. Nor would I have any idea how much to advance you on PC projects, because we still don't know what the entertainment software market is going to be like on what is essentially a business machine."

"A *crippled* business machine."

"With an inflated, monopolistic price," said Arkasian. "I don't like IBM either. But I think Neddy's right. I think IBM will make the PC go. I think it'll be ten times the CP/M market, and I think people will want color on it. And do you know *why* I think they'll want color on it?"

"So they can play games," said Step.

"Dead right."

Step laughed. "That's the only reason computers exist, isn't it? To play games."

"No joke," said Arkasian. "And the more gamelike the serious software is, the better *it'll* sell. Step Fletcher, I'll give you a development deal on Hacker Snack for the 64, just to start with. But it won't be enough money for you to quit your job."

"I understand."

"But if Ray Keene is as cheap and stupid a son-of-a-bitch as I think he is, he's going to decide not to develop for the PC. If that happens, you tell me, and we'll do a deal for the PC. A serious deal, maybe even including that atlas idea. You do *want* to do that, don't you? I mean, I know you were just making it up as you went along, and maybe—"

"I'd give my teeth to do it."

"So tell me when Ray Keene decides."

Step took a deep breath. "I can't do that," he said.

"What?"

"Mr. Arkasian, I work for Eight Bits Inc. I can't tell a competitor things that I find out about Ray Keene's plans."

Arkasian looked at him, perplexed. "Well, I'll be damned."

"The second I quit," said Step, "then I will be able to tell you whether my noncompetition agreement will allow me to develop for the PC or not, and then you can conclude what you like. But until I quit, I can't tell you what Ray decides about anything. I shouldn't even have told you that he hasn't decided yet, and I feel bad enough about that, I'm not going to make it worse."

"Well, then, if he decides not to go for the PC, quit your job and call me."

"I can't quit my job unless I already know I've got something lined up." What Step couldn't say was, There's a chance that you're only offering me work in order to get a spy inside Eight Bits Inc., and I won't do that. "I've got three kids and a fourth due in July."

Step almost held his breath, waiting to see what Arkasian would say.

"OK," said Arkasian. "I'll send you a contract for Hacker Snack for the 64. There'll be an option clause in it. Hacker Snack for the PC, and a development deal for the PC. If I decide, as I probably will, to take Agamemnon into PC development, then I'll exercise the option on Hacker Snack for the PC. At that point, if you come to the conclusion that your noncompetition agreement with Eight Bits Inc. would allow you to develop for the PC, then *you* can exercise the option on the PC development deal. And I'll make sure the bucks are big enough. What do you make now?"

"Thirty thousand a year, only that isn't enough to live on."

"I know how it is," said Arkasian. "A two-year deal, a hundred thousand dollars. You can't exercise your option unless I've already exercised mine, for the PC version of Hacker Snack, but after that, it's up to you."

"Up to Ray Keene, you mean."

"I'm betting on Ray Keene making the wrong move. Maybe only for six months before he changes his mind back, but if everything works out, your work is going to be coming out with the Agamemnon logo on it."

Step cocked his head. "You aren't just using me to stick it to Ray Keene, are you?"

"I don't invest money to stick it to anybody," said Arkasian. "I invest money where I think I'm going to make a shitload more." Then he grinned. "But if it also makes Ray Keene piss green, so much the better."

"You need my address," said Step.

"Give me your card."

"I don't have a card. I just moved and, well, I don't have a card."

"Write it on the back of mine. And keep one of these for yourself." Step pocketed one card, put the Chinqua Penn address and phone number on the back of the other, and returned it to Arkasian. Arkasian took it, put it in his pocket, and held out his hand. Step took it. Arkasian's grip was large and firm and it made Step feel . . . safe. Like he was in good hands now.

Arkasian didn't let go of his hand. "What I've said to you about *my* plans . . . ," he said.

"I don't spy for anybody," said Step. "And Ray Keene knows better than to ask me to." Though of course Ray *could* ask him to sneak around and run the programming behind Dicky's back, and Step would do *that*. I pretend to be so clean, but I'm really not.

That was what Step thought as he left the Agamemnon booth. I'm only *somewhat* clean. I only have *some* standards that won't bend. And if Arkasian had offered me enough money maybe I would have folded on all of them. He probably thinks I'm a good man who can be trusted, but I know that I can only be trusted until I think that being trustworthy won't get me what I want. Even as it is, I'm a sneak and a cheat, coming here to talk to one of Eight Bits Inc.'s most powerful competitors when it was Eight Bits that paid for me to come to this convention in the first place. I tricked them into paying for me to fly to a job interview with a rival. I'm even getting paid for the time that I spent here.

By rights I should share the idea for the atlas with Eight Bits Inc. My employment agreement says so, that any ideas I come up with while I work for them belong to them.

Then he thought: That's easy. All I have to do is propose the atlas to Dicky, and make him think that I really want to do it. He'll shoot it down. He'll kill it, just to spite me. If I get him to do it in writing, I'm home free. I'll have proof that I offered it to them and that clears me.

Sneaky. I'm so sneaky.

That night, Glass tried to get him to join him and the marketing guys and some young programmers at Apple who were working on software for the Lisa. They were going to drink their way through San Francisco, and Step begged off. "But we need a designated driver," said Glass.

"Take a cab," said Step.

"Oh, yeah," said Glass. "I forgot. This is a *real* city. Cabs."

So Step had the hotel room to himself when he called DeAnne and told her everything that had happened with Neddy Cranes and Dan Arkasian. He loved hearing the relief, the excitement in her voice. "It's not a sure thing," he said. "But the money for the 64 adaptation *is*."

Then she thought of something that could go wrong. DeAnne was good at thinking of things that could go wrong. "Only if you can get Eight Bits Inc. to stop working on their own 64 adaptation."

"I'll just tell them to stop."

"Right, you'll walk in and say, I sold it to Agamemnon."

"No, I'll just tell them that I won't sell it to *them*."

"And they'll ask why, since you work for them, and especially because they've got *so* much *invested* in it now."

"Not my fault."

"Not your fault, but then they fire you anyway because you're not a team player."

Step sighed. "This is all very complicated."

"It's all a matter of timing, isn't it," said DeAnne. "Because what if things come to a head about the 64 adaptation *before* we actually get a contract from Agamemnon, and then you tell Eight Bits Inc. they can't do it and they fire you and *then* you don't get the contract from Agamemnon after all."

"But what if the contract comes first and the 64 adaptation doesn't come to a head until after Ray decides *not* to develop for the PC and *after* Arkasian decides that he *will* develop for the PC."

"Everything depends on other people," said DeAnne.

"Everything always depends on other people," said Step. "And maybe the Lord is looking out for us a little. Maybe God has a plan."

"Well, if he planned for you to work for Agamemnon, why didn't he get us to move to California instead of this side trip to Steuben? Or even leave us where we were? We were happy in Indiana. Stevie wasn't playing with imaginary friends there."

That was something new. "Imaginary friends?"

"I realized it today. I mean, it's been going on for weeks. Almost since we *moved* here. He comes home from school so morose, I don't think he has *any* friends there, I mean I've asked him who he plays with at school and he says, Nobody, but I didn't worry because then every now and then he says, Jack and I did this, or Scotty and I did that. So I thought, he *does* have friends, he just wants me to feel sorry for him."

"Heck, I didn't even know he talked at all."

"He's not a *catatonic* or anything, you know. Just depressed."

"Oh, well, *that's* OK."

"On Saturdays I've been spending time with *you*, doing the shopping we had to do, all the work, all the unpacking, you know? But this Saturday you were gone, and I was lonely, and so I just sat on the patio for a while reading that Anne Tyler book you got me while the kids played. Robbie and Elizabeth were playing two-man tag or something, anyway they were chasing each other everywhere, but Stevie just sort of sat there on the lawn, and then he wandered around, touching the fence, touching the wall of the house, stuff like that. It worried me. He used to play with the younger kids, and here he is still sulking or something and he doesn't play with them, even though Robbie kept coming up to him and saying, Play with us. Anyway, then I went inside and did the laundry and stuff, but I kept checking on the kids because that's what I *do*—"

"Madame Conscientious."

"That's me, Junk Man. But what I'm saying is, I know Stevie never left the back yard and I know that no other kids were there. But then at supper I asked him, What were you playing there in the back yard today? And he says, Jack and me were searching for buried treasure. And I say, You mean at school? Because that's where I thought Jack was. And he says, Jack doesn't go to school."

"Are you sure he understood what you were asking?"

"Yes. I mean, I asked him right then, Well when did you search for buried treasure with him? and he says, Today, and I say, Where? and he says, In the back yard mostly."

"Isn't he a little old for an imaginary friend?"

"Yes, Step, of course he is. Way too old. It worries me."

"Maybe he's just pretending that his friends from school are part of his imaginary game at home. You know, including them even though they aren't there."

"I'm not making this up, Step. He actually *said* that Jack doesn't *go* to school. Doesn't that sound like an imaginary friend?"

"I forgot that you said that he said that. I haven't had a chance to think about this the way you have."

"Step, he doesn't have any friends at school, apparently, and at home he's not playing with his brother and sister, he's playing with imaginary friends—even when the kids are right there, when *I'm* right there. Tonight I tried to get the kids to play Life with me, you know Stevie's always liked that game, but he wouldn't play. I *made* him play, but he wouldn't move his car or handle his money, I ended up spinning for him even, like he was just a dummy player, and he just sat there staring off into space."

"Is he *still* punishing us for making him move and go to a new school?"

"What else can I think?" asked DeAnne.

"Things have to work out," said Step. "They have to work out so I can come home, work at home. So we can get life back the way it's supposed to be. I feel so *helpless,* so cut off, my boy is having these problems, he's so *angry* at us, and I can't do a thing, I'm trapped. How do other men do it? Going to work all the time? And then these housewives want to go to work just like the men, so they can be cut off from their families, too, when what *should* happen is all the men coming home, to put the family back together."

"I know, Step. At least that's how *we* need it to be."

"So pray for us tonight," said Step. "Pray for this contract to come through. For all the timing to be right."

"I don't know if I should be praying for things like that," said DeAnne. "It's so selfish."

"Listen," said Step, "even Christ expressed a personal preference before he said, Thy will be done."

"Yeah, but then look what happened to *him!*"

He hooted with laughter. "I can't believe *you* said that."

"I didn't mean it to be so—sacrilegious."

"It wasn't, Fish Lady, it wasn't."

"Things will work out," she said.

"I love you," he answered.

"I'll pick you up at the airport tomorrow," she said.

"We're all coming in on the same flight," he said. "So I can just hitch a ride home with one of the ones who parked there."

"I *want* to meet you at the airport, Junk Man. The *kids* want to meet you."

How could he tell her—he didn't want his children there when Glass got off the plane. He didn't want *anybody* from Eight Bits Inc. to see his family. The kids were still pure, still untouched by this slimy company, and he just didn't want them to be defiled by having Ray Keene tousle Robbie's hair or Dicky Northanger chuck Stevie under the chin or Glass *look* at Betsy.

"Please," he said. "Keep the kids home. Let me come *home* to them. To you. Please."

"Whatever you say, Junk Man." But he could tell she was hurt.

"Please understand," he said.

"Fine, it's fine," she said, though it was clearly not fine. "I love you."

"I love you more," he said. Another ritual.

"Not a chance," she said. The ritual answer.

"Hang up first," he said.

She did.

6

·INSPIRATION·

This is the career DeAnne found for herself: In high school she realized that the only way a decent woman with no skills could make money was as a burger flipper or a waitress. So she set about getting a skill. When she entered college, she could type a hundred words a minute. She earned enough money as a part-time secretary in the Child Development and Family Relations Department to pay for the materials to make her own clothes and the gas she used driving the old red Volkswagen to the Y and back. She mastered the mag-card electronic typewriter, got a raise, and saved enough to pay for a semester in Paris.

Her choice of major was less practical. She loved art and music and literature, and so she majored in humanities, even though she knew that there was no career on earth for which a humanities degree was regarded as a serious qualification. But that didn't matter. In the back of her mind she knew that motherhood was going to be her career, as it had been for her own mother. She studied humanities so she could create a home filled with art and wisdom for her children. If she ever needed a job, she could walk into any office, type a flawless 300-word page in three minutes or less, and be hired on the spot.

It turned out, though, that motherhood wasn't quite the career she had hoped it would be. For one thing, motherhood was always preceded by months of misery. If it hadn't been for Bendectin, which barely controlled her perpetual nausea during the first four months of each pregnancy, she would have vomited her way into the hospital with every child, and the nausea never really went away until the baby was born.

More important, though, was the fact that each newborn was a complete barbarian. She and Step put prints of great art on the walls and played records of great music of every kind, but that was background—her main activity was chasing, feeding, wiping, washing, changing, scolding, comforting, and containing her impatience with the little vandals. There were wonderful moments, of course, but they were few and far between, and while DeAnne loved her children and took pride in caring for them, she could never find any measurable accomplishment in her life. When Step finished working he wanted peace and solitude; she was dying to have an adult to talk to. And when Step helped her with housework or tending the kids, the fact that he was perfectly competent at everything told her that nothing she did could only be done by her—except nursing the newest baby, and *baboons* could do *that*.

Motherhood was not a career. It was *life*. A good life, one she had no intention of giving up, but it was not complete enough for her. She needed to do something that reminded her that she was human.

She had been saying this to her good friend Lorry Tisch, who managed the educational TV station in Salt Lake City, when Lorry started laughing at her. "You *have* a career, dimwit! Every bit as fulfilling as mine!"

"If you tell me that motherhood is supposed to be enough—"

"Listen, Deen, back before you and Step were married, when Step was back and forth between Mexico and Washington working on that project for the Historical Department and he was only home one Wednesday night right in the middle, why was it that you didn't have time to see him? Remember now, he was already the love of your life, and you couldn't spare him the *one* night in two months—"

"I had a responsibility," said DeAnne.

"Young Adult Relief Society president, and you had a presidency meeting. You could have changed the day! You could have canceled that week's meeting!"

"Why are you bringing all this up again, Lorry?"

"Because you'll sacrifice *anything* for your career. Even Step. You almost lost him over that one, you know. I had to talk to him for three hours that night to keep him from giving you an f.o. note."

"Please don't tell me what the letters stand for," said DeAnne.

"Your career is the Church, Deen. Whatever your calling is at any given moment, that's what you live for, and everything else better get out of your way. So don't give me any more b.s.—that stands for booger samples— about not having a career. You had a career when we were both in high school and you practically ran the whole Young Women program while the adult leaders just stood out of your way."

DeAnne had realized that Lorry was right. She had a career, one that she could pursue without setting aside her family. So she threw herself into her callings with renewed enthusiasm, and hadn't let up since, through their years in Salt Lake City, in Orem, in Vigor. Wherever they went, as soon as the strongest women in the ward realized how reliable, how competent, how inventive she was, they would go to the bishop and begin to ask for her to be called to a position in their organization. Almost immediately she would find herself in the inner circle of the best women in the ward, aware of everything, all the family problems and marriage problems and money problems, all the women who couldn't get along with each other, all the women who could be relied on and all the women who couldn't. Armed with this knowledge, she was able to make a difference. Her programs ran smoothly and she carried out all her assignments, but to her that was the minimum. Far more important was the work she imposed on herself—trying to help the sisters become a bit more patient with others' failings, more tolerant of strangeness, more loving and less angry, more obedient to the laws of God and less compliant with the mindless demands of tradition.

It was a life's work, because it never ended—and yet she had seen progress, she had made breakthroughs. And when she compared her career in the Church with the careers of her friends—even one as remarkably successful as Lorry, who was now programming director for a network station in a major market—she was not unsatisfied, for while she would never get the fame or recognition or money Lorry had, at the end of every working day what had Lorry accomplished? "M°A°S°H" reruns slotted between Carson and the new Letterman show.

If the Church was DeAnne's career, then moving to a new town—indeed, moving across town to a new ward—was like a job transfer. The Church was the same everywhere, in its broad outlines. There were the same callings to be filled, the same basic tasks to be performed. But the people were different; the way they fit together in the ward was always new. Each new ward had its own customs, its own traditions, its quarrels and its cliques.

Most important, though, was the fact that in each new ward, DeAnne never knew what her calling would be. It took time to become known, time for people to find out what she could do. And in the meantime, the bishop would be looking at the ward roster, trying to find someone to teach a Primary class or run the library. DeAnne would, of course, accept any calling she was given and do the best she could with it, but she had seen many times how someone could get put in one slot, and as long as they lived in that ward that's all that people ever saw them as. She had said it to Step as they prepared to move to Steuben: "I wonder who I'll be in our new ward."

"Who you'll be? You'll be DeAnne Brown Fletcher, of course."

She knew better. In Vigor she had been counselor in the Relief Society, one of the leading women in the ward, part of everything going on. In Salt Lake City she had been the young women's president; in Orem she had worked with the young women's organization at the stake level. Each role was different; in each place, because she had a different calling, the other Saints saw her differently, saw her as the role she filled.

And why not? That was how careers were *supposed* to function, wasn't it? That was the *difference* between a career and a job, wasn't it? A job was just something you did—but a career, that was who you *were*. Step had a history Ph.D., but nobody saw him as a historian because that wasn't his career; he *was* a game designer, because that's where his accomplishments were. Well, DeAnne had been an accomplished Relief Society counselor in Vigor, and now in the Steuben 1st Ward she would be someone else, and she was eager to know who.

They had moved often enough that they were now experts on how to get involved immediately in the new ward. Some people entered a ward shyly, quietly, just coming to the meetings and gradually getting to know people. But that could leave you without a calling for months and months, which would drive DeAnne crazy. So she and Step had perfected a technique of moving into a ward quickly and deeply, so they would be involved almost at once. They joined the choir.

Step had a strong baritone voice that could handle most tenor parts, and since every ward choir in the church was hurting for men, and especially for tenors, he was immediately the star of the choir. DeAnne's soprano voice was not quite so rare, but she learned parts very quickly and sang with strength—and on pitch. Besides, she played the piano and could fill in for a missing accompanist. There was always a core of music people in every ward, trading assignments and helping each other out in all the organizations. By becoming known to the music people, DeAnne and Step were soon known to everyone—known and valued. Because their attendance at choir was as faithful as possible, people also knew they were, as Mormons called it, "active." They could be counted on. If they were given an assignment, they would show up and fulfill it. Thanks to their choir connection, within weeks of moving into each new ward they were well and widely known.

They had followed the same program in the Steuben 1st Ward, and the technique worked just as effectively. When they showed up at the Sunday afternoon choir practice—their kids in tow and well armed with paper to draw on and books to read and, in Elizabeth's case, a few soft toys to play with while Stevie watched her—the choir director looked them over and immediately said, "We've got a new man in the choir!"

DeAnne always heard that statement with amusement. In a few moments the choir leader would apologize, whereupon DeAnne would reassure her that she understood that men were at a premium and sopranos like her were a dime a dozen.

As she took part in the familiar rituals of choir practice, DeAnne felt warm and comfortable and welcome. Even though she knew not a single one of the people there, they were Mormons and they were music people and so she knew them all, and knew that they knew her and her husband and already, already they belonged.

The next week DeAnne substituted for a Primary teacher—the Primary president's husband was one of the basses, and apparently when the Primary president was fretting about a teacher who was out of town, he must have said, "Why not ask the new sister to fill in? Sister—Fletcher, I think." And the following week Step substituted in gospel doctrine class. He had spoken up a couple of times in class the first two weeks, and word was getting around that he had a doctorate in history, which gave him great prestige in a mostly blue-collar ward, so it was only natural they gave him a try as teacher of the adult Sunday school class.

During the next week, the bishop called DeAnne and set up an appointment for her and Step to come see him. Saturday was the only day she could count on Step being home at any reasonable hour before Sunday came, and so Saturday it was. Sure enough, she was called to be a Primary teacher—the usual calling for a woman new in a ward—and Step was called to teach the gospel doctrine class. Step was elated. He loved to teach and hated administrative callings—he had not really enjoyed being elders quorum president back in Vigor. Besides, gospel doctrine class was a Sunday-only calling; there'd be no meetings during the week, and that meant that there'd be no conflict between his job and his calling.

DeAnne bided her time, however. She was a good

Primary teacher and loved working with the little children, but she knew that she would not be in Primary very long—something would open up in Relief Society and she would be brought in. She knew this because the Relief Society president, Ruby Bigelow, had made a point of sitting beside her the second Sunday they went to choir practice, and when the singing was done, they had chatted like old friends for a quarter of an hour, before the kids made it clear that they were hungry enough to start eating the pews. Sister Bigelow already knew that DeAnne had been education counselor in the Relief Society in Vigor—Jenny Cowper had told her— and they swapped stories about disastrous homemaking meetings they had lived through. "I hope I get a chance to know you better," Sister Bigelow had said after that first conversation.

It happened the last Tuesday night in April. A phone call from the bishop. He wanted to speak to Step first. Step talked for only a few moments, said, "Sure, of course, no problem," and then called DeAnne back to the phone. That told her at once that the bishop had a new calling for her, and had checked with her husband first—she didn't mind the custom; she only wished that they'd do the same when the shoe was on the other foot, and check with the wife before calling the husband to a new position.

"Hi, Sister Fletcher," said the bishop.

"Hi again," said DeAnne.

"I hate doing this on the phone, but I have to catch a plane in an hour and I won't be back before Sunday and Sister Bigelow would have my hide on the wall if I didn't get you called so you could be sustained this Sunday."

So it was going to be a Relief Society calling. She was almost relieved about that; because of her good experience in Vigor, she still thought of herself as a Relief Society person. And she liked Sister Bigelow. It

would be good to work with her, and good to be with
the women of the ward.

"Sister Mansard has just been called to the state
Relief Society board, and that leaves the ward without a
spiritual living teacher. Sister Bigelow and I both think
that you're the one the Lord wants in that position. Will
you do it?"

Of course she would do it, though she was aston-
ished that she was being given spiritual living. That was
far and away the most prestigious of the four Relief
Society teaching positions. In her most ambitious
moments DeAnne might have hoped to teach cultural
refinement. Sister Bigelow must have an amazing amount
of confidence in a newcomer.

Thus it was that, almost exactly two months after
they arrived in Steuben, DeAnne finally knew what *her*
career in this place was going to be. She was relieved;
she was delighted. Like Step, she would be a teacher, in
the organization she loved best and with the assignment
she valued most.

"When you think about it," said Step, "you and I
have probably the two most influential teaching positions you can have. If the Lord brought us to Steuben to
make a difference in this ward, he couldn't have put us
into better callings to accomplish it." DeAnne could
only agree. It felt good to have those callings, as if the
Lord was reassuring them that this move was the right
thing to do, that they were in the place where he
wanted them to be.

If only Stevie could get that same confidence in
where he was, in what he was doing. But it was harder
for a child, even one as bright and mature for his age as
Stevie. He hadn't yet had enough experience with life to
be patient, to know even when things were unpleasant
and hard that it all had a purpose, even fear, even pain,
that it would end up preparing him to be a fine man
who would understand the suffering and loneliness of

others. There was plenty of time, though. That was the nice thing, that in a couple of years she could say to Stevie, "Do you remember how hard it was for you when we first moved here? Why, you even had imaginary friends that you played with, you were so determined to be lonely! And now look at you, with all these friends, and doing so well in school!" If only she could skip over the next few years, and take him to that place right now, so that he could see that this crisis in his life would pass.

In the meantime, she had her career in this place, and so did Step. Actually, Step had *two* careers, so while he hated working with some of those strange people at Eight Bits Inc., he had the relief of Sundays, a chance to talk to people who understood the way he saw the world, to be a servant of the Lord instead of a servant of Ray Keene.

For Step, of course, teaching the gospel doctrine class was easy. He didn't think about it during the week, didn't even prepare it until sacrament meeting, usually. He'd read a couple of chapters in the Old Testament while the speakers droned on, jot some notes, and then a few minutes after sacrament meeting ended he'd stand up in front of the class and dazzle them. In a way he'd been preparing all his life to teach a class like this—all it took was a few moments of thought and he could draw out of his memory enough insights into the scriptures to keep the class members pondering and exploring for a week.

For DeAnne, though, teaching was a much more involving task. For one thing, women in Relief Society expected far more preparation from their teachers. There had to be visual aids, and sometimes handouts, and sometimes treats, which meant that DeAnne had to plan each lesson for days, for weeks. For another thing, DeAnne soon found that Sister Bigelow apparently relied on her teachers to be part of the leadership of the

Relief Society. She was often on the phone to DeAnne, asking her to help with this or that—to call a list of sisters, for instance, and ask them to take food over to so-and-so's house because her mother had been in the hospital and she shouldn't have to worry about cooking. "I'm so sorry to put all these things on you," Sister Bigelow said, "but our compassionate service leader isn't—well, isn't always *able* to do what's needed."

DeAnne understood perfectly—the compassionate service leader was no doubt one of those who were given callings that they weren't really capable of doing yet, to help them grow. In the meantime, others had to take up the slack and get the job done while the sister with the calling was learning how to get her act together.

DeAnne took on all these assignments gladly and fulfilled them at once. After all, this was her career. To make those phone calls while Robbie and Elizabeth were down for their naps, to cut out visual aids for her lesson while Elizabeth colored beside her and Robbie practiced his letters—that was how life was supposed to be lived, connecting always with her children, and always with the sisters of the ward.

But the most pressing part of her work was that spiritual living lesson—if she didn't do *that* well, then she'd be less effective in anything else she did. The sisters here had to learn to have confidence in her from the start, and it would be hard, since some would be a bit resentful of a newcomer being given such a plum of a calling. Furthermore, her first teaching assignment was right away, on the first of May. She had no choice but to let a few things slide at home—the remaining boxes could stay packed until after the lesson was done.

On Sunday she was so nervous she woke early and couldn't get back to sleep. When Step got up at eight o'clock, he found the children already dressed in their Sunday clothes, eating breakfast. "What, does church start at eight-thirty instead of nine?"

"I just wanted us not to be all in a rush going to church today," said DeAnne.

Step smiled and put his arm around her. She knew that he wasn't much of a hugger by nature, but he knew *she* needed physical contact, so when he noticed that she needed it, he gave it. Today she hadn't realized how *much* she needed the reassurance of his arm around her, but she felt calm go through her in a warm wave, and she clung to him for a moment. "You're going to be wonderful," he said. "You always worry so much, but you're a great teacher and they're going to love you."

All through sacrament meeting she could hardly listen to the people bearing their testimonies, she was so nervous. During Step's lesson in Sunday school, she kept glancing down at her notes, making sure that she knew exactly what she was going to say. For a moment, though, his words brought her out of her reverie. He was telling the story of the time when Joshua was all upset because a couple of men were prophesying in the camp of Israel, and he wanted Moses to come and stop them. Step paraphrased Moses' answer: "Don't be jealous on *my* behalf. I wish *all* the people were prophets." Then Step launched into his riff about how the Lord expects every Saint to receive guidance from the Lord, and not rely on anyone else, not even the prophet, to tell them every move to make in their lives. For one awful moment, DeAnne thought, He's going to give my lesson. I should have told him what my lesson was about because he's going to cover the whole thing right here and in Relief Society it's going to sound like I'm just repeating what my husband said, which would completely undercut the whole point I want to make.

But Step went on to a discussion of ritual, and DeAnne breathed a sigh of relief, though she drew a little star in her notes and wrote "Step" beside it, right at the spot in her lesson where she should refer to what Step had said in Sunday school. She'd make it work.

She wasn't counting on Sister LeSueur.

Because of Jenny Cowper's warning, DeAnne had noticed right away who Sister LeSueur was. A nice-looking lady, probably in her early sixties, hair dyed blond, and always dressed to show both money and dignity. She always had a smile and a word for everyone, and DeAnne rather liked her. She couldn't understand why Jenny would have said such unpleasant things about her. Perhaps Sister LeSueur's sweetness was a bit excessive, a bit too ostentatious, but there were many worse things that could be wrong with a person. Jenny must simply have misunderstood something that she said. Or perhaps she just has a low tolerance for people who are too careful to show that they are really good at being Christlike. DeAnne didn't have too much use for people like that, either, but Sister LeSueur didn't seem all that obnoxious.

She began to understand what Jenny was talking about, though, when her lesson was over and it was time for the sisters to bear their testimonies. The lesson had gone very well. It was *about* testimonies, and after telling several stories she got to her main point, that each sister had to have her own relationship with the Spirit of God. "The only mediator between us and our Father in heaven is Jesus Christ, and no one else, not the bishop, not our husbands, can stand between us and the Lord. Your testimony of the Lord is the one that you will be judged by at the last day, not someone else's. As the Savior said, it is the words that we *speak,* not the words that we *hear,* that can damn us—or lift us up. Your husband's testimony can't possibly carry you into heaven." They nodded, many of them, when she said that.

Then she spoke about how she and Step had not discussed their lessons with each other, and yet both of them had ended up making exactly that point—that the Lord wanted *all* his children to be prophets, to receive the Spirit in their lives. "Perhaps the Lord really wanted you to hear that lesson today. But I didn't have to go to my husband to find out about it—if either of us was inspired, then we were *both* inspired, and that's how it should be with our testimonies." Again, they nodded. And when she finished with her lesson, more than a few were dabbing at their eyes.

The testimony meeting that followed was lovely, and that, too, was part of what DeAnne had tried for. It was the job of the spiritual living teacher to set the right tone, so in this one meeting each month the sisters would feel hungry to stand on theie feet and bear their testimonies to each other. There was such an air of fervor and excitement as the first few spoke. Then Sister LeSueur got up.

She began crying at once, of course—that was what one expected of people who were ostentatiously spiritual, just as from those who really were. It was Sister LeSueur's words, not her tears, that told DeAnne that Jenny Cowper might just have been correct about this woman.

"My heart is so *full* after that wonderful lesson," said Sister LeSueur. "I just had to tell my sisters how wonderful it is and how blessed I am to have my dear husband Jacob. He is such a strength to me, and I want you to know that he makes all the decisions in our lives, because he is the true head of our home, and the Lord shows him the way for us both. If I ever get into the celestial kingdom, it will be because his wonderful strong testimony carried me there. I'm so grateful that the Lord has given his daughters into the hands of good men, because without our husbands we would be utterly lost and alone. I just wish I were as spiritual as Sister Fletcher, here—I would never dare to teach a lesson without talking it out with my husband first, because that's the reason the Lord gave me my husband, to be my guide and teacher in all things."

She went on but DeAnne hardly heard. She felt as if she had been slapped in the face. It was bad enough that what Sister LeSueur said was false doctrine; what made it almost unbearable was that she had deeply undercut DeAnne's position as spiritual living teacher by directly contradicting the main point of her lesson. From all that DeAnne could tell, Dolores LeSueur had enormous prestige in the ward, and if she contradicted DeAnne, then who was going to be believed? DeAnne had now been branded as an unreliable teacher by one of the leading women of the ward. It was all she could do to keep from crying. Especially when the next sister got up and bore her testimony about what a spiritual giant Sister LeSueur was, and no wonder the Lord had healed her of cancer so she could continue to live in the Steuben 1st Ward and give such wonderful guidance and such a wonderful example of faith to all of them.

Then, mercifully, the meeting ended. DeAnne immediately gathered her things together and headed for the door, wanting nothing more than to leave and get to the car where perhaps she could cry for a few moments before Step gathered the kids and brought them out to the car so she would have to start being cheerful again. However, she got caught in the crush at the door leaving the Relief Society room, and before she could get through, there were hands plucking at her sleeve. It was the choir director, Mary Anne Lowe. Tears were streaming down her face. "What a wonderful lesson," she said. "It was just what I needed to hear today." And then she was gone, back in the crowd.

Jenny Cowper was next to tug at her sleeve, drawing DeAnne away from the door after all. "I heard what Mary Anne said, and I just want you to know—her husband went inactive when blacks got the priesthood, he's such a bigot, and it breaks Mary Anne's heart every time a certain pinhead bears her testimony about how wonderful her husband is and how a woman is nothing if she doesn't have a good husband. So when she said she needed to hear your lesson about how your husband can't stand between you and God, well, it's true."

"Oh," said DeAnne. So her lesson had been good for *somebody*.

"That witch with a *b* talks that way about her husband all the time, you know."

"You mean Sister LeSueur?" asked DeAnne.

"With a capital *B*," said Jenny. "So when you gave that lesson, it was like you cleared the air of a lot of smog that we've been breathing in this ward for *years*. What a great start."

"Great start!" said DeAnne. "I'm doomed."

"Doomed! Nonsense. Everybody here with any brains is so glad you're the teacher that they could *kiss* Sister Bigelow for calling you. You took a horrible weight off their shoulders. There are only about six good marriages in this whole Relief Society, and when the Queen *B* talks about her dear Jacob like that, it stabs everyone else to the heart."

"She must not have any idea of the effect of her words, then," said DeAnne.

"In a pig's eye," said Jenny. "But look who's coming."

DeAnne turned and there was Sister LeSueur, smiling and holding out her hand. "Oh, my dear Sister Fletcher, what a wonderful lesson! I was just telling Sister Bigelow that it's so dear of her to give someone so young a chance to grow into such a big calling—and you *are* up to it, I'm telling everyone, in a few months they'll see. I have such *confidence* in you." Then she winked and squeezed DeAnne's arm before she glided away.

"Kind of makes you want to wash your arm, doesn't it?" said Jenny.

"Or cut it off," said DeAnne. "She really *is* nasty, isn't she?"

"But it helps to know that you aren't the only one who realizes it, doesn't it! Otherwise you just sit there feeling guilty for hating her, because she's so *sweet* and *spiritual* and you know that hating her must mean that you're ripe for destruction."

"Forgive me for thinking you had a problem with malicious gossip," said DeAnne. "It was pure charity. Like warning somebody that there's a tornado coming."

"Oh, you haven't seen anything yet," said Jenny cheerfully. "Call me tomorrow, or tonight if you get the chance. I've got to round up the monsters before they tear out the satellite dish by the roots."

DeAnne laughed.

"I wasn't joking," said Jenny. "When the satellite dish was first installed a few years ago, my oldest two climbed the fence and pushed it over. But they've got it bolted down to a concrete pad now, so I suppose it's safe enough as long as we don't let the kids bring tools to church. Bye."

With Jenny gone, DeAnne once again headed for the door—without the same urgency now to get away and cry. Again, though, someone stopped her. "Sister Fletcher, I need to talk to you," said Sister Bigelow.

Uh-oh, thought DeAnne. Now it comes.

DeAnne walked over to the table where Sister Bigelow was stacking up the hymnbooks. "Better put down all that stuff you're carrying," said Sister Bigelow.

She's going to ask for the manual back, thought DeAnne. She's going to release me as spiritual living teacher right now. I'm not even going to get a second chance.

But if that's what happened, that's how it would be, DeAnne decided, and she set down her lesson materials.

"*Now* I can give you a hug without getting the corner of a book in my eye!" said Sister Bigelow. She *was* half a head shorter than DeAnne, but her hug was large and enthusiastic. When Sister Bigelow pulled away, DeAnne saw her glance around to make sure they were now alone in the room. "DeAnne, I know for sure that the

Lord truly brought you to Steuben, North Carolina to be our spiritual living teacher."

"Then the lesson *was* all right?" asked DeAnne.

"I think it was obvious how much that lesson was needed," said Sister Bigelow. "I won't say another word because I don't speak ill of any of my sisters, but I saw that one of the testimonies might have made you feel discouraged and I wanted you to know that there's not a blame thing for you to be discouraged about, and that's that. You are manna from heaven to me. Now go home and feed your family."

It was going to be fine.

Or was it? Jenny had warned her that Sister LeSueur always got what she wanted. That one way or another, she would not be thwarted. The last thing DeAnne wanted was to spend the next few years in a constant struggle—or, worse, an open war. No, she simply *wasn't* going to do that. She would win over Sister LeSueur with love and kindness. She would never give Sister LeSueur the slightest cause to think of her as an enemy.

DeAnne left the Relief Society room and began to comb the halls for her children. They were nowhere to be found. Step must have rounded them up, she realized, and she headed for the car, hoping Step would have the back of the wagon open so she could set down her lesson materials and Elizabeth's diaper-and-toy bag without having to fumble with keys or wait for Step to do it. Now that she was no longer keyed up about giving the lesson, everything seemed heavier and slower and she began to feel how much she needed some sleep. Not that she'd have much chance. Maybe Step would throw together some sandwiches for the kids while she took a nap before choir practice.

The back of the wagon *was* open. I may not need Step to save my soul, she thought, but he's pretty useful when I need someone to save my weary arms.

"How'd it go, Fish Lady?"

"It went interestingly."

"I sense a story."

"I'll tell you when there are fewer ears."

"I won't listen," offered Robbie from the back seat.

"Speaking of ear counting," said Step, "didn't you see Stevie in there?"

"Isn't he here?" asked DeAnne. She looked into the back seat. He *wasn't* there. How could she have failed to notice that one of her own children was missing? She really *was* tired.

"I didn't see him in there," she said.

"No problem," said Step. "I'll just go in and get him."

"Never mind," said DeAnne. "Here he comes."

Stevie was walking very slowly, looking down. Moping, thought DeAnne, that's what he's doing. He mopes to school from the car, he mopes from school back to the car, he mopes around the house all day, and he even mopes at church. "Sometimes I think he isn't even trying, Step," she said.

"Come on, Stevie!" Step called. "You have starving siblings in the car!"

"*I'm* not starving," said Robbie. "*I* had three cookies."

"Cookies?" asked DeAnne.

"Treats in class."

"Oh, sugar. Wonderful. I thought you didn't *like* cookies."

"These ones were chocolate chip," said Robbie.

"Were they as good as *my* chocolate chip cookies?" asked Step.

"Nope," said Robbie. "They were terrible."

"Then why did you eat them?" asked DeAnne.

"'Cause I *won* them," said Robbie.

"Won them how?" asked Step.

"I answered all the questions."

"Hmm," said Step. "I wonder what your teacher would have given you if you answered them *right?*"

"I *did* answer them right!" shouted Robbie, only he sounded cross instead of playful.

"Oh, I guess we're getting tired now," said Step. "OK, I'm through teasing."

Stevie opened the door behind DeAnne and got into the car. "Glad you could make it," said Step. "Hope it wasn't too much trouble, coming all the way out to the car like this."

"It was OK," said Stevie.

"Your father was teasing you," said DeAnne. "He was suggesting that you ought to come right out to the car after church. I worried about you."

"Thanks for translating for me," said Step. He sounded a little testy himself now.

"I wasn't translating," said DeAnne. She felt weary to the bone. "Let's just go home."

Step started the car and they pulled out of the parking lot onto the road.

"I really *do* want to know what you were doing," said Step.

Stevie didn't answer.

"Stevie," said Step.

"What?"

"I said I really *do* want to know what you were doing that made you late getting out to the car."

"Talking," said Stevie.

"Who with?" asked DeAnne. Maybe Stevie had found a friend, in which case she was *glad* he was late getting to the car.

"A lady."

Not a friend, then. "What lady?" she asked.

"I don't know."

DeAnne could feel Step suddenly grow alert. She wasn't sure what it was, but she always knew when he started to pay serious attention. He was still driving, but perhaps was a bit more tension in his muscles, a slowness about his movement. Deliberate, that was it.

He became intensely deliberate. Dangerous. Someone has come too close to his children, and the primate male has become alert. Well, she rather liked that; it felt comfortable to feel him bristle beside her. Of course, that feeling of hers was probably the primate female, gathering her children near her mate at the first sign of danger. We are all chimpanzees under the skin.

"What did she say to you, Stevedore?" asked Step.

"I didn't like her," said Stevie.

"But what did she say?"

"She said she had a vision about me."

His words came to DeAnne like a flash of light, blinding her for a moment: She had a vision. "Dolores LeSueur," murmured DeAnne.

"Yeah," said Stevie. "Sister LeSueur."

"And what did she say about her vision?"

"I don't want to say."

"You've got to," said DeAnne, barely able to control the emotion in her voice.

Step reached over and gently touched her on the thigh. He was telling her to keep still, that she was too intense, that she wasn't going about it the right way. For a moment she resented him for daring to police her comments to her own son, but then she realized that she was simply transferring the anger she felt toward Dolores LeSueur to the nearest target, her husband. And he was right. They'd learn more from Stevie if he didn't know how upset they were.

"The reason we need to know, Stevie," said Step, "is that no matter what she thinks she saw, and no matter whether it was really a vision or just a dream or just something she made up, she had no business telling *you* about it."

"It was *about* me," said Stevie.

"In a pig's eye," murmured DeAnne.

"Sister LeSueur doesn't have a *right* to get visions about you, Stevie. She's not your mother and she's not your father, she's not your *anything*," said Step. "The Lord's house is a house of order. He isn't going to send visions about you to somebody who has nothing to do with you. So if she got a vision, I bet it didn't come from the Lord."

"Oh," said Stevie.

Step had laid the groundwork well, but now DeAnne was ready to know. "So what was the vision?"

"He'll tell us," said Step, "as soon as he realizes that it's right to tell us. You had a bad feeling when she was telling you, didn't you, Stevie? That's why you said you didn't like her."

"Yeah," said Stevie.

"Well, don't you think that maybe that bad feeling was a warning to you that the things you were being told were lies? It made you feel bad, didn't it?"

"Some bad and some not," said Stevie.

"Did she tell you not to tell us?" asked Step.

"Yes," Stevie said quietly.

"What?" said DeAnne, outraged.

"He said yes," said Robbie.

"I heard him," said DeAnne.

"Then why did you say 'what'?" asked Robbie.

"Your mother was just surprised," said Step. "Stevedore, Stevie, Stephen Bolivar Fletcher, my son, you know what we've told you before. If someone ever tells you children that you mustn't tell your parents something, then what do you do?"

"*I* know," said Robbie. "We promise that we'll never tell, but then the very first chance we get we *do* tell you."

"And why is that?"

"Because no good person would ever tell us to keep a secret from our mom and dad," said Robbie.

"Remember that, Stevie?" asked Step.

"Yeah," said Stevie.

DeAnne heard something in his voice. She turned

in her seat, turned all the way, and saw that he was crying. "Stop the car, Step," she said.

Step pulled the car at once into the driveway of a Methodist church parking lot. The parking lot was emptying out—apparently the Methodists got out of church about the same time the Mormons did.

"Why are you crying, honey?" asked DeAnne.

"I don't know," said Stevie.

"Stevie, whatever this woman said to you, it's time for you to tell us."

"She said . . ." He started crying in earnest now, so it was hard for him to talk.

"That's all right, Stevie," said Step. "Just tell us slowly. Take your time."

"She said I was a really special boy."

"Well, *that's* true," said Step.

"And she said that the Lord had chosen me to do wonderful things."

"Like what?" asked Step.

"Like Ammon," he said. "A missionary."

"Yes?"

"But first she said that I had to prove that I was good enough."

DeAnne felt as though she needed to spit something awful out of her mouth.

"Did she say what it was you had to do to prove yourself?" asked Step.

"T-teach my parents, she said."

"Teach us what?" asked Step.

"R-righteousness," said Stevie.

DeAnne felt the baby kick. Only it wasn't a kick, it was more like a push, a hard, sustained push against her ribs. The child must have felt her anger; the adrenaline must have crossed the placenta, and now she had made the baby angry, too, or at least excited, upset, energized. I must calm myself, DeAnne thought. For the baby's sake.

"Well now," said Step, "what do you think she meant by *that?*"

"I don't know," said Stevie.

"I do," said DeAnne. "Stevie, I taught a lesson today in Relief Society, and Sister LeSueur didn't like it."

"Why not?" asked Stevie.

"Because the lesson I taught said that every person can talk to the Lord and you don't need anybody else to tell you what the Lord wants you to do, because the Holy Ghost can talk right to your heart."

"After I'm baptized," said Stevie.

"Which is only a little more than a month away," said DeAnne. "And even now the Spirit of God can whisper in your heart, if there's a reason. But she didn't like me saying that."

"Why not?" asked Stevie.

"Because Sister LeSueur likes going around and showing other people how spiritual she is." DeAnne found herself remembering everything that Jenny Cowper had said to her, and now she believed it all, and spoke of it as if she knew it from her own experience. "She likes to tell people about visions the Lord has given her. She likes to have other people *depend* on her and do the things she tells them to do. So if people start realizing that *true* inspiration from the Lord will come right to them, and not to somebody like Sister LeSueur, why, she won't be as important to them anymore as she is now. Do you understand that?"

"Yes," said Stevie.

"So she wants me to stop saying things like that," said DeAnne.

"Me, too," said Step. "I gave a lesson that said things like that, too."

"So she went to you to try to get you to think that she was having visions about you," said DeAnne, "so that instead of learning from your parents, you'd always come to *her* to find out what you should do with your life."

"Why would she tell a lie like that?" asked Stevie.

"She's trying to steal you from us," said Step.

"Like a bad guy!" said Robbie.

"Just like a bad guy," said Step. "Only bit by bit, and slowly, starting with your heart. Starting by making you doubt us. Making you wonder if maybe we *aren't* righteous, and if maybe you need to learn righteousness from somewhere else and then teach it to us. And where do you think that somewhere else would be?"

"From her," said Stevie. "That's what she said—that she knew that the Lord would tell her more about my g-glorious future."

"Such poison," said DeAnne.

"That's called flattery, Stevie," said Step. "The truth is that anybody who knows anything about you knows that you'll have a glorious future. You're so bright and good, how could it be otherwise? So it doesn't take a vision from the Lord to tell her *that*. But she hopes that by telling you wonderful things about your future, she'll get you to put all your hope in the things she tells you and not in what *we* tell you."

"It's just what phony fortune-tellers all do," said DeAnne. "They tell you wonderful things that you really *hope* are true. You believe them because you want them to happen. And so you convince yourself that the fortune-teller isn't a fake, that maybe somehow she really knows, but in fact she's really a phony all along."

Stevie chewed on this for a minute. Step pulled out of the parking place and then headed back into the street, driving home.

"But what if she really *had* a vision," asked Stevie.

DeAnne wanted to scream. She had no vision! She has poured poison into your ear, just like Hamlet's father! But she held her tongue, trusting Step to be calmer than she was, because he hadn't already had a run-in with Sister LeSueur today.

"Stevie," said Step, "if she really had a vision, and it

really was from the Lord, she had plenty of chances to tell your mother and me about it today. But she didn't, did she?"

"Because the vision said you were unrighteous," said Stevie. But DeAnne could hear a bit of sarcasm in his voice now. A bit more stress on the word *said*. She *said* you were unrighteous. He's beginning to move over and stand with us against her. She isn't going to win this round.

"If it was a true vision," said Step, "she wouldn't be afraid to tell us right to our faces that we were unrighteous. The Lord's prophets are always brave about that sort of thing. They always tell wicked people about their wickedness, right to their faces. I mean, haven't we told you stories about that? Like Samuel the Lamanite?"

"They almost killed him!" cried Robbie. "He stood on the wall!"

"So you *were* listening on Christmas Eve," said Step.

"That's right," said Stevie. And now there was certainty in his voice. He had put the pattern together. "If it was true, she would have said it right to you, instead of sneaking around."

"Like Abinadi," said DeAnne.

"He got burned!" Robbie yelled.

"Bird!" Elizabeth screeched, looking around to see where Robbie might have seen one.

"Not *bird*, Betsy Wetsy," said Robbie. He explained to her the concept of fire, none of which she understood, but that was fine with Robbie, he didn't actually need other people to understand what he was saying as long as they'd sit still and listen. And with Elizabeth belted into her carseat, she was the perfect audience.

DeAnne could see that Step wanted to say more to Stevie—she understood, because she wanted to, too. But instead they both held their peace. Stevie understands. He sees how this woman has tried to manipulate him. So there's no need to say any more.

And yet when they got home, while Step was carrying Elizabeth in from the car, DeAnne couldn't resist adding one more bit of teaching. "Stevie," she said, "I want you to know something."

"What's that?" he asked.

She had the door unlocked and Robbie assigned himself to hold it open for Step and Elizabeth. She carried her lesson materials and the diaper bag into the kitchen and set it all on the table. Stevie was right behind her.

"What I want you to know is this." She got down on one knee, so she could look him in the eye. "You really *are* a special boy, with a wonderful future. I've known it from the start. I even knew it, I think, when you were still inside my tummy."

"Uterus," said Stevie. Step had given him the first birds-and-bees lesson back last fall, and now he insisted on not using childish language.

"Yes, my uterus," said DeAnne. "But certainly when you were a baby, and ever since. You have a sensitive spirit. You *know* things. You know when things are right. It's like what you felt when she was talking to you. Even though she was flattering you, you still didn't like her, right?"

"Yeah," said Stevie.

"That's because there's something inside you that knows, just *knows* when someone is good and when someone is not good. Or maybe you just know when *you* need to do something because it's right. And believing in Sister LeSueur's story just wasn't the right thing for you to do, and so you knew it. Do you understand what I mean?"

"Yeah."

"Stevie, trust in that place inside your heart that knows the right thing to do. Trust in it, and do what it tells you."

"Even if it tells me to disobey you and Dad?"

"It will never tell you to do something wrong, Stevie. I promise you that."

He nodded soberly. "OK," he said. Then he turned and headed out of the room.

She felt weak, shaky. What had she just said to her son? To trust in some feeling inside himself, in preference even to the things that she and Step told him! How could she have said something so irresponsible, so insane! Yet at the moment she had felt as if it could not go unsaid. Only how could they possibly counter this LeSueur woman, this Queen B, if DeAnne was giving Stevie permission to ignore them? No, not giving him permission. Insisting on it.

She headed for the kitchen to tell Step what she had just done and get him to help her clarify it with Stevie, but Elizabeth was alone there, rooting through the Cheerios that still survived inside the Tupperware box DeAnne always took to church in the diaper bag.

DeAnne went down the hall, looking into Step's office on the way. Not there. Not in Elizabeth's room. Not in the boys' room, where Stevie was lying on his bed, staring at the ceiling. Poor kid, so much confusion, so many strange things in his life! How could he make sense of it all?

She expected that Step would be in their bathroom, but he wasn't. He was sitting on the bed, talking on the phone.

"I'm so sorry that she isn't feeling well," said Step. "But I can certainly understand it, Brother LeSueur, she had a very busy day in church. Listen, if she can't come to the phone, Brother LeSueur, perhaps you can simply relay a message to her for me. Can you do that?"

DeAnne waited, holding her breath, to hear what Step would say, especially since poor Brother LeSueur probably hadn't a clue about what his wife had been doing today. DeAnne rather imagined that he hadn't a clue about anything his wife did, ever.

"OK, here's the message. She raised a doctrinal question with me today—about what a father should do if someone tried to steal away his children." Brother LeSueur must have said something, because Step paused a moment and then answered. "No, it wasn't in class, it was after the meeting. Anyway, here's the best answer I could come up with. I truly believe that if someone tried to steal away a man's children, that man would be completely justified in *anything* he might do to protect his family. . . . Yes, that's right, anything at all . . . even killing, yes. I don't think it would be murder, I think it would be defense of the helpless. Don't you think so, Brother LeSueur? . . . Yes, I thought you'd agree with me. Why don't you tell her that, then—that you agree with me, too, that a man would be perfectly justified in killing someone who tried to steal away his children? I think she'll be quite satisfied with that answer. . . . Yes, I think that particular question will never come up again. . . . Thanks so much, and tell her I hope she gets well soon and lives a long and happy life. . . . Oh, thank you! Bye!"

Step looked up at DeAnne and grinned. "He said he liked my lesson a lot."

"I can't believe you said that to her own husband!" said DeAnne.

"Yes, well, I said it because I wanted to make it clear to her that this was the last time she ever pulls a stunt like this."

"She really is an awful woman," said DeAnne. "Jenny tried to warn me, but I never thought anyone would be so low as to try to get to the parents by poisoning the hearts of their children against them."

"Oh, heavens," said Step, "people have been doing that for years. The Nazis did it, and the Communists, and a lot of divorced parents do it, too."

"All right then," said DeAnne, "I guess a lot of people are just that low. But she's certainly one of them."

"Oh, yes," said Step. "She definitely crawled out from under a rock."

"How can you be so calm about this? Aren't you angry?"

Step only smiled—a tight little smile. "Hey, Fish Lady. I just got a man to deliver to his wife a message that if she messes with my family again, I'll feel perfectly justified in killing her. You think I'm not mad?"

"But you wouldn't really do it," she said.

"Wouldn't it be sad if Sister LeSueur thought the same thing," said Step.

"You aren't a violent person."

"I've been thinking about that," said Step. "And I think that maybe I'm only pretending not to be a violent person. Because the need for violence simply hasn't come up till now."

"Well, I really don't think violence is the answer against her."

"Oh, I know," said Step. "The real answer is to keep our children away from her and then teach people the truth every chance we get. That's the thing we have going for us—she really *is* wrong, and we really *are* right, and so good and wise people will eventually see through her and recognize what she really is."

She walked over to him and sat beside him on the bed and then laid her head in his lap. "I liked it when you talked on the phone about killing people," she said. "I must be the most terrible person in the world, but it just made me feel so—delicious."

"Me, too," said Step.

"Aren't we awful?" said DeAnne.

"Personally," said Step, "I think we're terrific."

Late that night, she awoke suddenly from a dream, but the dream slipped away even as she tried to cling to it. She rolled over and saw that Step's bedside lamp was on, and he was reading.

"Can't sleep?" she murmured.

"That was some dream you were having," said Step. "Didn't understand a word you were saying, but you sounded *very* firm."

"Don't remember," said DeAnne.

Then she *did* remember. Not the dream, but something else that she had wanted to talk to Step about, and she hadn't done it. She confessed to Step how she had as much as told their oldest son that he should trust his own judgment more than his parents' instructions.

"Well," said Step. "Well."

"That's it? Just 'well'?"

"No, not just 'well.' I distinctly remember that I said, 'Well. Well.' Two wells."

"I'm serious, Step."

"DeAnne, it's like you told me. It was just something that you had to say, right up till the moment it was said, and then you suddenly couldn't understand why you had to say it."

She was still half asleep, that must be why she didn't get the point of what he was saying.

"Fish Lady," he said patiently, "you were following your own advice. You did the thing that you knew, in that moment, was the right thing to do. You told Stevie something that you would *never* have dreamed of saying if you were in your normal mind."

"So I'm going crazy?"

He sighed.

"Do you really think I might have been *inspired* to say that?"

"How should I know?" asked Step. "We believe it's possible, don't we? And in the meantime, I'm certainly not going to say anything to Stevie to get him to *doubt* what you said. Because the fact is that what you said is true. In the long run, every human being is accountable for what he chooses to do. Stevie won't be able to hide behind us and say, But I did what they said! He'll have to stand before the judgment bar of God and say, This is what *I* did, and this is why I chose to do it."

"But he's only seven."

"He's not just a seven-year-old," said Step. "You know that. It's something my mother once said to me. That there were moments that she thought, Maybe, before we were all born, when we lived with God in the pre-existence, maybe her children were older than her. Maybe they were very old and very wise, and God simply saved them till now because he needed to have some of his very best children on the earth during the last days. Maybe Mom was right. Not about *her* children. About *ours*."

"He's seven, Step, even if his spirit is very old."

"You said what you said, and Sister LeSueur said what *she* said. And you know what, Fish Lady? I like what you said a lot better. She said to him, Depend on me, lean on me, do what I tell you to do, and I'll make you a great man. You said to him, Stand on your own, make up your own mind, you already *are* a man, and maybe you'll make yourself into a great man by and by. What's so wrong about that?"

"You make me feel so good, Junk Man," she said.

"It's my job," he said. "It was written into the marriage contract. When wife wakes up in the middle of the night and needs some reassurance, husband must provide it or go without hot meals for a week."

"Oh," she said. "Well, then, you're living up to the contract."

"I do my best," he said. "But I still miss most of the hot meals."

"Not because I don't prepare them," said DeAnne.

"Maybe the contract will come from Agamemnon. Maybe tomorrow."

"Even if it doesn't come, Step, even if Mr. Agamemnon or Akabakka or whatever—"

"Arkasian."

"Even if he changed his mind or couldn't do it or whatever. Even if that comes to nothing, things will still work out."

"I hope you're right, Fish Lady."

"I am. You can count on it. Because I get inspiration, don't I?"

"Sometimes you just give it," he said. "To me."

She nestled closer to him in bed and closed her eyes, feeling comforted now, feeling ready for sleep. "You make me feel so good, Junk Man."

He leaned down and kissed her forehead. Then she must have fallen asleep, because she remembered nothing else till morning.

7

·CRICKETS·

This is what happened with Stevie's second-grade project: He brought home a one-page ditto that listed the requirements, which were not very specific. The end-of-year project had to show "an environment" and the creatures that lived in it. It was due on April 22nd, and it had to include a written report and a "visual depiction."

"Most of the kids are doing posters," said Stevie, "but I don't want to." He had been reading about octopuses, and he wanted to do his project about the undersea environment. And instead of cutting pictures out of magazines and pasting them to posterboard, he got his mom to buy some colored clay, which he shaped into fishes, clams, coral, and an octopus. He arranged them on a cardboard base that DeAnne cut from the side of one of the boxes they had used in the move. Then he wrote his report, typing it himself on Step's word-processing computer and stapling it in the corner.

It was the first thing Stevie had shown any real interest in during his whole time at this school, and DeAnne showed it off to Step with real pride, the night before Stevie took it to school. "This is incredible," said Step. "You didn't help him?"

"I did nothing. In fact I advised him against doing something so hard. Who knew he could make fish that looked like fish?"

"Not to mention an octopus that looks like an octopus," said Step. "And look at the clam. There's a starfish prying it open!"

"He still never talks about school," said DeAnne. "Not even when I ask. But he did *this*, so it can't be all bad."

Then came DeAnne's new calling, and she was so involved with preparing her spiritual living lesson that she didn't think about Stevie's project now that it had been turned in.

On the first Monday in May, however, her lesson was over, and as she drove Stevie to school she remembered his project and asked what the teacher thought of it.

"She gave it a *C*," said Stevie.

"What?" asked DeAnne.

"And it got mooshed."

"It got mooshed! How? Did somebody drop it?"

"No," said Stevie. "They put them all out on display in the media center, and when the other kids walked past it they mooshed it."

"On purpose?" asked DeAnne.

"Yeah," said Stevie.

"How can you be sure? Did you see them do it?"

"Raymond said, 'Tidal wave!' and then after him they wadded it up even more so finally it was just a big mess of clay."

"Where was your teacher when they were doing this? Where was the librarian?"

"Mrs. Jones was there."

"And she didn't do anything?"

"No," said Stevie.

"She must not have seen what they were doing."

"She saw," said Stevie.

"She *saw*? And she didn't *stop* them?"

"No," said Stevie.

DeAnne felt sick. No, she thought. Stevie just misunderstood the situation. The teacher hadn't really been watching. She could never have let such a thing happen.

"I'm going in to talk to your teacher," said DeAnne.

"Please no!" said Stevie, urgently.

"This has to be cleared up. There was no way that your project deserved a *C*."

"Please don't come in!" he pleaded.

"All right," said DeAnne. "But why not?"

"It'll just make things worse if you do," said Stevie.

"Worse?"

But they had just reached the turnaround in front of the school, and Stevie bounded out the door and raced for school—the first time she had ever seen him *hurry* toward class. Somehow it didn't make her feel any better. There was something seriously wrong here, and not just his moroseness because of the move. Mrs. Jones could not have given that project a *C*. No teacher could have stood by and let the other kids destroy a child's project, either. It simply couldn't happen.

Well, if she couldn't talk to Mrs. Jones, she could at least talk to the librarian and find out from *her* what had happened. "Come on, kids, we're going in," said DeAnne.

DeAnne pulled the car into the teachers' parking lot, where a visitor space was open, and within a few minutes she was leading the kids down the hall to the media center. DeAnne supposed that she ought to check in at the office, but the receptionist there was so snotty, and DeAnne was already so upset, that she decided that if she wasn't going to get really furious today she'd better pretend that she didn't realize she needed to stop in at the main desk.

The librarian was a sweet-voiced older lady, and when she smiled DeAnne thought for some reason of the time she had an eye injury and when the bandages were on and she couldn't see, someone laid a cool damp cloth on her forehead. "I'm so glad when parents come by the library," said the librarian.

"Oh, I thought it was a media center now," said DeAnne.

"Well, so it is. We have two video carts and an Apple II computer, so we *are* a media center, but look at all these books. Wouldn't you call this a library?"

"Yes I would," said DeAnne. "And I like it all the more, knowing that you call it a library, too."

The librarian smiled and patted DeAnne's hand. "Aren't you the sweet one." Then she bent over—not far, because she wasn't very tall—and soberly greeted Robbie and Elizabeth with a handshake each. "When will *you* be a student here, young man?"

"I start kindergarten next fall," said Robbie.

"Oh, and I see you have been well taught," she said. "You said *kindergarten* and not *kindy-garden*."

Robbie beamed.

The librarian turned back to DeAnne. "Did you just stop by to visit? Or is there something I can help you with?"

"I understand that the second-grade projects were displayed here."

The librarian looked mournful. "We just barely took down the display over the weekend. I'm so sorry you missed it. We're so *proud* of our second graders."

"It is rather remarkable, to have second-grade projects," said DeAnne. "I've actually never heard of such a thing before. I don't think we even had senior projects in high school when I was there."

"I think it's because our school is only K through 2," said the librarian. "Dr. Mariner wanted our students to mark the children's departure from our school in a special way—something they would remember, perhaps, in time to come."

"That's certainly the way my oldest boy responded to the assignment," said DeAnne. "Perhaps you noticed his project when it was on display."

"Oh, I don't think I'd remember any one in particular, Mrs. . . . um . . ."

"I'm DeAnne Fletcher."

Suddenly the librarian's eyes grew wide, and she flashed her wonderful smile again. "Oh, you must be Stevie Fletcher's mother!"

"I am," said DeAnne.

"What a very special boy," said the librarian. "I *do* remember his project, in fact. It was a sculpture garden—an undersea environment, I believe. With an octopus and that clam with the starfish opening it—and I noticed that the shark had a tiny little fish that the shark was swallowing. A little gruesome, perhaps, but *very* creative. You must have been proud for your son to be given the first-place ribbon."

"First place? Stevie told me the project got a *C*."

"But how could that be possible? Dr. Mariner came here and judged them all herself, and before she had even seen the rest of the children's posters, she laid the blue ribbon down beside Stevie's project and said, 'This will stay here until I find something that makes me take it away again.' And of course she never did, because he ended up receiving it. Isn't it just awful what those other children did? They were so jealous, I suppose, but still, I think it was churlish of them to moosh it up that way."

So *that* part of Stevie's story was accurate. And the word *moosh* was apparently current enough in Steuben that a gracious, educated lady like this one could use it. "Yes, Stevie was rather disappointed, I think," said DeAnne.

"He's such a quiet boy," said the librarian. "He spends every recess here, did you know? I think he must have read half the . . . um, *media* . . . in my little . . . um, *media center*." She winked.

"Every recess?" said DeAnne. "I know he loves reading, but I had hoped he would play with the other children."

"I know," said the librarian. "I think it's better when children play together, too. But as long as he keeps to himself, better to have the company of a book than no company at all, don't you think?"

"Oh, yes," said DeAnne. "Well, I didn't mean to trouble you. And I can't wait to tell Stevie's father about the blue ribbon. I wonder where it is!"

"Well, of course it was given to Mrs. Jones to display in Stevie's classroom. They usually keep them there until the end of the year, and then send them home with the student who won."

DeAnne made her polite good-byes and left, feeling much better. Except that Stevie hadn't told her the truth about his project. Was it possible that he was still trying to make his parents feel bad about putting him in this school? Was it possible that he was refusing to let them know anything good about his experience there, so that they'd continue to feel guilty? That just didn't sound like Stevie, but what other explanation could there be? He must be so *angry*.

For the first time DeAnne wondered if they shouldn't perhaps find a therapist who could talk to Stevie, who could help him find his way through this thicket of problems. Imaginary friends. And now lying. She called Step at work and he agreed not to be late tonight.

◦   ◦   ◦

None of Step's usual rides would be able to take him home today—not if he was leaving at five, because none of the programmers ever left until well after seven. So he hitched a ride with two of the phone girls, the ones who took orders for Eight Bits Inc. software on the 800 number. All the way home he kept thinking that there was something strange about the drive, and it wasn't because of the two girls chattering in the front seat or the fact that in the back of a Rabbit his knees were up around his ears. Not until they pulled up in front of his house and he realized that the lawn was overgrown and very badly in need of mowing did it occur to him what was so strange. It was daylight! In the two months that he'd been working at Eight Bits Inc., he had never once come home in daylight.

He thanked the girls for the ride and came into the house. DeAnne was in the living room, playing the piano while Robbie sang and Elizabeth hooted and beat two rhythm sticks together. The song was "Jesus Wants Me for a Sunbeam."

"Somehow I never thought of this as the sort of song that needed a percussion section," said Step.

"Daddy!" cried Robbie.

"Robot!" answered Step. Robbie ran to him and Step tossed him in the air and caught him.

"Daddy!" screamed Betsy.

"Betsy Wetsy!" answered Step.

"Someday you're going to smack their heads into the ceiling," said DeAnne.

Step tossed Betsy into the air. Then, after catching her, he lifted her up and bumped her head against the ceiling. "Owie ow ow ow!" howled Betsy.

"Don't be a poop, Betsy," said Step. "That didn't hurt at all, I was just teasing."

"Owie ow!" Betsy reached for DeAnne.

"What did I tell you?" said DeAnne.

"Betsy's a poop!" shouted Robbie. "Betsy's a poop! You can bump *me* into the ceiling, Daddy!"

"Better not," said Step. "*Your* head might cause structural damage."

"I don't mind!" insisted Robbie.

"I can't believe you came home so early," said DeAnne.

"I said I would, when you asked me to," said Step.

"I never thought it would be a quarter after five," she said. "Or were you fired?"

"Not yet," said Step. "Though I may be, after today."

"Because you left at five?" asked DeAnne.

"The lawn is really overgrown," said Step. "I never noticed that before."

"Well, that's because it wasn't as overgrown yesterday as it is today. Why might they fire you after today?"

"Because I finally worked up the guts to go in and make Cowboy Bob give me a copy of that agreement I signed with him."

"You mean you only just got it *today?* I assumed you had that weeks ago."

"I *asked* for it right after San Francisco. Well, not *right* after, or somebody would think that I was doing exactly what I'm doing. But the Friday after."

"And they didn't send it to you till today?"

"They didn't even send it to me today. I had to go get it. And not from Cowboy Bob, in fact, because he wasn't in and his secretary was on lunch and so it was somebody *else's* secretary who got it for me out of my personnel file and made a copy for me."

"So you only have a copy?"

"They weren't going to give me the original!" said Step. "Anyway, I have it, and it's possible that Cowboy Bob doesn't know that I have it even now."

"Well, then you won't get fired."

"Except what if he finds out that I came and got it behind his back? Then he'll be *really* suspicious."

"Well, I've got to admit, it wouldn't break my heart to have you home every day," said DeAnne. "This is such a treat, Step."

"Treat!" scoffed Step. "Hardly. It's where I ought to be, and it makes me sick that you actually had to call me and practically make an appointment to get me home to talk to my own son. I'm living like one of those high-powered stockbroker types, like a Madison-Avenue live-for-the-job hyper-ambitious robot, except that I'm not getting the money they make. Where *is* Stevie, anyway?"

"He's either outside in back, playing with—Jack and Scotty—or he's in his room."

Step nodded grimly at her mention of Stevie's imaginary friends. *And now lying to her . . . I've just been too cut off from the family. I'm practically a stranger here.*

Stevie was in his room, lying on the top bunk, reading a book.

The conversation did not go well at all. Step leaned on the safety bar and said, "Your Mom tells me that your undersea project did really well."

"No it didn't," said Stevie.

"She said it got the blue ribbon."

"J.J. got the blue ribbon," said Stevie.

"Well, the first-place ribbon, anyway, she didn't actually say what color it was."

"First place was blue," said Stevie.

"Stevedore, I've got to tell you—your mom went to the school and checked. Dr. Mariner gave your underwater garden the first-place ribbon."

"My project got mooshed," said Stevie. "So it couldn't get first place."

"Son, Dr. Mariner judged the projects over that first weekend, *before* your project got ruined by the other kids. And she gave first place to *you.*"

"No she didn't!" said Stevie, and now his voice was full of emotion. "She said that my project was nothing but a lump of clay and it didn't deserve to be shown to anybody at all! And I got a *C* on it."

"Dr. Mariner actually *said* that?" Step could not, *did* not believe it.

"Yes," said Stevie.

"She actually stood there and told you that to your face?"

"No," said Stevie. "She told Mrs. Jones and Mrs. Jones told us."

"Us? What do you mean us?"

"Us," said Stevie. "Me and the other kids."

"The whole class?"

"Yeah."

Step tried to imagine it—a teacher repeating such a remark in front of all the other students. It would be too cruel to say it even in private, but in front of everybody—unthinkable.

"Stevie, are you sure that you aren't just—pretending this story?"

Stevie looked up into his father's eyes. "No, Daddy," he said. "I don't tell lies."

"I know that you never have before we moved to Steuben, Stevie. But you've got to realize that this story is a little hard to believe. I mean, isn't it possible you exaggerated it a little? Or maybe pretended?"

"I'm not pretending."

"I mean, you pretend to have two friends, Jack and Scotty."

Stevie looked at him silently. "I never said that," he said.

"Not to me," he said. "But you told your mom about things that you and Jack and Scotty did."

Stevie said nothing.

"I don't mind you pretending. Maybe that's what you need to do in order to get through a hard time at school. But you can't tell Mom and me pretend things as if they were true."

"I don't," said Stevie.

"You mean you won't from now on," said Step.

"I mean I never do!" shouted Stevie.

His vehemence made Step pause. Was it possible

that Stevie wasn't lying about this? That in fact it happened the way he said? Then how to account for what
the librarian told DeAnne? Impossible, it couldn't have
happened the way Stevie described. And yet he insisted
on being believed, and it made Step remember the
times when he was a kid and adults didn't believe *him*
because they were so sure they knew how things were.
He remembered very clearly saying to his mother,
"Well you weren't there so how do you *know?*" And
now here he was, contradicting Stevie's account when in
fact Step wasn't there, so how did he know?

"Stevedore," said Step, "have I been making a mistake here?"

"Yes," said Stevie.

"I've got to tell you that if Mrs. Jones stood up in
front of class and said such a terrible thing, even if it
was true, then she should be fired from her job as a
teacher."

"Yes," said Stevie. "I wish she was dead."

Step was horrified. "Do you really mean that?"

"Yes," said Stevie. "I think about it all the time. I
look at her talking and I think of blood coming out of
her forehead from a bullet. I think of her falling over
dead in class and then I'd laugh and I'd sing a song. I'd
sing 'In the Leafy Treetops' because it's the happiest
song I know."

This was worse than Step could have imagined. No
matter what was true about the project, it was certainly
true that Stevie hated Mrs. Jones beyond all reason. It
was awful to think of his sweet little boy—a child who
had always been forgiving and generous—having such
hatred in his heart for anyone. And these feelings must
have been smoldering for some time now, yet he had
said nothing.

"Stevie, why do you hate her so much? Is it because
of the blue ribbon?"

"She never calls on me," said Stevie.

"Sometimes it feels like that," said Step. "It's because you're so smart, and she has to give other kids a chance to answer sometimes."

"She always calls on the other kids."

"Yes, that's how it feels."

Stevie looked at him with hot anger burning in his eyes. "I said she *always* calls on the other kids! That's not how it feels, that's how it *is!*"

Step again realized that he had just spoken like a typical adult, taking a child's clear, plain language and twisting it to fit the adult's preconceived notion of reality. But what if Stevie meant it? What if it was literally true?

"You mean she really *never* calls on you? *Ever?*"

"Never once," said Stevie.

"Are you sure she sees you raising your hand?"

"Yes," said Stevie. "She always sees me."

"How do you know?"

"Because she says so."

"She *says* that she sees you raising your hand, and yet she doesn't call on you?"

"Yes," said Stevie. And the tears in his eyes forced Step to believe that this must be true, or at least *seem* true to Stevie, because it was certain that Stevie believed it himself.

"Son, you have to understand, I'm not there so I can't see it for myself. You have to help me. What does she say when she sees that you've raised your hand, but she doesn't call on you?"

Stevie took a deep breath, and then, with his voice trembling, he said, "She says, 'Of course Stephen *Ball-lover* Fletcher knows the answer. *He* knows *everything.*'"

Step heard the words with a sickness in the pit of his stomach. It couldn't be true. No one could ever talk to his son in a tone like that. But if they did . . . if they did, he'd . . . he'd do something. Something. "Son, does she really say your name that way? Ball-lover?"

"Yes."

"Haven't you told her it's Boh-*lee*-var? That you're named for one of the greatest liberators in history?"

"How can I, Dad, when she never calls on me?"

"No, I guess you couldn't," said Step. "And she really does make fun of you like that when you raise your hand?"

"I don't raise my hand anymore," said Stevie.

"No, I imagine not." Step tried to think, tried to make sense of it all. "When did she start doing this?"

"The first day."

"Your very first day in school?"

Stevie thought for a minute. "The first day she said I was really stupid because she kept saying things and I didn't understand her and so I raised my hand and I asked her what she said, and then she said it again and I still didn't understand her."

Step thought back to what the problem had been that first day. "Because of her accent?"

Stevie nodded. "I got most of what she said, but it was like the first couple of words or a couple of words right in the middle, I wouldn't understand them. And she said I was really stupid. And all the kids made fun of me."

"Gee, why doesn't that surprise me, if the teacher called you stupid," said Step. "But then the next day you stayed in Dr. Mariner's office and took those tests, and then you came back to class the next day. What happened then?"

Stevie started to cry. "She made me stand up and she said, she said . . . " He couldn't go on. He just lay there on his bed, sobbing.

Step reached over and gathered Stevie up in his arms and slid him off the top bunk, and then sat on the edge of Robbie's bed and held Stevie on his lap, held his son tight against his chest while he cried. "There, there," he said. "I know this is so hard for you. It must be so hard. Why didn't you tell us any of this before?"

"I'm supposed to do my part," said Stevie.

"What do you mean?"

"I'm supposed to do my job at school like you do your job at work," said Stevie.

"Yes, Door Man, that's true," said Step. "But when things go bad at work, I don't keep it a secret, I tell your mom about it. And when she has a hard day, she tells *me*."

Stevie's crying grew quieter, stopped. "I didn't know that," he said.

"Of course, how *could* you know?" said Step. "We talk that way to each other late at night, after you kids are asleep."

"I didn't know," said Stevie.

"Can you tell me now what happened the day after you took those tests? You said that she made you stand up in front of the class, and then she did what? She said something?"

"She said that she was wrong to say what she said about me that time before. She said that I wasn't stupid at all, I was very very very smart, I was the smartest boy in the whole world, and when I didn't understand what people said it was because I was too *smart* to understand them because they were all really stupid compared to me, and so there was no point in anyone talking to me, *ever*, because I was way too smart to ever understand or care about a word they said."

Unbelievable, and yet now Step believed it. There was too much detail in it—Stevie could not possibly have made it up. And it rang true. Maybe when Dr. Mariner called Mrs. Jones to talk to her about Stevie's first day, Mrs. Jones assumed that Stevie had repeated to his parents what she said in class—though he hadn't, not till now. And so she assumed that Dr. Mariner knew and was simply too nice to mention it openly. And so she assumed that Stevie had told on her, had gotten her in trouble with her boss, and so she decided to get even with him.

"Son, I think I believe you. I'm sorry I didn't

believe you before, but you have to understand, this is such a terrible thing for a teacher to do that it's hard to believe that any teacher would *ever* do it. I mean, I had some strict teachers in my life, but never one who was downright *mean* like this. You should have told us this before. We thought everything was going along all right."

"It is," said Stevie. "Except for that."

"So you have friends at school?"

"No," said Stevie.

"Then it's not all right, is it?"

"How can I have friends when Mrs. Jones said for nobody to talk to me?"

How far did this go? "You mean that she actually told the other kids never to speak to you?"

"A couple of them tried to at recess but she yelled at them and said, 'Let's not bother Mr. Fletcher, please. He's thinking higher thoughts and we wouldn't want to disturb him.'"

Step held him closer. "Oh, Stevie, I didn't know, I didn't guess. How could I know this?"

"Jaleena talks to me sometimes," said Stevie.

"Is she one of the girls?"

"She's the black girl so Mrs. Jones doesn't really care what she does. But she doesn't talk to me *much* because it really is hard to understand her. She has to talk slow. And so she doesn't talk to me much."

So that was what Stevie's two months in second grade in Steuben had been like. Isolation. Ridicule. Utter loneliness. And he hadn't breathed a word of it at home. No sign of it except his reluctance to go to school.

"But you're still doing your schoolwork," said Step. "You *are* learning things."

"We did most of it in my old school," said Stevie.

"At least you had fun *doing* your project, didn't you?"

Stevie nodded.

"Son, I'm going to have a talk with Mrs. Jones."

He leapt from Step's lap and stood on the floor in the middle of the room, his eyes wide with fear. "No!" he said. "Don't talk to her! Please, Dad! You can't! You can't talk to her! Please!"

"Son, parents talk to teachers. That's how the system is supposed to work."

"You can't, you just can't do it. It'll get worse if you do, she'll be worse!"

"Stevie," said Step. "I promise you this. I absolutely promise you. Things will get *better* after I talk to her. And if they don't, I will keep you home from school."

"Yes!" he cried. "Keep me home!"

"Only if things get worse after I talk to her," said Step.

"No, keep me home now!"

"Stevie, I can't just keep you home now. There's a law that says that you have to go to school, and in North Carolina they're very strict about it. If I keep you out of school, it could mean going to court. Or moving again."

"Let's move back to Indiana!"

"Son, I can't afford to. If we moved, we'd have to move to Utah, to live in Grandma and Grandpa Brown's house. I'd lose my job. I'm just telling you that I'll do all those things if I *have* to, if talking to Mrs. Jones makes things worse for you. But I think when I talk to her things will get better, do you understand? The last month of school won't be so bad. I promise you."

"A whole month," said Stevie, his voice sounding dead.

"Think of it this way," said Step. "Think of it as if you had been convicted of a crime you didn't commit. You aren't guilty, you didn't do anything wrong, but the system worked wrong and you got convicted for it and now there's nothing you can do except hang on and live through the last month of your sentence. And then you'll get out and you'll never have to *see* Mrs. Jones again. And next year you'll be in the middle school and there'll be a whole bunch of new kids from other schools—*everybody* will be new, not just you. Next year will be better. You just have to live through this year."

"Don't talk to Mrs. Jones," said Stevie. "Please."

"Trust me, Stevie," said Step. "When I talk to Mrs. Jones, I will make things better."

Clearly Stevie did not believe him. It frustrated Step, made him almost angry, that his son didn't believe that he could do it. But Step had taken a good little while before he believed in Stevie, too. Turnabout is fair play.

When he left Stevie's room a few minutes later, he found DeAnne leaning against the door of the room they shared, right across the hall. She looked grim as she opened the door and led him inside. She closed the door.

"You heard?" asked Step.

"I couldn't stand not to listen," she said. "I've been so worried."

"Well, then, you know everything." He laughed bitterly. "At least now we know why he was so desperate to believe Sister LeSueur's flattery. If the kid's been hammered at school, he's got to be starved for praise."

"Do you really believe his story?" asked DeAnne.

"I think so," said Step. "Partly at least. I've got to."

"But what about the librarian? Step, I *know* the librarian wasn't lying. She's the sweetest woman, she sounded like she really *loved* Stevie. She talked about how he comes in during recess every day and reads, and she talked about his project with such *pride*." Then DeAnne stopped herself. "Listen to me. I'm standing here telling you that I would rather believe a woman I only met this morning than my own son."

"We don't believe something out of loyalty," said Step. "We believe it because it sounds plausible to us.

And Stevie's story didn't sound plausible until he told so much more of it that it began to fall into place. For instance, why *should* the librarian have been lying? Maybe she was telling the truth. Maybe Stevie's project *did* win first place, and maybe Mrs. Jones simply lied to her class about it."

"Oh, Step, she couldn't possibly imagine that she could get away with it, could she?"

"Who knows?" said Step. "There are a lot of crazy people in the world."

"But not teaching school."

"Why not? I mean, all those crazy people in mental institutions, they weren't *born* there. The day before they were in the asylum, they were *outside* the asylum, and a lot of them probably had jobs, and some of them were probably teachers. You don't think teachers could go crazy? Heck, they probably have a higher percentage than most, when you think of what they go through. So maybe she's just three months away from getting committed because she has come to hate children so deeply. Like a disease inside her. And this year she found a scapegoat, somebody she could pour out all that bile and venom onto, and it was Stevie."

DeAnne shook her head.

"It's possible," said Step. "I've at least got to find out."

"You made a promise to Stevie that you can't keep," said DeAnne.

"Oh, I'll keep it," said Step. "One way or another."

"How can you stop her from punishing him even more as soon as you're through talking to her?"

"If necessary I'll go to class every day."

"She'd never permit that. The *school* would never permit it."

"A parent, observing his child's class?"

"You'd lose your job."

"I'll quit the job!" said Step, and to his own surprise he was talking loudly, angrily. He brought his voice back down, spoke quietly, intensely. "I will quit the job. I hate the job. The job is keeping me from being a decent father to my children. The job is killing me and my family. *Screw* the job."

DeAnne visibly recoiled from him. "Step, please," she said.

It made him irrationally angry, to have her get upset at him for his *language* when he was talking about something that actually mattered. "Oh, don't you like the way I said it? The word *screw* is too rough for you? It's a *euphemism,* DeAnne. You can't get mad at me for using a *euphemism!* I mean, I *could* have said—"

"I'm not mad at you for saying *screw,* you dunce! I'm not mad at you at all, and don't be mad at me either, I can't stand it!" She burst into tears. "You were about to say the *f*-word! You were about to say that to your own wife."

"What is this about?" asked Step. "You *were* mad at me, I know you well enough to know what it looks like, you were mad at me for saying *screw* and—"

"So I was! For one stupid second! And then I realized it was stupid and I'm sorry, I can't help getting some look on my face for one split second, I don't deserve to have you *swearing* at me!"

"What are we doing?" said Step. "Why are *we* fighting?"

"Because our son has been tormented in school and we didn't do anything to help him—"

"How could we? He didn't tell us—"

"And we're both so angry we want to beat somebody up and the only person within easy reach is each other." DeAnne stopped talking for a moment. Then, to Step's surprise, she laughed. Laughed and lowered herself to the edge of the bed.

"OK, share the joke with the rest of us in this room," said Step.

"I was just thinking—this is so stupid, it isn't even funny . . ." She wiped tears away from her eyes.

"I know, I can see how funny it isn't," said Step.

"I just thought, when I said we're so mad and the only person we can reach is each other, I thought, 'Let's go beat up Sister LeSueur.'"

She was right. It *wasn't* really funny, and yet Step had to sit down beside her on the bed and laugh and laugh.

Step didn't actually ask for permission to leave work in the middle of the day. He just leaned his head into Dicky's office and said, "I'm taking lunch at two-thirty this afternoon because I have to go meet with my son's teacher after school."

"Your wife can't do that?" asked Dicky.

"Dicky," said Step, "it's my lunch hour, and I'm taking it at two-thirty. I'm only telling you because I want you to know where I'm going to be during that time period. I wasn't asking permission."

Dicky made no argument, just shrugged and gave a sort of half smile that made Step say to himself, You're too sensitive, too prickly, Step. Dicky didn't mean anything by what he said, and you jumped all over him.

Then, at twenty after two, as Step was sliding his microcassette recorder into his right pants pocket just prior to leaving, Dicky buzzed him on the phone. "Come by my office, please," he said.

"I'm on my way out," said Step. "To lunch."

"On your way, then, please stop by my office."

Step felt a sick dread in the pit of his stomach. Is he firing me? Because I spoke rudely to him? Impossible. Or maybe Ray Keene found out that I snuck a copy of my employment agreement, and so he thinks I'm looking for another job and so I'm being sacked because of *that*.

Instead, Dicky was all smiles when Step came into his office. There was another man there, a tall, thin fellow with a dark complexion and a sepulchral face that would have been rather frightening if he hadn't been smiling so broadly. In fact, his head was so narrow and his smile so wide that it looked for a moment as if he really were, literally, grinning from ear to ear. A mouth like a Muppet, thought Step.

"Meet Damien Weinreiter," said Dicky. "We're interviewing him for that programming position we have open."

"Oh? I didn't know we were looking for a programmer." Step never knew when they were hiring or firing people—he wasn't exactly part of the personnel process.

"Oh, yes, and I thought we couldn't very well have him come through without you having a chance to interview him."

Interview him! When Step had to get to Stevie's school?

Of course, he realized. This was how Dicky was getting back at him for speaking so sharply to him earlier today. Trying to put him into a position where he *had* to stay and miss that appointment. And the worst thing was that it was going to work. There was no gracious way that Step could tell Dicky to sit on his thumb, Step was taking his lunch *now*.

"Dicky, why me? I write manuals."

"Oh, Step, don't be so modest. You're not just our manual writer."

I knew it! thought Step. He knew about my secret assignment all along.

Dicky went on. "You're also the programmer of Hacker Snack. So of course Damien wants to get a chance to meet you."

"Great game," said Damien. "You're the best."

Yeah, right, thought Step. And you want a job here and you have the delusion, you poor thing, that sucking up to me will help you get it. Dicky here has probably already decided that you're not going to get an offer, and he's just using you to screw up my family life.

Well, Dicky, it isn't going to work.

Step did as Dicky asked—came in and sat down while the interview continued. But he knew Dicky had no intention of actually letting Step take part in the conversation. This was a humiliation game, so Dicky was going to make Step sit there in virtual silence while he conducted an interview in which Step was obviously not needed for anything.

So Step opened his attaché case, took out a yellow notepad, and wrote a brief note to Dicky.

> *Dear Dicky,*
>
> *I'm putting this on a note so I don't embarrass you in front of your interview. I'm going to meet with my son's teacher, as I told you I would. And I can't wait to be there at the meeting when you tell Ray Keene that you are now including me in the hiring process for programmers. With such a broadening of my responsibilities, I'm sure I'll get a raise!*
>
> *Affectionately yours,*
> *Step*

He stood up, wordlessly put the note on Dicky's desk, and left, closing the door behind him.

On the way to the school, Step tried to calm himself down. His anger at Dicky would do no good if it made him approach Mrs. Jones carelessly. He had to handle this exactly right with her, or he *would* do more harm than good. Being angry wouldn't help.

DeAnne had let him take the car today. He had been trying to catch more rides with other employees more often lately, because he knew how trapped she felt, being home all day without a car. Somehow he knew they had to come up with a second car—especially after the baby was born this summer. No way could he leave her home with a newborn without transportation. And yet it really didn't work out well for him to ride with others. He always ended up keeping them late. Or coming home with Gallowglass, and he hated bringing Gallowglass to his home. He didn't even want Glass knowing where he lived, though of course it was far too late for that. And Glass still asked him, every time, when Step was going to call on him to babysit. No, Step needed a car and DeAnne needed a car and there was no way they could scrape together the money right now even to buy a junker, let alone something dependable.

He pulled up in front of the school as the last buses were pulling out. Too late he remembered that DeAnne had told him that he had to take Fargo Road so he could park in that hidden lot up on the hill. Oh, well, thought Step. What are they going to do, shoot me? So he pulled in behind the last bus and followed it around the turnaround and pulled into a visitor parking place.

Dr. Mariner was at the door as he approached the school. "I'll bet you didn't know that parents aren't supposed to use the turnaround after school," she said.

"Actually, I did," said Step, "but I forgot until I was here and then I saw the last bus was leaving so I figured it wouldn't do any harm."

"Why, in fact, I think you're right. No harm done at all. Can I help you with something?"

"I hope so, ma'am. I'm Step Fletcher, and I'm here to—"

"Stevie Fletcher's father?"

"Yes," said Step, "I am."

"Oh, what a remarkable young man you have! And your wife is such a sweetie. And I think you have a little boy who's going to be in our kindergarten next year."

"Yes, that's Robbie."

"Well, I can hardly wait, though of course I'll be sad to see Stevie leave us. He's the sweetest boy, and so *smart*. Why, Mrs. Jones is always telling me how well he does in class, and of course you already *know* how he did with his second-grade project."

"I did hear something about it," said Step. He wanted *her* to tell him, in part because he didn't know which story was going to be true.

"Hear something about it indeed," said Dr. Mariner. "First-place winner, and you 'heard something about it.' We don't get many students of his caliber. You must know that."

"Oh, yes," said Step. "But I'm glad to know *you* know it."

"Well, of course," said Dr. Mariner. "But I mustn't keep you—I'm sure you came to have a consultation with Mrs. Jones, and we don't want her to be kept waiting."

"Actually, she doesn't know I'm coming."

"Oh, well, all the more reason to hurry—you want to get there before she goes home. My, I hope she hasn't already left! Do you know where her classroom is?"

"Actually, no," said Step.

"Then let me take you."

"No, just tell me, I don't want to inconvenience . . ."

But she was already five steps ahead of him down the corridor.

Mrs. Jones was still there, though she was already shrugging on her coat and if Step had waited to get directions instead of having a guide, he probably *would* have missed her. So he thanked Dr. Mariner profusely, even as he wondered whether this interview was even necessary. Clearly the librarian's version of reality had been the true one.

"Why Mr. Fletcher," said Mrs. Jones, after Dr. Mariner had left. "We don't have many fathers come to school. If only you had made an appointment, I could have stayed longer."

"Perhaps this won't take long," said Step. "I mostly came to talk to you about Stevie's project."

"His project?" she asked.

"His second-grade project. The—environment thing. He did an underwater scene. Out of clay."

"Oh, of course, yes. That was so *creative*."

His heart sank. He *should* be relieved, of course, to know that Mrs. Jones had not given him a *C*. But it meant Stevie had lied.

No, he told himself. Don't give up on Stevie so easily.

He reached into his pocket and switched on the microcassette recorder. He had already tested it in the pit at work. It picked up very well through the denim of his jeans.

"I wondered if you could tell me, Mrs. Jones. What grade did you give Stevie for that project?"

"Oh, I can hardly remember, that was so long ago."

"A week ago," said Step.

"Oh, here it is." She had her thumb down on the gradebook, but Step noticed that she glanced toward the door. Why? To see if Dr. Mariner was still there? "My," she said. "I see here that he got a *C*."

"Ah," said Step. He felt himself to be on fire inside. Stevie *had* told the truth. And so had the librarian. The project won first place, and yet somehow, somehow it got a *C*.

"Yes, that's it," said Mrs. Jones. "Definitely a *C*."

"Well, now," said Step. "That's hard to understand."

"Not really," said Mrs. Jones. "There's nothing wrong with a *C*. It means average."

Step had already scanned down all the other grades in the column of her gradebook where Stevie's *C* was marked. "It's hardly average," said Step, "when everybody else got *A*'s and *B*'s."

"Now, Mr. Fletcher. We don't let parents look at other children's grades, and you clearly were peeking at the wrong column of my gradebook."

But Step was looking around the classroom, not at her. "I was hoping," he said, "to see what an *A* project looked like, if Stevie's was only worth a *C*. It would help us as his parents, you see, to know what the standard is that he must meet, so we could help him do better on future projects."

There was the thing he was looking for. A blue ribbon, pinned to a bulletin board. Nothing written on it or by it. Just a blue ribbon.

"Oh, the projects have all been returned," said Mrs. Jones. "Stevie chose to throw his away, I'm afraid, but it was just a mass of clay by then. It was a shame what those ill-mannered children did to his project, but then, we really didn't have any practice at dealing with sculpture. If Stevie had brought a poster like everyone else, it wouldn't have happened."

Step reached into his shirt pocket and pulled out the folded-up assignment sheet DeAnne had armed him with. "I've looked and looked on this assignment sheet you sent home, and it says nothing about a poster. It just says, 'A depiction.'"

"Well, you see," said Mrs. Jones, "that *means* a poster."

Step looked back at the blue ribbon. "Ah," he said. "And how was I supposed to know that? I mean, the Mona Lisa is a depiction, isn't it? And yet it isn't a poster. And wouldn't you call Michelangelo's David a depiction?"

"All the other parents managed to figure out that a poster was what was intended," said Mrs. Jones. Her tone was getting quite frosty now.

"I see," said Step. "Perhaps they knew the local custom. But we're new here, and we did not."

"Obviously," said Mrs. Jones.

"But surely you're not telling me that Stevie's project was given a *C* because it wasn't a poster, are you?" asked Step.

"Not at all. As I said—it was creative."

"Then I still need your help to figure out what Stevie did wrong."

"And I keep telling you, Mr. Fletcher. You don't have to do something *wrong* to get a *C*. That signifies *average*. It was an average project."

Short of calling her a liar right now, there wasn't much Step could say to that, not directly. It must be time to talk about the ribbon. "Well, Mrs. Jones, it makes me wonder why Dr. Mariner would give the first-place ribbon to an average project."

"Dr. Mariner has her judgment, and I have mine," said Mrs. Jones.

Yes, thought Step. She is definitely sounding quite cold. "Oh, of course," said Step. "But you see, you didn't give your grades until after Dr. Mariner had made her decision, did you?"

"My judgment was completely independent."

"But wouldn't you say, Mrs. Jones, that for you to give the lowest grade in the class to the very project that won first place, you must surely have found something *wrong* with it?"

He faced her. Her expression was hard, but she was holding her hands together in front of her very tightly. Oh, yes, she's afraid. She's very much afraid. Because everything that Stevie told me was true.

"Very well, Mr. Fletcher," she said, ending the silence at last. "I will tell you what was wrong with Stevie's project. It was the written portion of the project, the report. The other children turned in reports of five or six pages. Stevie's report was only two pages."

With great difficulty, Step controlled his rage. "Stevie's paper was typed. Was anyone else's paper typed?"

"That hardly matters," she said.

"They were all written in big letters, weren't they— like these papers on the board. Right?"

"Of course. This is the second grade, Mr. Fletcher."

"My rough count here gives me . . . let's see . . . about fifty or sixty words per page, handwritten. Is that right?"

"Oh, I suppose."

"But Stevie's paper was single-spaced, and that means he got between four and five hundred words to a page. So each of his pages was about the same amount of content as—"

"A page is a page!" said Mrs. Jones.

"And the assignment sheet," said Step, "said nothing about a minimum number of pages."

"Everyone *else* managed to figure out that four or five pages were required! And they didn't have their mothers type it for them—*they* used their own handwriting."

"The assignment sheet didn't say anything about penmanship being part of the assignment," said Step. "So naturally Stevie thought he should do the same thing I did with my dissertation. He went to my computer, turned it on, brought up WordStar, and typed every letter of every word himself. Then he printed it out and stapled it—himself."

"That was another problem," said Mrs. Jones. "The other children's reports all had very nice plastic covers, and your son's report was nothing but two sheets of paper with a staple. It showed a lack of respect."

"The assignment sheet didn't mention a cover," said Step. "If it had, there would have been a cover. But in graduate school, you see, I turned in my papers with a staple in the corner. So of course Stevie thought that that was the grown-up way to do it. And in fact, Mrs. Jones, it is, isn't it? Surely you're not telling me that the difference between an *A* and a *C* is a twenty-nine-cent cover?"

"Of course not," said Mrs. Jones. "It's just *part* of the difference."

"Don't you think that computer literacy and college-level presentation should count *for* him rather than *against* him?"

"Other children don't live in wealthy homes with

computers in them, Mr. Fletcher. Other children don't
have fathers who went to college. I'm hardly going to
give one child an advantage over others because of
money."

"I'm not rich, Mrs. Jones. I work with computers for
a living. I have a computer at home the way car salesmen
sometimes bring new cars home." Watch it, Step. You're
letting her sidetrack you. "What matters is that Stevie's
paper was probably ten times as long as any of the other
children's papers. He did all the work himself, and he
did not violate the assignment sheet in any way. Now,
why did the first-place project get a *C* in your class?"

"I don't have to justify my grades to you or anyone
else!" said Mrs. Jones.

"Yes," said Step mildly. "In fact you do. You can justify it to me, today, or you can justify it before the
school board."

"Are you threatening me?" asked Mrs. Jones.

Step almost brought out the tape recorder then, to
confront her with it. But he knew that the moment she
saw it, she would say nothing more—and there was
more that he needed her to say.

"No, Mrs. Jones. I wouldn't dream of it. If my son
earned a *C*, then he earned a *C*. I'm not trying to get
you to change the grade. I just want you to help me
understand it."

"This discussion has gone on long enough. It isn't
right for you to be here alone in this room with me anyway, Mr. Fletcher."

"Perhaps you're right," said Step. "Let's go get Dr.
Mariner to join in this conversation with us. I haven't
mentioned Stevie's *C* to her yet, but I'm sure she'll want
to know the reason for that grade as much as I do."

Mrs. Jones glared at him, then sat down at her desk
and began rummaging through a file drawer. She came
out with Stevie's paper. Sure enough, there was a big
red *C* at the top.

And not another mark.

"I guess all the flaws in the paper are on the second page," said Step.

"What?" she said.

"There aren't any marks on the first page, so the errors must all be on the second page. I'd like to see them."

She handed him the paper.

He opened it. There was only one red mark on the second page. Mrs. Jones had circled the word *octopuses* and in the margin had written *octopi*.

"Oh, but you must be making a little joke here," said Step.

"A joke?"

"Look," he said, showing her the paper. "You must be kidding, right?"

"I'm not kidding when I correct errors on my students' papers."

"But Mrs. Jones, surely you know that the plural of *octopus* is either *octopus*, with nothing added, or *octopuses*."

"I think not," said Mrs. Jones.

"Think again, Mrs. Jones."

She must have realized that she was not on firm ground here. "Perhaps *octopuses* is an alternate plural, but I'm sure that *octopi* is the preferred."

"No, Mrs. Jones. If you had looked it up, you would have discovered that *octopi* is not the preferred spelling. It is not a spelling at all. The word does not exist, except in the mouths of those who are pretending to be educated but in fact are not. This is because the *us* ending of *octopus* is not a Latin nominative singular ending, which would form its plural by changing to the letter *i*. Instead, the syllable *pus* in *octopus* is the Greek word for 'foot.' And it forms its plural the Greek way. Therefore *octopoda*, not *octopi*. Never *octopi*."

"Well, then, *octopoda*. Your son's paper said *octopuses*."

"I know," said Step. "When he asked me the correct

plural, I told him *octopoda*. But then he was still uncertain, because my son doesn't think he knows something until he *knows* it, and so he looked it up. And to my surprise, *octopoda* is only used when referring to more than one *species* of octopus, rather than when referring to more than one actual octopus. What Stevie put in his paper is in fact the preferred dictionary usage. Which you would have known, too, if you had looked it up."

"So I'm human, Mr. Fletcher. I made a mistake."

"As did I, Mrs. Jones, as did I. But the fact remains that the only red mark on this *C* paper is in a place where you have taken a correct plural and replaced it with an incorrect one. Isn't that right?"

"If you say so," said Mrs. Jones.

"So I'm still baffled," said Step. "How can I possibly help Stevie do better next time? You haven't really pointed out a single thing wrong with his paper—oh, except that he didn't put a plastic cover on it."

"There won't *be* a next time," said Mrs. Jones. "Your son will never have to do another second grade project as long as he lives. So it doesn't matter, and therefore you're wasting my time as well as your own. Good afternoon, Mr. Fletcher!"

"One more question, Mrs. Jones."

"No," she said. "I have to go home, right now."

"It's just one more question," said Step, mildly. If she didn't stop, however, the tape recorder would definitely come out. She would not be going home anytime soon.

"Very well, what?"

"Who is going to take that ribbon home?"

Mrs. Jones looked at the ribbon that Step was pointing to.

"That *is* the first place ribbon for Stevie's project, isn't it?"

"It might be," said Mrs. Jones.

"Then who will take it home?"

"*If* it's the particular ribbon you're referring to, then of course Stevie will take it home at the end of the school year."

"Ah," said Step. "Then what in the world are you going to tell J.J.?"

She blanched.

Stevie's story was completely vindicated now.

"What do you mean?" she said.

"Why, I mean that Stevie's whole class is under the impression that J.J. received that award."

"That's impossible," said Mrs. Jones.

"Is it? Let's call J.J.'s parents and see," said Step.

"I certainly will not bother my children's parents over such a thing."

"Then I'll go to Dr. Mariner's office right now and she and I will place that phone call together," said Step. "You won't mind, will you?"

Mrs. Jones was barely holding herself together now, Step could see that. She was wringing her hands and he could see that she was trembling. "It's possible that someone might have gotten a false impression. That perhaps someone made a mistake and . . ."

No, thought Step. You aren't going to weasel out of this. You're going to say it outright. "You stood in front of the class and announced that J.J. won the prize, didn't you?" he asked.

"Oh, now, don't be silly," she said.

"What if lawyers representing the school board came to your students and asked them how they got the idea that J.J. won the ribbon? What would they say?" Step knew that of course such a thing would never happen, but he figured that Mrs. Jones was not going to be confident of that, not in the state she was in right now.

"I may have said something that gave that impression," said Mrs. Jones.

"May have, or did?"

She looked toward the window, weaving and

204 • ORSON SCOTT CARD

unweaving her fingers. "I thought that Dr. Mariner had judged very hastily, and so she missed the superior merits of J.J.'s project."

"Ah," said Step.

"If you want," said Mrs. Jones, "I will change Stevie's grade. And of course I will correct the mistake about the ribbon."

Yes, I'm sure you will, thought Step. And then you'll torment and ridicule Stevie even more mercilessly every day until school ends. "No," said Step. "I don't want you to change Stevie's grade. In fact, I insist that you *not* change it. I want it there on the books, just as it is now."

Mrs. Jones looked at him narrowly. "Then what is all this about? Just the ribbon? Very well."

"The ribbon—yes, that would be nice. You can tell the students that there was a mistake and in fact the ribbon belongs to Stevie."

"Very well, I will do that tomorrow."

"But that's not all," said Step.

"I think it is," said Mrs. Jones. "Unless you changed your mind about the grade."

Step pulled the tape recorder from his pocket, pressed rewind for a few moments, and played it back. It was fuzzy, but it was clear. " . . . the superior merits of J.J.'s project." Then Step pushed *stop*.

Her face turned white, and it occurred to Step that perhaps he had overplayed this moment—it wouldn't be very good for anybody if the woman fainted right now.

But she didn't faint. And when she did speak, her voice was stronger than he expected. "That's illegal," she said. "To bug a conversation like that."

"On the contrary," said Step. "It's only *inadmissible* when it was obtained by a government employee without a warrant. I'm not a cop. I'm just a man who carries around a tape recorder. Besides, I don't intend to use this in court. I only intend to play it for Dr. Mariner and every member of the school board as I put an end to your career."

"Why are you doing this to me?"

"The real question is, why have you been doing all the things you've been doing to Stevie?"

"I haven't been doing anything to him," she said defiantly. "Go ahead and use that tape."

"All right," said Step. He put it back in his pocket and walked around her, through the door, and down the corridor toward Dr. Mariner's office. With each step he became more uncertain. Maybe she really *could* talk her way out of this. Maybe she understood the system here better than he did, and even this tape recording would end up being worthless. Maybe he had broken his promise to Stevie that he wouldn't make things worse.

"Mr. Fletcher!" she said. Her voice echoed down the empty corridor.

"Yes?" he said, not turning around.

"There was one more thing that I forgot to show you about Stevie's work."

He turned around and headed back down the hall.

When they were alone again in the room, she looked tired, defeated. "I didn't mean anything by it," she said. "Is that thing *off* now?"

He pulled out the recorder, took out the tape, and put them back in different pockets.

"I didn't mean anything. I just—it's very hard being a teacher and having parents come down on you all the time. And so when Dr. Mariner called me that night— at *home*—because Stevie was upset and *you* were upset, when all I did was make a foolish little joke—I mean, everything I said, he made me say it over and over and over, and it was disrupting the class. So I made a joke—"

"Calling him stupid."

"A *joke*," she insisted. "And then he tells his parents and you call Dr. Mariner—well I was just sick of it, and when he came back to class I was just so angry the moment I saw him, and so I said things that I shouldn't have said and I'm sorry."

"But you've kept on doing it," said Step.

She started to cry. "I know it," she said. "And I felt bad about it, but I just couldn't seem to stop, I just . . . couldn't seem to stop. And then he stopped raising his hand, and so . . . I thought it was over."

"If you thought it was over, why didn't you let him have the blue ribbon?" said Step. "Why didn't you let him have the A on his project?"

"I don't know," she said. Her voice was so small and high, like a little girl's voice. It made Step feel like a bully, like a tyrant, coming in here and pushing this woman around until she cried.

Then he remembered how Stevie had cried. And how this woman had tormented him, and even if she talked now about how she felt bad about it and tried to stop, the fact was that she could have stopped at any time and she did not. She even lied about something as utterly stupid as the ribbon awarded by the principal. Surely she must have realized, in some rational part of her mind, that this could not possibly go undiscovered. That this was far too public, too open for her ever to get away with it.

She wanted to be caught, Step realized. The most obvious psychological insight of them all. Maybe because she hates teaching. Or she hates the children. She doesn't want to teach anymore, and yet she can't stop because that's how she makes her living. So she gathered up all her hatred and poured it out on my son, again and again and yet he continued to take it; nothing happened, so she pushed harder and harder, and still Stevie took it, absorbed it all; and then finally she pushed so hard that she succeeded. Stevie broke. Stevie wept out the truth to his father, and now I have finally come to give her what she wanted all along.

"There's a month left in school," said Step. "From

now on if Stevie raises his hand, I want you to call on him. Not every time, but as often as you'd call on any other bright kid. Do you understand me? I want you to treat him *normally*. If he gives the right answer, you don't say anything snide to him, and if he gives the wrong answer, you correct him kindly. Do you understand?"

She nodded, dabbing at her eyes.

"If a kid talks to him, then you let the friendship develop. You do *nothing* to interfere. I don't mean you're to *order* kids to be friends with him, because then they'd hate him even more. I want you treat my son fairly and normally. Can you do that?"

Again she nodded.

"Yes, I think you *can*," said Step. "It's whether you *will*. Just keep this in mind. If you get the urge to say something spiteful or cruel to Stevie, or for that matter to *any* of your students, just remember that this tape exists. Along with however many copies I feel like making. For the rest of your life, if another child suffers anything like what Stevie has been through, you can expect to hear this tape again. I'll be watching."

"You aren't a Christian, then!" she said. "Christians believe in forgiveness!"

"I'm a Christian who believes in repentance *before* forgiveness. If you never again mistreat a child, then you have nothing to fear from me. This tape will never surface. All you have to do is control your hate. If you can't do that, Mrs. Jones, then you shouldn't be a teacher."

"It's my life!" she said.

"No," said Step. "The woman on this tape is not a teacher, Mrs. Jones. The woman on this tape is a Nazi."

She buried her face in her hands. Step remembered Stevie weeping the night before. More than ever before in his life, he found himself longing to hurt someone, to tear at her. It frightened him to feel such a hunger for violence. Nor had he felt it so strongly until she was helpless and weeping. It was a terrible thing to know about himself, that he could feel such a lust to punish a submissive enemy.

He turned and fled from the man he had found in that room.

In moments the rage was gone, replaced by satisfaction. He had fulfilled his promise to Stevie. As he walked down the corridor toward the front door, it occurred to him that he had confronted evil and subdued it. The mythic theme of half the movies and TV shows and novels and of a good deal of history as well. Of course, it had been too clean and simple for the movies. She should have had a gun in her purse, the one that Mr. Jones had bought for her to defend herself. She should have taken that gun out of her purse and followed him and shot him and taken the tape, right now, before he could make copies of it.

What if she *did* have a gun? What if she *was* going to follow him?

It was an absurd thought, a childish sort of thought, and yet he walked faster. She won't shoot me in the corridor here, he thought, because there are still other teachers in the building, and the custodial staff—witnesses. No, she'll do it in the parking lot, around the corner, where no one can see and she can drive away. He hurried, almost ran out the door and around the corner to his car. He fumbled with his keys, dropped them. Picked them up, looked around, and yes, there she was, coming out the door of the school. He unlocked the door of his car and opened the door and then looked up and saw that she was heading past him, that in fact she didn't even see him, or at least didn't give any sign that she saw him. She got into her car, a sad-looking little Pinto, and backed out of her parking place.

A Pinto. She drives a Pinto. She's a *teacher,* for

heaven's sake, making a pathetic salary and getting no respect from anyone, putting up with people's miserable children all these years and all the flak from stupid angry parents yelling at her over nothing, when she was trying to do her best, and here he was, the ultimate angry parent, the parent from hell, destroying her, when all she ever wanted to do was teach. What am I, he thought, to set myself up as an angry god, deciding who needs to be punished, who deserves to have a career and who doesn't.

Then he remembered Stevie crying, and he thought, some things, some *people,* simply have to be stopped. It doesn't mean that the person who stops them is noble or great or some kind of hero. I'm no hero. But maybe I've stopped her. Maybe now she won't end up doing something even worse to some other kid, driving him to suicide maybe. And who's to say she hasn't done this before? Maybe she's always had a goat in all her classes, some poor kid who becomes the target of her vicious abuse, only this time she just happened to pick the wrong kid. This time she picked the kid who would put an end to it.

I shouldn't feel proud of this, thought Step. But I also shouldn't feel ashamed. I should just feel glad that it's over. *If* it's over.

She drove away.

He got into his car, started it, pulled out, and headed home.

The song on the radio was the one by Hall and Oates that had been a big hit back in January when Step came to Steuben for interviews. "Maneater." That's what I saved Stevie from, a maneater. Mrs. Jaws. Doing all she could to chew up this child and spit him out. So why don't I feel better?

Because I'm *not* better. I just chewed *her* up and spit *her* out, and I don't like how it feels. I don't like being cruel. I don't have the stomach for it.

And yet I do, don't I, because I did it. Maybe that's a good thing and maybe it's not.

When he pulled into the driveway, he noticed that something was different about the lawn. Then he turned the engine off, and the radio stopped, and he heard the lawnmower. DeAnne was mowing the lawn.

But it wasn't DeAnne. When he got out of the car and went around to the back yard, there was an old man mowing the grass. One of the neighbors?

Suddenly DeAnne was beside him, slipping her arm around his waist. "How did it go?" she asked.

"Who's he?" he asked.

"Oh, he's Bappy. You know, I told you about him, the landlord's father. I called him to ask if he knew any neighbor kids who mowed lawns, and he said he'd do it."

"I can mow our lawn," said Step. "We can't afford to pay a grown man."

"When are you going to mow it, Step?" she asked. "You don't have time. And if you *did* have time the kids and I would much rather have you spend that time with *us* than mowing the stupid lawn. And besides, he's doing it for free. He says that living at the condo he never gets an excuse to get outside and have some exercise."

Step looked at Bappy. He waved. DeAnne waved back, and so did Step, halfheartedly.

"So come inside and tell me how it went."

As they headed for the house, he said, "She agreed to everything I said. The harassment stops. The last month at school should be better."

"But will she actually *do* it?" asked DeAnne.

"Oh, yes," said Step. "I think she will."

"Well tell me what you said, and what did *she* say? Was it as bad as Stevie said?"

"Every word that Stevie said to us was true," said Step.

"How *could* she? How could *anyone?*"

"I'll tell you what," said Step. "Tonight, I'll make sure you hear *every* word. Word for word."

"What, you memorized it?"

He pulled the tape recorder and the tape out of his pockets. She looked from one to the other and then whooped once with laughter and then got a frown on her forehead. "You *did* have the tape *in* the recorder, I hope!"

"You'll hear it all, Fish Lady," said Step. "The Junk Man really got the junk this time."

She threw her arms around him, as far as they would go, with her belly so large and solid in front of her. And she kissed him. "Come on inside," she said. "Stevie's been so nervous, you need to tell him everything went well. This is great, you having the afternoon off work like this."

"What am I doing?" said Step. "I can't believe that I even came home. I'm on my lunch hour. I've got to go back."

"Oh, no!" she said. "It's four o'clock, there's only an hour left anyway."

"Yes, but Dicky and I had a run-in about me leaving, so I've got to show my face there, but I'll tell you what, I'll get home as early as I can, all right? Tell Stevie it went fine, tell him that his teacher will never pick on him again—and if she gives even one hint of it tomorrow, I'll get her fired, and I can do it."

DeAnne laughed. "I'll bet you can."

"And thanks for getting the lawn mowed," he said.

"I'll pass it along to Bappy."

But he couldn't go. "Aw, Fish Lady," he said, in his mock-sorry voice, "I gotta tell him myself."

"Oh, of course, you goof," said DeAnne. "He's in the family room playing computer games."

Step leaned through the doorway from the kitchen to the family room. Stevie was sitting at the Atari, playing some game with a pirate ship, talking at the screen. "Come on, Scotty!" Stevie said.

"Stevie," said Step. "I've got to go back to work, but I wanted to tell you."

Stevie pushed the *reset* button on the computer, and the screen went blank and then blue.

"You didn't have to turn it off," said Step. "I was just telling you, everything went fine with Mrs. Jones. The tough days are behind you, I promise you."

Stevie nodded—glumly. Well, of course, Step thought. Even if I'm right, he knows that getting the teacher off his case won't instantly give him a whole bunch of friends at school. But at least maybe some of them will *talk* to him.

Step kissed DeAnne again, got back in the car, and headed back to work. When he got there, he saw three notes on his desk. All three were messages from Ray Keene. They all said the same thing: Ray called. Wants to know where you are.

Dicky was so low, so petty, so spiteful that after months of trying to make sure that Step *never* got a chance to talk to Ray Keene directly, he got Ray to attempt direct contact when he knew Step was gone in the middle of the afternoon.

Step immediately picked up the phone and punched in Ray's extension. As he had hoped, it was Ray's secretary who answered. "Hi," he said. "I'm returning Ray's call."

"Oh, I'm sorry, Ray's in a meeting right now," said the secretary.

"Isn't that the way it goes?" said Step. "I'll bet the meeting is with Dicky, isn't it?"

"Well, Dicky's *one* of the guys in there, anyway," she said.

"Isn't that the silliest thing?" said Step. "Ray was trying to call me, and yet Dicky was with him, and Dicky *knew* that I had taken a late lunch today so I could meet with my son's teacher. You'd think Dicky would have told Ray so Ray wouldn't waste his time trying to reach me."

"Oh, Dicky probably just forgot," said the secretary.

"I'm sure you're right," said Step. "Would you tell Ray that I'm sorry he called me during my late lunch today? And give Dicky a poke in the ribs for me, forgetting to tell Ray where I was like that!"

"I sure will," said the secretary. "Isn't that just the way things go?"

"Ain't it the truth," said Step, and hung up.

Maybe the scene would play right and maybe it wouldn't, thought Step, but at least Dicky might have an embarrassing moment or two, if the secretary actually relayed the message even halfway accurately, and if Ray just happened to be standing there when she did.

Because he hadn't been there for much of the afternoon, Step wasn't deeply involved with any projects and so he was able to get away by five-thirty. When he walked past the pit on his way to the door, Glass called to him. "Hey, Step!"

"Hey, Glass," said Step. He came a little way into the room. There were several programmers there, but they were goofing around, not working—he knew that, because he recognized the games that were on the screens, and none of them were published by Eight Bits Inc. They did that sometimes, staying after work and fooling around with other companies' games. They called it "industrial espionage" but the truth was that they loved computer games, and here were all these machines and all this software lying around, and most of them didn't have families anyway except maybe parents, and so why the hell not stay late and play?

"Heading for home?" asked Glass.

"Wish I had time to play," said Step. "But yeah, I'm going home."

"Ray was looking for you," said Glass.

"I got the messages. I was taking a late lunch."

"It sounded important."

"Well, when I got back, I called in and so Ray knew that I was back and he didn't call again, so it can't have been *too* important."

Glass rolled his eyes. "Do you know what the term 'deep shit' means?"

"Glass," said Step, "Dicky knew where I was. Dicky didn't *like* where I was, but it was my lunch hour, and I wasn't cutting out on work. So if this is even a halfway rational universe, I'm not in deep shit."

"I didn't say you were in it," said Glass, grinning. "I just asked if you knew what it meant."

Step faked slapping him across the face. "Why, I oughta . . ."

"Oughta what?"

"Never mind, you're too young," said Step. "In fact, *I'm* too young. I don't get it myself. Seeya tomorrow, humans. Seeya tomorrow, Glass."

Step headed out to the car. On the way, it occurred to him that he'd seen practically every game on the market for the Atari, and he didn't remember any of them with that pirate ship he had seen Stevie playing with. He'd have to check and see what the game was. Probably just one of the games he brought home from work to look at—it was one of the perks of working for a software company, that you could bring games home as long as you brought them back. Stevie must have found one that Step hadn't actually seen on a machine yet.

By the time he got home, his mind had turned to other things, and when he finally stood there in front of the Atari, he could only remember that there was something he wanted to do with it but he couldn't remember what. Oh well, it would come back to him.

The family actually had dinner together, and he was able to coax Stevie into playing some games with them afterward. He wasn't much fun, though, but at least he was playing, and after he saw that things were better at school, maybe things would also start to get better at home.

Step was all set to help DeAnne get the kids through bathtime and bed when the phone rang. It was Sam Freebody, the elders quorum president. Freebody was a tall man, sloppily fat, and he seemed determined to prove every cliche about the joviality of fat people. So it took a bit of convivial chitchat before he finally came to the reason for the call. It was what Step had expected— and, truth be known, dreaded. "I'd like to give you your home teaching assignment," Brother Freebody said.

"You know," said Step, "if you could hold off on that for a while, I'd be grateful."

"We're really short-handed in the quorum," said Freebody. "Everybody has to do his share or the Church will grind to a halt."

Step remembered giving the same speech many times when he was elders quorum president back in Vigor. "Brother Freebody," he said, "I know what you mean, and I believe in home teaching and I'm actually an excellent home teacher, but right now at work I'm putting in twelve-hour days most days and I never get to see my family and I don't think it'd be fair to them or to me if I spent one of my few days home going out—"

"You're home *now*," Freebody pointed out.

Step wanted to scream over the phone, It's none of your business! But he knew Freebody was only doing his calling, and doing it well. "Yeah, I guess so," said Step. "OK, look, I'll do my best. I just warn you that I might not get to everybody every month."

"Right now, Brother Fletcher, you would improve our quorum average if you just got to *any*body, *any* month."

Step laughed and then wrote down the names of the families they were supposed to visit and a few notes about each of them. Freebody was an excellent elders quorum president, Step realized—he actually knew who these people were, they weren't just names on the roster to him. Home teaching wasn't just something Freebody had to get other people to do, it was an enterprise that he cared about and understood. It made Step determined to take the time to do his home teaching, to help Freebody and because Step, too, believed in the program. Really believed in it, except when he forgot to think about it at all, which was most of the time.

"And your companion is a young prospective elder named Lee Weeks. He's a new convert, nineteen years old, and I'm hoping to get him ready for a mission maybe in a year or so. So set him a good example!"

"You mean, like, don't take him out for a beer afterward?"

Freebody guffawed. "I mean show him what a normal member of the Church is like. He has a lot of enthusiasm, but some of it is directed toward some kind of weird ideas."

"Weird ideas?"

"How can I put this, Brother Fletcher? Let's just say that he was first contacted by Brother and Sister LeSueur, and he took all the lessons in their home."

"I'm not sure I know what that means," said Step. Of course, he knew exactly what Freebody meant—the kid had been exposed to the strangest, most self-servingly charismatic version of the gospel that could be imagined. But Step was already getting into the spirit of the way things worked in the Steuben 1st Ward: You know that certain people are difficult, but you just work around them as best you can and try not to put the nastiness right out in the open. As a westerner, Step was used to a more direct way of doing things. But if this elaborate effort to avoid hurting anybody's feelings or provoking any conflict was the southern way, then Step would learn to act southern.

So Step wasn't surprised when Freebody's only

explanation was to say, "You'll see. He's a good kid, though."

Step wrote down Lee Weeks's name and phone number. "Does he live at home or will I maybe get a roommate when I call?" he asked.

"Lives at home. His mom's a shrink. Divorced, so I haven't met the father. She approved of Lee joining the Church, though, so there's no problem with hostility."

"So she'll deliver messages."

"Heck, she'll probably push him out the door to go home teaching with you. She even drives him to church on Sunday."

"He doesn't have a license?"

"I guess not, or maybe he cracked up the car once too often or something. She drives him, anyway."

That was that. Step said his good-byes and hung up the phone and sighed as he sat back down at the kitchen table.

"Home teaching, right?" said DeAnne. She was loading the dishwasher.

He got up and started helping.

"No, Step, I'm almost done, and you've already been the hero of the day. I just want to hear the tape."

"The kids are all bathed?"

"I'm real fast now," said DeAnne. "Splish-splash and I pop 'em in bed. And Stevie takes his own bath. Done in record time. I'm a wonder."

"You are, you know," he said.

She smiled. "Let me hear the tape."

So they sat in the family room and listened as Step copied the tape from the microcassette recorder to the cheap little Panasonic that clearly wanted to be a boom box when it grew up but would never, never make it. The quality of the recording wasn't that good, especially when Step had been across the room from her, but it was certainly good enough to hear pretty much everything, and even the copy was OK.

"Oh, Step," said DeAnne when the tape was finished. "You are *sly*."

She meant it as a compliment, but to Step it had a hollow ring. He didn't like thinking of himself as a sly person.

"You should have heard me later," said Step. "I stopped being sly, and turned into a bully." Then he told her in some detail what he had done after he stopped recording. And how Mrs. Jones had called it blackmail, and he wasn't sure but that she was right. At some level, anyway.

DeAnne slapped him playfully on the arm. "There, I hereby punish you. Case dismissed."

"I just thought it would feel better than it did."

"Come on, didn't it feel just a little bit good when you pulled out the recorder and showed her?"

"Yes," said Step. "But afterward . . ."

"Afterward you found a way of making yourself the villain of the piece," said DeAnne. "But you weren't. You were rescuing your little boy."

"Yeah," said Step. "When I remember that, I feel better. But I don't always remember it."

"Then I'll remind you," she said. "Again and again and again." To his surprise, she kissed him long and soft and deep, and he realized that she was going to make love to him tonight.

"Maybe I should bully defenseless teacher ladies more often," he said, when the kiss was finally done.

"Shut up, Junk Man," she said, and kissed him again.

"Step! Step!" He dreamed that DeAnne was very, very upset and she was calling to him, softly so she wouldn't wake the kids but her voice was full of fear. Then he opened his eyes and looked at the clock and at the same time heard her call his name again and he realized that it wasn't a dream at all, it was three in the morning and something was wrong and DeAnne was calling out for help, she needed him to help her.

He threw back the covers and got up and realized that he was naked; he must have fallen asleep as soon as they were through making love. *I hope I stayed awake long enough to actually finish,* he thought. And then remembered that yes, he had. DeAnne had not been left unsatisfied tonight, as she had so many nights before.

He inwardly slapped himself for the churlish thought and went to get his bathrobe out of the closet. The only light in the room was what spilled in from the kids' bathroom, which was around the corner and down the hall, so he could hardly see anything; but he found the robe and put it on. She called again.

"I'm coming," he said, trying to be loud enough and yet soft enough at the same time.

"Put on your slippers first," she said.

"I don't need them," he said.

"Yes you *do!*" she said, and her voice rose almost to a scream at the end, and so he put on his slippers and then went to the door into the hall and just as he was turning on the light he realized that he had just *stepped* on something, and something had just bumped against his leg, and now the light was on and he saw that the floor was jumping with crickets. Dozens of them, hundreds of them.

"Holy shit," he said. "I mean good heavens."

"Where are they coming from, Step?"

"What an excellent question," he answered. He bent over and brushed several of them off his legs. It was almost impossible to take a step without crushing one under his feet while others jumped at him, landed on him.

DeAnne was standing there holding a can of Raid. "I don't think I should be breathing insecticide fumes when I'm pregnant," she said.

"There isn't enough Raid in a can to kill them all,"

he said. "We'd asphyxiate the children long before we got the crickets."

"What, then? Sweep them up into garbage bags?"

"Sounds better than trying to stomp them all," he said. "Where are the seagulls when you really need them?"

"I'll get the garbage bags," she said, heading for the kitchen.

While she was gone, he tried to find the source. The hall was the worst place, it seemed—there were only a few in Betsy's room and in the bathroom. But when he turned the light on in the boys' room, it was even worse. The crickets were so thick on the floor that in places he couldn't even see the carpet. The crickets jumping on him made him want to scream, and walking was very slow when he had to keep brushing them off, and finally he just *stopped* brushing them off, even though he couldn't stand the way it felt to have their feet on his naked legs. He couldn't brush them off because they were here in his children's bedroom and he had to get rid of them and so what did it matter whether he was comfortable or not?

They were coming up from a small gap in the back of the boys' closet. He could see them crawling out, first the antennas and then their black, mechanical bodies, their legs like pistons. Robot crickets, that's what they are, he thought. Somebody made them.

And then he thought, *I* made them. Crickets from hell. A plague of crickets. A sign to me that God saw the way I bullied that woman today and he knows that I secretly loved doing it, that I loved the power I had over her. So just like Pharaoh, I get a plague.

DeAnne was in the room now, holding several garbage bags—and a broom and dustpan. "You'll have to hold the dustpan while I sweep," she said. "I can't bend over that far these days."

"Forget the dustpan," said Step. "They'd just jump

off. I'll hold the bag open for you. But first we've got to stop them from coming in."

"You found the place?"

"A crack between the floor and the wall in the back of the closet. Do we have any rags?"

"All the old socks," she said.

"Get them wet and we'll jam them in," he said.

"Wet? Why?"

"Oh, please, DeAnne, I don't know, just do it." He wasn't really sure why. He just had some vague idea that if the socks were wet then he could jam them in tighter and they'd stay in place better and it would do a better job of keeping the crickets from coming through.

It took all the socks DeAnne had been saving for dustcloths, but when he had jammed them in, no more crickets were able to come through.

Then the hard part started. The crickets were not inclined to hold still, and so it seemed an almost sisyphean task. Step would keep the bottom of the garbage bag flat on the floor by holding down two corners with his feet, and then hold the top open as far as he could with his hands, while DeAnne tried her best to sweep them in. All the while, of course, they were jumping up at Step's head and onto his arms and legs; yet he couldn't let go of the bag to brush them off, he could only shudder and shake his head. The boldest of the crickets seemed to enjoy this, and hung on for the ride until Step finally asked DeAnne to sweep them off.

Gradually they began to make progress, especially after Step figured out that by spraying Raid into the garbage bag itself from time to time, he could convince the ones they had already caught to stay put. It took an hour before all the visible crickets were collected and the bags tied tightly and carried out to the garage. Then began the hunt for the strays.

They pulled the kids out of their beds, one by one, and perched them sleepily in Step's and DeAnne's room, where there were no crickets remaining; then they closed the door. Since the kids had slept right through the time when masses of crickets were moving around, there was a good chance that they wouldn't see any of the crickets at all, and therefore wouldn't have nightmares about them later.

I hope we're so lucky, thought Step.

They found three crickets that had crept down into Robbie's sheets, which meant that DeAnne would not think of anything less than stripping down all the beds and changing the sheets—even the top bunk, Stevie's bed, where no cricket could possibly have reached. But finally it was done. All the crickets were gone, or at least if there were any left they had the sense to stay out of sight and not chirp. DeAnne proposed bathing the kids again but Step told her to forget it. "These weren't dung beetles, honey, they were crickets, and let's let the kids get back to sleep."

They already *were* asleep, sprawled in a tangle on top of Step's and DeAnne's bed, but one by one Step carried them back to their rooms and DeAnne tucked them into bed. In moments they were sleeping again.

"Wouldn't it be nice," Step said to DeAnne as she tucked Betsy into her clean sheets, "wouldn't it be nice if all the bad things in life could happen in their sleep and we could make them go away without them ever knowing what happened?"

"I've got to wash," said DeAnne. "I can still feel cricket feet all over me." She shuddered. "I'm surprised I didn't go into labor."

Now that she mentioned it, he still felt the tickling of those tiny feet, and it got worse the more he thought about it. "You get the first shower," he said, "but make it snappy."

She didn't make it snappy, but he understood. When it was his turn, he had to soap himself up and rinse himself off three times before he finally felt clean enough to dry off and go to bed. And even then, he inspected the sheets, though no cricket had jumped on their bed and he knew it, he *knew* it, but he still had to look. He had to be sure.

"Tomorrow, the exterminators," he said as he finally pulled the covers up over him.

"Yes," she said, "I already thought of that. I'll call Bappy to find out if they have some kind of contract, like with Terminex or somebody."

The next morning he was late to work, of course, later than usual, because he had lost so much sleep the night before. He came in to find a memo sitting on top of his desk. It was from Ray Keene, and even though it was addressed to everybody, Step knew that it was aimed at him.

> It has come to my attention that some employees have been abusing our relaxed attitude toward work hours. Therefore a new policy is instituted beginning tomorrow. All employees must be at their work stations promptly at eight-thirty. Lunch is to be taken from twelve noon to twelve-thirty, the only exceptions being that those who must work the telephones will be assigned half-hour shifts between 11:30 and 1:00. Anyone arriving even five minutes late in the morning or taking a lunch even five minutes over thirty minutes will be dismissed on the spot. The only exceptions are for medical reasons or genuine, documented family emergencies.

Step wanted to storm into Dicky's office and call him every name he could think of. But he couldn't. If only Arkasian had come through. If only Step had a contract with somebody else, a way to get out of this place. It would be such a joy to tell Dicky Northanger exactly what he thought of him. Instead, Step put the memo into his attaché case, locked it again, and then headed for the pit.

The pit was silent when Step came in, and for a moment he thought that they all blamed him for this. But their silence, he realized, was because Dicky was in the room, leaning over the shoulder of one of the programmers. Since Dicky rarely came into the pit, this was in itself significant—but then, perhaps Dicky was doing it in order to stifle the outrage that they were all no doubt feeling. Well, that was fine with Step. The longer Dicky hung around in the pit, the more their anger would focus on him instead of on Step.

"Glass," said Step. "I need you in my office, if you can. I'm having some trouble with the way hyphenation is handled and I think there's a system to it that you can explain to me." They had worked all of this out the week before, but Dicky certainly wouldn't know that.

It didn't matter. "Glass will *not* go into your office right now," said Dicky. "And there is no reason for you to be in the pit. Glass is helping me work with my programming staff, and that takes precedence over anything the manual-writing staff needs. In fact, you should make a list of your questions and leave them on my desk, and I will get the answers *for* you. The programming staff has been inclined to goof off, and I am not allowing any further distractions."

"Documentation is not a distraction, Dicky," said Step.

"No, it's not," said Dicky. "But people walking into the programming center and talking loudly *are* a distraction, and I won't have it. Leave your questions on my desk."

Step stood there a moment, looking at him, and then he thought: We didn't get all the crickets last night. There's one left, waiting to jump on me the second he thinks I'm not watching. Well, Dicky, I'm a champion cricket killer. I'm an expert at it. And if I can slaughter those crook-legged hordes, I can handle one lone whining fiddler like you.

Step went back to his office and wrote a memo.

> *Dear Ray,*
> *Dicky has barred me from the pit, and wants me to funnel all my questions for the programmers through him. If that's the way you want it, fine with me. But if that isn't the way you want me to do my job, then the change will have to come from you.*

Step signed it and carried it to Ray's secretary, Ludy. "Is Ray in?" he asked.

"Yes, but he's not seeing anyone," she said.

"Does he have anyone in there with him?"

She looked a little startled. "Step, I can't see that that's really any of your business."

"I just wanted to know if, when I walk in there and lay this memo on his desk, I'm going to be embarrassing him in front of someone else or not."

Ludy didn't blink an eye, and her smile didn't fade. "Compared to barging into his office, Step, embarrassing him in front of somebody else is hardly going to be a problem. I really advise you against it."

"Well, then, tell me what else I can do to make sure he gets my memo. I've written him a couple of dozen memos about different things since I've been here, and as far as I know he's never got them. He never answers them anyway, and the only time he ever phoned me was yesterday when he knew perfectly well that I wasn't in."

Ludy reached her hand closer to him across her desk; if he had been sitting by her, the gesture probably would have been a touch on the arm. "Step, he gets all your memos."

"Cross your heart?"

She smiled. "And hope to die."

He handed her the memo. "And you might tell him that if he doesn't answer this one, he's going to be looking for a new manual writer."

"I'll tell him," she said, "that you'd really appreciate an answer as soon as it's convenient. That way, if he does want to send an answer, you'll be around to receive it." She winked at him.

"You've got a twitch in your eye." Then he winked back. Ludy rolled her eyes, and he left.

When DeAnne called Bappy to find out about what exterminator to call, he seemed almost excited. "I do that myself!" he crowed. "I worked for one of them companies way back and I've kept up! I'll be right over, and you just make sure all the containers in your kitchen is closed up tight."

"The kitchen?" she asked. "Do you have to spray stuff in the kitchen?"

"That's where the bugs like to be best, where the food is," he said. "And you best get the kids out of the house while I'm doing it."

She had plans for today. And Step had taken the car, since he was so late to work. Maybe she could take the kids over to Jenny's house. And most of her work could wait. Mostly checkbook balancing, not that there was much to balance. She could do it after Bappy was done. And her little hope of perhaps taking a nap at the same time as the children, to make up for last night's lost sleep—well, she had scheduled naps before, but she didn't often get to actually take them, and that was OK, it was part of the territory. Part of the never-ending struggle to get organized. When she finally got organized, there'd *be* time for naps. "How long will it take?" she asked.

"Couple hours," said Bappy. "Got to get under the house and up in the attic, you know. Do it right. You said you already got the place plugged where they came up through?"

"With old socks is all," said DeAnne.

"'Bout what I'd use myself, anyway," said Bappy. "Just so it's plugged. Anyways, two hours after I'm done the stuff will all be settled and then y'all can come on back into the house and open up the windows and air it out. But don't you be thinking of coming back too soon. Got to take care of your precious burden."

It took her just a moment to realize that her "precious burden" was the baby, who even now was pressing hard against the distended wall of her stomach. Well, she didn't need Bappy to tell her that she shouldn't be inhaling bug-killer when you never could tell what might cross the placenta. And she didn't want her older kids to be breathing it straight into their lungs, either.

She called Jenny, who really sounded delighted about having sudden all-day company, and when Bappy pulled into the driveway in his pickup truck and started pulling what looked like scuba gear out of the back, DeAnne gave him the spare housekey, shouldered an extra-heavy diaper bag, and led the kids off on the walk to the Cowpers' house.

DeAnne had driven Stevie to school this morning, but, knowing that Step would be late enough getting up that he'd need the car to get to work, she told Stevie to take the schoolbus home. He would have no idea that the house was being fumigated. It was only eleven o'clock, so maybe they'd be back in the house before the schoolbus dropped Stevie off—but maybe not. She'd have to make a point of being there to meet him. She hated the idea of any of her children ever, even once, coming home to an empty house.

Life in Jenny Cowper's house was hard for DeAnne, at first. Chaos bothered her, the children running every which way, yelling at each other or coming in at odd intervals to scream out a report of some disaster to Jenny, who, likely as not, said, "Thanks for telling me, dear," and then did nothing. At first DeAnne was horrified at how lackadaisical Jenny was about her children's safety. And when DeAnne saw Jenny's five-year-old sitting on top of the crossbar of the swing set in the back yard, riding it like a pony, she could not restrain herself. "Jenny, you've got to *do* something."

Jenny looked up at her and smiled. "Like what, staple his feet to the ground? The first time he climbed up there I nearly had a heart attack, but the fact is that he's a good climber and he never falls. I've watched him, and he's careful. So I figure, he's going to climb, and better if he does it where I can see him, where he can show off to me, instead of doing it when I'm *not* watching. Now *that's* dangerous. So we have a deal—he can climb up there, but only when I'm watching."

"Forgive me, Jenny," said DeAnne, "but you're *not* watching. You're talking to me."

Jenny laughed. "OK, then, I'm listening. If there's a scream, I know I need to do something."

"There've been fifty screams already."

"I know, but they weren't the kind of scream you worry about. And half of them were you, anyway, DeAnne."

"Did I scream?"

"This little high-pitched scream, yes. I know you think I'm the worst kind of mother, and I'll tell you, I used to be like you. After my kids all the time. Hovering over them."

"Do I hover?"

"Don't you?" asked Jenny.

"I want them safe," she said. "If something happened to them . . ."

"But things *will* happen to them. You think just because you're watching them, stopping them from having any fun, they won't still break their arms or split their lips? And what are you going to do when your Elizabeth starts dating, make it so she never gets a broken heart? God gave our children *life,* and it's not our place to take it away from them just because we're afraid. That's what I think."

It sounded so sensible, so wise. And yet, and yet. "What about this missing child?" DeAnne said, pointing to the newspaper.

"Isn't that awful?" said Jenny. "And there was that other one I told you about not six months ago. I tell you, you see those faces on the milk cartons, and you think, there's some mother out there, and one day she looked for her little boy and called his name and he didn't answer, and she went out and called and called, and he didn't answer, and then all of a sudden it comes into her heart that he never will, he'll never answer her again, and oh, DeAnne, doesn't it tear your heart out?"

"Yes," said DeAnne. "He was just walking over to his friend's house, three doors away, and he never got there."

"And that mother's going to blame herself, DeAnne, I know she is," said Jenny. "She's going to say, If only I had watched him. Walked out in the front yard and watched him till he went in the front door of that house."

"Yes," said DeAnne. "Yes, and she's *right!*"

"No she isn't," said Jenny. "Because inside that house there could have been a gun with bullets in it, and so what should she have done about that, stood over him the whole time he was playing? Forbid him ever to go to a friend's house? Lock him in his room? Do you think that the boy wouldn't have *known* that his mother was watching? That she didn't trust him to get from his house to a friend's house *three doors away?*"

"But he *couldn't!*"

"This time he couldn't," said Jenny. "But maybe

he's already done it a hundred times. Like when your kids learn to walk, you don't hold their hand anymore, they get to a point where you just let go of their hand and they walk by themselves. Do you think that means they never fall down again?"

"Turning up missing isn't quite the same thing as falling down."

"Do you think I don't know that? Do you think I don't know that one moment of carelessness and my Aaron could be lying there under the swing set with a broken neck? Dead or paralyzed for the rest of his life? Do you think I don't have a stab of fear go through my heart when I see him up there?"

"Then why do you let him?"

"Why does God let us live on this earth?" asked Jenny. "Why doesn't he come down and watch every move we make and keep us from ever, ever, ever doing anything wrong? Because we can't grow up if somebody's doing that. We can't *become* anything. We'd be *puppets.*"

DeAnne didn't know how to answer. Anguish was twisting her inside. Partly it was the newspaper story about the mother of that little lost boy. Partly it was the strain of not being in her own home, of having her kids playing with these wild hellions that Jenny was raising so free. Partly it was what Stevie had gone through at school for weeks and weeks, without DeAnne having any idea. It was Dolores LeSueur taking him aside and sowing the seeds of some terrible life-sucking weed in his mind, and by the time DeAnne knew about it, the seeds had already taken root, and there was nothing she could do except hope that Stevie's native goodness and common sense would help him get rid of those thoughts on his own.

"I just can't *stop* watching out for them," said DeAnne, "even though I know that I can't protect them from everything. I *know* that. I know that they're out of my protection for so much of the time. Stevie at school, and when I'm out of the room even. Anything could happen. But I can still do something, I can still try."

"For what it's worth, DeAnne, I actually *do* step in and stop my kids from doing really dangerous stuff," said Jenny. "It's just my, um, my threshold isn't as low as yours is."

"Jenny, I'm not talking about you now," said DeAnne. "I'm talking about me. Because I know you're right, and I'm just—I don't want to overprotect my children and turn them into frightened little hamsters in the corner of a box. But I can do *something*. I can maybe save them *sometimes*, can't I? It's like my neighbor across the street in Orem. There was this guy with a pickup truck who used to roar down the street, going too fast, and she just hated it, and her husband even spoke to him about it but he just laughed and told him to drop dead. So one evening, it's dusk, you know, when it's dark enough that you can't really see anymore but you still *can*, sort of, and she realizes, I've let the children play too late, I've got to get them all into the house, and she goes outside and she's calling out for them and then she hears that truck turn the corner and gun the motor and there's the headlights coming down the street and then she hears the sound of her son's Hot Wheels on the asphalt of the street. Not on the sidewalk, on the asphalt, and she thinks, he's in the street, he's going to die, and sure enough, there's her son tooling across the road, his legs churning, and there's the truck, and she knows the truck will never see the boy in time to stop, and her son is twenty yards to her right, much too far for her to run to him in time, and the truck is coming from the left, and he'll never hear her shouting at him, not with that engine, and so without even thinking about it she just steps into the road in front of the truck. Just steps into the road."

"Good heavens," said Jenny.

"And the truck guy saw her and he slammed on his brakes and it turned out that he really *could* stop in time, but then *she* was a full-sized person, who knows whether he would have seen her little boy? And he gets out of his truck just yelling and cussing at her, you know, what kind of idiot are you, and she just stood there crying and crying until finally the guy sees the little kid pull up to his mom on his Hot Wheels, right there in the middle of the road, and the guy realizes that he never saw the little kid until right that minute, and he says, 'My God,' and they didn't have any trouble with him speeding down that road anymore."

"I don't know if I could have done that," said Jenny. "I would have stood there on the curb and screamed or something. I don't know if I could have just . . . stepped into the road."

"She didn't know either, till she did it," said DeAnne.

"Well of course you save your kid from a speeding car," said Jenny. "Even a lousy mother like me would try to do *that!* But what she did—I mean, that's beyond love, that's all the way into crazy. What if the truck *couldn't* stop? What does that do to the little boy, seeing his mother killed right in front of his eyes? And he grows up without his mom."

"He grows up knowing that his mom gave her life to save his. That's got to help."

"Or he feels guilty all his life because he feels like it's his fault she died. DeAnne, I'm not saying she was wrong—I mean, she was *right* because it all worked out. But even saving his life, she might also do harm. Anything can do harm, anything might work. Well, not *anything,* but you know what I mean. Maybe you're right to be so protective, and maybe I'm right to run a looser ship. Maybe maybe maybe."

"So no matter what we do, we're probably wrong."

"No, DeAnne, don't think of it that way. Think of it that no matter what we do, as long as we're trying to do our very best for our kids, it will work out. Maybe they'll get hurt. Maybe they'll grow up so mad at us that they don't speak to us for twenty years. Maybe they'll get *killed*—that's part of life. It's the worst thing in the world, to lose a child. At least I can't think of anything worse. But it happens. And when the child dies, God takes him into his home the same way that he takes old people who die. I mean, even if his life was short, it was life, and was it good? Was he happy? Did he have a chance to taste it, to choose things for himself, to—"

"I know," said DeAnne. Despite her loathing for herself when she was weak enough to cry in front of someone else, her tears started flowing. Just thinking of children dying, and the mother whose son was lost today, and her friend in Orem who knew, *knew,* that she would give her life for her child. And Stevie. "I'm sorry. It's just . . . what we've been going through for the past while with Stevie . . . ever since we moved here. I've just felt so *helpless.* And now things are going to be OK with him, because Step went to school and took care of it, I mean things are going to be *fine* now, if he can just get rid of these imaginary friends. So why am I crying *now?* Why do I just feel shaky and cold and—"

Jenny slid her chair over next to DeAnne's and put her arms around her and DeAnne cried into her shoulder. "You can't stop bad things from happening," said Jenny softly. "That's why you're crying. You think I didn't ever have a day like this? *Days* like this? And then I came out of it and I realized that I can only do what's possible, and I stopped expecting myself to make life perfect for my kids, perfectly happy, perfectly safe. They cry sometimes, they hurt sometimes, and it still tears me up inside, but I can only do what I can do, and that's what you've got to realize too, DeAnne. I saw that the day I met you, that you just expect too much of yourself, and so you're bound to fail all the time, because you don't count it as success unless you've done what nobody can do."

It sounded so good, so comforting, and yet DeAnne didn't believe it. Oh, she knew that she spent too much time feeling like a failure, Jenny was right about *that*. But Jenny was wrong when she responded to it by deciding not to try very hard anymore. How could you ever learn to be perfect if you didn't try to reach beyond yourself and do more than you could do? And then the Lord would take you the rest of the way. Wouldn't he? If she honestly did everything she could possibly do, then the Lord would do the rest, and things would work out, the way they were finally working out for Stevie. Because you had to *try*.

But she would be less protective. She would try to do that, too. Jenny was right about that. Kids had to have a chance to be kids. Like when she was a girl and played in the orchard behind her house. It was dangerous back there, with old metal equipment and wires and things lying around, especially along the irrigation ditches, and she and her friends did crazy things. She had climbed much higher into cherry trees than little Aaron Cowper ever got on the swing set. And those were wonderful times and wonderful years. She couldn't let her children miss out on that, just because their mother felt so afraid for them. But she also couldn't sit back and get so—so *distant* from what her children were doing and feeling. It just wasn't in her.

"You are the kindest person," DeAnne said, withdrawing from Jenny's embrace. She wiped her eyes on a paper napkin from the kitchen table. The paper was rough on the tender skin of her eyelids. "I really wasn't coming over here to cry my eyes out," she said. "I came over because an old man is spraying bug poison in my kitchen."

"And if I know you at all," said Jenny, "you're going to throw away every box of cold cereal that was open. In fact, I'll bet you even throw away the ones that were closed, because you won't be able to convince yourself that the bug spray didn't get through the cardboard or something."

DeAnne had to laugh. "Jenny, I already *did* throw them away. Before he even got there. Isn't that stupid?"

"It's just you, DeAnne. And one thing you are *not* is stupid. Why, you're the teacher who finally gave the women in the Steuben 1st Ward permission not to pretend to worship their husbands in that sicky-icky way that Dolores LeSueur does. I mean, you stood up to the she-spider right in her own web."

"I think that *proves* that I'm stupid," said DeAnne.

The tumult outside spilled back into the house and it was time to fix lunch. About two o'clock, when DeAnne finally had her kids down for their naps—and Robbie actually went right to sleep; he had run around so much with Jenny's kids that he had worn himself out—she headed back over to her own house to see if Bappy was done and the smell was gone. Then she realized that she should have gone over at noon to see when he actually finished, so she'd know when the two hours were up. But no, he had left a note on the side door:

Finished at noon. Key on table.

Such a thoughtful man.

Thoughtful, but dead wrong about how long it would take for the poison to settle out of the air. Her eyes stung when she went inside. The stink was awful. She fled back outside, leaving the door open behind her. She could smell it from here. It wasn't going to go away, either, not if she left the house closed up tight.

She ran back inside and held her breath the whole time she was rinsing a dishtowel and wringing it out. Then she held it over her mouth and nose as she went through the house, opening all the windows and doors. The living room windows didn't have screens, so she couldn't very well leave *them* open. Nor could she bring herself to leave the doors standing open, even with the screen doors closed. Of course a serious burglar could easily get through any of the windows, so why not leave the doors open? But she just couldn't do it.

She left the dishtowel hanging over the inside knob of the side door that led to the carport, and then went out to the street to wait for Stevie's schoolbus.

Immediately after lunch, Dicky appeared in the doorway of Step's office. Step thought at first that he was there to make sure that he hadn't stayed out longer than his allotted half hour, and maybe that was part of the reason, but the main reason was to deliver a message. "Ray seems to think that you can't do your work properly unless you have unrestricted contact with the programmers, and in fact I agree with him."

Of course you do, thought Step.

"So you can go back to visiting them in the pit," said Dicky. "But I'd appreciate it if you held your distractions to a minimum."

"Sure, Dicky," said Step.

"And I'd still like a report from you on everything you ask them about."

"That's a wonderful idea, Dicky. That will cut my productivity almost in half, I'd say, if I not only have to *do* my work, but also have to write a detailed report of all of it for you."

"Nevertheless," said Dicky.

"When hell freezes over," said Step cheerfully. "My report to you on each project is the finished manual."

Dicky stood there, looking at him with that steady, animal-like gaze of his, showing no more expression than a sheep. At last he left.

I shouldn't have goaded him, thought Step. I shouldn't have pushed.

But it felt good to push. It felt good to know that Ray Keene still thought Step, or at least Step's role in the company, was valuable enough to put Dicky in his place. It was Dicky who had pushed too far this time, not Step, not Step at all. Besides, Dicky still had his victory over the schedule.

A few minutes later, Step was in the pit, so the guys could see exactly how short a time Dicky had been able to make his absurd restriction stick. As soon as he came in, one of the programmers murmured, "Dicky check," and a couple of them got up and sauntered out into the halls for a moment. "No Dicky," they reported. Immediately they all turned their chairs to face the center of the room. It was as if they had been waiting for Step to show up in order to have a meeting.

Step plunged right in. "Guys," he said, "I'm sorry. I think this schedule thing is all my fault, because I took that late lunch hour yesterday and threw it in Dicky's face."

"Screw all that," said Glass. "Dicky's not a force of nature or something. He does what he does because he chooses to, not because of anything *you* did."

"He does what he does because he's an asshole," said one of the programmers.

"So the thing is this," said Glass. "If they're going to make us show up at eight-thirty and take lunches exactly one damn half-hour long, then our response is obvious."

"We quit," said one.

"We burn the place down," said another.

"Nothing that dramatic," said Glass. "In fact, it's simple and it's elegant. We leave at five."

They sat there looking at him, and then they all began smiling and chuckling and some of them pantomimed slapping their knees.

"Five sharp," said Glass. "Every night. In the middle of a line of code, if need be. Save your work, shut down, and leave this place dark at five oh one. Everybody agreed?"

"With all my heart," said Step. The others echoed him.

"One for all and all for one," said Glass.

"Now," said Step, "everyone back on your heads."

Step was home by five-fifteen. He found a note on the side door:

Pls chk to see if bug spray still bad. At Cowpers'.

When he went inside, the stench was unbearable. He felt like he could taste it, it was so intense. The house was a bit chilly—it was going to be a cool night, and there was already a stiff breeze. If it rains, Step thought, all these open windows are going to mean soaked carpets and furniture. But we can't close them, either. Just have to keep watch on the sky.

No way will we be able to sleep here tonight.

He set the lock on the front-door screen and left the door open. Maybe somebody could break in and steal everything, but they could do that with the windows open anyway, and the living room just wasn't airing out at all—when he went in there his eyes stung. Then he closed and locked the side door, got back in the car, and drove to the Cowpers'.

"You're home so early again," said DeAnne, happy to see him.

"Maybe from now on," said Step. "Unless they back down. But I can never be late again in the morning." He kissed her. Jenny Cowper was standing right there watching, but Step only waved as he kissed DeAnne again.

"Don't mind me," said Jenny. "I already guessed that you two knew about kissing."

"We're still beginners at it," said Step, "so we need all the practice we can get." Jenny laughed and then went back into the kitchen or somewhere.

"How did things go with Stevie?" asked Step.

"Not what we expected," said DeAnne. "A substitute."

"Ah," said Step. "So she couldn't face it."

"And Stevie came home with his ribbon. Mrs. Jones must have said *something* to Dr. Mariner, because she came into class today and said something about—"

But at that moment several children charged into the room. Robbie and two unidentified Cowper children—Step hadn't even bothered to *try* to tell them apart; they all looked like identical twins of different ages. Stevie followed, carrying a book. Not part of the game, apparently. But at least he was talking.

"Hi, Dad."

"I hear you had a substitute today."

He nodded. Step squatted in front of him, then realized that his knees didn't respond well to that position anymore, and he knelt on one knee. "Hear you got your ribbon."

"I didn't care about the ribbon," said Stevie.

"Well, I guess Dr. Mariner *did*."

Then Stevie looked Step in the eye and said, "Did you kill Mrs. Jones?"

"No!" Step said, appalled. "No, of course not! I didn't touch her, I didn't hurt her at all. Son, she stayed home today because she's *ashamed*."

Stevie didn't look convinced. "Dr. Mariner said she was sick. She said Mrs. Jones wouldn't be coming back the rest of the school year and our substitute would be our teacher from now on."

Mrs. Jones had taken the coward's way out, after all. She could be bold as brass when it came to heaping scorn on a seven-year-old in front of his classmates, but when it came to making up for it a little, she just couldn't face it. Well, too bad.

"Dad," said Stevie, "what did you *do* to her?"

DeAnne, realizing that they needed some privacy for this, herded Robbie and the Cowper creatures out of the living room. Thanks, DeAnne, Step said silently. "Door Man, all I did was tell her the truth about what she was doing, and I made it clear that if she didn't stop, I was going to tell the truth to everybody else, too. So she stopped. In fact, she stopped so completely that I wouldn't be surprised if she never teaches again, even after this year."

"Wow," Stevie whispered.

"I mean, that's what you do with bad people, when you can. You just name their sin to them. That's what the prophets always did," said Step. "Just name their sins, and if they have any spark of goodness in them at all, they repent. Maybe she's going to repent."

"What if they're bad all the way through? What if they got no spark?"

"Well, it's like Alma and Amulek. The Lord wouldn't let the evil people harm them, even though a lot of other people got killed. They finished giving their message and then they left."

"The bad guys burned Abinadi," said Stevie.

"Yes," said Step. "But not until he finished naming their sins. And that's what eventually stopped the wicked people from doing their wickedness. Telling the truth about them. They can only do their evil when they think that nobody knows."

"But Abinadi was *dead*."

"Son, I guess he knew and the Lord knew that death isn't the worst thing in the world. The worst thing in the world is knowing that something really bad is going on and then not doing anything about it because you're afraid. So when Abinadi died, death tasted sweet to him."

"*Burning* to death?"

"No, I don't think *that* was sweet. But then it was over, and he went to live with his Father in Heaven. Anyway, Stevie, that isn't the point. Nobody was going to burn me to death for telling the truth about Mrs.

Jones. I'm no Abinadi, I was just a very angry father of a very wonderful son who had been treated very badly and now it's over. Mrs. Jones won't be able to hurt you ever again, and my guess is that she won't be able to hurt *any*body."

Stevie threw his arms around Step's neck and clung to him for a long time. Then Stevie pulled away and took off out of the room, probably a bit embarrassed.

Step got up and wandered into the kitchen and joined in the conversation there. "You're going to sleep on our bed because you're pregnant, DeAnne," said Jenny.

"*I'm* not," said Step.

"Uh-oh," said Spike. "Hyper-courtesy alert."

"Oh, please," said Jenny. "We all know how this conversation goes. You protest that Step can sleep on the floor while DeAnne sleeps on the couch, only you both know perfectly well that DeAnne would wake up perfectly dead if she did that and *we'd* feel so guilty we couldn't sleep a wink. Besides, what you don't realize is that Spike and I went *camping* on our honeymoon."

"There's a way to zip two bags together," said Spike, in a confidential tone. "I'll show you sometime."

"It does *not* hurt our feelings to sleep in sleeping bags on the floor," said Jenny. "We actually find it romantic, not that anyone who knew our kids would think we needed any more romantic opportunities. So please, let's just skip the arguing part and all agree right now, you on the bed and us in the bag."

Step and DeAnne were laughing, and DeAnne said, "That's just fine."

It wasn't until about nine that night, with the children bedded down, that DeAnne realized that she had never even checked the mail.

"We can always get it tomorrow," said Step.

"Or we could take a walk over there tonight," said DeAnne. "And check on the house while we're at it."

Why not? The Cowper house was so intensely extroverted that Step was glad for a chance to get away for a while.

On the way to the mailbox he told her what had passed between Stevie and him. "So I guess we've finally gotten over the hump," he said. "Stevie's going to be fine."

"I hope," said DeAnne.

"You only *hope?*"

"Today when he got off the bus, I started to explain to him about the bug spray and how we couldn't get in the house, and finally he says to me, 'I know, Mom. Jack already told me about it.'"

The imaginary friends. "Well, I suppose we couldn't expect them to just suddenly go away."

"I'm worried, Step. He's way too old to have an imaginary friend. And besides, who ever heard of somebody having more than one? I mean, aren't imaginary friends supposed to be like Snuffy on Sesame Street? Just one big strange creature or something?"

"Give him some time," said Step. "As things get better at school, he'll let go of this fantasy life. I mean, let's face it—these imaginary friends got him through what amounts to a concentration camp experience. Let's not be too quick to kill them off!"

"It's not a joke, Step," said DeAnne. "Stevie just absolutely refuses to admit that they're pretend. I think he really believes in them."

"So what if he does? The fantasy wouldn't have done him much good if it hadn't seemed real."

"But these imaginary friends *aren't* real, Step, and what if they don't go away? What if he insists on having one of these imaginary friends as the best man at his wedding? It's going to start interfering with his social life sometime, you know."

"But not today," said Step. "Give him some slack. He's just come out of hell into daylight, and it takes a while to shake off the shadows."

They were at the mailbox. Step opened it and checked for spiders, as he always did, ever since the black widow had scooted right up his sleeve when he was getting the mail one time in Orem. He had never known that you really could rip all the buttons off your shirt in one smooth movement and tear a whole shirt off your body in less than a second. It hadn't bit him, but he hadn't forgotten, either.

DeAnne started tilting the letters so she could see the return addresses under the streetlight. "We can take them inside," said Step. "We do live here."

"I'm not going in there again till that stink is gone," said DeAnne.

"The Cowpers aren't going to be thrilled about having us live with them forever, you know," said Step.

"They might. I was very helpful today with the housework. Here's one from your brother." She tore it open and started scanning it.

"You know what Spike Cowper said to me?" said Step. "He said, I know you folks need a car, and we've got this ugly beat-up rusted-out Datsun B-210, it runs fine but it's so ugly we'll never get what it's worth. So why don't you take it off my hands? Five hundred bucks. And I said, We can't afford anything right now. And he said, So we'll send you our address, and you pay us when you can."

"I hope you said yes," said DeAnne.

"You think I'm an idiot? I almost kissed him. I can take the Datsun to work, and you can keep the wagon."

"It'll feel like emancipation day," she said. "I think your brother's letting you know that he needs you to pay him back the money we borrowed for the move."

"Blood from a stone," said Step. "I'll call him. He's probably just afraid that we've forgotten we owe it to him."

"I didn't make the house payment in Indiana this month," said DeAnne.

"I didn't think we could anyway," said Step.

"This is the second month in a row," said DeAnne. "I don't think we're going to be able to make up these missed payments unless we get a surprise royalty check or something."

"I know—I'll ask Ray Keene for a raise. No, I'll ask *Dicky* for a raise."

She held out the last envelope to him. A big manila envelope. "Agamemnon," she said.

"You're kidding," said Step. He tore it open.

"I can't believe we're reading our mail out here on the street," said DeAnne, looking around the neighborhood. There was nobody outside.

"Isn't that what everybody does when their house has been turned into a gas chamber?" asked Step. "It's the contract. Arkasian came through."

"Took him long enough," said DeAnne.

"It just *felt* like a long time. It's only been a few weeks. In fact, he probably did this right away and it just took this long to process it." He looked up from the letter. "You know, Fish Lady, if you had got the mail at the regular time and called me and told me this was here, I would have quit my job right then, before lunch, and that would have been really stupid and totally unnecessary, because after lunch things got better again at work. I mean, it was a really lucky thing that you *didn't* get the mail then. Because I really can't quit yet, not until I know whether Eight Bits Inc. is going to do IBM games or not."

"Lucky thing," said DeAnne.

"Yeah, right," said Step. He put his arms around her, there under the streetlight, each holding handfuls of mail behind the other's back. "Maybe the Lord really is looking out for us a little bit."

"Or maybe the law of averages said it was about time," said DeAnne.

"Yeah, well, who do you think *wrote* the law of

averages?" He kissed her and they headed back to the Cowpers' house. As they walked away, Step stole a look back at the house, wondering whether Stevie's imaginary friends had also been driven out by the insecticide.

8

·SHRINK·

This is how it happened that Step found a psychiatrist for Stevie, even though he had vowed that he would never take his son to one of those charlatans.

Not that Step had anything against psychiatrists individually. Their best friends in grad school in Vigor had been Larry and Sheila Redmond; Larry was a fellow history student, while Sheila was just starting a private practice as a psychotherapist. Step had made himself obnoxious, teasing her about how she had gone into the ministry. "The only difference between psychotherapists and ministers is that psychotherapists charge more, and more people believe in their brand of miracle cure."

Sheila took it all in good humor—after all, patience was the mark of a good therapist—and, because of her,

Step had to admit to himself that even though he thought all psychological theories were nothing more than competing sects in a secular religion of self-obsession, it was still possible that an individual therapist might do genuine good for a patient, much the same way that a good friend might help someone who was going through inner turmoil. And even the money angle began to make sense to him when he remembered that in America, people tended to think that anything with a high price tended to be worth more—so that paying a whole lot of money to have someone listen to you and apply meaningless theories to your troubles would feel more valuable and therefore provide more solace than getting nonsense advice from a friend for free.

But the one thing Step knew he would never do, despite his new tolerance for the possibility of helpful therapy, was take one of his children to one of those witch doctors. "Why should we?" said Step to DeAnne. "If we took him to a Freudian, we'd find out that he wanted to kill me and sleep with you. A Jungian would link up his imaginary friends to the collective unconscious and some kind of dual hero myth. A Skinnerian would try to get him to perk up and smile at the ringing of a bell. And the new drug guys would dope him up and he'd sleep through the rest of his life."

"We're out of our depth," said DeAnne. "And we need help."

"So does that mean we put our faith in the theories of men," said Step, "instead of trusting in what we *claim* we believe in? Is Stevie a physical machine, genes acting out the script we gave him? Or is he an eternal intelligence, responsible for his own actions? Do we try to help our own son find his own way out of his own problems? Or do we pay for a therapist to teach him strange new lies to believe in?"

DeAnne looked at him coldly, then, and said, "We're not Christian Scientists, you know."

"And psychiatrists aren't doctors, either," said Step.

"Yes they are," said DeAnne.

"Having an M.D. doesn't make you a *doctor*," said Step. "People on the waiting lists at clinics get better at exactly the same rate as the people who are being treated."

"I read that article, too," said DeAnne. "But I also noticed that the clinics seemed to do no *harm*. And maybe if we take Stevie to a doctor he'll realize how much we care about him."

"He'll realize that we think he's crazy," said Step.

"He plays with imaginary friends," said DeAnne.

"And psychiatrists cost thousands of dollars," said Step, knowing that his secret weapon in any argument with DeAnne was to say that they could not afford it.

"Ninety dollars," said DeAnne.

He realized how very serious she was about it. "You've already checked."

"On the cost, yes," said DeAnne. "I went to Jenny's pediatrician, Dr. Greenwald, and he gave me the names of three child psychiatrists in Steuben, and I called them all and asked what they were charging and it's ninety dollars an hour. The only question now is whether the insurance from Eight Bits Inc. will cover a psychiatrist."

"It won't."

"You won't even ask about it?"

And then it was Step's turn to confess. "I already did."

She laughed, but she was angry. "You hypocrite."

"You've been hinting around about this ever since you noticed these imaginary friends," said Step. "I knew you were going to want to do it, and I had to know whether it would be covered. And it won't."

She looked at him, wanting to say something really dangerous—he knew the look, knew she was deciding whether it was worth the fight that would ensue if she said what was on her mind.

He saved her the trouble of deciding. "You're about to accuse me of lying about it," said Step.

"I was not!" she said.

"You were deciding whether or not to tell me that you were going to call Eight Bits Inc. and find out for yourself if it's covered."

"That's not calling you a liar," she said. "That's checking to make sure. What if they thought you meant adult psychiatric treatment, and that's not covered, but psychiatric treatment for children *is.*"

"Oh, I see. It's not that I'm a liar, it's that I'm so incompetent that I can't carry on an effective conversation with another adult. You have to check up to see if I missed a little thing like that."

"People can make mistakes!" she said.

"Yes, ma'am, they certainly can," said Step, and he started to leave the room.

"Don't do that!" she shouted at him.

"Don't do what?" he asked.

"Don't walk out on me."

The words hung in the air.

"There's a world of difference," said Step, "between walking out on *you* and walking out of a *room.* I'm walking out of a room right now." She started to say something, but he didn't give her a chance. "Right *now,*" he said.

He opened the bedroom door and went into the hall and realized that Robbie and Betsy were playing quietly in Robbie's room, not in the family room as he had thought. Step and DeAnne had raised their voices during this argument—did the children hear? "Hi, kids," he said. "What brings you back here?"

"Stevie told us to get out."

"Are you fine here?"

"Yes."

But Robbie looked so solemn that Step knew that he had heard, that he was worried. "What's wrong, Road Bug?"

"Stevie doesn't like me anymore," said Robbie. His face twisted up to wring out his tears.

"Sure he does, Robot Man," said Step. He sat down by Robbie and put his arm around him. Betsy, of course, began to cry, too, since crying was getting Robbie so much attention from Daddy. Step put an arm around her, too, but his attention remained on Robbie. "Stevie's just having a hard time right now."

"What's so hard about it?" asked Robbie. "He just sits around and plays computer games or he plays with Jack and Scotty and he never plays with me."

"Jack and Scotty?" asked Step.

"He's always playing pirates with them, or playing train or something, and he won't play with me, and Betsy's no fun."

"No fun," said Betsy.

"I mean she's just a baby."

"Baby in Mommy's tummy," said Betsy.

"Road Bug, it's hard, you think I don't know that?" said Step. "Stevie's having a hard time at school and I think he's still a little mad at me for making him move. And so he needs to be by himself a lot."

"Then how come he's always playing with Scotty and Jack?" asked Robbie.

Step had to think for a minute. What in the world could he say to *that*? You have to understand, Robbie, that your brother is retreating from reality into a wonderful magical world full of good friends, which has only one drawback—none of the rest of humanity can get to that place.

"Robbie, can't you just be patient with Stevie for a little longer?" said Step. "He doesn't hate you. He loves you, he really does. He just isn't able to show it as much right now. A year from now you'll look back on this time and you'll say—"

"Don't say 'a year from now,'" said Robbie disgustedly.

"Why not?"

"That's what Mommy always says. 'A year from now you'll look back and laugh.'"

His imitation of DeAnne was dead on. Step had to laugh. "Can you do *my* voice?"

Robbie immediately deepened his voice and said, "Life's a bitch, ain't it?"

"Bitch," said Betsy.

Step was appalled. "I've never said that to you."

"No, you say it to Mom when you think we're not listening," said Robbie. He was very proud of himself.

"Well, now I know that you *are* listening," said Step.

"What's a bitch, Daddy?" asked Robbie.

"It's just a word for a mommy dog," said Step.

"Woof woof," said Betsy.

"Why did you say life's a mommy dog?" asked Robbie.

"That what a mommy dog say!" shouted Betsy. "Woof woof woof!"

"Believe me, Robbie, when you get older, you won't even have to ask. The answer will just come to you."

Step unfolded himself and stood up. DeAnne was standing in the doorway to the boys' room, jiggling with silent laughter. "If you hold all that laughter inside," said Step, "it might make the baby pop out."

She laughed all the harder—but still silently.

"Could it really make Mommy pop?" asked Robbie.

"No, Road Bug, I was joking," said Step.

"Why is it a joke when *I* don't think it's funny," said Robbie, "but when *I* tell a joke and *you* don't think it's funny, then you say, 'That's not a joke'?"

"Because I'm the official funny-decider of America," said Step. "Back in 1980 when they elected Ronald Reagan to be president, I got elected to be the national funny-decider, and so if I say it's a joke it's a joke, and if I say it isn't it isn't. Next year they'll elect somebody else, though, because I'm not running again."

"Is that true, Mommy?" asked Robbie.

"What do *you* think?" asked DeAnne, her eyes wide in a mockery of innocence.

"I bet this is a joke, too," said Robbie.

"You are right indeed, my brilliant boy," said Step.

"If Mommy's laughing does that mean you aren't going to yell at each other anymore?" asked Robbie.

At the word *yell,* Betsy opened her mouth and let out a full-throated holler.

"Betsy, don't do that!" said DeAnne. "They can hear you on the street. People will think we're child-abusers."

"We weren't yelling at each other," said Step.

"Yes you were," said Robbie.

"We were arguing because we didn't agree about something," said Step. "That happens sometimes. And maybe we got too loud because we both care very much about the thing we were discussing."

"What were you discussing?"

Thank heaven he didn't understand the actual words we said, thought Step. "We were talking about stuff that only grownups talk about."

Robbie chanted derisively: "Grown. Up. Grown, up."

"Yeah, well, someday *you'll* be a grownup and then you won't think it's so cute. Now play with your sister."

That's where they left the question of taking Stevie to a psychiatrist—nowhere. It was the first clause in article one of the unspoken constitution of their marriage: If they disagreed about something it was a tie vote, and no one had the power to break a tie, but they both had to promise to think about the other person's side. So Step was thinking about DeAnne's point of view, and DeAnne was thinking about Step's, but this time Step knew that he would never, never agree with her, and he knew that she would never see things his way, either.

Except that in the back of his mind, he knew that

he *would* see things her way. That somewhere in the future he would realize that they really *were* out of their depth in dealing with Stevie's problem, that Stevie wouldn't just give up on these imaginary friends, and Step would end up walking through the door of a psychiatrist's office one day, taking his own son to the witch doctor to get an incantation that would make the evil spirits go away. It made him angry to think about that, though, and so he put it to the back of his mind and hoped desperately that the whole issue would just stay there, would just go away along with Stevie's imaginary friends.

The memo finally came down from Ray Keene that it was time for all the creative staff to evaluate the IBM PC and come up with a recommendation. This is it, thought Step. This is what will decide whether I can sign the contract with Agamemnon, the big one that will let me quit this job and never see Dicky Northanger or Ray Keene again. As long as Eight Bits Inc. decides *not* to support the IBM machine.

And there were plenty of reasons not to support it. The biggest reason was that it was a crippled machine from the start. The operating system was a kludged-together imitation of CP/M; color graphics was only an option, and even if you paid some obscene amount extra to get it, all you got was four colors on the screen at a time, and it was no compensation that you could switch between a set of cool colors and a set of warm colors. The only sound came from a repulsive little onboard speaker that made you want to answer the door whenever it buzzed. It was like somebody had examined the Atari 800 and the Commodore 64 and said, "How can we strip these machines down so there is nothing left that would be remotely interesting to any human being?"

And that's what the other programmers were all saying. It would be easy enough for Step just to let their words go unchallenged. Dicky would take his negative report to Ray, the machine would be dropped, and Step would walk away clean.

Only he would not be clean. Because he knew that a failure to support the IBM PC would be the death knell, in the long run, for Eight Bits Inc. If he didn't speak the truth as he saw it during this time when Eight Bits Inc. was paying for his expertise, then he was a cheat and a liar, even if no one ever knew it, and Step couldn't live with that.

So he spoke up. "OK, it's crippled," said Step. "But it has one feature that no other microcomputer made today has."

"What's that?" asked Glass. His voice was full of challenge, since he was the most vociferous opponent of the PC.

Step pointed to the letters *IBM* on the case.

"What is *that!*" demanded Glass. "That's nothing!"

"That's everything," said Step. "That's a vast national sales force, that's *credibility,* that's reputation, that's big corporations being willing to spend a hundred thousand dollars or half a million dollars putting these things on people's desks."

"We don't do business software," said Dicky quietly.

"Business software will be done by somebody," said Step. "Somebody will do a terrific word processor loaded with features because you can put 256K of RAM in this thing, 512K, you can have a word processor that will stand up and dance if you want it to."

"Nobody will ever put 512K on this thing," said Glass. "You can't *fill* 512K with meaningful code!"

"Don't get mad at me, Glass," said Step. "I'm just telling you what I think. The machine's a piece of shit, but it's an IBM piece of shit, and where we're looking at maybe half a million 64's in use today, we'll see a million, two million, three million of these on people's desks."

"What does it matter what's on people's *desks*?" said Dicky contemptuously. "We don't do *business* software. We write programs for the home market."

"You think a businessman doesn't want to play a game now and then? You think a businessman doesn't want to have a real computer at home?"

"Not for this price," said Dicky. "Not when he can get a Commodore 64 with a printer and a monitor for half what he pays for this overpriced box alone."

It occurred to Step that by being honest he had accomplished what he really wanted. With Step firmly committed to voting *for* developing software for the IBM PC, Dicky would be even more firmly committed to killing any possibility of Eight Bits Inc. turning to the IBM. I couldn't have set it up better if I had planned it, he realized. So it was with a light heart that he said, "You're wrong, Dicky. We're going to see the IBM market take off until it's the *only* market."

"Except Apple," said Glass. "That piece-of-junk company just won't die no matter how useless its computers are."

"You're forgetting the Lisa," said Dicky. It was a joke, and so everybody laughed. The poor, pathetic Lisa, a vast overpriced machine whose only selling point was that it made pictures of your disk files instead of just giving them names—as if you needed a picture of a file folder to tell you that your file was a file! "Step probably thinks there'll be nothing around but the IBM and the Lisa."

"Make whatever recommendation you want," said Step. "I can't disagree with a single bad thing anybody's said about the IBM PC. Just tell Ray that I cast a dissenting vote, OK?"

"Oh, I'll be sure to tell him," said Dicky. "I'll tell him that you agree with our assessment as *programmers*, but that in your great wisdom and vast experience as a *businessman* you think we should support the IBM PC based solely on *business* considerations. I'll go see Ray right now, I think."

Dicky left the room, almost swaggering.

Step could have shouted for joy.

"Man, you just been shat on," said one of the programmers.

"But it was only Dickyshit," said Glass, "so it smells like little roses."

"Little pansies," said another programmer.

"Chanel Number Two," said Step. They all dissolved in laughter.

Robbie and Betsy were safely strapped into seatbelts, while Jenny's innumerable herd was bouncing around in the back of the Renault like Ping-Pong balls in a room full of mousetraps. "Don't you believe in seatbelts?" asked DeAnne the first time they rode anywhere together.

"I believe in seatbelts all right," said Jenny, "but carmakers don't believe in big families. There are never enough."

"You could belt in as many as you can," DeAnne suggested.

"And the ones without seatbelts, what's the message they get from that?" asked Jenny. "Mommy loves the other kids and doesn't want them to die in a crash, but *you* don't *need* a seatbelt."

DeAnne laughed, but it still made her feel queasy. "So the solution is to protect *none* of them? Why not double them up?"

Jenny just looked at her. "DeAnne," she said, "I bet I'll have as many kids live to adulthood as you will. I'm leaving Steuben next month, so let's just figure that there are some things about each other's lives that we aren't going to be able to fix."

"I'm sorry," said DeAnne. "I wasn't criticizing. I just didn't understand."

"I don't understand either," said Jenny. "And we've got to get this dinner over to Sister Ho's house." DeAnne reluctantly pulled the car out of the Cowpers' driveway, even though she and Step had never before violated their rule that their car never moved without every passenger strapped down.

Now it was late in May, and it seemed as though once or twice a week there was something that required her and Jenny to do some kind of Relief Society compassionate service together. "Compassionate service" invariably meant fixing a meal for somebody. Child in the hospital? The Relief Society brings you dinner. Husband lost his job? Again, dinner. Down with pneumonia? Dinner.

No, thought DeAnne. That isn't fair. The Relief Society does a lot of other things—hospital visits, taking old widows shopping, and that time Sister Bigelow spent three days getting that woman and her two sons with a car that broke down on I-40 installed in a rented mobile home with borrowed furniture. It's just that meals seem to be the main thing that Jenny and I get asked to do.

DeAnne was getting just a little bit tired of it. "Isn't there a compassionate service leader in this ward?" she had asked Jenny on the phone that morning. The kids were in the back yard playing, and DeAnne was sitting down resting her back because the baby was sticking about nine feet out in front of her now and just standing up took as much work as lifting heavy crates all day.

"There is one," said Jenny. "Sister Opyer. She was called because of inspiration. I know that because no *rational* person would have called her to do it. Amazingly enough she's been sick every time Ruby Bigelow calls on her to do anything, and now Ruby just calls us."

"Why not release her and call someone else to the position?"

"You don't do that around here," said Jenny. "Sister Opyer wants the position—she just doesn't want to do the work. So if Ruby released her, she'd be hurt and she'd go inactive and all the women in the ward would say that Ruby drove her out of the Church."

"But that's nonsense!"

"You just don't understand the South yet, DeAnne," said Jenny. "I give you about a year. Then it'll suddenly dawn on you that all these sweet, nice, kind-talking people are stabbing you in the back, and you'll think, What a bunch of hypocrites! Then a year later, you'll realize that they aren't hypocrites, they're just so polite that they talk in code. When they say, 'Why I'd be glad to, soon as I can,' that means 'Better do it yourself because I never will.' When they say, 'You think up the most interesting ideas,' it means 'You are plumb loco, woman!' You just have to learn the code."

"How long did it take *you* to learn it?"

"I'm still learning it," said Jenny. "They still surprise me. But the basic rule is, *yes* means *maybe* and *maybe* means *no*."

"Why don't they just say what they mean?"

"Confrontation!" cried Jenny. "That would mean confrontation! To say *no* right out in front of God and everybody? Impossible. No true southerner is capable of it. It would be unseemly. It would be *rude*."

"Well, I always say what I think, and I prefer it when other people do, too."

"Of course," said Jenny. "You're a westerner. And the southerners in the ward all think that us westerners are the most crude, pushy, bossy, obnoxious, contentious, cantankerous fight-pickin' chest-pokin' rapscallions as ever crossed the Mississippi going the wrong way. If you catch my drift."

"Was that cowboy talk?" asked DeAnne.

"Trust me," said Jenny. "You'll never get a southern Relief Society president to release somebody who doesn't want to be released. Oh, she'll hint around about how it must be such a burden for poor Sister Opyer and I just don't know how you manage, you sweet thing, what with being so poorly all the time and still having to carry on the burdens of your calling. And if Sister Opyer ever said, It does seem so hard sometimes, but I can manage, then Ruby'd know to release her right off. But instead Sister Opyer says—I was there once, and I think I can remember—she said, 'Oh, Sister Bigelow, it's my calling that sustains me, it gives meaning to my life to know that in the midst of my own suffering I can go out and relieve someone else's.' And you know that after that, Ruby's got no hope of releasing Sister Opyer even if she dies."

"So we do her job," said DeAnne.

"Hey, it's the Lord's work and it needs to be done and we can do it."

"You're more of a Christian than I am."

"So do you want to make the salad or the casserole?"

"I'd *like* to make the biscuits."

"Not a chance," said Jenny. "You don't know how to make southern biscuits yet and I don't have time to teach you."

"They just look like Bisquick drop biscuits to me," said DeAnne.

"Don't ever say Bisquick around the women of the ward. Might as well sew a scarlet *B* on your dress after that."

"Salad, then," said DeAnne.

So instead of resting, DeAnne made a Jell-O salad and put it in the fridge to set. And then, along about one-thirty when the kids *should* have been napping, DeAnne strapped Robbie and Betsy into the car and drove over to pick up Jenny and her brood. They had talked about maybe one of them just tending all the kids while the other took the meal over, but then they realized that DeAnne was too pregnant and tired all the time to deal with Jenny's rowdy crew and DeAnne also couldn't deal with the terror she felt whenever her kids were at Jenny's house and besides, Jenny knew the way and DeAnne needed to get out of the house so there was no other way to handle it—they both went and took the kids.

The family they took dinner to lived way out in the county, and on the long drive back home the kids all fell asleep. Quietly Jenny asked how things were going with Stevie. "Did you decide to go with any of the names that Dr. Greenwald gave you?"

"Step's against taking Stevie to anybody like that," said DeAnne. "I mean really against it. He's not rational about it. I think he'd rather that I had an affair."

"Men," said Jenny. "And they say *we're* irrational."

"Well, there's some reason for it, but he never says," said DeAnne.

"Does he have some relative who's a shrink?" asked Jenny.

"No," said DeAnne. "Why?"

"I mean, I have an uncle who's a real estate agent and so I hate all real estate agents. I just see one and I want to go get my gun."

"Because of your own uncle?"

"The sleazeball of all sleazeballs," said Jenny. "I can't go into detail because of the little pitchers in the back, but believe me, if you knew this guy you'd want to impose the death penalty for general offensiveness."

"Well, he's got no shrinks in his family, anyway," said DeAnne.

"So," said Jenny, "when are you going to take Stevie in?"

"I said, Step won't do it."

"You're at home," said Jenny. "Now that he works human hours, he carpools, so you have the car. You also have the checkbook. Take Stevie in and what's Step going to know till you've done it?"

DeAnne was appalled. "Would you really do such a thing to Spike?"

"If Spike ever dared to put his foot down and forbid me to do something that I knew my child needed, hell yes!"

"Well Step *didn't* put his foot down," said DeAnne. "We just didn't agree, that's all."

"Well then what's the problem?" asked Jenny. "If he didn't forbid it, then you can just go and do it."

DeAnne was nonplussed. It was as though Jenny came from a different tribe with strange marriage customs. "Jenny," she said, "Step and I don't do things about the children until we agree."

"I can see it now," said Jenny. "The child bleeding to death on the lawn, and you on the phone talking it out with Step."

"It's not like that," said DeAnne. Then she closed her mouth and decided it would be better if she said nothing else.

After a minute, Jenny broke the silence. "Um, if you want to kill me, could you wait till we've got the kids out of the car?"

"What?" asked DeAnne.

"You're going about sixty and this is a thirty-five zone."

It was true. DeAnne immediately put on the brake and the kids lurched around in the back, making grumbling noises in their sleep. "Sorry," said DeAnne.

"Look, be mad at me if you want," said Jenny, "but it's Step you're mad at and you know it. Call it what you want, he's stopping you from doing what you know is right for your child. The mother bear in you is not happy, DeAnne. Besides, one of those doctors is even in the ward. Well, she's not a member herself, but her son just joined."

DeAnne made a connection in her mind. "Step was just assigned to a home teaching companion like that. A young man whose mother isn't a member but she drives him to church."

"That's the one," said Jenny. "She's a shrink. Dr. Greenwald told me she was probably the one most likely to have an opening, too."

"Why, because she's no good?"

"Because she's a woman," said Jenny. "Most men have a harder time going to a woman therapist, and a lot of women have an *easier* time going to a man. Or they think they will, anyway. Dr. Greenwald said. It's like gynecologists. I for one don't understand why any woman would go to a male ob-gyn ever, now that there are women doing the job, but they still dominate the business. Anyway, she's got a connection with the Church and she's sympathetic. She's more likely to understand."

"Understand what?"

Jenny laughed. "I can see you've never *been* to a shrink. They think religious people are crazy."

"Not true," said DeAnne, thinking at once of Sheila Redmond back in Vigor. "I knew a therapist and she and her husband were serious Christians. Not Mormon, but they certainly didn't think it was crazy to be religious."

"Have you ever taken the Minnesota Multiphasic?"

DeAnne vaguely remembered that she had taken it once, but couldn't recall anything more than that.

"It's got questions all over it like, Do you believe that God sometimes talks to you? I mean, that's our whole religion, isn't it? That God still talks to human beings. And by their rules it means we're crazy!"

For the first time DeAnne began to think that maybe Step was right. If psychiatrists were really like that, then it could be a disaster to take Stevie to see one. As Step said, they didn't really cure people that often. And if the psychiatrist actually did talk Stevie out of his belief in the gospel . . .

"What I'm saying," said Jenny, "is that maybe you can talk Step into it if he knows the shrink and trusts her. So just make sure he does his home teaching and meets Lee Weeks's mom."

Step came home with his trophies: a copy of his employment agreement, excluding Hacker Snack and any work he might do for computers not being supported by Eight Bits Inc., and the memo from Ray Keene stating that Eight Bits Inc. would not be supporting the IBM PC. He thought DeAnne would be overjoyed.

"I can quit now," he said.

"Not really," she said.

"The option in our contract with Agamemnon says that at any point in the first six months I can send them a letter saying I'll be working on PC programs for them, and that's it. We get a check. And when I turn in Hacker Snack for the 64 we get another check. And when I turn in Hacker Snack for the PC, we get *another* check. Which means that before Christmas, if I work hard enough and learn 8088 machine language quick enough, we'll have had a total income this year of more than fifty thousand dollars."

"That's fine when all that money comes," said DeAnne. "But what about right now? You may have noticed that we have a baby due in July. I don't think we're going to be able to get a new insurance policy that will cover a preexisting pregnancy."

Step looked at her belly for a moment, as if the baby might come up with an idea.

"You can't quit till the baby is born," she said. "As it is, the first check from Agamemnon will barely catch us up on the house in Vigor." She held up a letter. "They're warning us that we have thirty days to bring the loan current before they'll begin foreclosing on the house."

"But don't you see?" said Step. "If I quit right now, we'll have enough money to pay for the house *and* the baby."

"Do you think I haven't gone over the figures?" said DeAnne. "Do you think I haven't read the Agamemnon contract? Do you think I haven't calculated all our payments down to the penny? If you quit now, and anything goes wrong with the pregnancy, we'll be in such deep trouble that we'll never get out. We need the insurance. We've got to be covered."

She was right, but she was also wrong. "DeAnne, Ray's decision not to support the PC is a deep and serious mistake. Somewhere along the line—and I think it'll be soon—Ray will realize that and there'll be another memo. We have a brief time right now when I can quit and go straight into PC projects. But if Eight Bits Inc. is supporting the PC when I quit, then I have to wait a *year* before I can do anything but Hacker Snack for Agamemnon, and we really *can't* live on just Hacker Snack for one year, even if it sells brilliantly."

DeAnne looked away from him; he could see that she was trying to control her emotions. "I don't know what to do, then," she said.

"I can't even afford to *buy* a PC until we exercise our option and get the check from Agamemnon," said Step.

"If we lose the house in Indiana," said DeAnne, "that'll be on our record forever. Every loan application there'll be a question—have you ever been in default on a loan? Have you ever had a mortgage foreclosed?"

"We won't *lose* the house," said Step. "We'll lower the selling price, what about that? We won't even get our equity out. That's fifteen thousand down the toilet, but—"

"It's more than that," said DeAnne. "It's the money we spent on the new furnace and the air-conditioning and the rewiring and the Andersen windows and I wish we'd never moved! If we had stayed there and you had just gone to San Francisco on your own, you could have signed with Agamemnon and we'd still be in the house and—"

"DeAnne," said Step, "what good will it do for us to start second-guessing ourselves? We had no way of knowing Agamemnon would take me on—we wrote to them, didn't we? And how would I have gone to San Francisco? We were already broke."

"I know," she said. "But I feel us circling and circling around in a whirlpool, getting sucked down, and this job is something to hold on to."

"What we need to hold on to is my ability as a game designer," said Step. "I'm good at it. I've seen it at Eight Bits Inc. I really do see things that other programmers don't see. I have a knack for it. You've got to trust *me*, DeAnne, not the check from Ray Keene."

"Don't put it that way!" There was fire in her eyes. "Don't you dare put it that way! Trust in you—I've trusted my whole life to you, the lives of my children, my whole future *forever!* So don't tell me that if I ask you not to quit your job until after the baby is born it means I don't *trust* you."

"We're fighting about money," said Step.

"We're not fighting at all," said DeAnne. "We're worrying together."

"I'll stick with the job for a while. But if it starts looking like Ray's going to change his policy, I'm quitting on the spot. Not even giving notice. I can't afford to give up this Agamemnon thing."

"Fine, that's good."

But it wasn't good, Step knew. Ray Keene wouldn't give any advance signals that he was going to change his mind. He'd just send around another memo, announcing that Eight Bits Inc. was going to support the PC. It wouldn't even mention that there had ever been a different policy. And there Step would be, holding that new memo, feeling his future slip away. I'll be under Dicky's control, then, Step thought. For years and years and years.

Still, at the moment he knew that DeAnne's fears were more important than his. So he would stay on the job, and they would just have to pray that Ray Keene would be really stupid.

To help ease the tension, Step took over fixing dinner. It was simple—toasted tuna and cheese sandwiches— and while he was doing it, DeAnne could go lie down. But she stayed in the kitchen and tore up lettuce for a salad. Step knew that her way of relaxing was to be with him, to talk to him. *His* way was exactly the opposite. What he needed was to be alone in the kitchen, fixing dinner, concentrating on the task at hand, letting his tension slip away. But DeAnne could never seem to understand that. When she saw that he was tense or upset or worried, she tried to minister to him, fuss over him, chat with him until he wanted to scream, Just leave me alone! He never did, though. Now he stayed in the kitchen with her as she talked about her day, letting her unwind, knowing that he would be able to get off by himself later, that when he sat down at the 64 in his office and started working on the Hacker Snack adaptation again, he could shut everything out and that would be good solo time for him.

As Step was still mixing up the tuna and Miracle Whip, the phone rang. It was a woman. "Is this Mr. Fletcher?"

"Yes," said Step. "And who is this?"

"I'm Lee Weeks's mother. I understand you want to take him somewhere tonight."

Step was puzzled. He hadn't called Lee Weeks yet. He was too busy. It was nearly the end of the month, and so he *needed* to call him if he was going to get any of his May home teaching done. He had even said so to DeAnne. But he hadn't actually called Lee Weeks. And he certainly had *not* planned on going out home teaching tonight.

"Just a second," he said on the phone. "Can you hold on for a second?"

"Of course," said Mrs. Weeks.

Step covered the handset and looked at DeAnne. "It's my home teaching companion's mother. She thinks I'm planning to take him somewhere tonight."

"Yes," said DeAnne. "I called her for you. I thought you wanted me to help you get it scheduled."

"*Tonight?*" asked Step. "You didn't mention it to *me.*"

"I didn't actually talk to anybody," said DeAnne. "I left a message on her machine, that's all. That you wanted to take him home teaching. I don't think I said tonight, but maybe something I said gave her that impression."

Step uncovered the phone. "Sorry for the delay," he said. "Yes, I wanted to take Lee home teaching. I've been assigned as his companion. What we do is, we go visit in the homes of a few families in the ward. We teach a little lesson, we see if they need anything. Like a permanent Welcome Wagon, without the gift certificates."

She laughed. "Well, that certainly sounds fine. But I'd like to meet you before you take him. You know that he doesn't drive. Sometimes he tries to, and you must understand that he is not to drive. He doesn't have a license. And I need to meet you, I think."

"Yes," said Step. "I'd be glad to meet you, and I won't let him drive." How old did she think her son was? At nineteen, the poor kid still had his mother screening anybody who came to pick him up and take him anywhere. And she made such a point of his not driving.

Maybe he's an epileptic or something. Maybe he can't drive and it isn't just that she's being overprotective. Give the woman the benefit of the doubt.

"Lee will be ready at seven-thirty," said Mrs. Weeks. "Do you think you can have him home by nine?"

"Between nine and nine-thirty," said Step. "We wouldn't be able to visit anybody later than that anyway."

"Well, I'll look forward to meeting you, then."

She gave him the directions and they said their good-byes.

Step went back to the tuna fish, feeling glum. "I was all set to really plunge into Hacker Snack tonight," he said. "This wasn't a night that I wanted to go home teaching."

"I'm sorry," said DeAnne. "I've been thinking through what I said, and I'm sure that all I said was that my husband, Stephen Fletcher, wanted to set up an appointment to go home teaching with Lee Weeks. She's the one who interpreted that to mean tonight."

"Fine," said Step. "I wasn't blaming you." DeAnne seemed really upset. Or worried, anyway. She still hadn't calmed down since the conversation about quitting. "She sounds nice."

"So you're going home teaching then?"

"Yes," said Step.

She seemed relieved. What, had she worried that he was somehow drifting away from the Church? Why would it *relieve* her when he went home teaching?

Never mind.

He turned the heat on the griddle. "If the salad's ready then I'll start toasting the sandwiches," he said.

"Yes, sure," said DeAnne. "I'll call the kids." She struggled to her feet and left the room.

Two months left, thought Step, and she's already so big she's got the pregnant-woman waddle. What's it going to be like for her by the end of July?

Lee Weeks lived in a simple ranch-style house out in the county, but there was a lot of yard around it and it was all meticulously landscaped and manicured. And the driveway was a turnaround. La-di-da, thought Step as he drove up and parked at the front door.

Mrs. Weeks answered the door. She was slim, and Step imagined that she probably thought of herself as tall, though of course she was much shorter than he was. She brought him into the living room and engaged him in conversation; he was aware that she was extracting information from him, but it wasn't really the information he expected her to be interested in. She did ask what he did for a living—the standard American status measurement—but then she went on to talk about an odd array of things, including local politics.

Gradually it dawned on him that she was testing him. But for what? She found out that he thought the mixed-race city schools should be consolidated with the mostly-white county schools. That he opposed Jesse Helms and his racist attacks on Governor Hunt, his probable opponent in the next election. What could this possibly have to do with Lee? Yet it was only when Lee's mother was certain that Step was a staunch civil rights supporter that she finally called her little boy into the room.

Little boy! When he walked into the room, Step realized that the kid must be at least six-five, because Step, at six-two, found himself staring straight into Lee's chin. Nineteen years old, tall enough to be an NBA guard, and his mother still wouldn't let him drive or go out with strangers until she interviewed them. Strange indeed. Especially since he was really a good-looking kid. Surely somewhere along the line he would have found out that he was attractive to women and got himself out from under her thumb.

Lee was cheerful enough, though, and when they finally got out into the car, Lee started laughing. "Mom's really something, isn't she!"

"A very interesting woman."

"She treats everybody like a patient." Lee seemed to be full of barely smothered mirth.

"A patient?"

"Oh, she's a shrink, didn't you know? Couldn't you feel yourself being analyzed?"

"I guess I could," said Step.

"She's nice, though," said Lee.

That was a weird thing to say about your own mother, thought Step. And he said it with such detachment that she could have been anybody. His teacher. His chauffeur.

Which, in fact, she was.

It was already well after eight o'clock, so Step had been right when he guessed that they'd probably only get to make one visit tonight. Step had decided on Sister Highsmith, an elderly widow, since she would presumably be glad to see them and wouldn't throw him any curves as he was introducing Lee to the idea of home teaching. On the way to her house, he briefly told Lee what home teaching was all about.

"Oh, so we're not, like, giving a lesson," said Lee.

"A message is all. Very brief. And then drawing her out, letting her talk. She's been a widow for twenty years, and she's kind of a talker. Doesn't get much company, so whoever comes over is going to get an earful. But that's fine—that's part of what we're coming for. To help her feel connected to the Church. To *life.*"

"I thought you said this was your first time visiting these people."

"That's right. I've never met this sister, in fact. Or anyway, not that I remember."

"Then how do you know so much about her?" asked Lee.

"I don't know *anything* about her."

"She's a widow for twenty years, she's lonely, she's a talker . . ."

"Oh, well, that's just stuff that the elders quorum

president knew about her. I mean, she's had home teachers before us."

"So we *report* on these people?"

"Man, you make it sound like we're spying," said Step, laughing.

Lee didn't laugh.

"Lee, it's not like that. We don't pry. People tell us what they want to tell us. Most of it's just like stuff you'd tell any friend. And we don't talk about it except if the Church needs to get involved. Like, for instance, this one family back in Vigor, Indiana, the dad was a trucker but he broke his leg playing touch football. They weren't even active in the Church, but I was their home teacher and I went to their house and the mom spilled her guts about how they didn't have any money and no insurance and they didn't know where to turn. She had a job, but as she said, she was getting paid like a woman, so they were *not* exactly going to make ends meet. They didn't have anything to *eat* till she got paid on Monday. So I invited them over to dinner at our house. And then I went and got her visiting teachers and we went to the store and did a week's worth of grocery shopping and dropped it off at their house."

"Oh," said Lee.

"We didn't tell anybody else in the ward except the bishop, and he got in touch with them about welfare assistance and it was all very discreet. You see what they need, and then you do it. If that's spying, I wish I had more spies in *my* life." Which was true enough—presumably someone had been assigned to home teach Step's family, but they had never shown up. Home teaching was a great idea, but it just didn't happen all that often, and when it did it usually wasn't much more than dropping by, taking up a half hour with empty conversation, and then saying, Well, let us know if you need anything, and then they were gone till the last day of the next month. No need to tell Lee that yet, though. Why not let him think that Mormons actually took home teaching seriously and watched out for each other faithfully? There'd be plenty of time to be disillusioned later, and in the meantime Lee might have got into the habit of doing it right.

When they got to Sister Highsmith's apartment building, Step and Lee waited in the car for a moment while Step led them in a short prayer. Help us know what she needs and provide it for her, help her know that she can rely on us—that sort of prayer. Then they went up to the door and knocked.

It took forever for her to get to the door, but when she got there it was as if she were receiving royalty. She was dressed to the nines and her stark white hair looked as though she had just stepped out of a beauty parlor. She was gracious and elegant, as was her home, though it tended to be a little too knick-knacky for Step's taste. A grandma house, he decided, a grandma house where the grandchildren never came, so that nothing had ever had to be put up out of the reach of children.

But there *were* pictures of children, and so Step asked about them, and that was good for fifteen minutes of talk about how wonderful they were but their parents just didn't seem to take the gospel seriously and the children were downright frivolous sometimes, all except her son's eldest girl, who was quite a serious child and wrote to her once a month, without any prompting from the girl's parents, which is a very fine thing in this day and age when children have no respect.

When that subject wound down—that is, when Sister Highsmith started asking about *his* family—he answered her briefly and then commented on the fact that she didn't seem to have a southern accent. That was good for another fifteen minutes about all the moving around that she and Nick had done before he retired from the military and they settled in Steuben. He died a year to the day after he retired, even though he had just invested most of their savings and all of her inheritance in a little fast-food franchise, but it turned out that Der Wienerschnitzel just didn't do all that well in Steuben. It just wasn't a southern franchise, they realized too late—southerners didn't want mustard and onions on their hot dogs, they wanted chili and cole slaw and they also wanted a place to sit down and they weren't going to pay Der Wienerschnitzel prices to do it. So the business wound down and even though she lost all that money, she didn't mind, because she had plenty of pension money on top of social security and her life with Nick had been a good life and if he had lived he would have made the franchise work, she was sure of it. So now it was just a matter of waiting until the Lord saw fit to take her home to heaven so she could be with Nick again.

"Do you really think he's in heaven?" asked Lee.

It was the first thing he had said in Sister Highsmith's house after the initial greeting, and the question just hung there in the air for a moment, as Sister Highsmith tried to discern whether he was challenging her assessment of her husband's righteousness.

"Brother Weeks here is new in the Church," Step explained. "I don't think he's suggesting that Brother Highsmith isn't in heaven, I think he's asking a doctrinal question."

"Oh, yes," said Lee. "I didn't think of it that other way—no, of course he's in heaven! I mean, even people who open hot dog franchises can still go to heaven, right?" He laughed, and Sister Highsmith and Step politely laughed along, though Step was meanwhile thinking, OK, let's get this boy out of here. Apparently Mommy hasn't given Lee much chance to learn what you do and don't say, and what you do and don't joke about.

"What I was asking," said Lee, "was whether you think your husband is a god."

274 • ORSON SCOTT CARD

Step cringed inside. What had the LeSueurs taught this boy? Step loathed the way that some Mormons bandied about the idea of godhood as if it were first prize at the county fair and really good Mormons would bring it home like a giant stuffed bear.

"I mean that's what first attracted me to the Mormons," said Lee. "Was the idea that human beings can become gods. I've always felt that. And then I saw this movie about how that's what you Mormons all believe and so I phoned up the church here in town and the missionaries came by."

"What was the movie?" asked Step. "Was it by any chance called *The Godmakers?*"

"Yes, that was it," said Lee.

"That's an anti-Mormon film," said Step. "It distorts our doctrines beyond all recognition. And the answer to your question is no, Sister Highsmith does not believe that her husband is a god. He's a man, and a good man—am I right, Sister Highsmith?"

"The very best sort of man," she said. "He became a colonel before he retired."

"Yes," said Step, "and now his spirit has left his body behind and he lives on with those of his family who died before him. But Lee, becoming holy and perfect enough to fully share in God's work is very rare and when it does happen it would happen only after *long* development and a long, *long* time after death and to most people it never comes at all. It's not like becoming a colonel." And then, to help Lee realize that the discussion should now end, Step added, "And it's not a doctrine that we discuss much." Or at least, if we have any sense of proportion we don't discuss it much. We don't even understand what Joseph Smith meant by it, for heaven's sake! Much better to concentrate on things like loving your neighbor and trying not to screw up your life and the lives of everybody around you than to get into mysterious doctrines.

Apparently mysterious doctrines were all that Lee wanted to talk about. "I think about becoming a god all the time," he said. "I think it would be neat to design planets and stuff. I could sure do a better job than *this* world."

Sister Highsmith blanched, and Step knew that she would not be reluctant if he now got Lee out of the house. "Well," Step said, "it was wonderful to meet you, Sister Highsmith. Can we have a word of prayer before we go?"

"Oh, do you have to go already?" she said.

Step cringed again, waiting for her to say the obligatory Don't go, wait awhile, it's early yet.

But she didn't say it. "Well, how sweet of you two to come by. And I'd be glad if *you'd* say the prayer, Brother Fletcher."

Yes, Lee had really put the stamp of strangeness on *this* evening. Sister Highsmith was glad to see them go—not exactly the best finish for the evening.

Out in the car, Lee seemed oblivious to the idea that he might have said something wrong. "That was neat," he said. "To be able to talk like that about things that I've just kept bottled up inside for years. I mean, that's the best thing about the Mormons, I can tell my secret thoughts and people *understand.* Not like Mom, I can't tell her anything or she just analyzes me to death."

I can understand that, thought Step, if you talk very much about becoming a god. To a psychologist, no less!

"I can feel it inside me, you know," said Lee. "All the time. Sometimes even a voice. And I know that it's the voice of God, it's the presence of God, just like Sister LeSueur told me. She said she had a vision about me, that I had the seeds of godhood inside me and I was just waiting for the gospel to bring it out of me. Sometimes I think that if I could just strip away all the weakness of this body that just ties me down to earth I could *fly*. And I don't mean just flapping around like a sparrow or something, I mean soar up to the stars, go from planet to planet. I feel like that sometimes. I mean, sometimes I think that I really *have* done it, that yesterday I was on another planet just like this one, only the old one wasn't as real, *this* one is the real one, the other one was just an imitation and now, for the first time, I can see what reality is, what it means to be alive, and I think, No one else can see this, I'm the only one who can see this, because the god inside me has opened my eyes. Everybody else *sees* it, I mean, but they don't really *see* it. They see but they don't—they can see but—"

He was beginning to sound almost frantic, as if the right word were just out of reach and he couldn't quite find it. So Step offered a finish for this impossible thought. "You're saying that they apprehend it with their eyes, but you *comprehend* it."

"With my *soul*," said Lee, "yes, just like that! That's got to be the Spirit of God, making the connection between us so you know what I'm saying even before I say it!"

Brother Freebody might have warned Step a little better about what he meant by Lee Weeks having some weird ideas about doctrine. Or maybe Lee hadn't been this extreme about it when Freebody talked to him. Or maybe Freebody hadn't believed that he was hearing what he was actually hearing when Lee said it.

"And sometimes I know that I'm the only real person in the world. No offense," Lee added quickly.

"No, that's not an uncommon feeling," said Step. "It's called solipsism. The idea that nothing is real except the self."

"No, I don't just mean a feeling, like anybody can get. I mean I *know* that God sees me and recognizes me as his kindred spirit, like a lost twin. Nobody but me ever feels like that. Only I can't tell that to anybody but the Mormons, because *you* understand! You've known about it all along."

Patiently Step tried to explain the fact that the gospel of Jesus Christ was mostly about how we treat other people, and not at all about becoming the most powerful being in the universe and getting into a first-name relationship with God. That was for the bozos on TV who talked about *Jeeee*-zuz as if he was their old high-school chum or something. Lee listened to everything that Step was saying, nodding wisely and agreeing to all of it. But Step was sure that Lee was missing the whole point of everything.

When they got to Lee's house, his mother was waiting at the door. She seemed to size them up as they came from the car, and by the time Step got up to the house, she was beaming. Only on the porch did it occur to Step that there was no reason for him to have walked Lee to the door. That was what Step did with thirteen-year-old babysitters, to make sure they got in safely. Home teaching companions over the age of eighteen you could just let out of the car. But for some reason Step had just expected himself to come to the door.

"Please come in," she said warmly. Her whole demeanor was different. This was the woman on the telephone. What had happened since eight o'clock?

"I can't stay," said Step. "Got to get home. I don't see my family half enough as it is."

"Oh," she said, looking disappointed. "Perhaps some other time."

"Well, in fact you'll probably see me a couple of times a month. We home teach four families, and we do it every month."

She raised her eyebrows, but she seemed to be pleased all the same. "How nice," she said. "What a very social church you have."

"I suppose so," said Step, thinking how wearing that sociability could sometimes be.

"And how was Lee?" she asked.

Lee was standing right there. It was so outrageous,

to ask about him as if he were a small child in another room, and not an adult, a *man*, standing right beside her. Yet Lee beamed. He seemed to expect a good report card, and so Step delivered one. "Lee was great," he said. "He spoke right up and we had a good visit."

No need to tell Mommy that Lee got a bit weird about doctrine. To explain *that*, he'd have to explain the doctrine, and it always sounded deeply weird to non-members. Or it *should*, anyway—it wasn't quite natural, the way Lee had taken right to it, and all the wrong way. You had to build up to understanding it, and it was a sure thing that Lee had neither the buildup nor the understanding.

But there was plenty of time, if he stayed in the Church. A lot of people came into the Church with serious misconceptions about the gospel—no matter how clear the missionaries were, people were going to filter ideas through their own preconceptions and come out with something skewed at least a little bit off plumb, and sometimes a lot more than a little bit. If they stuck with it, though, and realized that correct opinions about doctrine weren't anywhere near as important as learning to serve other people, to accept and fulfill responsibility, then eventually they'd loosen up enough to come around and change their beliefs, too, or at least not be upset that most Mormons didn't see things the same way.

Outsiders usually seemed to think of Mormons as automatons, obeying a charismatic prophet the way Jim Jones's followers obeyed him in Guyana. The reality was almost the opposite—stubborn, self-willed people going off every which way, with bishops and other ward leaders barely able to hold them all together, all the while tolerating a wide range of doctrinal diversity as long as people would just accept their callings and then be dependable. There was room even for Lee Weeks, who seemed to be obsessed with a rather inflated view of his own divine potential; given that the 1st Ward already had Dolores LeSueur, Lee's ambitions could certainly be taken in stride.

"I'm so glad," she said. Step was relieved to see Mrs. Weeks smile.

But no, it was *Dr.* Weeks, wasn't it? "Lee says you're a psychologist," said Step. The idea of her being a psychologist seemed somehow very important. Then he realized why—Stevie. Stevie and DeAnne's idea of what they ought to do for him. Suddenly Step looked at Dr. Weeks in a different light.

"Not a psychologist," she was saying. "A psychiatrist. The M.D. isn't much—just years of medical school and internship and residency." She chuckled.

"I'm sorry," said Step. He almost added, What Lee actually said was, She's a shrink. But he decided that he shouldn't get on her bad side because maybe she was the one who could bring Stevie back from the company of Scotty and Jack.

"Oh, I'm used to people getting the different branches of our profession confused," said Dr. Weeks. "I'm called a psychoanalyst just as often, and of course that's wrong, too. That's more of a priesthood than a profession, anyway."

She spoke with a light, amused tone, but Step took the words as a very good sign. He *liked* this woman, this shrink.

"Well," Step said. "Till next time, OK?"

"Right!" said Lee.

When Step got home, DeAnne was in the kitchen, waiting for him. Everything was cleaned up, and she was reading a book. It was the Anne Tyler novel he had bought her more than a month ago. "You just getting around to that?" he asked.

"No, I started it back when you first gave it to me," she said. "But then I didn't like her for a little while."

"Oh," said Step. "And now you've kissed and made up?"

She made a face at him. "It was just something that the character said in the beginning. This old woman is in bed, probably dying, and she thinks how her children ought to have had an extra parent instead of just her. The husband ran off."

"And that made you mad?"

"No, it was that she had decided to have her second and third *child* for just that reason. So she could have extras. When the first one almost died of croup. I thought it was the most awful idea, to have your later children as spares in case you lost the early ones."

"It's not really so awful," said Step. "People thought that way for thousands of years. What does it say in Proverbs about a man having lots of sons? Blessed is he who has a quiverful, or something like that."

"A quiver," said DeAnne. "How phallic."

"Actually, it's the arrow that's phallic. A very confused sexual image."

"Anyway," said DeAnne, "I just couldn't believe Tyler really meant that. So I just reread that opening again and I realized that that was just what the character had thought, not Tyler herself. And in fact the character realized right away that each child had become an irreplaceable person and not just a spare in case one of the earlier ones didn't work out."

"So now you can read it."

"Oh, who has time? But I thought I'd just check it out to make sure I liked it well enough to take it into the hospital with me."

"You've got two months till the end of July," said Step.

"I like to plan ahead. What if I got stuck in there with just *People* magazine?"

"If you like I can bring you the *Enquirer* as soon as the baby's delivered."

"I thought you had enough of me throwing up already."

Truth was, she hadn't thrown up that much with this

baby. The best morning-sickness period of all four pregnancies. Maybe that was a good sign. Maybe this baby was going to be no trouble. Maybe Step wouldn't have to lie beside his bed every night for the first three years of his life, humming "Away in a Manger" over and over again. Maybe this one wouldn't wake up with screaming nightmares. Maybe this one wouldn't periodically decide to hit a sibling over the head with something heavy.

Then it occurred to him that DeAnne was not waiting up at the kitchen table to read a book—she could have done that in bed. She was waiting up to talk to him at the opposite end of the house from the children.

"What's up?" he asked.

"Nothing," she said. "How did it go?"

"Fine. Lee's a little weird, but Sister Highsmith was fine. A nice old lady who likes to talk but then she's never boring, so it's OK. Not a lot of woes and troubles, either. Most of what she talks about is bragging about her late husband or her wonderful children or her even *more* wonderful grandchildren who are being spoiled or overprotected by her very *stupid* children."

"I thought her children were wonderful."

"Only when they were children," said Step. "Now they're parents and so they've become stupid. Hey, it happened to *our* parents, didn't it? And it's happened to us, too."

"Are we really stupid parents, Step?"

"By definition," said Step. "I was a brilliant parent till Robbie was born. Then all the things I'd learned about parenting went right out the window. Robbie was completely different from Stevie and so nothing that worked with Stevie worked with Robbie. I think that's why second-child syndrome develops. You know, nice cooperative first child, rebellious and troublesome second child. The first child was raised by confident parents. The second child was raised by parents who were nervous wrecks, trying to apply first-child methods to second-child problems. No wonder second kids want to spend most of their teenage years screaming at their parents."

"Poor Robbie. And what explains Elizabeth's temper?"

"I haven't analyzed third-child syndrome yet," said Step. "Give me time. She's still very, very short."

They sat in silence for a few moments.

"Did you meet Lee's mother?" asked DeAnne.

"Sure," said Step. "It's kind of impossible not to. She guards Lee like a tigress. I felt like I was going through a job interview just to get her to call Lee into the room so we could go."

"I can understand being protective."

"Yeah, well, especially with Lee. The kid's got a twisted sense of what it means to be Mormon."

"Oh really?"

"It's not so much that he can hardly wait for God to retire so he can move into the job, like Sister LeSueur. It's more like he thinks that he already *is* God, or at least *a* god, and he thinks Mormonism is cool because we seem to be the only ones who understand that a divine person like him is possible."

"How strange," said DeAnne.

"But he's young. Young people fantasize about a lot of things." Step had been thinking about his own youthful thought that maybe someday he would be president, or a great conquering general like Frederick the Great, or a doctor who discovered the cure for cancer. But now, when the words came out of his mouth, he instantly thought of Stevie. Of what Stevie was fantasizing. Not some grandiose megalomania. Just having a friend, that was all. A couple of friends. Did that make him *crazy*? It was Lee Weeks who was crazy if anybody's child was, and *his* mother was a psychiatrist, for heaven's sake.

"She's a shrink, too," said Step, following his own thought and not the thread of the conversation.

"Who is?" asked DeAnne.

"Lee's mother," said Step. "She's a shrink. That's

what he called it. He said, She's a shrink. But she's nice, though."

"I'm glad to hear it."

"No, I mean, that's what he said. That she was nice *though*. As if to be nice was sort of a contradiction to being a shrink."

"So now we actually know a psychiatrist," said DeAnne.

"Well, not like we're intimate friends."

"But at least we wouldn't be sending Stevie to a stranger."

It came to him all at once. DeAnne knew perfectly well that Dr. Weeks was a shrink. And it wasn't just that. DeAnne had set up the home teaching appointment, had *pushed* him into doing his church calling, which she had never done before, just so that he'd meet a psychiatrist. In fact, Dr. Weeks might well be one of the shrinks on the list she got from Jenny's pediatrician. There couldn't be *that* many shrinks in town. DeAnne had *manipulated* him. It made him feel sick and angry, and he wanted to say something really cruel and walk out of the room.

Instead he just sat there, thinking. What had she done, really? Just helped him to do his home teaching. Just helped get him into a position where he'd meet a psychiatrist. What was so bad about that?

She didn't tell me, that's what was so bad. She maneuvered me to this position instead of persuading me to it.

But Step hadn't left her much room to think that he'd be open to changing his mind. And so if she really felt strongly about getting help for Stevie, maybe she thought there was no other way. So it isn't that she manipulated me. No, I feel angry and sick because I'm ashamed that I'm the kind of husband whose wife thinks she *has* to do this kind of manipulation in order to get from her husband what she thinks her child needs.

I must be a really terrible husband, in her view, that

she has to fool me. Like the giant's wife in *Jack and the Beanstalk.* Doing her best to save the life of the small person in her care by keeping him out of the way of the cruel, awful, tyrannical husband.

When the silence had grown very long, he said, "Maybe you could find out her office number and set up an appointment for Stevie. If she takes children."

"Do you think she'd be good for him?"

No, Step thought. I don't think any more of psychiatrists now than I did before. Less, in fact, because she's so weirdly protective of her own son. Treating him like a child at this age. No wonder he has power fantasies, with her shepherding him through life as if he were incompetent to zip his own fly after peeing. What's she going to do for *my* child when her own is Lee Weeks?

That wasn't fair. Just because she couldn't see the problems in her own family didn't mean she couldn't see clearly the problems in others'. When Step had been elders quorum president, he had seen a lot of things clearly about other people's lives, but his own was just as murky to him as ever.

"She might be," said Step. "As good a chance as anybody else. And like you said, we know her."

"*You* know her," said DeAnne.

"Well, anyway," said Step. "Make the appointment. And then we have to figure out how to break it to Stevie that we're taking him to a shrink."

"It will help if you don't call her a shrink in front of him."

Oh, you've already thought this all through, I'm sure. "Well don't call her a psychiatrist, either," said Step. "Call her a therapist."

"Why? A psychiatrist is a doctor, and a therapist isn't. *Sheila* is a therapist."

"In contemporary American culture," said Step, "going to a psychiatrist means you're crazy. But going to a therapist means you're rich and stylishly uptight."

"I hate it when you talk about 'contemporary American culture' this and 'contemporary American culture' that."

Well, I hate it when you treat me like a puppet you can maneuver however you want. I didn't know how *much* I hated it till now, because up till now you had never done it.

"Can I get you anything to eat?" asked DeAnne.

"I've already gained about fifteen pounds working at Eight Bits Inc.," said Step. "The candy machines are killing me. The last thing I need is a snack."

"Just asking," said DeAnne. "Are you upset about something?"

Yes. "No. I'm just tired. I wasn't planning on spending tonight home teaching."

"I'm sorry," said DeAnne. "I told you, I wasn't trying to set it up for tonight, I just figured you wouldn't mind if I tried to establish contact with your companion. Are you coming to bed soon?"

"I suppose," said Step. "Is there anything good on Thursday nights?"

"We have forty channels," said DeAnne.

"Yeah," said Step, "but thirty-three of them are Jimmy Swaggart clones trying to heal hemophiliacs with the hemoglobin of the Holy Spirit. Or was that Ernest Ainglee?"

"It was that weird crewcut guy with the crazy eyes," said DeAnne. "Don't stay up too late. You have work in the morning, you know."

DeAnne left before she could see how Step tensed up at those words. Yes, I have work in the morning. I don't *have* to have work in the morning, though. I could walk in and give notice tomorrow and tell Keene where to stick his Dicky. I could let them fire me and collect unemployment. But no, *you* won't let me get out from under Dicky's thumb, because you don't trust me to make enough money to pay for the baby, you don't even trust me enough to talk to me rationally about getting a psychiatrist for Stevie. You have to trick me into it.

Step hated feeling such rage toward the person he loved most. And it wasn't the yearning love of young romance, but rather the kind of love that made her feel like part of his own self, so that he couldn't imagine a future without her beside him. To be so savagely angry at *her* was terrible.

He went to the sink to get a drink of water. Is this how divorce begins? he wondered. A feeling of terrible rage, of betrayal, a sudden discovery that maybe the marriage isn't as real and honest and strong as you thought it was? Then it builds up and builds up and builds up and then you find yourself living in an apartment somewhere and seeing your kids on weekends.

No, he said to himself. No, I forbid it. I will not let it happen, and neither will she. I'll just have to work on being the kind of husband she doesn't think she *has* to manipulate. Lord, help me to be whatever it is she needs me to be so we can hold this thing together. Just get us through this summer. Through this year. And then we won't need any more help, we'll be OK.

He set down the glass and turned around. There she was, in the doorway, her eyes red-rimmed.

"I knew she was a psychiatrist," said DeAnne.

"What?"

"I set up that home teaching appointment for you because her name was on Dr. Greenwald's list, and I thought that if you met her maybe you'd like her and even trust her and then you'd take Stevie to her. I didn't actually lie to you but I still didn't tell you the truth."

The tears spilled over her eyes onto her cheeks. She angrily wiped them away with her shirtsleeve.

"I know you hate me now," she said. "We don't trick each other and lie to each other, ever, and now I did it."

Step walked to her, put his arms around her. "I knew that you knew," he said.

She leaned away and looked up at him. "You did?"

"Not earlier, but here in the kitchen, I realized it. That you set me up."

"And you aren't mad?"

"Yeah, I was mad," said Step.

"But you didn't say anything," she said.

"No," said Step. "I got a drink of water instead."

She gave a little laugh that was almost a sob. "That doesn't make any sense at all," she said.

"I know," said Step. "But that's what I did. And I'm not angry now, because you told me."

Now she cried in earnest. Clinging to him. Tears of relief, of release. "Step, you can quit your job. You really can. It's wrong of me to make you stay. You hate it there, and we'll make it anyway, I know we will. So what if we lose the house in Indiana. It's just a house. It's just money. I can't stand the thought of you going every day to a job you hate just because I'm so scared of things being so out of whack in our lives."

"That's OK," said Step.

"I mean it," she said. "You can quit. And we don't have to take Stevie to a psychiatrist, either. I really don't have to have everything my way, you know."

"I know," he said. And he knew that, for the moment at least, she really meant it. But he couldn't take this capitulation of hers seriously. Her need for him to stay at work till the baby came was real and deep. And as for taking Stevie to a psychiatrist, it was the only solution she had thought of for her sense of helpless frustration with Stevie. He couldn't deny her that unless he could come up with something better, and he couldn't.

"I mean it," she said.

"I know you mean it," said Step. "But I won't quit. For now, anyway. But it means a lot to me that if I just can't take it anymore, you'll understand."

"I will, Step, I really will. It's up to you. I'll just

expect that one of these days you'll come home and say, It was time, and that'll be fine with me. I *want* you to come home! I want you here with me and the kids. Our life was so good in those days."

"It was, wasn't it," said Step.

"And it still is," she said. "My life is still good because you're in it. Everything good in my life comes from you."

Step shook his head. He knew she meant it, but in fact he knew that it wasn't true. Even the good she found in him was really the goodness she had put into him, the goodness he had put on himself like a disguise in order to get her to marry him. He had known that she could only be happy with a husband who was good in certain distinct ways. Like going to church with absolute faithfulness, and fulfilling his callings, the whole nine yards. And so for her he started going to church again, and she never realized that it was a sacrifice he was making out of love for her, in order to be part of her. She thought it was his own desire, and she loved him for it. But what she was really loving was herself, reflected back to her. And even now, when she clung to him, it was not Step the historian or Step the programmer she was clinging to. It was Step the faithful Mormon, and she had given him that role herself. It was Step the father of her children, and those, too, had been her gift.

"Make the appointment with Dr. Weeks tomorrow," said Step. "We'll start him as soon as school lets out a week from tomorrow. So he never has to leave class to go see his psychiatrist."

She clung all the tighter to him. "You're really something, Junk Man," she said.

Yeah, thought Step. When you get your way.

And then he pushed the nastiness out of his mind and just held her. This is what love is, he thought. Doing what you don't want to do, because she needs it so much. And it isn't that bad. And it isn't that hard.

9

· J U N E   B U G S ·

This is what Stevie got for his eighth birthday, on
June 3, 1983: his first wristwatch; a large Lego
set which could be made into a castle; four pairs of
shorts and four tank tops; his first dress slacks, white
shirt, and kid-size tie for Sunday; and a computer game
called Lode Runner for the Atari. It was a decent number
of presents, despite their financial situation, but Step
and DeAnne suspected that the present he liked best
was that when school was dismissed at noon on his
birthday, he was through with second grade, through
with that school, through with those kids, and home at
last for the summer.

In fact, that was what Step wrote to Stevie on the
inside of his birthday card: "You made it, school's out,

you were brave and strong and we're proud of you." Stevie read the card silently, looked up at his father without a sign of emotion on his face, and said, "Thanks."

That Sunday at church Stevie wore his new Sunday clothes for the first time, and when the bishop called him up to the stand to announce that he was going to be baptized that afternoon, it almost broke Step's heart to see how small he was, and yet how much he had grown; how young and how old their eldest had become.

After sacrament meeting, DeAnne took the kids and led them off to Primary. While Step was still gathering up his notebook and scriptures to head for gospel doctrine class, Lee Weeks came up to him, obviously bursting with excitement about something.

"Your son's getting baptized!" said Lee.

"That's right," said Step.

"Well I'm a priest," said Lee. "They ordained me a priest right after I was baptized myself."

"That's right," said Step. He knew what was coming next, but he could hardly believe that anyone would have the gall to intrude so badly into someone else's family.

"Well I can baptize your boy!" said Lee.

Brother Freebody happened to be standing nearby, talking to somebody else, but Step saw that he heard what Lee had said, and Brother Freebody rolled his eyes in sympathy.

"You have the authority to baptize," said Step. "But we have the custom in the Church that if a father is a worthy priesthood holder, he baptizes his own children."

"Sure," said Lee. "But I've never baptized anybody. This is my first chance. You've baptized a lot of people. On your mission, right?"

"You're nineteen," said Step. "Prepare yourself and in a year you can be ordained an elder and go on a mission yourself and baptize everybody who receives the gospel from you."

"But why should I wait?" asked Lee.

"Because Stevie is my son," said Step.

"All the more reason," said Lee. He lowered his voice a little. "I told you, God is with me. I'd give him a *real* baptism. Like John the Baptist gave Jesus."

"Lee, I have the same priesthood you have, when it comes to baptizing. He'll be just as baptized when I do it as he would be if anybody else with that same authority did it. And now I have to get to class."

Lee looked . . . not hurt, really, but . . . what? Angry. Yes, angry, thought Step as he slipped along the space between benches and emerged into the aisle of the chapel. Great, Step, great, you've offended a new convert who was given to you as a home teaching companion specifically so you could strengthen him in the gospel.

But no way in hell is anybody but me going to baptize my oldest son.

Later, in priesthood meeting, Lee seemed to have forgotten all about it—he was talking and laughing with the other men and boys, and a few times with Step himself. Things were fine.

That afternoon, though, at the baptism, it became clear that Lee had not understood anything at all. It was a simple service. DeAnne played the piano and Step led the music; the bishop spoke for a minute, and then Sister Cowper gave a talk about the meaning of baptism. At that point Step led Stevie out of the Primary room, heading for the font entrance by way of the dressing room where they had earlier changed into the white baptismal clothes.

Lee was in the hall with his mother, waiting. Already behind them the bishop and Brother Cowper were opening the folding doors between the Primary room and the corridor, and people were coming out, and there was Lee, dressed in white clothes, right down to white athletic shoes. "Are sneakers OK?" asked Lee. "We couldn't find any white dress shoes."

"Lee," said Step, trying not to embarrass him too much in front of his mother, "only the person getting baptized and the person doing the baptizing wear white clothes. I'm so sorry that you misunderstood." He turned to Dr. Weeks. "I hope that it wasn't too much trouble, coming up with all these white clothes."

"But isn't Lee performing the baptism?" asked Dr. Weeks.

Lee was smiling as if nothing at all was wrong. He clearly intended Step to stand aside and let him perform the baptism. But that was not going to happen unless Step dropped dead in the next few minutes. "No, Dr. Weeks. I told Lee this morning when he offered to do it that in the Mormon Church, whenever it's possible a father baptizes his *own* children."

Dr. Weeks's expression hardened. "Then this is an inappropriate behavior?" she asked.

"I don't know how Lee could have misunderstood," said Step.

"But you said I could do it," said Lee. His voice was quite loud, to get the maximum sympathy from the onlookers. Step could sense DeAnne coming up beside him, standing with him.

"No, Lee," said Step, also loudly. "I clearly told you that you would have chances to baptize if you serve a mission, but that *I* would baptize my firstborn child today. I'm sure you realize that there is no chance that I would ever have said otherwise under any circumstances."

"Come along, Lee," said Dr. Weeks icily. Step couldn't guess whether she was angry at him or at Lee or—worst of all—at the Church.

DeAnne touched Dr. Weeks on the arm. "I hope you understand," she said softly. "No one meant to embarrass your son. It was just a misunderstanding."

"Oh, I'm sure Lee understood perfectly all along," said Dr. Weeks, also softly, and with a slightly pained smile. "He simply has a way of adjusting reality to fit his desires and then expecting others to go along. I hope you will overlook this."

"Of course," said Step. He was relieved—she knew where the blame for this belonged.

"You've embarrassed me, Mother," said Lee.

"It's time to go home," said Dr. Weeks.

"Why not stay and see the baptism?" said DeAnne.

"I saw Lee's baptism," said Dr. Weeks. "I imagine this will be much the same."

"I want to stay," said Lee.

"Come home now, Lee," said Dr. Weeks.

There was a moment's silence between them, and then Lee turned to Step and, with a cheerful smile, said, "You really should have let me baptize him. That would have been the best thing." Then he turned and walked with his mother down the corridor toward the southeast door of the meetinghouse.

DeAnne squeezed his arm. "They're leaving, and everybody else is waiting," she said.

"Yes," said Step. "Sorry." He looked down at Stevie and smiled. "What do you say we go through with this?"

Stevie nodded.

Inside the dressing room, where their Sunday clothes were hanging up on hooks, Step paused for just a moment, feeling a need to explain. "Lee Weeks is just excited about being a priesthood holder," he said. "He misunderstood, that's all."

Stevie looked up into Step's eyes and said, "I think he's crazy as a loon, Dad."

And I think *you're* as sane as I am, thought Step. But you've got to go to a psychiatrist, while Lee only goes home teaching.

"I love you, Stevie," said Step.

"I love you too, Dad," said Stevie. But it was perfunctory, the obligatory answer.

They went to the door that led from the dressing room into the font itself. The water was just above the second step from the top. The water bent the light to make the font seem no deeper than a child's wading pool, but as Stevie stepped down into it, it seemed to swallow him up, bending him at the legs and then at the hips until he was so short that this shallow water came up to his shoulders. Step followed him. The water was cold, but he got used to it quickly. It came up only to his hips. Stevie is so small, he thought. He's too young to take on himself the consequences of all his future choices.

Then he thought, Stevie's been making his own choices, taking responsibility for himself ever since he was old enough to walk. For Stevie, baptism is probably years overdue. The Lord just picked eight years old as a convenient middle ground, that's all. Some children are ready for it as toddlers, and some aren't ready until well past their teens. Stevie was born with wisdom and goodness in him, like the high priest Samuel, like Solomon, like Joseph who was sold into Egypt, like Jesus.

Step took Stevie's right wrist in his left hand. "Hold on to my arm," he whispered. "Just like we practiced."

Stevie reached up his left hand and took hold of Step's left wrist. His hand was so small, his grip so tight and yet so feeble.

Stevie tried to move his right hand up to plug his nose.

"Not yet," Step whispered. "After the words."

Stevie waited as Step raised his right hand to the square and spoke loudly, so the official witnesses could hear and make sure he said it right: "Stephen Bolivar Fletcher, having been commissioned of Jesus Christ, I baptize you in the name of the Father and of the Son and of the Holy Ghost. Amen."

"Amen," murmured the crowd.

"Amen," whispered Stevie.

Step lifted Stevie's right hand toward his face, and Stevie took hold of his nose to pinch it closed. "Bend at the knees," Step whispered. Stevie closed his eyes and

Step pushed him backward into the water, then shoved him down. The water resisted as it always did, but Step pushed Stevie downward, downward, burying him under the water until he was completely immersed. Only then did he let the water have its way, float him back up; and when Stevie reached the surface, gripping tightly to Step's arm, Step pulled him back up to a standing position. Stevie gasped, let go of Step's arm, wiped at his eyes.

Some of the onlookers chuckled affectionately. They had all been through this. They knew how it felt to come out of the water. The disorientation. The hunger for breath. Like being born, gasping for air. The body's instinct for survival in control of you, so all you can think about is, live. Breathe. Then you think, I'm cold. Can they see through the white clothes? Did I look stupid? Did everything go right? Did some part of me stick up out of the water so they'll have to dunk me again?

Step looked from the bishop to Brother Cowper, who were serving as the official witnesses. They both nodded.

"We're OK," said Step. "Got it right the first time."

Stevie nodded gravely.

The bishop and Brother Cowper closed the sliding doors between the font and the corridor. Everybody else went back into the Primary room to wait. Step and Stevie climbed up out of the water, their clothes heavy, dripping, cold.

In the dressing room they dried off and changed back into their street clothes. Stevie was very shy about his body, asking Step not to look and making sure that his back was always turned to his father while he dressed. A far cry from the days when he used to run stark naked into the living room with company there, shouting "Teebee go toe-let now! Hurry-up Daddy!"

Step wrung out the wet clothes and then they

returned to the Primary room, where some of the younger children—all Cowpers, by Step's rough census—were running around hooting and screeching. They soon got things quieted down, Brother Cowper gave a short talk about the meaning of confirmation and receiving the gift of the Holy Ghost, and then Stevie came forward, sat in a chair facing the small congregation, and Step laid his hands on his son's head. The other priesthood holders there—the bishop, Brother Cowper, and the Primary president's husband—then laid their hands lightly on his, with perhaps a finger also touching Stevie's head. And Step began the confirmation as he had done so many times on his mission in São Paulo—except in English, not in Portuguese. He confirmed Stevie a member of the Church, and then commanded him to receive the Holy Ghost.

Technically that was all that was needed, and Step could have stopped there—but that would have caused talk, a lot of gossip, because the custom was to add a few minutes of blessing and admonition, and the omission of that blessing would have been shocking.

Yet as Step stood there, ready to speak the words of blessing, nothing came to mind. It was not that he had given it no thought. In fact, for days he had been replaying in his mind the ways he might obliquely address the problems Stevie had been having. He couldn't say, I bless you that your imaginary friends will go away without your having to bother going to a psychiatrist, but there were ways of phrasing the same idea, such as, I promise you healing, and that all your visions will be true ones—things like that, which would sound ordinary enough to people who knew nothing about Stevie's problems, but whose true meaning DeAnne and Step and God would understand.

Now, though, Step could not remember a single thing that he had planned to say. He stood there in long silence. This was not unusual. Many men took a moment or two to gather their thoughts. But this time the moment became longer and longer, and one of the men in the circle around Stevie shifted his weight, and a woman in the congregation cleared her throat.

Is there nothing I can say to my son? Is his life as bleak as that? Or is it me? Am I unworthy to give any kind of blessing to this good boy, who needs blessing so much?

Suddenly there were words in his mind; and he spoke them almost before he thought of them. "The Lord knows your heart, Stephen, and he trusts you. He brought you into this world to perform works of love, and I promise you that if you listen to the Holy Ghost and make your choices as the Spirit of God directs you, then you will bring joy and peace into the lives of everyone who loves you, both your family and your friends."

As quickly as the rush of words had come, it was gone. "Amen."

The men in the circle immediately turned their attention to Stevie, shaking his hand. Solemnly Stevie shook hands with each man, but without looking them in the eye. And as Stevie headed back to his seat, Spike Cowper glanced at Step a bit quizzically, as if to ask, What was going on there during the confirmation? The bishop put his hand on Step's shoulder and squeezed. Meaning what? thought Step. Encouragement? Consolation? Sorry you couldn't give your own son a real blessing at the time of confirmation.

Yet it *had* been a real blessing, Step was sure of it, or at least he was pretty sure that he was sure. It had happened a couple of times before, on his mission in Brazil, the words just flowing into his mind like that. It meant something.

On the way out to the car, after the closing song and the prayer, DeAnne hung back from the kids and asked Step about it. "Was that really all? I mean, you didn't even mention him getting married in the temple or anything."

"This was his confirmation, not a patriarchal blessing," said Step.

"Yes, but Step . . ."

"I said what I was given to say," he answered, a bit uncertainly. That's the problem with spiritual things, thought Step. You knew what was going on, and yet you also didn't know. Because if you *really* knew, then it wouldn't take faith anymore, would it? And yet you had to live in perfect trust, as if you *did* know for sure when God had spoken in your heart. Only later, looking back, could you see with any kind of certainty whether there seemed to be meaning in what had happened, whether there was some purpose or plan in things.

On the drive home, it happened that there was one long silence that for some reason made Step uncomfortable, and he filled it with the first thing that came to mind. "Well, Door Man, feel any different now?"

As soon as he said it, Step regretted it. It was exactly the sort of stupid question adults were always asking children. Now Stevie would think, Am I supposed to feel different? Uh-oh, I *don't* feel different, except maybe still a little damp, and so now what do I say? If I don't say I feel different, Dad will think that he failed. Or that *I* failed. But if I *do* say I feel different, then that will be a lie. My first lie after baptism. All my sins washed away, and now this is my first sin and so the baptism was only good for about half an hour. At least, that was what had gone through Step's mind when he was eight years old and his father baptized him.

From the back seat, Stevie answered quietly, "Yes, Dad."

He had opted for the white lie.

"Son," he said, "actually most people don't feel all that different, really. It's OK if you don't."

"I do, though," said Stevie. He didn't sound insistent. Just reporting a fact.

"Oh really?" asked Step. "What does it feel like?"

Stevie seemed to think about this for a moment. "Like the Holy Ghost is in me."

For a moment it seemed like the perfect response. For a moment Step thought, Of course Stevie feels the gift of the Holy Ghost, though I never did as a child, because *he* has always been sensitive to spiritual things, and I never was.

Step thought then of how much Stevie sounded like Lee Weeks just before Sunday school today. God is in me. God is speaking inside me. Whatever it was that Lee had said. Stevie might be spiritually sensitive, or he might be deluded.

Step realized that he was seeing him through the psychiatrist's eyes. How easy would it be for a psychiatrist to distinguish between Stevie's simple language of faith and Lee Weeks's weird certainty that God had chosen him? Probably it wasn't a problem—Lee might be strange, but he wasn't certifiable or anything. And of all people Dr. Weeks would certainly take Stevie's pure faith in the religion of his parents in stride.

Certainly DeAnne was taking Stevie's answer without any kind of skepticism. She reached over and cupped her hand over Step's right hand where it rested on the gear shift. Our son is so pure in heart, she seemed to be saying, that he can sense the Spirit of God when it enters him.

"What did you think when your father was confirming you?" asked DeAnne.

"I don't know," said Stevie.

"I mean, what did you think of the blessing he gave you?"

"Fine," said Stevie.

"Let's not quiz him," said Step to DeAnne. But what he was really thinking was, Do you have to remind him of how inadequate my blessing was?

"Sorry," said DeAnne, her feelings hurt a little.

"Nothing to be sorry about," he said.

Stevie spoke up from the back seat. "Dad?"

"Yes, Door Man?"

"You said that I'd bring joy and peace to my friends."

"And family," said Step.

"Well I don't know how," said Stevie.

"But that's what the gift of the Holy Ghost is for," said Step. "To show you how."

"But what if the Holy Ghost doesn't tell me?"

"Then maybe it isn't time for you to do anything about it yet. Or maybe you just haven't learned how to hear what the Spirit of God is saying. Or maybe you aren't supposed to do anything yet."

"Oh," said Stevie.

A moment passed. Stevie said, "I'd really like to."

"Like to what?" asked DeAnne.

"Make them happy."

"Make who happy?" asked DeAnne.

You know who he means! Step wanted to shout.

"Jack and Scotty and David," said Stevie.

The imaginary friends. Only now there were three.

"Stevie," said DeAnne. "Who is David?"

"Just another kid we play with," said Stevie. "Me and Scotty and Jack."

Stevie might have been confirmed, and the Lord may or may not have given Step words to speak in his confirmation, but the fact remained that Stevie was still living in a world where invisible friends came to play with him. And today he had added another. Or was it today?

DeAnne asked, "Did David just . . . move in or something? I don't remember you talking about him before."

Move in, yes, that's a good one, thought Step. Let's pretend that these friends actually live in the neighborhood and have families and new ones just "move in" from time to time.

"He's been around for a while," said Stevie. "I think he was born in Steuben 'cause he talks southern and I can't understand him all that well yet. I mean I can, but I have to listen slower."

All right, DeAnne, thought Step. You were right. He needs to see a psychiatrist or somebody, anyway. I've never heard him talk about his imaginary friends this way. As if they had real lives. He must be spinning out their biographies faster than Step was coming up with code for Hacker Snack on the 64. You knew this, DeAnne. You've heard this sort of thing before. No wonder you were so upset. No wonder you insisted. This is too much for us alone.

When they pulled into the driveway, Bappy's pickup truck was out front. "On Sunday?" asked Step.

As if he had heard the question, Bappy came around from the back yard. "Y'all at church?" he asked. "I come by at about four thinking you was bound to be back from church but nobody was here."

"We had a special meeting," said DeAnne. "Stevie got baptized today."

"Well that's something," said Bappy. "That's really something. So y'all don't baptize babies either, eh?"

"Are you Baptist?" asked Step.

"Well, my daddy was a Pentecostal minister, and he was a real dunker, he put 'em all the way under and held 'em down till the sins were all drownded and so were the ones who found Jesus, I'll tell you. Why, some of 'em came up with a mouthful of mud, he pushed 'em down so far!" DeAnne and Step joined in Bappy's laughter, but Step was thinking, I don't like making light of baptism, not today, not in front of the kids.

"Well," said Step, "anyway, I'm sorry we weren't here. Have you waited long?"

"Oh, I didn't wait at all," said Bappy. "I figured, I know I oughta ask 'em first, but here I am and there's the tent flies in the back yard and I gotta do *something* about 'em, and it's not like I'm gonna make a mess that I don't clean right up."

"Is that what those cobwebby things on the trees are?" asked DeAnne. "Tent flies?"

"Them eggs hatch and the worms can eat every leaf right off the tree," said Bappy. "So I bag 'em up and prune 'em off. Got my truck mostly filled now, and you won't have any more of them wormy things droppin' off on your kids under the trees."

"Yay!" shouted Robbie. "Those are really icky!" He charged around back, Betsy hard on his heels.

"Well I got 'em all," said Bappy. "Or almost. I *will* have 'em all by the time the day's over."

Step wasn't comfortable having Bappy doing yard-work on the Sabbath. But he knew that it really wasn't his business. Bappy wasn't his employee, he was the landlord's father, and if he chose to do yardwork on Sundays, well, it wasn't Step's job to control it.

"Step, would you go round the kids up out of the back yard?" DeAnne asked.

Step headed into the back yard and found Robbie and Betsy circling the tree like the tigers in *Little Black Sambo,* though they would never know the reference because somewhere between Step's childhood and his children's, that story had been discovered to be a mon-strously poisonous thing that would turn otherwise innocent children into bigots. I guess there's no hope for me, thought Step. I see kids running around in circles, I think of tiger butter.

Bravely Step stuck a hand into the circle of children and emerged with a child attached to it; then the other hand, and the other child. "Come on into the house," he said, "if you want supper."

"He got the webs!" shouted Robbie.

It was true. The tree had been pruned back, and now was missing all but two of the branches that had been covered with a mass of white web; even those were now wrapped in large plastic garbage bags, waiting to be cut off and disposed of. It wasn't hard to imagine Bappy's wiry body climbing around in the trees. He's in better shape than I am, thought Step. But then, he doesn't have to work around the corner from a candy machine.

When Step got the kids into the kitchen and DeAnne had sent them off to change out of their Sunday clothes, she asked him, "Where's Stevie?"

"He wasn't in the back yard," said Step. "I thought he came in with you."

"I thought he took off when the other kids did."

"He's in here somewhere."

"No he's not, Step. I unlocked the back door, and he'd have to come in past me, and I know for a fact that he didn't. So he's still outside, and I don't like it that you didn't see him with the other kids."

She had good reason to be worried. This morning's paper had told of another kid who had turned up missing last night at a Weavers baseball game. It was a minor league team, of course, but there were a lot of loyal fans in Steuben and so the games were crowded. Kid just disappeared. Scary times. He'd be on a milk carton soon, no doubt. Or turn up at a neighbor's house. Or dead. Where was Stevie?

Step went out into the back yard again. Bappy was up in the tree, sawing away at one of the limbs wrapped in plastic. He waved, and Step waved back. "You seen my oldest boy?" asked Step.

"No sir!" shouted Bappy. "You lost him?"

"Oh, he's around here somewhere," said Step.

"Keep your eyes on your kids, young man!" shouted Bappy. "It ain't safe these days. The devil is loose in the world!"

"Oh, I have no doubt of it!" Step called back.

Stevie was around in the front of the house, sitting on the doorstep.

"Stevie, we've been looking for you," said Step. "Your mom and I were worried, we didn't know where you were."

"Sorry," said Stevie. He got up.

"You can't go running off without saying anything."

Stevie frowned. "I was right here, Dad."

"You weren't in the house, and you weren't where we could see you, and so we were scared. That's just the way it is with parents, and you have to humor us and make sure we know where you are all the time or we'll end up putting you on a leash or locking you in the house or something, and you won't be very happy with *that*."

"Sorry," said Stevie again.

This wasn't how it should be on the day a kid was baptized. Off by himself, and then having to apologize for it. "What were you doing here in the front yard, anyway?" What were you thinking about? What was going through your mind?

"Sitting," said Stevie.

Step knew when he was defeated. "Well, come on in, it's time for supper."

Dutifully, Stevie followed him inside.

The next morning should have been the first weekday of summer. Stevie out of school, a chance for DeAnne to get a little more sleep in the morning, get things moving a little later. But DeAnne woke up before her alarm anyway, and not just because the baby was pressing so hard on her bladder that it held about a half an ounce these days. She lay there for a moment and then knew why her stomach felt like it was tied in a knot. She was taking Stevie to Dr. Weeks at ten.

DeAnne and Step had decided not to tell Stevie about the psychiatrist until the morning of his appointment. Why have him worry unnecessarily for days in advance? Why spoil his birthday and his baptism?

Stevie wasn't so young that they could play the "this is just a different kind of doctor" game that might have worked with Robbie. Stevie knew that there were crazy people in the world, and doctors who treated them, and places where they were shut away from everybody else. It was the child's version of mental illness—all the old prejudices about madness survived in the subculture of children, passed from nine-year-olds to eight-year-olds, year after year. The loony bin. The nuthouse. Shameful, terrifying. Somehow Step and DeAnne had to make Stevie understand that that was not what was happening here. It would be especially difficult because DeAnne was afraid, deep inside, that that was exactly what was going to happen somewhere down the road.

DeAnne showered. Step had installed a handheld showerhead, which was a lifesaver when she was pregnant—not so much bending and reaching while standing on a slick, wet surface. It felt good to be clean. There were times, late in her pregnancies, when she felt like she was permanently ugly and vile; her hair seemed to get oily faster during pregnancy and it matted to her head, and she felt awkward and bumptious and her back hurt, and her legs, and she got charley horses and she was tired all the time, too tired to want to clean herself up, and there was always this belly between herself and anything she was trying to do, and there were times when she just didn't want to go through the bother of getting out of bed. Yet if she just stripped off her clothes—a lot of trouble right there, of course—and washed herself, letting the water beat on her body, scour her all over, then she felt better, invigorated. She felt like maybe it was worth dragging herself around for another day.

Step staggered out of bed and into the shower as soon as she got out of the bathroom. Twenty minutes before his usual getting-up time. He had remembered, too. She watched him as he stripped off his nightclothes and pitched them into the plastic laundry basket in the closet. His body was definitely going to seed at this job.

His old regimen of bike-riding back in Vigor, along with some serious attention to what he ate, had kept him trim for the past few years, but the belly was coming back again, the thickness in the buttocks, the softness in the face. He had been pasty and overweight when she fell in love with him, of course; she hadn't really minded, but *he* minded so much that she knew he wasn't happy with his body that way. So when he got himself under control a few years back and shed the weight and built up his strength in a way he had never done in high school or college, she loved it mostly because he was so much happier, so much more confident. Looking at him now, she thought: Eight Bits Inc. has been destroying him in every way it could.

She wanted to say, Quit your job today, Step. Get back on the bicycle. Join a health club. Get away from the candy machine.

If only we hadn't moved to Steuben.

It had felt like the right thing to do at the time. Even though she was already pregnant before Step even thought of applying for jobs, it felt *right*. Almost inevitable. We just have wandering feet, she supposed. We can't stay rooted anywhere for long. Pioneer spirit. It was built into Mormon culture, to be ready to pick up and move to a new land every couple of years. And maybe there was some genetic component to it. People who were born to be nomads.

Then she thought of chopping down trees and building log cabins and sweeping a dirt floor and cooking at a hearthfire and never being able to bathe and having to use an outdoor latrine and giving birth alone in the dark, squatting over the straw, and she decided that she had no desire to be a pioneer. Wanderlust was fine, as long as you could wander from one place with flush toilets, electricity, and a good local hospital to another.

She headed for the kitchen to fix herself a bowl of

raisin bran, but when she had the fridge open, getting out the milk, it occurred to her that it was awfully dark. Most mornings the sunlight streamed into the east-facing kitchen window.

The plastic gallon jug of milk in hand, she turned around and glanced toward the window to see what the weather was. Weather had nothing to do with the darkness of the room. Most of the gap between the window and the screen, up to about six inches from the top, was filled with june bugs, their translucent bodies glowing a ruddy brown as the bright sunlight tried to get through into the room.

It was so startling, so repulsive, all those bugs tumbled onto each other, that DeAnne screamed. Then she felt something cold spatter on her legs, and she screamed again. Only then did she realize that she had dropped the milk jug and the cap had burst off, spattering milk everywhere. Now it was lying on its side, gurgling out the remaining milk. She squatted down as quickly as she could to pick it up before it all poured out, but she moved so slowly that before she could get it the flow had reduced to a trickle. About a third of the milk remained inside, but most of the nearly full jug was all over the floor.

I can't deal with this, she thought. This horrible house. The bugs in this place, the milk all over the floor, the cupboard that still smells like coffee after all these months, I hate this place.

She struggled to her feet and used paper towels to wipe the milk off her legs and her bare feet, and then she went back to the linen closet in the hall and got out the old towels, which she then dropped onto the milk to soak it up. Then she laboriously squatted again to pick them up, dripping with milk. "Damn, damn, damn," she said.

"And good morning to you," said Step. He stood in the kitchen doorway.

"I dropped the milk," said DeAnne.

"What a relief. I thought maybe you had poured it out. The world's largest bowl of Grape-Nuts Flakes."

"I was going to have raisin bran this morning."

"Well that explains everything."

She hated it that he was joking when she felt so awful, but then he helped her stand up again, saying, "You shouldn't be doing that, Fish Lady," and she was able to sit down by the table and watch as he picked up the towels and rushed them into the laundry room. While he was gone, she dared to look back at the window, hoping that she had exaggerated the quantity of june bugs. She hadn't.

Step came back, heading for the paper towels to finish wiping up the milk, when he finally noticed the window.

"Oh," he said. "Now I know what you meant by *damn damn damn.*"

"*Damn damn damn* was for the milk and being pregnant," said DeAnne. "For the bugs in the window I screamed, only you must have been in the shower so you didn't hear me."

"Too bad, it must have been a doozie." Step leaned over the sink to look closely at the bugs. "How did they get in there?"

"I don't know," said DeAnne. "Maybe some bug entrepreneur sold tickets." He laughed, and she laughed, too, though it wasn't that funny.

"They're all dead," said Step. "Not one of them even twitching. Weird, isn't it? Like all the june bugs who knew their number was up came here last night to die."

"So we have the world's largest bug collection, only it's all one species."

"Well," said Step, "good thing we woke up early today. This roll of paper towels is nearly out, do we have any more?"

"Yes, but we still have to speak with Stevie," said DeAnne. "I want it to be when you're still here. I can mop the floor later."

"It'll only take me a minute to finish wiping it up," said Step.

"You can't just mop up milk," said DeAnne. "I have to scrub the floor."

"Pregnant?"

"I've done it before, you know," she said. "That's what Bendectin is for. To allow pregnant women to keep scrubbing floors while their men watch mud-wrestling on ESPN."

He looked at her, his eyes narrowed in a mockery of a glare. "Feminist bitch," he said.

She pretended to glare back. "Male chauvinist pig."

"Let me guess," he said, looking at the window again. "You don't want these guys to be up here all day."

"It's more important to talk to Stevie."

"He's not in here yet." Step went to the laundry room and got out a green plastic garbage bag. "This time it's your turn to hold the bag," he said.

"Oh, Step," she said, shuddering.

"It's either that or you climb up on the counter to open the window."

"Can't you do it outside?" asked DeAnne. It made her sick to think of those bugs *inside* her kitchen.

"I don't have a ladder," he said, "and I don't want to fuss with unscrewing the whole screen when I can just slide this window up. It's not like I have time for a half-hour job this morning."

"I can call Bappy," said DeAnne.

"And have him spray again?" asked Step. "I can do it, and I don't like Bappy doing jobs that I can do. That *we* can do, if you'll just help me."

She was already up. Step had anchored the bottom corners of the bag on the windowsill using the big red salt and pepper shakers from beside the stove. "Don't use those," she said. "If they get bugs all over them I could never stand to use them again."

"Well, unless you have four hands, Fish Lady, we've got to anchor them with *something*."

She squatted awkwardly to reach inside the cupboard under the sink and came up with two large wrapped bars of hand soap.

"Excellent work, my beloved assistant," he said. "That's what I keep you around for, your extraordinary resourcefulness."

Now, with the bottom corners anchored, DeAnne held the bag open against the window as Step slowly opened it. The bug bodies rattled out of the bottom of the window, tumbling into the bag like popcorn. The sound of it, the vibration of the bag, knowing what was falling into it, it was all too much for DeAnne. A bug-loathing instinct far deeper and more powerful than her common sense took over, and for a moment she lost control. She moaned, her body was racked with a huge, irresistible shudder, and she let go of the bag.

At once the top of the bag dropped down below the opening in the window and the bugs started spilling out on top of the bag instead of inside it. "Shit!" said Step. "Can't you—"

He didn't finish the sentence, as he reached down and lifted up the corners of the bag again, so the bugs went back to falling inside it. Of course, the ones that had already spilled onto the outside of the bag now slipped off onto the counter and into the sink and onto the floor, still damp with spilled milk.

"Can't you do anything right," said DeAnne, finishing his sentence for him.

"That's not what I was going to say," said Step.

"Yes it was," said DeAnne.

"I was going to say can't you at least hold it open again, and then I realized that you couldn't, and so I did it. Don't put words in my mouth, especially when they're mean and nasty words that I didn't even think of saying."

"Now you're supplying the mean and nasty words just fine by yourself," she said.

"Just get out of the kitchen until I get this cleaned up, will you?" said Step. "Do you think *I* enjoy handling dead june bugs? Do you think it makes it any easier to have you standing there not helping at all and trying to pick a fight with me in the meantime?"

Struggling against tears of anger, biting off the retorts she thought of, DeAnne fled the kitchen. Had any of the bugs touched her hands? She rushed into the kids' bathroom and washed with Lava soap, gritty and rough, trying to get them clean. Only it wasn't bug-touches she was washing away, it was the pointless argument.

She rinsed and dried her hands and then went in to waken Stevie. During the school year she had started the custom of waking him by rubbing his back as he lay asleep. Usually at some point his eyes would suddenly fly open and he'd say, "Morning." Today, though, his eyes stayed closed and he murmured, "No school."

"I know there's no school, honey," she said softly. "But your father and I want to talk to you about something this morning before he goes to work."

Now his eyes flew open. "OK," he said.

She knew now that he would quietly climb down from the upper bunk and get dressed without waking Robbie. She headed back for the kitchen.

Step was using a paper towel to pick up dead bug bodies from the kitchen counter and put them in the garbage bag. In the meantime, water was running in the sink and the disposal was on. She imagined him hosing dead bugs into the drain and then the garbage disposal blades chopping them into tiny bits. It made her shudder again, and she felt her empty stomach churn with nausea. "Thank you for taking care of that," she said.

"You might want to wipe off the milk carton and put it back in the fridge," he said coldly.

Well, she deserved to have him speak coldly to her. She had let her revulsion about the bugs turn into sniping at him, and he hadn't deserved it. Still, she had to eat something to settle her stomach, and she couldn't eat it in the kitchen, not till all the bugs were gone. "Step, I'm sorry," she said.

"Fine," he said.

She knew that when he was angry with her, it was better not to try to force a conversation. Better to wait, to let him calm down, and then he'd be gentle with her and they'd apologize to each other and he'd insist it was his fault and that would be fine. But sometimes she just couldn't stand to do it that way because while *he* needed to be alone after a quarrel, she couldn't bear to be alone, she felt the separation as sharply as if he had struck her and so she *had* to speak to him, *had* to explain herself, *had* to get his reassurance that he didn't hate her, that he still loved her and wanted her with him. It was completely irrational, she knew. But then so was his need to be alone after a fight.

"Step, I'm sorry," she said.

"And I said fine." His tone said it was not fine.

"I mean I'm sorry but I have to say this."

"So say it," he said impatiently, not looking at her.

"I need you to wash the counter. Everywhere that the bugs touched. I know it makes no sense at all but I don't think I can stand to do anything in the kitchen today if you don't wash it for me first. Please."

"I was already planning on it," said Step. He tossed his paper towel into the bag after the last june bug corpse. Then he gathered the top of the bag together, held it up in one hand, and spun the bag so that there was a hard twist right under his hand. He pulled the plastic tie tight around the twist. He was so deft about it, thought DeAnne. As if he had everything down to a science. As if his hands already knew all the secrets about how to do things, to make things happen. She wondered how it felt, to know that you could just think of doing something and your hands would know how to do it.

He carried the garbage bag outside, and while he was gone she dared to go into the kitchen and it wasn't hard after all, as long as she didn't go near the sink, didn't go near the window which was still partly open. She could hear him outside, lifting the lid of the garbage can to put the bag inside. She wiped down the milk bottle and got out a bowl and a spoon and poured the raisin bran and the milk and put the milk back into the fridge and then she knew that she couldn't stay in the kitchen another minute. She fled into the family room.

Stevie was there, playing a computer game. It must be the new one Step bought for Stevie's birthday, she thought, even though it cost fifty dollars that they could ill afford. There was a pirate ship in full sail, and not far off there was another ship, and they were maneuvering to fire broadsides at each other. It reminded her of the movie *Captain Blood,* which she had never seen before she got married, but Step had seen it as a boy, he had read the book and loved it, and when it came on cable he had taped it and made the whole family watch and it *was* a good movie, wonderful dumb fun. Errol Flynn, a real swashbuckler. This game was like that. She ate spoonfuls of cereal that got steadily soggier, and she watched from the couch as Stevie played.

"Come on," Stevie said softly. "You can do it."

He spoke with an intensity DeAnne hadn't heard from him since they moved here.

"Come on, Roddy."

Had he even named the tiny people in the computer games?

"That's right, help him out, Scotty. You can *do* it."

He was pretending that his imaginary friends were part of the computer game. Well, that's all right, thought DeAnne. At least in the computer game they were really up there on the screen, you could *see* them. Maybe by playing this Lode Runner game Stevie would move his imaginary friends out of the back yard and up on the screen, where they'd just go away whenever he switched the computer off. Maybe this was a problem that would heal itself and they wouldn't have to take him to a psychiatrist after all, or at least maybe they wouldn't have to take him for very long.

"Hurry up, Jack! Roddy's in trouble and Scotty can't—that's *it!* Smooth! Got him!"

And with that the two ships swept each other with broadsides and then grappling hooks flew through the air. DeAnne was very impressed. It was almost like a movie, there was so much realistic movement on the screen. Not so . . . so *limited*-seeming, like all the other computer games she'd seen. Like Hacker Snack, for that matter. If this was the competition, Step was going to have to do some superb programming to match it.

"Well if you'd get into it instead of just standing there, David, you'd have more fun," said Stevie.

Her heart chilled. He was talking to the computer figures as if they were alive. As if they could hear him. Not just the "come on, come on" stuff that people said while watching football or basketball games on TV, but a full conversation, as if the screen were talking back. Stevie wasn't getting any better, and the computer game wasn't any help.

She thought back over the names. The regulars, Jack and Scotty, and the new one he had mentioned yesterday, David, and now a fourth. Roddy. It was getting worse.

She could hear Step turning off the water in the kitchen and she was finished with the raisin bran and it was almost time for Step to leave for work. "Stevie, maybe you better pause the game for a minute so your Dad and I can . . ."

Before she finished the sentence, Stevie had reached

behind the Atari and switched it off. Just like that.

"Honey, you could have saved your game," she said. "You didn't have to switch it off."

"It's fine," he said.

Step came into the family room. "Hi, Stevie," he said. "Sorry you had to get up early on your first day of summer, but your Mom and I wanted to tell you what's going to happen today."

Stevie waited. Not even curious, it seemed.

Step looked at DeAnne.

Oh, is it suddenly *my* turn? Well, she supposed that was fair. "Stevie, we've been worried about you ever since we got to Steuben. You've been so sad and quiet all the time."

"I'm OK," he said.

"The problems in school that we didn't even know about—the Stevie that we knew last fall in Vigor would have *told* us if a teacher was acting like Mrs. Jones did."

"She's gone," he said.

"We know she's gone," said DeAnne. She could hear herself starting to sound impatient. It was so *hard* dealing with Stevie, with the way he deflected questions. "But even after she left, you didn't seem to get any happier."

"I'm fine," said Stevie.

Step came to her rescue, for the moment at least. "It's not just the way you've become so sad and quiet, Door Man. It's the way you don't play with Robbie and Betsy anymore."

Stevie looked down at his hands.

"And your friends," said Step. "It worries us that you play all the time with imaginary friends."

Stevie seemed to bristle.

"Don't get mad at me, Stevie, *help* me here," said Step. "You've been talking about Jack and Scotty for months, and yet when we watch you playing, there's nobody there."

"I'm not lying," said Stevie.

"Well what are we to think, honey?" asked DeAnne.

"I never lie," said Stevie.

"We're not saying that you're lying," said Step. "This isn't about lying. It isn't about right and wrong or anything like that. We just want to take you to a doctor."

"You think I'm crazy," said Stevie. He seemed even angrier, but he wasn't looking at either of them. He was looking into the gap between them.

"Stevie, no way," said Step. "We do *not* think you're crazy. We just think you're having a hard time dealing with things and we want you to get help from somebody who knows about hard times. An expert. A doctor."

Stevie said nothing.

"Her name is Dr. Weeks," said DeAnne. "Her son is a member of the ward, so she's not even a stranger, really."

"She's not a Mormon herself, though," Step said.

"That's right," said DeAnne. "But your father has met her and she's a really nice lady. She'll just want you to talk to her. Nothing more. Can you do that?"

Stevie nodded.

"Will you speak honestly and openly to her?" DeAnne asked.

Now his angry glare was turned directly on her. "I always tell the truth," he said.

"I know," said DeAnne. "I didn't mean that I thought you'd lie, I just want you to *talk* to her. To tell her what's happening in your life. How things seem to you. You don't talk very much to your father and me, so we thought maybe somebody else, you could talk to somebody else, outside the family."

Stevie just sat there, looking into the space between them again.

"Can I come home sometimes?" he asked.

"Oh, Stevie, it's not like that! I'm just going to take you for a ten o'clock appointment. You'll go in and meet her and talk to her and then we'll come home. It's just once a week, and you won't even be there a whole hour. We wouldn't send you away from home, Stevie!"

Because Step wasn't pregnant he was able to get off the couch and kneel beside Stevie and put his arm around the boy. For once, Stevie responded, turning his face toward his father's shoulder.

"Stevie," said Step. "Stephen, my son, you are the brightest star in the darkest night, do you think we'd ever ever let you go? You belong with us until you *want* to go, and I hope that doesn't happen until you're old enough to go on a mission and then get married. Years from now. We will *never* send you away, no matter what."

But you mustn't say that, thought DeAnne. What if he needed to be hospitalized? What then? That would make a liar out of you, Step. Unless you really mean it, and even if he *needed* treatment like that you wouldn't let him go. Some love *that* would be!

Then she thought, I wouldn't let him go, either.

"Stevie, if you tell us you won't go to this doctor," said Step, "then we won't make you go. It's up to you. We don't think you're crazy or anything like that, but we think you're having a hard time and we think that maybe Dr. Weeks can help make things better for you, help *you* find a way to solve things for yourself. That's all. We'd really like you to try, but if you say no, we won't make you go."

How can you say that! cried DeAnne silently. Leaving it up to him—that's like asking a little kid whether he wants his tetanus booster! What if Stevie says no, what then, Step, what about your promise to *me* that you'd take him?

"I don't want to," said Stevie.

And there it was. Thanks a lot, Step!

But Stevie hadn't reached his decision yet. "Can she really help people solve hard problems?" he asked.

"Sometimes," said Step.

"Then I'll go," said Stevie. He didn't seem angry anymore.

"Thanks, Door Man," said Step. "And if it doesn't work out, or if you don't like her, then we won't make you go to her anymore, OK? This isn't like school, there isn't a law that says you have to go. Got it?"

Stevie nodded. Then he got up and left the room. DeAnne wanted to hold him, comfort him. But if he had wanted her right then, he could have stayed. He wanted to be alone, and that was his right.

Step sat back down beside her on the couch and put his arm around her. "It went pretty well, I'd say," he said.

She said nothing.

"I know what you're thinking," said Step, "and it isn't true."

"What am I thinking, smart guy?" she asked.

"You're thinking that you're the worst wife and mother who ever lived on the face of the earth and I'm telling you, that's just the pregnancy talking."

"No it's not," she said.

"I know you hate it when I point out things like this, but you've *always* spent the last couple of months of every pregnancy in the slough of despond. The worst mother, the baby would be luckier if it was stillborn—"

"I've never said such an awful thing!"

"You said it about Stevie and you said it about Betsy."

"So I'm just a machine that hormones use to accomplish their evil purposes in the world," she said.

"I'm not saying that the feelings you have aren't real, Fish Lady," said Step. "I'm just saying that you can't *believe* the things they make you think. You're a wonderful wife, and I wouldn't have any other."

"Oh yeah? Well what have I done this morning that was so wonderful?" asked DeAnne.

"For one thing, you've kept my fourth child alive

for another day, and that's a full-time job all by itself. And you didn't tell me to stop when you thought I was letting Stevie decide not to go to the shrink."

"What, have you suddenly decided that you're a mind reader?"

"You sat on the edge of that couch like it was all you could do to keep from leaping at me and stapling my mouth shut," said Step. "I don't have to read minds. But you didn't do it. You trusted me, and it worked out. I'd say that gives you the hero-of-the-morning medal."

"No it doesn't," said DeAnne. "Not after the way I talked to you in the kitchen."

"Nothing that anybody says on the same day they find five hundred thousand june bugs staring at them through the kitchen windows is allowed to count against them," said Step. "Now give me a kiss before I go to work because my ride is outside."

She kissed him. Then: "You didn't get any breakfast," she said.

"Why do I need breakfast," he answered, "in a world with candy machines?"

Then he got up and left.

Taking Stevie to Dr. Weeks was almost an anticlimax. She piled the kids into the car. Stevie was silent on the way to the doctor's office, but then he was usually silent, and there was no waiting when they got there, the receptionist just greeted Stevie with a smile and told him that his mother and brother and sister would be waiting for him when he got through and why not come in right now and meet Dr. Weeks? Stevie didn't even give DeAnne a backward glance. He just let the receptionist usher him into the office like a soldier letting the sergeant herd him into battle.

This has to work, thought DeAnne as she told stories to Robbie and Betsy in the waiting room. Please, Lord, let Dr. Weeks find a way for us to help get Stevie back to his old self.

Then the hour was up and Stevie came out. DeAnne raised a questioning eyebrow to Dr. Weeks, but the psychiatrist was not going to confide anything in front of Stevie. She just smiled and shook DeAnne's hand and then graciously shook hands with Robbie, who asked if he could come in and talk to her sometime, too, because he was really good at talking to people and he liked to do it a lot more than Stevie did. Dr. Weeks laughed and said, "Maybe someday you will, Robbie, but not for now."

On the way home, DeAnne wanted to ask Stevie about what happened, but she resisted the impulse. He couldn't be free to speak openly to Dr. Weeks if he knew he would face an inquisition as soon as he got into the car. So she confined her questions to one: "How was it?"

"Fine," he said.

The next morning, alone in the kitchen at 8:30, she called Dr. Weeks at home, hoping to catch her before she went to work. A man answered; it must be Lee, DeAnn realized. "May I speak to Dr. Weeks?" she asked.

"Who may I say is calling?" asked Lee.

"This is DeAnne Fletcher."

A pause.

"What's this about?" asked Lee.

"Is she not at home?" asked DeAnne. She wasn't about to confide in this young man, not after his display at the baptism.

"I need to tell her what it's about," said Lee.

"Then I'll call back later."

As she spoke, however, there was a click on the line. "Hello?" It was Dr. Weeks.

"Dr. Weeks, I'm so sorry to bother you at home, but I wanted to speak to you before you had other patients in the office and while the kids were still asleep."

"That's fine," said Dr. Weeks. "And who is this?"

"Oh, I'm sorry, I thought Lee had told you. This is DeAnne Fletcher, Stevie's mother."

"Lee was on the phone with you?"

"Yes, he answered the—"

"Lee, hang up the extension right now."

A long silence.

"He must already have hung up," said DeAnne.

"Lee, hang it up now. This conversation will not continue until you hang up the phone."

Another silence. And then a click.

"I'm sorry, Mrs. Fletcher. Sometimes it's like living with an oversized four-year-old."

"Yes, I understand," said DeAnne. But she did not actually understand.

"You wanted …?"

"I just—I needed to know if you—if there's anything I can help you with. Information or whatever. After your first visit with Stevie yesterday."

"Not really," said Dr. Weeks. "You already gave me the basic information before. Oh, I would appreciate it if you would make a list of all the names of his imaginary friends and mail it to me at the office."

"I could tell you all the names right now," said DeAnne.

"At the office, please," said Dr. Weeks. "That is how I maintain things in the strictest confidence."

"All right," said DeAnne. "Thanks. And I won't bother you at home again, I promise."

"That would be best," said Dr. Weeks. "Good morning." Then she hung up.

In the moment before DeAnne hung up, she heard a second click.

Lee had not hung up before. He must have listened to the whole thing.

No wonder Dr. Weeks was having her mail the list to the office. No wonder she said "That would be best." It wasn't rudeness, it was simple recognition of reality. Lee was spying on his mother every chance he got. Lee was out of control at home.

DeAnne sat down at the table at once and wrote down the names she could remember. Jack and Scotty, of course. But yesterday morning while Stevie was playing Lode Runner . . . what were the names? Roddy. And David was the one Stevie had mentioned after the baptism. Four now. Jack, Scotty, Roddy, and David.

Then she set that paper aside and wrote another:

Names of Stevie's friends in the order we heard them:
>   *Scotty*
>   *Jack*
>   *David*
>   *Roddy*

She sat there for a while, looking at the list. Imagining those imaginary friends herself. Four boys, Stevie's age. Maybe Scotty was a redhead like that child actor Johnny Whitaker, and Jack was a freckled round-faced brown-haired boy like Artful Dodger in *Oliver!*, and David was quiet, shy, holding back, perhaps a medium blond. And Roddy, bold as brass and inclined to get himself in trouble from which others had to rescue him. All hanging around the house here, always coming into the kitchen and she had to keep shooing them away from the fridge or there'd never be anything left for dinner, but then they'd come in and tell her all about the game they were playing in the back yard, and they'd be sweaty from running and have that acrid little-boy smell that DeAnne remembered from her brother, probably the worst smell in the world she had thought then, but now she thought that she would love to smell it on Stevie, on his friends, the stink of sweat from hours of hot play in the afternoon as the summer vacation got under way and the still-lengthening days left them with so much time, so much time in the evening, the lightning bugs like tiny meteor showers on the lawn as the children ran and ran, and they would never stop until at last she called them in and said, "Time for you boys to go home, don't you think? But first here's some milk and I made these cookies after supper, Stevie remember to let your friends choose first, *one* to a customer please, and maybe if you washed your hands you wouldn't catch a vile disease. I suppose I'll have to teach you how to work the faucet, from the look of you none of you boys has ever turned on a watertap in your lives. The square thing by the sink is a bar of soap." And they would laugh and protest and Stevie would say, "Mo-om," and then they'd eat the cookies and flecks of chocolate would cling to the corners of their mouths.

Oh God, why can't Stevie have real friends? Why can't I hear my son's voice crying Ollie ollie oxen free in the front yard as dusk settles over the street?

She folded up the list and put it in an envelope and addressed it to Dr. Weeks's office and then took it out front and put it in the mailbox at the curb.

When she got back into the kitchen, Robbie was kneeling on a chair, sounding out the names on the first list DeAnne had written.

"You forgot Peter," said Robbie.

"What?" asked DeAnne.

"Peter," said Robbie. "He won't come out and play though. He just watches."

"Do you know what this list is?" asked DeAnne.

"Stevie's friends," said Robbie. "He won't ever let me meet them, though."

"No, I don't guess he would," said DeAnne.

"What you writing them down for, Mommy? Is Stevie having them come over?"

"Don't worry about it," said DeAnne. She put the list up on top of the serving dishes in the top cupboard. "I was just writing names. What do you want for breakfast?"

"Cream of Wheat!" cried Robbie.

DeAnne let him help make the mush, and within moments the list was forgotten.

Dicky came into Step's office on Tuesday afternoon. "Good news," said Dicky.

"Oh, really?" Step immediately felt a thrill of dread: Ray had decided to support the PC after all.

"Ray has decided to publish a Commodore 64 version of Hacker Snack."

How ludicrous! thought Step. No one had *ever* spoken to him about Hacker Snack, not even after he walked in on the programmers working on it as a secret project just before the San Francisco trip. He had assumed that the programmers told Dicky and Dicky told Ray and they just dropped the whole thing. But no, apparently it was still alive and now Dicky had the gall to walk in here and say that Ray had *decided* to publish a game that didn't belong to him.

"Oh, that's a shame," said Step.

"What do you mean?" asked Dicky.

"I already sold it to another publisher."

Dicky sat there in stunned silence as the blood flowed into his face, turning it red. "You sold Hacker Snack to a *competitor?*"

"No one here made me an offer for it. It's not as if I was hard to find. So I figured you weren't interested."

"Don't give me that bullshit," said Dicky. "I know perfectly well that you've been aware of our interest in Hacker Snack for months."

"On the contrary," said Step. "I knew that Glass had disassembled my code and that the programmers had been goofing around with it, but since I had not sold the rights to anybody and no one at Eight Bits Inc. had ever so much as whispered the name of Hacker Snack to me, it never occurred to me that there was any official interest in it at all."

"Well, now I'm telling you that Ray has decided to publish Hacker Snack."

"And I'm telling you that I've signed a contract selling those rights to someone else."

"You had no right to sign such a contract," said Dicky. "Your employment agreement specifically gives the rights to any and all—"

"My employment agreement specifically excludes all games I published before coming to Eight Bits Inc., Dicky. Before you go quoting people's employment agreements, you ought to read them. They aren't *all* the same."

Dicky looked as though his face was going to explode. "You ungrateful little shit."

"Grateful for what?" asked Step. "I've worked here for more than four months, and not once did anyone make any kind of offer about Hacker Snack. You even forbade me to do any programming, remember? It has been crystal clear to me all along that Eight Bits Inc. valued me only for my manual writing. Or am I mistaken in that? Should I have thought of myself as a gamewright all along?"

"Do you realize what you've just done?"

"I've done nothing," said Step. "*You're* the ones who went behind my back and invested time in developing a product for which you hadn't the decency even to ask about the rights. Is that my fault? All I did was sell what was mine to a company that expressed an interest in it."

"Who? Who did you sell it to?"

"There is nothing in my employment agreement that obligates me to tell you what I do with my property, Dicky."

"We're going to sue their asses off!"

"Which is precisely why I have no intention of telling you."

"Ray will fire you for this."

"He'll fire *me?*" asked Step. Actually, he thought this was quite likely. But to Step being fired wasn't that bad a prospect. DeAnne could hardly blame him for leaving his job if he got *fired,* could she? So he even found himself enjoying this confrontation. There was nothing Step valued that Dicky could take away from him. "I don't think I'm the one whose job is on the line. I think the person whose job is on the line is the one who suggested developing an adaptation of my game behind my back. The one who didn't even bother to find out that my employment agreement is different before committing Eight Bits Inc.'s resources to a game that you didn't own."

"You fool," said Dicky. "That was Ray himself who did all that."

"Oh?" asked Step. "And is that the way Ray will remember it? Will he remember all the times you advised him against such a dangerous course of action?"

Dicky looked at him in livid silence.

"Dicky, now's a good time for you to lift your fat cheeks out of that chair and carry them through that door. If Ray's going to fire me, then have him send me a memo to that effect and I'll be out of here collecting unemployment in a hot second. And if he's not going to fire me, then I've got work to do and you are in my way."

Step turned back to the page proofs he was checking.

After a while he heard Dicky get up out of his chair and leave the room. Softly, softly, on little cat feet.

When Dicky was gone, Step got up on shaking legs and gently closed the door. Then he leaned against the wall, breathing heavily. He felt so light-headed. Is this how a soldier feels when he has leapt from the trench and run toward the enemy lines and reached them and discovered that not one bullet touched him? Step had missed Vietnam with a draft lottery number of 225—a number that sounded as magical to him now as 7 or 3 or

12 or 40 sounded to other people. He had no experience of war, of real courage, of struggle between man and man. But this might just have been a taste, he thought. Dicky came in here prepared to bestow some pittance on me as if it were a great gift from Eight Bits Inc., and I laughed in his face and dared him to do his worst. I don't know how I did it without wetting my pants.

He went about his business as best he could, considering that he expected at any moment to have Dicky come in with his pink slip. At the end of the day he hadn't seen Dicky again at all, and he hadn't been fired. It was almost a disappointment.

The Cowpers moved on the tenth of June. "I wish you could have waited till Saturday," DeAnne told Jenny. "Step wanted to help load up the truck. You've been so good to us, and we've never been able to give anything back."

"Nonsense," said Jenny. "I've had a wonderful time since you got here. In fact, if you had been living here when Spike accepted the transfer, I don't know if we would have taken it. But that's the way it goes, don't you know? We were each other's best friend, except for our husbands—I had to say that real quick to get it in before *you* said it, I know—anyway we were best friends, as long as it lasted, and I'll never forget you. But don't bother promising to write, you know we won't. Except Christmas cards every year. I'll never be bored reading your year-end family newsletter, you hear?"

"Can't I write if I want to?"

"Phone me. I'm not a writer. If you're broke, phone me collect."

"And vice versa," said DeAnne. "You're the one who knows my phone number, so you have to call first."

"Of course," said Jenny. "How else will you know

where to send the five hundred dollars for the Datsun?"

"Eight hundred dollars," said DeAnne.

"Make it ten thousand if you want," said Jenny. "But *we* think the price was five hundred dollars and we don't really care if you never pay *that*. Think of it as a law-of-consecration car, a church-service car. Take it out visiting teaching and take teenagers to youth activities in it. And whenever you do, think of us."

"I'll think of you more than you know," said DeAnne. "And I'll miss you more than you know."

"You'll make a new best friend within a month," said Jenny.

"Someone else can be my best friend," said DeAnne, "without ever being half as good a friend as you."

"Are you just trying to make me cry so I can't drive straight and I run us into a bridge abutment or something?" asked Jenny. "Now make sure none of your kids is standing behind the U-Haul or the car when we drive out." Jenny looked at the U-Haul in disgust. "They're a big enough company to transfer our family across the country and buy our stupid house, but they're not big enough that they can afford to pay for a real moving company. Tell Step to quit his lousy job, they're all thieves." Then Jenny kissed DeAnne on the cheek and they hugged each other and then Spike finally locked the house and got into the cab of the U-Haul with two of the kids as Jenny got into their nice car with the rest of the kids. DeAnne made sure that Stevie and Robbie and Elizabeth were in plain sight and nowhere near the cars, and then she waved and the Cowpers pulled out into the road.

She watched them out of sight and then felt the baby inside her do his stretching thing, pushing against her ribs until it hurt, until she thought she couldn't stand it anymore. She wanted to swat the baby, to yell at it, to *demand* that it stop hurting her, that it just leave her alone for a minute.

The baby pushed all the harder. He was probably

responding to the grief hormones flowing through her body, the chemical anguish.

At last the pressure subsided and she could think of walking again. "Come on, kids. This isn't the Cowpers' house anymore, so we better go on home."

When she got home, there was the Cowpers' old beat-up Datsun B-210. The car that made her and Step a two-car family for the first time in their marriage. She walked up and touched it, examined it, the paint pitted and faded, the doors rusted through at running-board height. She caressed the car as if it were a horse that no one had been able to tame but her. Thank you for Jenny, she said. But why did you have to take her away from me so soon?

She stopped herself from thinking that way, and said, very clearly and definitely inside her mind, Thank you for Jenny. And then she forced herself to leave it at that, to go inside and concentrate on fixing lunch, which was long overdue.

There was a substitute mailman, so the mail didn't arrive till almost four o'clock. There was an envelope from Agamemnon, and inside was the check. The money that would catch them up on their payments on the house in Indiana. If the regular mailman hadn't been on vacation, she could have paid the Cowpers for the car before they left.

Oh, well. She'd make out the checks tomorrow and everything would be fine. Most of the money would be gone immediately, they were so far behind—and none of it could go to the IRS for their back taxes, so *that* still hung over their heads. Still, freedom was in sight.

But the next day when she sat down to write out the checks, she just couldn't bring herself to do it. It made her feel so stupid, to find it emotionally impossible to write the checks. Hadn't she and Step decided last night that they would definitely go ahead and pay the mortgage up to date?

Finally she wrote out a check for the amount of the oldest overdue mortgage payment, along with all the late fees that had accrued on that one payment. She put it in an envelope, piled the kids into the car, drove to the post office, and slipped the envelope into the box.

A month. That's all I'm doing, just paying for one month's delay before they foreclose. Why? It's stupid and dangerous—they'll probably still call the note; this one payment won't do anything at all. But I can't wipe out that five thousand dollars sitting in the bank. I can't bring it down to nothing because who knows when the next check will come?

10

·INDEPENDENCE DAY·

This is what the Fletchers did on the Fourth of
July: The 1st Ward had a flag-raising ceremony
at dawn, along with a pancake breakfast. Step could
think of about three thousand things he'd rather do than
get up before dawn on the Monday morning of the only
three-day weekend of the summer, but the elders quorum
was cooking the pancakes and DeAnne was conducting
the choir's singing of "The Battle Hymn of the Republic."
Having a southern church choir sing *that* song was in
itself remarkable enough to be worth getting up early
just to hear it.

In the weeks since the Cowpers had moved, the
choir leader, Mary Anne Lowe, had been cultivating
DeAnne's friendship. To Step it seemed almost as if
Sister Lowe had been waiting for Jenny to get out of the

before she moved in, as if there were room for only one friend in DeAnne's life at a time. And maybe it was so. DeAnne didn't exactly have a surplus of time and energy. Still, it seemed to Step that this friendship was different from the friendship with Jenny. Where Jenny had seemed to revive DeAnne, to buoy her up, Mary Anne's ebullient energy only made DeAnne seem more tired. Most annoying to Step was the way that being friends with Mary Anne Lowe meant having more and more duties in the ward music program. Like conducting the choir for the sunrise flag raising and all those practices on Saturdays and Sundays getting ready for it.

When DeAnne had done compassionate service with Jenny, it almost always happened during the day, but the choir practices took place during the few hours that Step had home with DeAnne, with the family, and so he ended up either going to choir practice himself, as the only tenor, or staying home trying to tend the children while typing Hacker Snack code into the Commodore 64.

Even with Jenny gone, the compassionate service assignments continued. Sister Bigelow was still on the phone with DeAnne a couple of times a week, so that Step would come home from work and find DeAnne ready to rush over to Sister Something-or-other's house with a salad or a casserole or a plate of biscuits and a tub of gravy and could Step please just watch the kids for an hour and maybe slice up the cucumbers for the salad?

Sure, DeAnne. And I'll finish Hacker Snack in December, about three months after we're bankrupt.

Then he'd feel bad about being so childishly resentful and he'd go ahead and do the things she had asked and, usually, more, so she'd get back and find dinner ready to eat, or the kids already bathed, or whatever else he figured he could accomplish to make her feel cared for and help her get some rest because, after all, wasn't she the one carrying their child? What right did he have to think that she somehow wasn't doing enough?

After the sunrise service and the [...] tasted like they were cut from cardb[...] down like lead, the Fletchers came home [...] began to fuss and fight with each other. Step [...] problem by sending them all back to bed, sin[...] were obviously too tired to get along in human so[...]ty; and then he took DeAnne by the arm and dragged *her* back to bed. Within fifteen minutes Robbie and Betsy were both asleep and so was DeAnne. Stevie, of course, stubbornly lay there in bed with his eyes open until Step walked in and quietly told him he could read if he wanted to. Finally Step went to bed and lay there feeling physically worn out and very sleepy. He continued to feel that way for five minutes, ten minutes, fifteen minutes, until he gave up and went into the family room and slipped the Hacker Snack disk into the drive and turned on the computer.

It made the usual horrible grinding sound as it activated the disk drive—though it was not as bad as the metallic chewing noise the Commodore disk drive made—and then the familiar screen came up and Step began to move his little cartoon character, Rodney, with his nerdy glasses and perpetual melvin, through the maze of computer chips and hamburgers.

This is boring, thought Step. Not the first time, but each level is really just more of the same. You don't get that much pleasure out of the tenth time you play it.

The normal solution to this problem was to make each succeeding level so hard that you kept playing just to try to beat the machine and get your name on the vanity board. But for Step that wasn't enough. It had to be fun the first time, and yet the game had to be rich enough that at higher and higher levels better stuff happened, so that the game became its own reward.

What could he change without eating up too much memory? Well, it didn't have to be computer chips and burgers. He could work in other stuff—maybe different

ter brands! Eating a VIC-20 and a Timex and an
II on the way to finally reaching an Atari and
maybe a mainframe or something.

If I'm going to do an evolutionary sequence like that,
why not do evolution itself? Instead of starting with
Rodney, I start with a salamander or something that
climbs up out of primordial ooze and then at each level
he becomes something else. A dinosaur. A mammal. A
shrew, maybe. And then a chimp. And then Homo
habilis, and then some big athletic-looking guy, and then
finally, as the crowning pinnacle of evolution, the computer
hacker, the nerd with glasses and a melvin! OK, that
would be fun, but it would chew up disk space, especially
since he couldn't very well have dinosaurs collecting
computer chips, so he'd have to change the thing they ate
at every level. Leaves for the dinosaurs—and maybe
salamanders, the guys from the previous level! And the
shrews could eat dinosaur eggs. And the athletic guys
could trample Homo habilis guys and leave them in a car-
toony pile of arms and legs like Beetle Bailey after the
sergeant gets through beating him up. And then Rodney
could leave athletic guys behind him holding pink slips!

Would anybody get the joke? No, not pink slips,
then. Too hard to show on the computer. No, they'll be
left wearing Burger King uniforms!

That's it, that's it, he thought. It's still Hacker Snack,
but it's a better game. This is going to blow Agamemnon
away.

Step went into his office, pulled out a piece of
paper, and began calculating how much memory the
new graphics would eat up. He actually found himself
wishing for the 128K of the IBM PC. Lousy as it was,
the PC would still give him the room to do it right, with
better animation and more levels. It could be a bigger
game, with large mazes that extended off the screen.
And what if I had 256K? He could forget character-
based graphics and do smooth full-screen animations,

like that pirate ship game he had seen Stevie playing.

What was the name of that game? He had looked for it once before, and never found it. Sometime he'd have to borrow Gallowglass's disassembler program and figure out how the programmer of that game had done it.

DeAnne came sleepily into his office. "I must have dozed off," she said.

"That was the idea," said Step.

"We have to get to the Eight Bits Inc. party, don't we?"

"It's an all-day picnic," said Step. "We can show up anytime."

"Well, the kids might want to stay and play awhile, and I imagine they'll be serving the food around noon, won't they?"

Step shrugged. "What time is it now?"

"Eleven."

"So what's the rush?"

"No rush," she said. "Do you know what they'll be serving at the picnic?"

"Hot dogs and stuff," said Step. "And fried chicken, I think. Good old magnanimous Ray is having it catered by Colonel Sanders and Oscar Mayer."

"Don't be snide," said DeAnne. "I think having a company picnic is a good idea."

"I'm sure it is," said Step. "I'm just tired."

"Why didn't you sleep?"

"I tried," said Step. "And then I got to thinking."

"Oh, *that's* a mistake. I gave it up years ago."

"Well, I'll finish this later," he said. "Let's get the kids ready and head out before the temperature gets up to a hundred. The humidity is already at a hundred percent by now, I'm sure."

"You're just a desert boy, Step."

"I'm not used to sweating and having it not evaporate until the next day." He turned off the computer and got up from the chair and stretched. "*Now* I think I could sleep."

"Well, then, go lie down," said DeAnne. "We'll go later in the day."

"No, let's go now and get it over with. At some point we'll see Dicky in a bathing suit and then we'll throw up the pancakes from this morning and we'll all feel much better."

Robbie and Betsy woke up sluggish, as much from the pancakes as from their nap, and it was almost one o'clock before they got to the picnic. Eight Bits Inc. had rented UNC-Steuben's private lake, and there were about a hundred people in the water or milling around on shore. The food was being served under a canopy, and they headed there from the car. Ray Keene himself was nowhere to be seen—he had been getting more and more reclusive over the past few months, and some of the programmers had started referring to him as Howard Keene, in reference to Howard Hughes. But Keene's wife was there, and their five-year-old daughter, and every *other* employee of Eight Bits Inc. had shown up. They knew this because Dicky greeted them by the condiment table with the cheery announcement, "At last, the Fletchers? Finally we have a hundred percent."

"I didn't know we were taking attendance," said Step with equal cheer. "I would have brought a note from my mom." And then he and DeAnne concentrated on getting hot dogs into the kids.

Afterward, since they couldn't swim, Step took the boys over to where people were playing games—horse-shoes and lawn darts. After a few moments of watching, though, Step concluded that these were no safer than sending nonswimmers into the lake—the lawn darts were being thrown by careless, unsupervised children, and the horseshoes were dominated by adults, mostly from the business end of Eight Bits Inc., including Cowboy Bob, and the iron shoes were whizzing through the air with enough velocity to break a child's head open. Stevie, of course, was quite careful, but Robbie had a way of getting excited and running straight toward his goal without noticing things like darts and iron shoes flying through the air. So Step kept a firm grip on Robbie's hand and soon led both boys away from the games.

Which left precious little for them to do. Well, fine, thought Step. I'll go collect DeAnne and Betsy and we'll head on out of here. After all, attendance has now been taken and we won't be missed.

Step saw DeAnne standing near the food canopy, talking to Mrs. Keene, who had lit up a cigarette and was now puffing away as she talked. Even outdoors with a slight breeze, Step knew that the cigarette smoke would quickly make DeAnne sick and light-headed, hardly a good thing for a pregnant woman in the afternoon heat. So, with Stevie and Robbie in tow, Step headed over and broke into the conversation.

"I'm sorry, Mrs. Keene, but DeAnne's probably just too shy to tell you that cigarette smoke really makes her ill. If she weren't pregnant, it wouldn't be a problem outdoors like this, but—"

"Oh, that's just fine," said Mrs. Keene pleasantly. "I was hardly smoking it anyway." She dropped the cigarette to the ground and twisted her foot on it. "You should have said something, you sweet girl, I just didn't even think, I smoked right through my own pregnancy with Allison and so I forget that some people just need to have fresh air all the time."

"It really wasn't bothering me outside in the breeze like this," said DeAnne.

"Oh, heavens, girl, I'm the boss's wife, you think I don't know that? But just between you and me, I'm not half so impressed with Ray as Ray is, and Ray isn't all that impressed with *me*, so kissing up to me won't help anybody keep on his good side anyway!" She chuckled, a low, throaty smoker's laugh.

Mrs. Keene was charming and funny and nice, but

also dangerously disloyal. Was the marriage in trouble? That would be no surprise, really, given the kind of autocratic, secretive man Ray Keene was becoming; the joke in the Pit was that Ray kept secrets so well that his wife had to hire a private investigator to find out where he kept his dick. But if the marriage *was* in trouble, Mrs. Keene could be a walking kiss of death, bestowing herself on selected employees and then leaving them behind without a thought of the consequences. Somebody was bound to be keeping track of whom she talked to.

"Dad," said Robbie.

Step turned away from the conversation. Robbie was excited about something. Behind him a little girl was standing in front of a clump of other little kids. "Allison wants me to go on the raft with them! Can I go, Dad?"

"No," said Step. "You know you can't go on the water, Robbie. You can't swim."

The little girl stepped forward and, in a voice that was accustomed to getting results, said, "He can *so* go. My daddy said it was perfectly safe."

"Then that means *you* can go," said Step. "But Robbie can*not* go, because *his* daddy says that it is *not* safe."

"Well my daddy is the boss of this company and what he says goes!"

Step remembered the three precious pieces of paper in DeAnne's filing cabinet at home—his employment agreement, the contract from Agamemnon, and Ray's memo stating his intention not to support the IBM PC—and his smile broadened. "Well, little girl, your daddy may be the boss of this company, but he is not the boss of my family, and so when it comes to the safety of my children, what *he* says matters about as much as a mouse fart."

The other children delighted in this—the one topic guaranteed to make little kids laugh is flatulence. But

Allison was not amused. "I'll tell my daddy what you said!"

"By all means," said Step. "He'll be proud to know that his little girl thinks she can boss around grown men. He's doing a fine job of raising you."

Allison was young enough not to realize she was not being complimented. "Well, thank you," she said. "I forgive you and I won't tell. Now come *on*, Robbie."

"You missed the point, little girl," said Step. "Robbie is not going on the raft. This is because I love Robbie and don't want him to fall into the lake and drown. But I can't wait for *you* to go on the raft. So please, hurry up, the lake is waiting for you."

Allison looked confused for a moment, and then stuck her tongue out at Robbie and led her little troop of friends off toward the water.

"She stuck her tongue out at me, Daddy," said Robbie.

"And it made her look really ugly and stupid, didn't it?" said Step.

When he turned back to DeAnne and Mrs. Keene, however, he was chagrined to realize that they had apparently been listening to the whole exchange. Mrs. Keene at once put him at ease by winking and saying, "She's got so much of her father in her, wouldn't you say?"

"I wouldn't know," said Step. "I haven't seen Ray in months."

"Well, you haven't missed much," said Mrs. Keene. "You must be independently wealthy or something, because it's plain that you don't give a rat's ass whether you keep your job. I like that in a man." Then she grinned at DeAnne. "I'm flirting with your husband, Mrs. Fletcher, but don't pay any attention to it, because I'm just a little bit drunk. My rule is no more than one martini—per hour." She laughed in delight. "Not really, of course," she said. "What I'm drunk on is the fact that

I can look around this whole group of people, more than a hundred of them now, and I can be absolutely certain deep in my soul that every single one of them hates Ray Keene. You don't mind my telling you this, do you?"

"Actually," said DeAnne, "we really need to be going."

"Oh, I'm not surprised," said Mrs. Keene. "I need to be going myself."

"Where's Stevie?" asked DeAnne.

"Right over there," said Step, pointing to the tree where Stevie was leaning, watching the activities on the water. "Where's Betsy?"

"Oh, that young fellow who used to drive you home a lot is taking her for a walk."

"Glass?" he asked. "Gallowglass?"

"No, he said his name was Roland McIntyre."

"That's Glass," said Step. He cursed himself for not having warned DeAnne, not having told her that she must not let Betsy out of her sight for a moment, and she must be especially certain not to let Roland McIntyre, alias Saladin Gallowglass, so much as touch a hair on Betsy's head. "Where did he take her? How long ago?"

"Oh, while I was talking to Mrs. Keene here. He took her off that way, up that hill."

Vaguely in the direction of the parking lot. Or the woods just to the left of the cars. In any event, the very area where nobody else was gathered.

"Is something wrong?" said Mrs. Keene.

"I hope not," said Step. "Here's Robbie." He put Robbie's hand in DeAnne's. "Don't let *anybody* take him or Stevie for a walk, please."

DeAnne clearly caught from Step's air of urgency the fact that she had done something very wrong by letting Glass take Betsy. "Step, I'm sorry, I figured he was a friend, I saw him drop you off so often . . ."

He didn't stay for the rest of her apology. He wasn't

much of a runner, and he was badly out of shape, but he still had breath enough when he got up by the parking lot to call out Betsy's name, then Glass's.

"Over here, Step!" called Glass.

Now Step could see him, standing behind a car at the far edge of the lot, beside an overgrown pasture. "Do you have Betsy with you?"

"Of course," said Glass. "Your wife said I could take her for a walk."

Step was halfway across the parking lot. Now his run up the hill was catching up with him—he was panting, and he hadn't enough breath for speech.

"I think she might be wet," said Glass. "I was just checking. I didn't know which car was yours, though."

At last Step was around behind the car and there was Betsy, holding hands with Glass. Her diaper was still on and she was waving a dandelion fuzzball, trying to get the last of the seeds to fall off. Step finally had breath to speak. "DeAnne said you could take her on a walk, not fiddle with her diaper, Glass."

"Well, I didn't think you'd want your daughter walking around getting diaper rash," said Glass.

Step scooped Betsy up into his arms and stood there looking Glass in the eye. "I don't know how to put this delicately, Glass, so I won't try. I like you, as a programmer, as a friend. But don't you ever, ever touch any of my children as long as you live. Because if I ever catch you alone with one of my kids again, then that will *be* as long as you live."

Glass looked him right in the eye, and for a moment it seemed that he was going to answer—angrily? With a joke? Step could not begin to guess. Finally Glass just shut his mouth tight and turned his head to look out toward the entrance to the park.

OK, so I've made an enemy, thought Step as he carried Betsy back down toward DeAnne. But I'm not making this up. Glass had Betsy for no more than a couple of minutes before he had her off behind a car, where nobody could see, and if I hadn't come up there he would have added her to his list of treasured stories of times he has cleaned the private parts of little girls. Until now Step had begun to think that Glass had never actually molested a child, that perhaps what he had said to Step in the hotel room in San Francisco had been nothing worse than a weird fantasy of his, an obsession that was still only in his imagination. Now Step knew better. Call it "checking her diaper" or "helping her wash," it was still sexual molestation and he had come *this close* to doing it to Betsy.

When Step got back to DeAnne, Mrs. Keene was still there—and she was frankly curious. "What was all that about?" she said.

"Just time for us to go home, I think," said Step.

"You certainly seemed upset when you heard that Bubba McIntyre was taking her for a walk. I can assure you, Bubba's the sweetest boy and he's very good with children."

Step remembered Allison Keene and had to ask. "Did Bubba ever babysit for you, Mrs. Keene?"

"He used to, back when Allison was just a toddler. He used to come around and *ask* if he could babysit, he was such a dear. That's how he got started programming on our old Commodore Pet—that's where he first wrote Scribe, you know—only when he started really working for Ray, Ray told me never to ask Bubba to babysit for us again. It wouldn't be right to have his best programmer also tending his children, I suppose!" But there was still a quizzical expression on her face.

"Is Betsy all right?" asked DeAnne.

"He was about to check her diaper," said Step. "To see if it was wet."

"Of course it isn't," said DeAnne. "I just changed her. I told him so."

"You told him?"

"He asked if she needed changing, and I told him I'd just changed her."

Mrs. Keene was not stupid. "Good God," she said. "You're not saying that Bubba—but that's—"

"No, I'm not saying anything about Bubba," said Step. "Except that if I ever catch him alone with my little girl again, a jury will be deciding between life imprisonment and capital punishment for me."

Mrs. Keene looked sick. "But he tended Allison all the time when she was your little Betsy's age."

"At least he doesn't tend her anymore," said Step.

"No, because Ray . . ." Mrs. Keene's expression darkened. "I knew he was a son-of-a-bitch, but even *he* wouldn't hire a . . . a . . . person that he knew was . . ." She shook her head firmly. "I'm not going to believe malicious gossip." She turned her back and stalked away.

"Oh, Step," said DeAnne, her face stricken. "Why didn't you tell me about that boy?"

"I forgot," said Step.

"You *forgot!*"

"No, I mean I forgot that when we brought the kids to the picnic, Glass would be here. He's been asking to babysit for us from the first moment I met him. But after San Francisco, when I realized what direction his fantasies go, I've been making sure he never gets a chance to meet the kids. And nothing happened today, not really. It was my fault things came so close, not yours, and now let's *please* get the hell away from this place."

DeAnne did not demur. In a couple of minutes they were back in the car, pulling out of the lot and heading home. Step was very calm all the way, and because Robbie and Stevie were in the car they hardly said anything—nothing at all pertaining to what happened with Betsy and Glass.

At home, DeAnne wasted not a moment before she

had Betsy undressed and in the bathtub. Step stood at the door and thought of all the times he had changed Betsy and bathed her and never once had he thought of anything except to talk to her and smile at her and be *close* to her, just as such times had always been close, affectionate times with his sons. But now the idea of watching DeAnne bathe Betsy made him feel guilty, as if the mere fact of knowing how Glass had looked at her made it so that any man's eyes that looked at her were vile, even Step's own.

The rage and shame he felt were too strong for him. He fled into the bedroom and threw himself on the bed and buried his face in the pillow and roared, a wordless animal shout that he couldn't contain a moment longer. Again. Again.

Panting, exhausted, he rolled over onto his back.

Gradually he became aware that he was not alone. He turned his head and saw Stevie in the doorway. "Hi, Stevedore," he said.

"Did that man hurt Betsy?" asked Stevie.

"No," said Step. Of course, he thought. Stevie isn't as young as Robbie. He isn't as oblivious. He watches more. He understood some of what had gone on at the picnic. "No, Betsy's fine."

"Then why were you yelling like that? You sounded really mad."

How much to say? The truth, as much as it was fair to tell someone as young and innocent as Stevie. "I *was* mad, but mostly at myself, because I didn't protect Betsy well enough. And also I was afraid, because we came so close to something bad happening."

"What?" asked Stevie. "What bad thing?"

"There are people in the world who do bad things to children," said Step. "People like that are the worst people in the world. Jesus said that if any man harmed a child, it would be better for him if he tied a millstone around his neck and threw himself in the sea. And if you think somebody like that might hurt your child, well, it makes you really angry and afraid."

Stevie nodded. "Yeah," he said.

"But nothing bad happened, OK? I was just upset because I thought maybe we came close to having something bad happen, that's all."

"Sometimes the bad things really *do* happen," said Stevie.

"Yes, I guess they do," said Step. "But if I can help it, it'll never happen to any child of mine."

"I know," said Stevie. "You and Mom are really good." He turned and went back to his room.

This was the most Stevie had said to him about *anything* since they moved to Steuben. He couldn't wait for DeAnne to get through bathing Betsy so he could tell her.

But when DeAnne came into the room Step had fallen asleep. He didn't get to tell her what Stevie had said until late that night, when they were in bed together, and when he told her what Stevie said at the end she nestled closer to Step and said, "Maybe we *are* pretty good parents, Junk Man. At least we're not Ray Keene or his wife."

That was why Step got back to thinking about Ray Keene, and realizing that Ray almost certainly knew about Glass's predilections, and yet he kept him around Eight Bits Inc., and hired other people to work with him, people for whom Glass would certainly offer to babysit, and Ray said not one word to help other people protect their children. Now, maybe Ray didn't really know, maybe it was just coincidence that he didn't let his wife hire Glass to babysit Allison anymore. But maybe Ray *did* know, and just didn't tell anybody because he needed Glass too much, needed Scribe 64 too much to risk losing the strange sick boy-man who had created it for him.

❖   ❖   ❖

Dr. Weeks didn't come to the door of her office any-more when Stevie's hour was up. He pushed the heavy wooden door open by himself, and came out, looking—or so it seemed to DeAnne—smaller every time he did. She really is shrinking him in there, she thought. Yet Stevie never complained about going and never talked afterward about what went on. It was as if it didn't really happen to him, or as if it was something not important enough to be discussed.

On Monday, the eighteenth of July, DeAnne got the kids home from the psychiatrist's office and let Robbie and Elizabeth run out into the back yard to play, while she and Stevie got the mail.

She headed for the side door that led from the car-port into the laundry room and then to the kitchen—it was the door they always used. But Stevie called to her. "Mom, there's a package at the front door!"

In fact, it wasn't a package at all. It was a manila envelope. It had been mailed, but the postman had left it at the door, probably because it had a rubber stamp on it, DO NOT BEND, and there would have been no way to get it into the mailbox without bending it. It had a Steuben postmark, but no return address, and the mail-ing label had been neatly typed: "Stephen & Diane Fletcher, 4404 Chinqua Penn, Steuben, N.C."

No zip, and while they had got Stephen's name right, DeAnne's was wrong. Usually people either got both right or got both wrong. It probably meant it was from someone who knew Step and not her. Or from someone who wanted to peeve her and not Step! Why was someone careful enough to get it stamped DO NOT BEND and then careless enough not to include a return address?

Stevie came into the house with her, and as she opened the mail at the kitchen table she heard him start up the Atari. It bothered her that he didn't go outside enough, even though it was summer. He was spending altogether too much time at the computer. It was probably time for her and Step to institute time limits on computer games just as they had for television. An hour a day—that wasn't unreasonable. And then let Stevie find something else to do. Something healthier, something that would get him out in the sun. He looked downright pallid compared to Robbie and Elizabeth, who were getting quite a golden glow, with nice highlights in their hair.

Most of the mail was ordinary. She set aside the letter from the mortgage company in Indiana—it could only be bad news, and it could wait. Then she opened the anonymous manila envelope.

Inside was a 45-rpm record, and nothing else. It was by a group DeAnne was only vaguely aware of. She really didn't follow rock music, not the way Step did. But she did enjoy watching the new videos now and then. Cable had MTV here in Steuben, the way they had in Vigor, and she left the TV tuned to that channel sometimes while she worked. She liked the "Billy Jean" video—the lighting sidewalk appealed to her. But that one where Michael Jackson became a monster had scared the children and she had stopped just leaving MTV on when the kids were up. Still, she was aware of rock music, however vaguely. She must have seen something by the Police before.

They never bought forty-fives, and so DeAnne had no idea where she could find one of those little plastic doodads you had to put in the middle of them to play them on the stereo. It had to be somewhere near the stereo. They certainly wouldn't have thrown it away—throwing things away was not their problem.

There was a knock at the back door, the one that led from the family room into the back yard. It was Robbie. "Can we have the sprinkler?"

"OK," said DeAnne. "Come on in, both of you, and get into your swimsuits."

Elizabeth trooped in after Robbie with an exaggerated lope. Giant steps. "Pink-*er*, pink-*er*, pink-*er*," she chanted. It took a moment to realize that Elizabeth was saying "sprinkler." Why it had become a chant, and what it had to do with taking great galumphing steps through the family room, DeAnne could not begin to guess. It was the great mystery of childhood—what they thought they were doing when they did such weird things.

Of course, that was also the great mystery of adulthood.

Then DeAnne glanced down at the stereo and saw immediately what she had missed before: the 45-rpm adapter was built into the turntable.

She got the record from the kitchen table and slipped it onto the adapter and turned on the stereo and set the needle on the record. It sounded like big dumb lummoxes singing lumberjack songs. She lifted the needle, changed the speed to 45, and set the needle down again. Now it was a rock song.

It was a strange kind of love song. No matter what the woman did, the man would be there watching her. It didn't sound like he loved her, either. Or even liked her. It talked about her faking smiles, staking claims, breaking promises. And the rhyming was relentless. "Every cake you bake," she thought, and almost laughed. "Every child you wake. Every thirst you slake. Every duck and drake. Every well-done steak." Amazing the number of words in English that rhymed with *take*. The songwriter had barely scratched the surface.

Then it didn't seem funny anymore. Because somebody had sent that record to them anonymously. Why would they do that? They wanted to send a message. And what was the message? That no matter what they did, somebody would be watching.

She went around the house, checking the locks on all the doors. In the meantime the record had ended. She came back into the family room and started it over. After just a few notes of the song, she lifted the needle and turned off the stereo. Step would play it tonight, and that would be plenty.

Elizabeth came into the room in her diaper, carrying her swimsuit. DeAnne laboriously sat on the couch to help her get it on. "I can't just put it on you like I used to, Elizabeth," said DeAnne. "I can't reach over my tummy. You have to step into the suit."

It took about a dozen tries, but Elizabeth was finally standing in her swimsuit and now DeAnne could pull it up and tie it behind her neck. "Are you going to come out into the sprinkler, too, Stevie?" she asked.

Stevie didn't stop playing even for a moment. "No," he said.

"You used to like to," said DeAnne.

Robbie ran into the room, wearing not only his swimsuit but also the Superman cape that DeAnne had made for him two Halloweens ago. "Ta-da!" he shouted. "Ta-*da!*"

"Here you are to save the day," said DeAnne.

"Turn on the sprinkler, Mommy!" shouted Robbie.

DeAnne leaned to the side and sort of rolled up onto her feet, supporting her weight on the front of the couch as she did. She felt like an elephant she had seen once in a movie, wallowing in the mud.

"Stevie," she said. "You used to like to play in the sprinkler."

"It wouldn't be fair," he said.

"What wouldn't be fair?" she asked.

" 'Cause I can and they can't."

She knew the answer, but still she had to ask. "Who can't?"

"Scotty and Jack and those guys."

She curbed her frustration and spoke in what she hoped was a reasonable tone. "Well, they can't play computer games with you, either."

"Yes they can," he said.

She opened the back door and Robbie and Elizabeth

burst out into the sunlight. She turned back into the dark cave of the family room, where Stevie now seemed to be only a shadow in the corner, his head silhouetted against the bright screen, where a train sped along a track.

"Stevie, even if they can't play with you in the sprinkler, if your friends are *really* your friends, they'd want *you* to play in the sunlight. Real friends wouldn't stop you from playing with your brother and sister sometimes. Your brother and sister need you, too."

She couldn't believe she was talking to Stevie as if his imaginary friends were real.

But if these imaginary boys were at the center of Stevie's life, then shutting them out would mean shutting Stevie out, too. She had to *try* to reach him, and if this was the only door he held open, then she would reach in through that door.

Stevie reached behind the computer and switched it off. "OK," he said. "I'll get my suit on."

She felt weak with relief as she turned the water on.

The sprinkler began its sweep back and forth across the lawn. Elizabeth ran through it, screaming. Robbie, however—the one who had suggested this—hung back. "Go on!" DeAnne said. "Just run through it and get wet. The water won't hurt."

Robbie still hesitated.

Then Stevie came out, walked over to where Robbie was, took him by the hand, and said, "OK, they're about to drop the bomb on us, let's *run!*" And, screaming, he and Robbie ran through the water.

DeAnne went back in the family room and brought out the folding chair she always used when she sat in the back and watched the kids play. She sat there, watching, and thought, Somebody wants me to think that *he's* watching, too. Somebody wants me to sit out here in my back yard and be afraid.

Well, it's working.

* * *

Step knew that something was bothering her, so when he woke up at three in the morning and found her side of the bed empty, he was not surprised. He knew why she couldn't sleep. The letter from the mortgage company had laid things out in no uncertain terms. "Your single payment was insufficient to keep this account open. If we do not receive in our office all back payments and late fees, along with the July payment currently due, for a total payment of $3,398.40, by 22nd July, we will begin foreclosure proceedings against the property." It was only then that Step discovered that DeAnne had *not* paid the back payments in June, when the first check from Agamemnon arrived. She hadn't spent the money on anything else; it was still there, ready to be paid. But it had been strange, to say the least, for DeAnne simply not to pay. It wasn't as if they didn't owe the money. It was their moral obligation to pay it. They had decided together that they *would* pay it. And yet the money still waited in the bank.

DeAnne had obviously been unwilling to discuss it with Step last night. She agreed at once that she would send the payment tomorrow, but she seemed distracted, as if she wasn't paying attention. She told him twice about Stevie playing with the other kids in the sprinkler, and she seemed jumpy. Now she couldn't sleep. Well, neither can I, thought Step. He got up and went in search of her. He found her in the family room and started reassuring her about the mortgage.

"It's not the *house,* Step," she said. "But you were so worried about it tonight that I didn't want to pile on anything more."

"You were protecting *me?* That's not how it's supposed to go."

"I'm sorry," she said. "We depend so much on your being able to concentrate on your work. But I can't handle this alone." She gave him the record and the envelope it came in. "It was waiting at our front door."

As soon as it started playing, he recognized it. He had the car-radio habit as DeAnne did not, and the song was hot right now. He had even liked it, the cleverness of it, the nastiness. But not when someone sent it anonymously to his family. He took it off the stereo before it finished playing. Then he broke it in half and carried the pieces outside to the garbage. There was nothing he could say that would reassure DeAnne. He could only take her to bed and hold her until finally she fell asleep.

He slept badly the rest of the night, and the next day at work, the question kept nagging at him. Who could have sent it? Who would want to disrupt their lives, fill them with fear?

DeAnne had figured that whoever it was knew Step better than DeAnne—but that didn't really leave anybody out, because it seemed as though Step had made all the enemies they had anyway. Who, after all, would want them to think that they were being watched? It might be Lee Weeks, of course, punishing them for the baptism thing. Or Gallowglass, after the Fourth of July picnic—he had been cool and distant at work ever since, and who knew what might be going through his mind in response to the clear accusation in Step's actions that day?

There were others who might harbor ill feelings, too. It might conceivably be Mrs. Jones, who had missed her last month of teaching and, according to Dr. Mariner, would not be coming back next year. Could she have sat at home, brooding, until she thought of sending that record to make the Fletchers suffer a little, too? It could even be Sister LeSueur, though that seemed beyond possibility—it was hard to imagine her ever *hearing* a rock song, let alone buying one, even as a satanic weapon.

Dicky? It couldn't be Dicky. He was a vindictive

man, Step already knew that, and they had already had one confrontation too many. But surely Dicky would confine his vengeance to bureaucratic infighting at work. Wouldn't he?

It was an appalling list, really: Lee, Glass, Mrs. Jones, Dicky Northanger, Sister LeSueur—these were the people who definitely felt they had cause to hate or fear or resent Step Fletcher after he had lived in Steuben, North Carolina, for less than five months. Just think how many enemies he could make by New Year's! Yet he hadn't set out to make any enemies at all. He had come to Eight Bits Inc. expecting to be friends with Dicky Northanger—he had liked him well enough during interviews. It was Dicky who decided to be Step's enemy. It was Sister LeSueur who intruded into their lives, not the other way around. It was Mrs. Jones who singled out Stevie and mistreated him—should Step have let it go on, in the effort to be a "peacemaker"? What kind of peacemaker would he be, how *blessed* exactly would he be, if he pursued peace at the expense of his children's happiness?

As for Glass and Lee, well, standards of reasonable behavior clearly did not apply. No one could blame him for *their* enmity, surely.

By ten o'clock he realized that he was not going to get anything meaningful done this morning. He might as well go hang out in the pit and see if he could pretend to be useful there.

On the way he passed the spare office where unused equipment was stored and noticed that someone had left the light on. Step opened the door just enough to snake his arm in and flipped off the light.

Someone inside the room bellowed.

Step flung the door open and flipped the light back on, already apologizing as he did. "I'm sorry, I just assumed somebody had left the light on, I didn't know anybody was using it."

He had already closed the door when he realized that it was Dicky who was in that room, sitting at a cleared-off desk, and the computer he was using was not a 64 or an Atari or any machine Step had seen before. He opened the door again. "Excuse me, is that the Lisa? We haven't got a Lisa here, have we?"

Dicky had already covered the machine with a tarpaulin and he was halfway to the door. Step's having opened it yet again clearly unnerved him. "Dammit, you sneaky son-of-a-bitch, haven't you spied enough for one day?"

"Since when is it spying to open the storage room?" asked Step. "Is this some sort of top secret project?"

"No, it's a Boy Scout computer, and it likes to sleep in a tent," said Dicky.

But by now Step had already seen what Dicky had carelessly left uncovered—the large empty box on the floor with the name *Compaq* emblazoned on it.

"Sorry, Dicky," said Step. "Perhaps a locked door would do the job."

"I was just getting up to lock it when you barged in for the third time—I hope you'll forgive me for counting."

"Sorry," Step repeated. "I'll never switch off another light at Eight Bits Inc., I promise." He drew the door shut behind him.

As he walked down the corridor, he heard Dicky open the door again and then slam it shut. Oof, Dicky, feel better now?

Step got to the door of the pit, set his hand on the handle, and then turned around and headed back to his office. He picked up the phone and called DeAnne. "Have you mailed that check to the mortgage company?"

"Not yet," she said.

"Don't."

"Why not? What happened?"

He told her about what he had seen, and how secretive Dicky had been about it. She didn't get it.

"The Compaq computer is an IBM clone. And Dicky is working on it secretly."

"Oh," she said. "The agreement . . ."

"If Eight Bits Inc. is supporting the PC when I quit, I can't do any programming for the PC for a year. I'll already be cut off from the 64 and the Atari as it is. I have to quit today, DeAnne. It may already be too late."

"If it's already too late," she said, "then what good will it do to quit? The baby isn't born. He's due on the twenty-eighth. But it might not be that long, he might be early. Elizabeth was."

"And Robbie was a week late and we had to induce him at that," said Step. "Don't you see? If I don't quit now, today, then I can't quit at *all*."

"But would that be so very bad, Step? It's been so much better since you stopped working such late hours."

He wanted to scream at her. No, it hasn't been any better, it's just been *shorter*. But he didn't scream. In fact, he lowered his voice, and he spoke rapidly, because he felt such urgency to persuade her. "My position here is deteriorating all the time. I'm not in charge of anything. My only authority comes from skulking around helping with programming and game design behind Dicky's back, and even that isn't all that valuable anymore because I've pretty much taught the programmers everything I know. In a month I could be so completely under Dicky's thumb that every hour of every day would be unbearable. He'd reject everything I wrote, make me do it over and over again for the stupidest reasons. In fact he already does that, I just ignore him and don't make the changes he suggests, but what if I *couldn't* ignore him anymore? You don't know what you're saying when you tell me I should just stay on."

"Step, I'm just asking you to stay until the baby—"

"No, you're not. You're asking me to stay *indefinitely*. No end in sight. Because Dicky knows that I've seen the Compaq. He knows that the secret will be out, and when he tells Ray, we'll get a memo announcing it so the news comes from them, not from me. Do you understand? It's now, this minute. I can't even give notice. I just have to *quit* and get out."

"You can't do that, Step, it wouldn't be right."

"Nothing has been right about working for them all along. Suddenly I'm supposed to be noble?"

"You have to give them two weeks notice and then if they challenge your right to do PC games, you can say that at the time you gave notice, Eight Bits Inc. was still not supporting the PC."

"Oh, right, I'm sure that that would hold up in court."

"It might," she insisted.

"Look, DeAnne. Call your Uncle Mike. He's a lawyer. Ask him what we should do. Tell him about my agreement with Eight Bits Inc.—*read* him the agreement—and see what he thinks. And for that matter, ask him what we should do about the house. What will happen to us if we hang on to that money to cover the cost of the baby."

"You mean let them foreclose?"

"That's what I mean."

"Oh, Step, we can't—that's not *honest*."

"No, DeAnne, if we had signed the mortgage intending not to pay, *that* would be dishonest. But the whole premise of the mortgage is that they recognize that we might not be able to pay, in which case they have the right to take the house. Well, we can't pay, and so they get the house."

"But we *can* pay, Step. We have the money in the bank right now."

"The money that's in the bank right now is not *house* money, it's just money. *Our* money. If we use it to pay for the baby, then I can quit the job today, right now, and we might still have a future with Agamemnon. Don't you understand that?"

"So you want to quit your job so bad that you'll walk off without giving them notice, you'll let them foreclose on the house, and you'll let us go into the birth of our baby without insurance?"

"I thought *you* wanted me to quit this job, too. I thought you wanted me to come home. To be with Stevie. To be a family again."

"Well, I'm not going to be the villain in this, Step. If you want to quit, then quit."

"Oh, so it's all right if I *am* the villain, is that it? This time we don't make the decision together, *I* have to make it alone, so if it works out wrong then it's my fault and only my fault forever. If I wanted that kind of life I would have married my mother!"

"That is the stupidest and cruelest thing you've ever said, Step."

"Oh, you think so? Then try this. Just imagine how you'd feel if I came to you and said, Oh, isn't it a little selfish of you to insist on having the baby *now?* If you really loved the family, you'd carry it another six months and you wouldn't complain about it, either."

Then, because he hated himself so much that he could hardly stand to hear his own voice on the telephone, he hung up without waiting for her answer.

Either she would call him back, or she wouldn't.

After a couple of minutes, when she hadn't called back, he sat down at the typewriter and wrote:

Dear Ray:

    I hereby resign my position with Eight Bits Inc., effective immediately. There is no need to pay me for today's work. Thank you for giving me the privilege of working with you for the past months. I'm sorry for any inconvenience my resignation might cause you.

                                 Sincerely,

He pulled it out of the typewriter and signed it.

He felt so free.

Then he tore it up into small pieces and dropped them into the wastebasket.

The phone rang. It was DeAnne. She was sobbing, barely able to speak. "Step, I'm so sorry, I'm so sorry, I was being selfish," she said.

"No, I was the selfish one," he said. "I won't quit. I'll wait till the baby comes, and if Eight Bits Inc. is supporting the PC by then, well, then that's the way it goes. Maybe that's what the Lord planned for us all along."

"No," she said, "no, that's wrong. What the Lord planned for us was Agamemnon. You know that, it all went so smoothly in San Francisco, and you really *like* Arkasian and he's kept all his promises and the money is good, you've got to reach out and take it, you've got to. It's only my fear, my stupid fear that made me say those things and try to get you to stay at Eight Bits and I was wrong, can't I be wrong? Can't I say I was wrong and then you just do the thing you were right about wanting to do?"

It was the same argument, only they had changed sides. When they both realized that DeAnne was now urging him to walk out immediately, they ended up laughing.

"Let's go back to plan A, DeAnne. Call your Uncle Mike. I'll be right here when you call me back."

"I'll call you right back. I love you, Junk Man."

"I love you, too, Fish Lady."

He sat down at the typewriter and wrote another letter. It was like the first one, except that it gave two weeks notice. The resignation would be effective as of August 2nd. And if the baby didn't come by the twenty-eighth when it was due, then they'd induce it, and it would be born under Eight Bits Inc.'s insurance policy. It was the best compromise Step could think of.

He set the letter on his desk and this time he didn't

sign it. He just sat there, eyes closed, waiting for DeAnne to call back. And he prayed, silently: Let Uncle Mike be home. Let him give us the right advice. Keep Ray Keene from sending a memo about the PC until after. Make it work out right, somehow.

The phone rang. It was DeAnne.

"He said to let the house go," she said.

"The house?" he asked. Was the house really the issue? Well, yes, it was—to DeAnne. Because to her it was a matter of honor to pay their debts, and so if her uncle advised them to let it go, it would ease her conscience considerably, and in the long run that would be very important.

"He said that there's a recession on, and Indiana is a hard-hit state. Chances are the banks there aren't being ugly about reporting on foreclosed mortgages. It may never come up in the future. And even if it does, it won't kill us. So let it go."

"All right," said Step. "So we can hold on to the money in the bank. What about the employment agreement?"

"He said it could go either way. If you resigned in the belief that the policy was one way, and then before you actually left they changed the policy, you'd probably be in the clear working on PC games, the way the agreement is worded."

"But I'm pretty sure they're going to change the policy," said Step. "That's why I'm resigning, and Dicky won't miss the fact that I resigned less than an hour after seeing him working on the Compaq."

"Well," she said, "that's why he said it could go either way."

"Hoo boy," said Step.

"He advised you to quit now. Just walk out. There'd be no ambiguity then."

"Except that from then on, Eight Bits Inc. could spread the word that I walked away and left them in the lurch. And it would be true."

"And our mortgage company could spread the word that we walked away from the house, and that would be true, too. It's like Uncle Mike said. Sometimes you have to walk away and let the chips fall where they may."

"Yeah, but he's a lawyer, what does *he* know from right and wrong."

"Step, he's my uncle, he—"

"That was a joke, DeAnne. I'll submit my resignation right now."

"Come home as a free man, Step. Come home to your family."

"I want to."

"Say you will."

"I love you."

"Oh, Step!"

"Say you love me before I hang up."

"I love you."

He hung up.

Why was he so reluctant, now, to walk out? It just felt wrong. The second letter, the one he had typed before DeAnne called back with Uncle Mike's advice—that was the letter he knew he had to submit. He didn't know why. It seemed like the stupidest possible course—the course that would leave him without a job, without the Agamemnon contract, and tied up in litigation with Eight Bits Inc. for a year. And yet when he looked at that letter he knew that it was the right thing to do, the only thing he could do and really live with himself. He could walk away from the mortgage because the bank would get the house, and the house was worth much more than the amount owed on it. But he couldn't be the kind of man who would walk out on a job without giving fair notice.

He signed the letter, made a couple of xeroxes of it, and took the original to Ludy, Ray's secretary, who looked it over, clucked her tongue a couple of times, smiled at him sadly, and said, "I guess I won't win the pool after all."

"What?"

"I thought you'd stick it out until after the baby was born."

"The baby's due before the two weeks are up."

She rolled her eyes. "Are you sure you don't want to wait to give this to him until your insurance has safely covered the baby?"

He shook his head. "Today," he said.

"No cooling off period? I could hold it till morning, for instance, and if you change your mind he'll never know you gave it to me."

"Ludy, you're a sweetheart, but give him the letter right away, please."

She smiled. "Mmm, you men are all so *attractive* when you think you know what you're doing. Of course, you never really do."

Step started to walk away, and then turned back. "Was there really a pool on when I'd quit?"

She laughed. "Of course not. Oh, maybe a teeny one. Maybe I bet myself an ice cream that you'd stay and a granola bar that you'd go."

"Crunch away," said Step.

"Bye-bye," said Ludy.

Step walked with a light step down the maze of corridors to the back, where he found Dicky's door partly open. He knocked.

"Come in."

Dicky was on the phone, mostly nodding. Step laid a copy of the letter down on top of Dicky's typewriter. Dicky glanced over it while he was listening to the phone, nodded, said "All right," and then hung up. He looked up at Step and smiled. "That was Ray. Your resignation is accepted."

"Very quick," said Step.

"But that two weeks notice shit is out of the question," said Dicky. "Two weeks in which a disgruntled employee can cause damage? Insert bugs in our programs?

Report to your new bosses on the secrets of Eight Bits Inc.?"

"What, you mean you guys are secretly developing nuclear weapons for the PLO or something? And I don't *have* a new boss. I'm going back to freelancing. I have a contract for Hacker Snack, I told you that."

"Sure, of course," said Dicky. "And you're just going to sit back and wait a year for your noncompetition clause and your nondisclosure clause to run out, right? Just remember, asshole, we're going to watch you and if we see one hint of a violation of that agreement we'll have lawyers up your ass so far you'll taste them whenever you burp."

"Ooh, nasty," said Step.

"Right, be flippant about it if you want, but we are going to march to your office together right now and you are going to put your personal belongings into that box while I watch. Nothing that is the property of Eight Bits Inc. will go out of this building with you, and when you leave here you will *never* come back, do you understand?"

"So you're saying that you reject my offer of two weeks notice, even though you've got nobody else up to speed on my projects?"

Dicky laughed derisively. "Step, the *janitors* could be up to speed on *your* work in half an hour. You are the most worthless, useless, completely replaceable person in this company."

"Gee," said Step, "it kind of makes you wonder why you'd bother replacing me."

"Let's get a box, Step. The sooner you're gone, the better this company will be."

The words stung, even coming from Dicky. And although Step's immediate departure was exactly what he had really wanted but hadn't felt right about asking for, it was still deeply offensive that Ray and Dicky understood him so little that they thought he would actually steal from them. But then, being dishonest and conniving themselves, of course they assumed that he would behave exactly as *they* would behave if the situation were reversed.

It took Step five minutes to withdraw his few personal papers from the desk. Dicky stopped him from taking copies of any Eight Bits Inc. memos, on the grounds that they were internal secrets, but that was fine with Step. He already had the only memos he needed safely at home.

The only problem they had was when Step tried to take a couple of disks with him. "No way," said Dicky. "Any code on any disk in this office belongs to Eight Bits Inc."

"This is just personal stuff," said Step. "Utilities I use. They don't belong to Eight Bits Inc. Look, let me put them in a machine and do a directory and you'll see."

"You could rename files to any other name, Step. Hand me the diskettes."

It wasn't worth it—the utilities he used most were already at home anyway. So he handed the disks to Dicky.

Dicky reached for the stapler on Step's desk and drove a dozen staples through the disks, bang, bang, bang, bang. He handed the mutilated disks to Step. Step held them up and dropped them on the floor. "When you bring a janitor in here to do my job, he can clean those up," he said. Then Step took the box of his personal papers and dumped it out into the garbage can. There was nothing he needed from Eight Bits Inc., because he had never brought anything here that really mattered. He hadn't invested any part of himself in these people, and so there was nothing that would bother him to leave behind. Except, of course, his attaché case, because that was a gift from DeAnne and because it was mostly filled with his lesson materials for his church calling, that and his home teaching information and a couple of magazines to read during lunch.

"Open the attaché," said Dicky.

"Not without a warrant," said Step.

Then he walked to the door, dug into his pocket, pulled out his keyring, pried off the key to the back door of Eight Bits Inc., and threw it toward the garbage can. To his surprise, it went right in. "You're so stupid, Dicky, that you didn't even ask me for my key."

Step closed the door firmly in Dicky's face and headed down the corridor to the pit. He opened the door, waved, and said, "I gave the bastards two weeks notice and they're throwing me out. It's been real, gents. Have a life!" Their cheers and applause rang in his ears as he went out the back door, got in his car, and drove home.

11

·ZAP·

This is what happened when the baby was born:
On Thursday, the twenty-eighth of July, DeAnne
went to her doctor's office to find out why the baby
hadn't shown any intention yet of entering the world. It
was the due date, and DeAnne had no desire for a
bonus week of pregnancy like the one she had with
Robbie. When Dr. Keese examined her, he looked surprised. "You haven't had *any* labor pains?"

"I don't ever get hard labor pains until I'm about to
deliver," said DeAnne.

"Well, get ready for them, then," he said. "You're at
six centimeters."

"Oh," said DeAnne. "I guess that means I don't have
time to plow the back forty before the baby comes."

"I think it means that if I were you, I'd go out and get in my car and drive to the hospital. I'll have Rochelle call your husband."

"This is really inconvenient," said DeAnne. "My mother is flying in from Utah tonight at nine-thirty. Do you think the baby will be here by then so Step can go pick her up?"

"Are you aware that you are speaking absolute nonsense?" asked Dr. Keese. "Things like that are no longer your concern for the next few days, and certainly not for the next few hours."

She stopped at the reception desk and borrowed the phone.

"Hi," said Step. "What's the news?"

"I'm at six centimeters and the doctor says I don't really have time to go home."

"OK," said Step. "Any pains yet?"

"None," she answered. "But I'm sure they'll make up for it later. Remember that Mother's arriving at nine-thirty."

"I've already arranged with Sam Freebody to pick her up if we happen to be at the hospital by then," said Step.

"Oh," said DeAnne. "How will he know her?"

"He'll look for the woman with short, tightly curled salt-and-pepper hair who seems lost and abandoned and who answers to the name 'Vette.'"

"You make her sound like a lost dog."

"And I'm going to call *her* before she gets on the plane and tell her to look for a man tall enough to change lightbulbs without a stepladder and wide enough that he couldn't get two rattlesnakes to reach all the way around him. I think they'll find each other."

"I know you're perfectly able to handle things, Step. But I have to ask about these things or I'll worry."

"I know," said Step. "Did I complain? I'm trying to reassure you so you *don't* worry."

"Well, you're doing a splendid job. Call Sister Bigelow or Mary Anne Lowe to stay with the children."

"Whichever one says yes, I'll get the other one to finish mowing the lawn for me."

"Very funny. As soon as whoever it is gets there, then I need you to bring me my bag, the one I packed with everything I'll need in the hospital."

"Yes," said Step. "I'm already standing in our bedroom and I have just opened that bag."

"Don't open it, Step, or something will fall out."

"I'm now putting into the bag your copy of *Dinner at the Homesick Restaurant,* which you told me you intended to read in the hospital but which you had neglected to put in the bag."

"I hate you when you're so superior-sounding."

"Now I'm going to sound bossy," said Step.

"Go ahead, I can take anything—I'm a woman."

"Get off the phone, leave everything to me, drive to the hospital, and I'll be there within thirty minutes."

"OK, Junk Man."

"Oh—wait—what was the name of the hospital again?"

"Step, you can't have forgotten the—"

He laughed and laughed.

"You are sick," she said. "I hope this little boy is nothing like you."

"I hope he's just like you," said Step, "except with a handle."

"I love you and I'm scared so please hurry."

"That's my plan. I love you, too."

She ran only one stop sign on the way to the hospital. When she walked into the room, they made her sit in a wheelchair. I drove myself here, she thought, I walked from the parking lot, and *now* I need somebody to take care of me?

Well, why not? She was no longer in charge of anything now, except the baby inside her that had finally decided he was coming. Without insurance, but with a mother and father who loved babies and had looked forward to this one with hope, as they had looked forward to all their children.

Step made the calls first, though he was dripping with sweat and covered with grass clippings. Sam Freebody would have no problem picking up DeAnne's mother— he would hold up a placard in the airport saying "Sylvette Brown, Grandmother again." Mary Anne Lowe was in her car heading over to the house to watch the kids almost before she hung up the phone. Bappy Waters would come over and finish mowing the lawn and put the mower away and bag the clippings. Step even called Ruby Bigelow, ostensibly to warn her that DeAnne probably wouldn't be teaching her class a week from Sunday, but actually because he was pretty sure that the Relief Society president would want to be informed of all childbirths-in-progress so that when sisters in the 1st Ward called her with the news, she could say, "I know."

Step told Stevie to open the door *only* if it was Sister Lowe, and then he headed for the laundry room, stripped off his grass-covered clothes, and bolted for the bathroom in his underwear. "You're not going to the hospital in your underwear, are you, Daddy?" shouted Robbie.

"I'm going to take a shower," he explained.

"In your *underwear?*" shouted Robbie. Robbie thought this was so funny he followed Step down the hall, repeating it. "In your *underwear?* In your *underwear?*"

"No, in *your* underwear," said Step. He closed the bedroom door, tossed his underwear into the laundry basket, and took the fastest shower of his life.

He got out, threw on his clothes, picked up DeAnne's bag, and when he got to the family room he discovered that Mary Anne Lowe was already there, armed with a bag full of coloring books, crayons, and little-kid board games. "Please help Sister Lowe all you can," Step said to the kids. And to Sister Lowe he said, "The kids don't like anything so don't bother fixing them dinner."

"Da-ad!" said Robbie.

"Robbie will eat anything with ketchup on it, including small live animals," said Step. "Stevie will only eat pasta with parmesan cheese on it, *no* butter, *no* salt. And Betsy doesn't actually eat food, she just Cuisinarts it and sprays it in a fine mist all over the kitchen."

"Don't believe him!" cried Robbie. "He's joking!"

"We'll do just fine," said Mary Anne.

Step looked at Stevie. "Will you help with your brother and sister?"

"Yes," he said.

Mary Anne turned to Stevie now. "What do you hope it is, a boy or a girl?"

"It's a boy," said Stevie.

"We had ultrasound," explained Step.

"Oh, so did we, on our last one," said Mary Anne, "but we wouldn't let the doctor tell us. We didn't want to know."

"We're gonna name it Zap!" said Robbie.

"Zap?" asked Mary Anne.

"For Zapata," said Step. "A great Mexican revolutionary." She grinned. "What's next, Pancho Villa?"

"Not likely," said Step. "DeAnne said that the only way I could name one of our kids for the bandit who drove her ancestors out of Mexico is if I give birth to it myself," said Step.

"Why are you still standing around?" asked Mary Anne. "Aren't you supposed to be telling her when to breathe or something?"

"Naw," said Step. "We believe in using epidural blocks. No pain. We work crosswords during labor."

"Go, please, you're making me nervous," said Mary Anne.

"Thanks for helping," said Step.

"Don't worry, I'll get even with you."

When Step got to the hospital he found DeAnne already wired up in a labor room. A nurse took the bag and the two of them settled down to their vigil. Everything was going normally now, which meant that the pains were starting, and that meant that DeAnne needed to have Step talk continuously, except when she couldn't stand to have anybody talking to her. By now he was pretty good at guessing when to be quiet and when to babble. Or maybe she was just better at hiding it when she couldn't stand to hear another word or when she was desperate for him to distract her from the horrible process that evolution had decreed for human women—giving birth to big-headed babies.

The nurse bustled in and out; the anesthesiologist punched a hole in her spine and fed in the tube for the epidural block.

Then came the bad news. "Dr. Keese's current patient is having a little trouble," said the nurse. "She may require a caesarean. If she does, there's a backup here for you—Dr. Vender. Is that all right?"

"Do we have a choice?" asked Step.

"Dr. Vender will be fine," said DeAnne. Then, when the nurse was gone, she said, "Vender is a woman. She just joined the same practice that Mary Anne's ob-gyn is in, and Mary Anne is thinking of switching to her. She says she's getting a good reputation."

"I don't like changing horses in midstream," said Step.

"Neither do I," said DeAnne. "But that's the way it goes—if your doctor's with another patient when your time comes, then he's not going to drop *that* baby on its head and come to *you*."

"Maybe we'll get lucky," said Step.

"Maybe that other woman will get lucky."

They didn't get lucky. DeAnne was ripe and ready to go, and Dr. Keese was still with the other woman. Dr. Vender showed up, solemnly businesslike—she looked to Step like one of those women who always wore midcalf brown skirts in college and put on little teeny half-smiles if somebody made a joke.

In the delivery room, it didn't take all that long. DeAnne had had enough babies now that she watched her own episiotomy in the mirror, though Step didn't think there were enough babies in the world to get him used to the idea, so he didn't watch. Then, just like clockwork, out popped the head, a little twist for the shoulders, and presto, boy number three. Zap.

"Hi, Zap," said Step.

"Oh, can't you let him hear his *real* name?" said DeAnne. "He'll want to go back if he thinks he's going to be Zap for the rest of his life."

"Hi, Jeremy Zapata Fletcher."

"Is he all right?" asked DeAnne.

"Twenty digits total, distributed normally," said Step.

Clip. Snip. The nurse took the baby from Dr. Vender and laid it on the scale. "Be useful, here, daddy," said the nurse. "Watch the baby and don't let him walk anywhere."

"He's shivering," said Step. "I think he's cold."

The nurses were preparing something over on the side counter. Dr. Vender was taking care of the placenta and stitching up the episiotomy.

"Can't we cover him or something?" asked Step. "He's really shivering."

"Now, don't worry mama," said Dr. Vender. "Everything's just fine."

Step wanted to snap back at her: Don't talk down to us like children.

"Here we go," said the nurse. She took note of Zap's weight and then dripped something in each of his eyes with an eyedropper. "Oh, I know you don't like *that*," said the nurse.

"This is definitely not normal," said Step. "He's shivering and you've got to do something about it."

"What's wrong, Step?" asked DeAnne.

"Nothing's wrong," said Dr. Vender. "Daddy's just being a worrywart."

"Can the babytalk," said Step, unable to endure it another moment. "DeAnne is a grownup and so am I, and we'd both like to know what's going on with the baby."

"We've already sent for a neonatal specialist," said Dr. Vender. "It appears that it may be some kind of seizure activity. There's no proximate cause. There was no oxygen deprivation and no anomaly in any of the baby's vital signs during delivery."

Step figured that what he was hearing was the standard disclaimer to avoid a malpractice suit. He also figured that it was probably true. But that still didn't answer the real question. "Is the baby going to be all right?"

"His vital signs are just fine," said Dr. Vender. "This isn't normal, but at the same time it may not be dangerous at all. Please, now, as soon as I know anything more I'll tell you, but it's time now for your wife to go into the recovery room."

Step leaned over DeAnne, kissed her, and squeezed her hand. "Can't I hold him?" she asked. "Can't I see him first?"

Step knew what she was thinking: Something is wrong with my baby. I don't want my baby to die without my having held him when he was alive. "Of course you can," said Step to DeAnne.

He looked at Dr. Vender, raised an eyebrow. She beckoned to the nurse who had the baby. The nurse brought Zap to DeAnne and laid him in the crook of her arm. DeAnne turned her head to see him. "He's beautiful," she said.

It was true. All newborns are squat and red, of course, but Zap was a genuinely pretty baby.

"He really is shivering," she said. "Don't be scared, Jeremy. We already love you. You've got a wonderful life ahead of you."

The nurse took the baby back. Another nurse wheeled DeAnne out of the delivery room, with Dr. Vender right behind.

"I'd like to hold the baby," said Step.

"The neonate's going to be here in a minute," said the nurse, "and we've got to get the measurements."

"He's not going to grow in the next thirty seconds," said Step.

"You're a feisty one," said the nurse. He could tell that she was *not* going to say I like that in a man.

"I'm sorry," said Step. "But this little guy is a lot more important to me than hospital routines, and there isn't a line of people waiting outside for this room."

She handed him the baby. Just like the three times before, the first thing he thought was: I never knew that babies could be so small. All his memories of the older kids were from later in their babyhood. The first minutes were always new again. "I think he's shivering a little less."

The nurse didn't say anything.

"Does this happen often?" asked Step. "This kind of seizure?"

"Everything happens," said the nurse. "And nothing's ever the same twice."

Which told Step that she had seen babies like this who died.

She was still measuring when the neonate came, a doctor named Torwaldson. "Why wasn't this already done?"

"I insisted that she let me hold the baby for thirty seconds," said Step. "I threatened to break the windshield of her car if she didn't."

"I'm done here," said the nurse. She did not think Step was at all cute.

Torwaldson started taking soundings with his stethoscope. "It's time for you to go to the waiting room, Mr. . . . Fletcher."

"Tell me about this kind of seizure," said Step.

"I'll tell you about this kind of seizure when I know what kind of seizure it is," said Torwaldson. "Pheno," he said to the nurse. "Let's get this under control."

Step left. There were times to be assertive and times to get out of the way.

He did not go to the waiting room. Instead he went to recovery, and the nurses there gave him no trouble about getting in to see DeAnne. Apparently she had been asking for him.

"Is he OK?" she said.

"The neonatal physician is checking him out. He said something about pheno. In my mind that seems to go with barbital. I assume that's something to stop the trembling."

"Did he seem worried?" asked DeAnne.

"He seemed competent and he seemed confident," said Step. "How are *you*?"

"It hurts," said DeAnne, "but they're being very nice and pumping me full of drugs. I think they're going to give me a sleeping pill or something because I'm so worried about the baby. Say a prayer with me, Step. Please?"

Step held her hand and prayed for the doctors to be able to find out what was wrong and to do whatever medical science could do to fix the problem and please let them have a long life with this little boy, they wanted him so much, but thy will be done. "I think he'll be fine," said Step. "I really do. They weren't doing any-thing dramatic. It wasn't an emergency."

In a little while she was asleep, and Step headed for the waiting room to start calling people. But first he saw

Dr. Vender in the hall. She waved him over. "I'm sorry if I was a little short with you," she said. "I was afraid you were worrying Mrs. Fletcher."

"If I saw something wrong with the baby, Dr. Vender, and I didn't tell her immediately, she would never trust me again."

"Well, some people need the truth and some people need anything but," said Dr. Vender. "I didn't know your wife or you, and so I did the safest thing. Or rather I tried to."

"Sorry," said Step. But he wasn't sorry, and she certainly knew it.

"Torwaldson is the best in Steuben," she said. "And he's on the phone right now with a neuro in Chapel Hill."

"Neuro?" asked Step.

"Neurosurgeon," she explained.

"Yeah, I know what a neuro *is*. I just wondered what it meant that he was calling one."

"I would guess," said Dr. Vender, "that it means he's run into something he hasn't seen before, or else he wants a corroborating opinion."

"Is the baby in danger of dying?"

"As far as I can see," said Dr. Vender, "no."

That was when Dr. Keese came bustling out into the hall. "Dr. Vender!" he called.

"This is Mr. Fletcher," said Dr. Vender.

Dr. Keese held out his hand, and Step shook it. "Nice to see you, I met you when I poked my head into the labor room, remember?"

Step shook his head. "Must have been before I got there."

"No, you were there," said Dr. Keese. "But I think you only had eyes for DeAnne. Sorry I couldn't be in there, but I can assure you that Dr. Vender did everything I would have done, and probably better."

How nice, thought Step. Doctors covering each other against a lawsuit.

"Mr. Fletcher," said Dr. Keese. "Dr. Torwaldson and I and Dr. Vender all agree that we need to stop the seizure activity, and for that we're giving your baby phenobarbital. We've given a fairly massive dose, for his body weight, but we've got to stop the seizures. Once we've got that under control, we'll step the dosage down to the minimum for maintenance. He's going into intensive care now, but I truly don't think he's in any danger of losing his life. So I urge you to go home. It's after midnight and you'll want to be up here in the morning. We'll know more then, and DeAnne will want to see you. All right?"

What choice did he have? He waited until he knew what room DeAnne was assigned to and where to find Zap the next morning, and then he went out to the car. He was just getting into the Datsun when he realized that there was no reason to leave the good car at the hospital. DeAnne wasn't going anywhere for a while. The rusty old two-door could keep its vigil here tonight. As he drove home, he couldn't stop thinking: My baby was born having a seizure and the doctors have never seen it before. Something's wrong with my youngest child, and I can't do anything but pray, and I can't think of a single reason why God should exclude the Stephen Fletcher family from the normal vicissitudes of life and so I don't think my prayers are going to be answered. Not my *real* prayer, anyway. The "thy will be done" part will certainly be answered, but the part about "Make this all go away so that nothing is wrong, so that the doctors say, I can't understand it, there was a seizure last night but now there's not a trace of a problem, and he'll definitely be brilliant and healthy and live to a hundred and four"—I don't think God's going to adjust his plan for the universe to make room for accommodating that particular prayer.

When he got home, DeAnne's mother, Vette, met him at the door. "Oh," he said. "I hoped you'd be asleep."

"And I hoped you'd call from the hospital," she said.

He had forgotten to call. "There were problems. They sent me home. I decided to call from here."

"Problems?" She looked stricken.

"DeAnne is fine. But the baby seems to have something wrong and they don't know what it is. He was trembling. They called it a seizure. Well, actually, they called it 'seizure activity.' But they said it didn't look life threatening."

"Oh, I hate this," said Vette. "I hate not knowing."

"You and me both," said Step. "I guess I ought to call everybody now. It's only eleven P.M. in Utah, right?"

"Also Mary Anne Lowe said to tell you to call her no matter how late."

"OK," said Step. "I'll call her first."

He went into the kitchen and suddenly found himself surrounded by tiny whining insects. He brushed his hands around his head but they wouldn't go away.

"Oh, aren't those gnats awful?" asked Vette. "I found a can of Raid and I've been spraying them, but new swarms just keep turning up. Do you get them all the time?"

"Never," said Step. "Where's the Raid?" The gnats all seemed to want to zoom right into his ear. "This is all I needed."

"I think they're coming from the laundry room," said Vette. "I haven't found any in the kids' rooms yet."

"We have this weird bug thing," said Step. He went into the laundry room and started looking around for where the gnats might be getting in through. As he looked, he told Vette about the crickets and the june bugs. "We don't have any regular bug problem, I guess," he said. "It just comes in waves. Every couple of months or so some group of insects decides that our house is ready to go condo."

He found that the dryer hose had come partly away from the outdoor vent. He tried to push it tight, but the pressure jostled it and it fell completely away. Suddenly another swarm of gnats arose. Only they didn't come from the vent—they came from the hose. As if they had been spawned somewhere inside the dryer.

"Here, give me the Raid," he said.

Vette gave it to him, and he first sprayed the swarm that was orbiting his head. Then he sprayed up into the dryer hose and then out through the vent and when he thought he had dosed them enough, he slipped the hose back over the vent and then got a screwdriver from the laundry room cupboard and tightened the collar over the hose so it wouldn't slip away again.

"What are we doing in this house?" he said, when he got back into the kitchen.

"Getting by," said Vette. "Doing what you must for your family."

"We never should have left Vigor."

"Step, you know that *I* think you never should have left Utah! But you are *not* having problems with little Jeremy because you moved to North Carolina."

"How do you know? Maybe the doctor did something wrong. In Salt Lake they have a billion babies every year, they've seen *everything*. Out here there just aren't as many babies and so they're learning on Zap."

Vette winced. "Do you *really* call him Zap?"

"Well, the first thing Robbie said when he heard the name Jeremy was 'Germy, Germy, Germy,' so maybe *Zap*'s the lesser of two evils."

"Step, things go wrong sometimes no matter where you live, and sometimes things go right, and you know something? Most things that happen aren't anybody's fault at all, so it's really kind of vain of you to think that your moving to North Carolina caused your newborn baby to have a seizure. *You* didn't do a single thing to cause it. For all you know whatever problem he has was determined at the moment of conception."

"Yeah, well, I was there for that, too." Then he was

appalled that he had said such a thing. He and DeAnne's parents got along really well, but still, you don't talk about the *conception* of your children to your wife's mother.

"Better call people," said Vette. "I'll keep watching for the gnats."

Step called Mary Anne first. It took longer than such calls usually did, because he mentioned that the baby was in intensive care and then he had to answer, "We don't know yet" to about fifty questions. It went that way with every call, but he couldn't very well *not* tell them the baby was having trouble, or when they found out they'd be deeply hurt. Besides, if prayer was going to be of any help in this situation, he wanted all the people praying that he could find.

He didn't finish the calls until nearly three. He had already sent Sylvette to bed, persuading her to go by pointing out that she'd be needed to take care of the kids in the morning while he went up to the hospital, and then she'd take her shift at the hospital while he stayed home with the kids—she'd need her sleep.

"So will you," Vette retorted.

"Yeah, but *I* can take a nap while I'm driving back and forth to the hospital."

She laughed and let him pull out the sofa bed, which DeAnne had already made up for her mother that morning. Then he moved his phone operations into the bedroom. When he finished the calls and took his last patrol through the house, she was asleep.

He looked in on each of the kids. Betsy, cuddled up to the stuffed Snoopy that—for reasons passing understanding—she had named Wilbur. Robbie, holding his real-fur stuffed bunny, which had been named Mammalee since his infancy. And Stevie, holding on to nothing.

You're all safe here in my house, Step thought silently, and yet I really can't keep you safe at all, can I? Because there's that new one, not six hours old yet, and his life is in danger and I'm not even there because I'm completely useless. And here you are, asleep, safe in your beds, only something's going on inside your head, Stevie, and I can't reach in and find out what's happening and make it get better. I can plug up one hole and sweep the crickets out, but then the june bugs get in somewhere else, and then the gnats. Even when you have a perfect child, nothing stays perfect. Something always gets in. The good things are always, always at risk.

In the bedroom, undressed and ready for bed, he did what he hadn't done in years, though DeAnne did it every night. He knelt down beside the bed, the way he had done on his mission, the way he had done as a child. He poured out his heart and asked for mercy for his new baby. Let him live. Let him have a good life. If it's within the power of my priesthood to heal him, then let me heal him when I give him a blessing tomorrow. I don't want to lose him. I want all my children, this one as much as any of the others, and all the children yet unborn that you might have for us. Don't take him away from us. Whatever he needs, we'll give it, if we have it to give.

Later, lying in bed, it occurred to him that he might have been praying for the Lord to grant him and DeAnne sixty years of caring for an invalid child. That perhaps what was wrong with Zap was so severe that it would be cruel to keep him here if the Lord was willing to take him home. So he re-entered the prayer that he thought he had closed, and added the phrase that he had deliberately left out when he was on his knees: Thy will be done.

DeAnne had recovered enough to go home, but she didn't want to. "I've never left the hospital without my baby," she said.

"You'll see him every day," said Dr. Keese. "And so will Step. And so will your mother. But you're not on insurance, I understand, and this is going to eat up your savings. You need whatever money you have to take care of Jeremy."

She said nothing.

"Good," he said. "They'll have you ready to go at noon."

To fill the empty time, she went back to the book. She had forgotten to pack it, and yet it had turned out to be the only thing that could keep her mind off Jeremy. She could read about the family in the book and say, We may have problems, but at least we'll never be like *them*.

No, it was more than that. The book kept speaking to her, characters kept saying things that echoed in her heart. Like when the nice son in the story said something about how life is like a cliff that's eroding away and you spend your whole life just shoring it up. It was the nightmare of her life, the one that lived always at the back of her mind, and he had named it. Only it wasn't *him*, of course. It was the author. Tyler wrote those words for me, she thought, so I'd know that I wasn't alone going through these fearful days.

This last morning in the hospital, she reached the passage where the mother in the book speaks of her "three lovely pregnancies" and how she counted down the months, waiting for something perfect to happen. "It seemed I was full of light," the mother said. "It was light and plans that filled me." DeAnne let the book fall onto the blanket and turned her face into the pillow and wept.

She must have cried herself to sleep, because when she next opened her eyes, Step was sitting there, leaning forward on the chair beside the bed, his chin resting on his hands, his elbows on his knees. He was looking at nothing, staring at the wall.

"Hello," said DeAnne.

"Hi, Fish Lady," said Step. At once the somberness left him, and if she hadn't had that moment of watching him unawares, she would never have known that he was anything but bright and confident. "I understand the doctor wants to kick you out and send you home. And I've got to tell you that I hope you come."

"I will," she said. "But please not yet."

"DeAnne, you'll be up here at least twice a day to nurse him. I'll drive you here, or your mother will. But in between those times, you need to be back home."

She reached out for his hand. "Step, I don't want to leave without the baby."

"He's doing better all the time," said Step. "And we couldn't very well give him all these tests at home."

"I don't like what they're doing to him here," said DeAnne. "I don't like the way he's drugged all the time."

"I don't like it either," said Step. "But we're not doctors."

"They don't know everything," she said.

"But they know something," said Step. "And sleeping in a hospital bed isn't going to make you or me any wiser about what we ought to do. Please—you've spent too much time here alone."

"I hardly have any time alone," said DeAnne. "I think every sister in the Steuben 1st Ward has been up here twice."

"At church this morning the bishop asked everybody to fast and pray for Zap next Sunday. The whole ward."

It filled DeAnne with emotion to hear that. They really weren't alone. And maybe with so many people fasting and praying, God would hear.

Or maybe not. Maybe it would be like in the book. Maybe things would always be just a little bit out of control, just out of reach.

Step reached down onto the floor. "You dropped your book," he said.

"I don't want to read it anymore," she said.

"Oh? I thought you liked it. Yesterday you even read me a passage from it."

"She knows too much," said DeAnne. "It hurts too much."

"Fine, I'll put it up on the shelf here—"

"No," she said. "No, give it to me."

"So you *are* going to read it."

"No," she said. "I'm just going to hold it. Is that all right?"

He looked at her strangely.

"I'm not going crazy, Step. It just . . . it's an anchor. It's another woman telling me she knows about things going wrong, and I just need to hold the book, OK? I mean at least it's not a Barbie doll or something."

"Fine," said Step. "I just wondered if this is going to become an icon to you. Like scripture. The fifth standard work?"

"Don't make fun," she said. "This is very hard for me, you know. I've always prided myself on making perfect babies. Now all I've got left that I make perfectly is my pie crusts."

"I wasn't making fun," he said, as he reached down and embraced her awkwardly. "And he *is* a perfect baby, DeAnne."

"You can't just deny it and make it go away," said DeAnne.

"He has the perfect body for the life God intends him to live. For the life he intends *us* to live."

God's plan. Nothing *we* can do about it. Might as well stop praying or trying or anything.

No, he doesn't really believe that, she realized. Because when we've talked about this sort of thing before, it was *me* who argued that God must plan all our lives or it wouldn't be fair, and he's the one who said, God doesn't have a plan for our lives, he just put us all into a world where no matter what our life is like, we can still discover how good and strong we are, or how weak we are, or how evil or cowardly. He's saying this about God's plan to make *me* feel better.

"I keep thinking," she said, "that we shouldn't have made love so soon after I used the spermicide the last time."

He shook his head. "It wasn't all that soon, DeAnne."

"You're supposed to wait longer. A week."

"DeAnne, the doctors don't even know what the problem *is*, let alone what caused it."

"And Bendectin—all these stories about Bendectin and birth defects—"

"In the *National Enquirer*, DeAnne, not in *Scientific American* or the *Journal* of the AMA."

"Step, I don't want to come home without my baby."

"But you *will* come home without him, DeAnne, because you know that's what's best for him, and best for you. And you always do what you know is right. That's who you are."

She thought about that for a while. "OK," she said. "Call for the nurse."

Later that afternoon, Step dropped by the pharmacy to pick up DeAnne's pain medication. While he was waiting for the pharmacist, he wandered over to the magazines. A woman was standing there, and he saw out of the corner of his eye that she glanced at him and stepped away. He scanned the covers of the newsmagazines, and then, out of sheer boredom, the professional wrestling fan magazines.

"You just can't give up, can you," said the woman.

Step glanced up, trying to see whom she was talking to. She was looking at him.

Did he even know her? She looked familiar, but he couldn't place her.

"At Kroger's, at the mall, I turn around and there you are. Can't you give me any peace?"

Step was baffled. "Excuse me, but I think you have me confused with somebody else."

"Wasn't giving up my job enough for you? Are you trying to hound me into suicide?" Her voice trembled; she sounded genuinely distraught. Whatever she imagined he was doing seemed real enough to her, though he could not think of why she would have fixated on him.

"Ma'am, nobody wants you to commit suicide."

"Then just *stop it*," she hissed.

Suddenly he made the connection. She hadn't chosen him out of madness; she really *had* given up her job because of him.

"Mrs. Jones," he said.

"You're a vile man," she said. "Whatever I did, I don't deserve to have you stalking me."

"I'm not, I swear it. This is the first time I've set eyes on you since —"

"Don't lie to me," she said contemptuously. "You stare at me every time. At the mall you laughed out loud at me."

"Mrs. Jones, how would I know you'd even *be* at this pharmacy? I'm here picking up a prescription for my wife."

"I won't go on with that tape hanging over my head. I just won't. It's worse than blackmail, it's torture."

It sickened him to have *her,* Stevie's tormentor, complaining about torture. But he didn't want to argue with her. She was a closed chapter. "Listen, Mrs. Jones. I just brought my wife home from the hospital and our newborn baby is still there because nobody knows why he's having seizures but he's in intensive care at a hundred dollars an hour and I don't have insurance and the bank is foreclosing on our house in Indiana and you know something? I don't care about you. I'm not following

386 · ORSON SCOTT CARD

you. I'm living my own life, and you go live yours and forget about me, because until this moment I had completely forgotten about you and I'd just as soon leave it that way."

He turned to go back to the pharmacist's counter. She snatched at his sleeve. "Give me the tape," she said.

"I don't even remember where it is," Step said. "Look, Mrs. Jones, we both live in the same town. We're bound to end up in the same store or the same fast-food joint or the same movie every now and then, and it doesn't mean *anything*."

"Is that how you plan to defend yourself when I ask the court for a restraining order?" she said. "That's what my lawyer suggests."

"Right now I think my prescription is ready and my wife needs it. Have your lawyer write me a letter." If there *was* a lawyer.

He picked up the prescription, had the clerk put it on his account at the store, and left. He was half afraid that Mrs. Jones would follow him out of the store, chase him all the way home, and beat on his door, insisting that he had to stop *following* her. But when he returned home with the medication, the only people who knocked on the door were more Relief Society sisters, coming by to help encourage DeAnne about Zap. Whatever happens will be part of Heavenly Father's plan, they said. After they left, DeAnne couldn't help but voice her exasperation to Step and Vette. "Of course it'll be part of God's plan, but God hasn't exactly been famous for planning nice things for all of his children."

Even though she was annoyed, Step could see that their visit had been good for her. In familiar surroundings, some parts of her life seemed finally to be under control again. She was back to being Relief Society spiritual living teacher instead of a helpless mother trapped in a hospital surrounded by doctors who didn't know what they were doing with her baby and wouldn't admit it.

* * *

On Monday morning, DeAnne arranged for Mary Anne Lowe to come over and tend Robbie and Betsy so that Step could take Stevie to the psychiatrist while Vette took DeAnne to the hospital to nurse Zap.

"We've been taking him to Dr. Weeks for two months," said Step. "Nothing's getting better."

"I know," said DeAnne. "But these things take time."

"After two months, we deserve a progress report," said Step. "We ought to be getting at least a diagnosis. Something. I mean, we're going through the same thing with Zap, the doctors searching to try to find out what's wrong, but *they* at least keep us posted. They explain what they're doing. And they learn things about the baby every day—at least they learn what *isn't* wrong with him."

"Psychiatry isn't precise," said DeAnne.

"Exactly my point. The hospital bill is already getting up around six thousand dollars for Zap alone, and who knows how much longer he'll be in there? We're putting in ninety bucks a week to the shrink—almost four hundred a month, almost as much as we're paying in *rent*—and we don't know what we're getting."

"So you don't want to take him? You want to give up? Stop cold?"

"I want to leave him home today. I want to go in myself, talk to her, find out what *she's* been finding out."

DeAnne looked at him suspiciously. "I think you want to pick a fight with her. I think you want to get rid of her the way you got rid of Mrs. Jones."

"If you want, I'll take the tape recorder and let you hear everything that's said."

"No," said DeAnne. "You can handle it."

"I promise that I won't do anything to antagonize her," said Step. "I wouldn't want to make it harder for Lee to continue in the Church."

"Or for Stevie to continue seeing her," said DeAnne.

"If that's in Stevie's best interest," said Step.

DeAnne just stood there, looking at him.

"I'm glad you decided not to say it," said Step.

"Say what?" asked DeAnne.

"That you don't think I'm capable of fairly evaluating whether Stevie should continue or not."

"That's not what I was going to say."

"No, but it's what you were thinking."

"Well, you can't get mad at me for what I thought and didn't say!"

"I'm not mad at you. I'm just reminding you that in all our years of marriage, I've never snuck off and done something about our family that you were against. Have I?"

"No," she said.

"So maybe I deserve a little trust here. You're not the only parent Stevie has who loves him."

"That is so unfair," she said. "I never said that, I never thought it, I never *would*—"

"I actually go through every day doing pretty well, DeAnne. I dress myself now, I carry on whole conversations with strangers, and I almost never have to call home for help. I've even used a credit card without confusion, and the grocery store lets me cash checks as long as I have a permission slip from my mother."

"Are you trying to make me cry?" asked DeAnne. "Are you trying to make me feel *guilty* because this is the first time you've taken Stevie to Dr. Weeks and I worry that you'll do something or say something to—"

"You see?" said Step. "You really don't trust me. For five months you've been in charge of everything at home, and now I'm back home again and you think that unless you program every word I say, unless I *stick* to your program every single moment, without deviation, without side trips, without *thinking* for myself, then everything will fall apart."

"Let's not fight," she said. "Please, please, please."

"We're not fighting," said Step. "I'm just expressing my resentment about the fact that you don't trust my judgment. Don't you remember that we decided *together* to send Stevie to Dr. Weeks? Or do you still think it was because you manipulated me into it and you don't dare let up on the manipulation?"

"Don't do this to me!" she said. "I have to go up there to the hospital and hold my baby who is so drugged up that he hangs like a rag doll in my arms and we have to suction the milk out of my breasts and force it into his throat in his sleep! I have to deal with all those doctors who think that I can't even understand English and force them to tell me what's going on so that I can have some idea of what's *happening* to my baby, and now you attack me like this—"

"Well if you're so tough and rigorous about finding out what the doctors are doing to Zap," said Step, "then why the *hell* have we gone two months sending Stevie to Dr. Weeks and you don't even know what goes on in the sessions? And when I say that I'm going to go up there and do with Dr. Weeks *exactly* what you're doing with Zap's doctors, you think that *I'm* too stupid or too emotional or too bigoted to do it. Well, I'm trusting *you* with Zap's life when you handle things up there. Don't you think I deserve the same respect in dealing with Dr. Weeks? Or am I the vice-president in this marriage? Will I just get trotted out for funerals?"

DeAnne gasped. "Don't say that!" she cried. "Oh, Step, you really think he's going to die!" She burst into tears.

Step was horrified. "It was just a figure of speech. I was just saying—Reagan sends Bush around to funerals, that's what I mean. Like when Sadat was assassinated. I wasn't saying anything about *Zap*. Really."

He put an arm around her. She turned toward him and wept into his shirt for just a moment. Then she lifted her head. "I'm not going to do this," she said. "I'm not going to cry. I'm not going to let go. Do you understand me?"

"Yes," he said.

"If I let go, then I won't be there for Zap. Or Stevie, or anybody. I'm just walking along the edge, Step. Right along the edge. You mustn't push me. You just mustn't. You're the one I've got to hold on to."

"So hold on to me," said Step. "Don't push me away. *Trust* me. Trust me the way I trust you."

"This whole argument, this is just because we're upset, that's all. We're upset and worried about Zap."

"And Stevie," said Step.

"Yes," she said. "And Stevie. I have to go."

"DeAnne," he said, "I have to know. Are you with me on this?"

"On what?" she said.

"On finding out from Dr. Weeks what's happening with Stevie."

"Yes," she said. "Do what you think is right."

"I won't *do* anything," said Step. "I'll just find things out. The way you find things out about Zap. All right?"

She looked at him steadily. "If you can see that Dr. Weeks isn't helping, you can discontinue the sessions. Without asking me or anything."

"But I won't," said Step. "Not without discussing it with you."

So it was that Step drove alone to Dr. Weeks's office, following the directions DeAnne had given him. When he went inside, Dr. Weeks stood up and greeted him warmly. "Mr. Fletcher," she said.

"Please, call me Step."

"Step, then. I've been thinking that it was about time I had a session with you and your wife."

"She's at the hospital. Our new baby is in intensive care."

"Oh, I'm so sorry. What's wrong?"

Step explained, briefly, and then said, "That's why

I'm here today. We're coasting along without insurance. The bills for these sessions are quite steep, and we thought it was time for us to evaluate where we stand— what exactly you've found out about Stevie's problems and what you think it looks like for . . . you know, down the road."

"Well, we've been making good progress, Stevie and I. He talks quite often during the sessions now. I think he's getting used to me."

Step wanted to say, He talks quite *often?* You mean we've been paying for sessions in which he hasn't talked at *all?* After two months he's only *now* getting *used* to you? But he remembered DeAnne's concerns about him and curbed his tongue.

"Beyond that," she said, "I'm still in the process of diagnosis. His reticence to speak is, of course, one of the symptoms of his disorder, but it also makes the process of diagnosis rather slow. I think that in another month or two I may be prepared to give you a prognosis. In the meantime . . ." She turned over a couple of sheets of paper on her desk.

Trying to keep his voice calm, Step interrupted. "What I'm interested in today, Dr. Weeks, is not a final statement, but an explanation of what you know so far, or what you *suspect* so far. DeAnne and I have to decide now, not two months from now, whether to continue treatment."

"I'd be happy to work out a payment schedule with you," said Dr. Weeks. "But I can hardly discuss an ongoing process, especially when you are not the patient."

"The patient is eight years old," said Step. "And if I were a fellow psychiatrist, you would have no trouble at all talking with me about what you think the diagnosis might turn out to be."

"But you are *not* a psychiatrist, Step."

"I have a Ph.D., Dr. Weeks. It's in history, which isn't an exact science like psychiatry, I know, but it does mean that I'm an educated human being, and I think that if you *try* to explain to me what's wrong with Stevie, I'll understand you." Thinking of what was going on at the hospital with Zap, he added, "For instance, you must have some idea of what his condition *isn't*. Things you've eliminated."

"It would be much more helpful to the whole process, Step, if you and your wife came in for some sessions with me yourselves. In fact, I suspect that your insistence on hurrying the diagnostic procedure may suggest possible sources for Stevie's abnormal reaction to stress."

I should have expected this, thought Step. The very fact that I want to hold her accountable is proof of *my* disorder. Well, he was not going to let Weeks establish a doctor-patient relationship with *him*. "Fine," he said. "If you explain to us what you think the problem might be and why our coming in for sessions might be helpful, then we might well agree that our joining in the therapeutic process might be the indicated course of action."

"Step," she said, "you seem to feel some hostility toward psychotherapists, along with an apparent fascination that has caused you to learn some aspects of psychological jargon. I wouldn't be surprised if you have unconsciously communicated this hostility to Stevie."

"Dr. Weeks, my efforts to find out what's going on between you and Stevie did not cause his problems."

"I wasn't implying anything of the kind," said Dr. Weeks. "Why do you think you felt a need to defend yourself just now?"

"Dr. Weeks, I think you misunderstand our relationship. I'm here as Stevie's parent. If I had brought him to a pediatrician with a bad cough, I'd have a right to expect the pediatrician to tell me what he thought *might* be causing the cough and what he intended to do about it, and he wouldn't give me any crap about how I couldn't possibly understand the ramifications of pulmonary function and, by the way, have I been short of breath myself lately? Stevie's been with you for two months, and apparently all you've observed about him is that he's morose and has imaginary friends, which is strikingly similar to what we already knew when we brought him here. I hope you'll understand that I'm not trying to interfere with Stevie's treatment. I simply have a responsibility to know what that treatment consists of and what it's designed to accomplish."

"Let me tell you why I'm reluctant to discuss this with you, Mr. Fletcher. Given the importance of parents in a child's life, it is inevitable that Stevie's parents are involved in the source of his problems. This idea is obviously threatening to you, and I fear that you may withdraw Stevie from treatment in order to protect your own ego. This might cause the boy great harm."

Step recognized that she was attempting to manipulate him into backing off—any objection he raised to her diagnosis could be dismissed as ego protection. But he held his temper and said none of the vicious retorts that came to mind. "Dr. Weeks," he said, "DeAnne and I knew from the start that solving Stevie's problems would almost certainly mean us changing our lives somehow. We're willing to do whatever it takes to help our son, and I'm not afraid to find out flaws in my own parenting. But I can promise you that if you *don't* tell me what you've learned about his condition, then we certainly *will* withdraw Stevie from your care."

She regarded him for a while, her expression aloof and uninvolved. She must have spent hours in front of mirrors during graduate school, Step thought, practicing that detached, I'm-above-emotional-engagement-with-mere-humans-and-their-petty-problems look.

"All right, Mr. Fletcher," she said, "I will tell you what possibilities I am currently considering as diagnoses for your son's condition. First, we may be seeing a simple factitious disorder. Second, we may—"

"Factitious disorder?" asked Step.

"*Factitious* means the opposite of what it sounds like, Mr. Fletcher—"

"I'm aware of the meaning of *factitious*," said Step. "It's the meaning of the phrase *factitious disorder* that I'd like you to explain."

"In layman's terms, it means that Stevie might be lying about these imaginary friends because he knows it upsets you and he's hungry for the attention that ensues."

Step stifled his desire to say, Stevie doesn't lie, he has never lied, he tells the truth even when it causes him to be embarrassed, even when he's sure that he'll be punished for it. If Stevie says that he's playing with imaginary friends, then that's because he really thinks he's playing with these friends, and it's not some damned cockamamy factitious disorder. Instead, he merely said, "And your second hypothesis?"

"It is possible that this is a mere adjustment disorder with depressed mood and withdrawal."

"And what would that mean?" asked Step.

"That he was seriously disturbed by your move to North Carolina. That he felt dislocated from his friends, from a familiar and safe setting, and instead found himself plunged against his will into a terrifying environment where he is incapable of making sense of what is going on and feels himself unable to protect himself from others. In that case, these imaginary friends would be a hallucinatory effort on the part of his unconscious to re-create the safe environment of the past, while his depression would be a sign that in fact the hallucinations are not successful in masking his unhappiness. He does not *quite* believe the falsely happy reality that his unconscious mind has created for him."

Step kept himself from saying, That's precisely what DeAnne and I thought before we ever brought him to you. "What do we do about it?" he asked.

"That was a hypothesis," she answered, "not a diagnosis, and therefore we will do nothing about it."

"But if it turned out to be the true diagnosis, what *would* be the right course of action?"

"We are getting into dangerous territory here," said Dr. Weeks. "Highly speculative."

"I understand that, and I'm not proposing that you do anything improper. I just want to have some idea of what the treatment might consist of if this turns out to be the diagnosis."

"Well," she said, "we might begin by having you contact the parents of some of his former friends back in Indiana, to get them to write to him or telephone. However, that may not be effective because at his age children are not very adept at making meaningful emotional contact through indirect media like the telephone or letters."

"And?" asked Step.

He meant for her to propose other possible treatments that might be used if Stevie's condition really was adjustment disorder with depressed mood and withdrawal. But she took it as a request for the third hypothesis.

"The third possible diagnosis, and the one that I think is most likely, is also the one that will be most difficult for you to hear impartially, and therefore I ask you to keep an open mind as best you can."

Step nodded, even though it was clear that she didn't think him capable of it.

"I think we can best account for Stevie's behavior if we view it, not as a new condition brought on by the move to North Carolina, but rather as an exacerbation of a preexisting condition of some severity, one which remained unobserved because it had gone on so long that you thought it a part of Stevie's underlying character."

"So why would we only have noticed it since—"

"Please," said Dr. Weeks. "An open mind. The stress of the move changed his pattern, you see, and it was the *change* you noticed, not the actual onset of his condition."

"And the condition would be . . ."

"Atypical dissociative disorder," she said. "This has been primarily documented in people who have undergone intense brainwashing experiences, but it is my belief that it shows up far more commonly and merely remains undiagnosed."

Step was baffled. What experience could Stevie have undergone that would produce the same effects as brainwashing?

"Actually, most children in America are subjected to a particular form of indoctrination from their earliest years, in which they are repeatedly reinforced in their belief in a powerful figure who does not actually exist. However, evidence is given to them to support that belief, accompanied by stories to make the child believe that the whole world believes in this particular mythic figure."

"You're saying Stevie's problems are because we taught him to believe in Santa Claus?" asked Step, incredulous.

"On the contrary. I think Santa Claus is, by and large, quite beneficial, for when the child is finally allowed—or forced—to recognize the nonexistence of Santa Claus, then the child is able to go through the vital intellectual process of reconstructing reality in light of new evidence, complete with back-forming new stories to account for past events. This prepares the child for many other disillusionments and gives her vital and well-supported experience in maintaining her grip on reality independent of the stories told to her at any given time."

"So Santa Claus is good," said Step.

"Santa Claus is usually not maladaptive," said Dr. Weeks, "and can be turned to a good end. I doubt many parents actually have that outcome in mind when they tell their children the ludicrous chimney story."

"No, I imagine not," said Step.

"Santa Claus is certainly not at the root of Stevie's problem. He has a healthy skepticism toward that story already."

We paid you ninety bucks an hour to find out whether Stevie believed in Santa Claus?

"Stevie has been subjected to another nonconsonant belief system whose implications are far more all-pervasive in his interpretation of events in his life. He feels an enormous weight of pressure to demonstrate his loyalty to this belief system, and therefore has for a long time been forced to come up with supporting personal experiences to tell you and your wife about. However, Stevie also has been taught to have an absolute commitment to truth, and cannot do as many children do and simply lie, claiming to have experiences that they do not have. Nor, being a child of a rather placid temperament, has he been able to work himself up to a level of emotion in which hysterical phenomena appear, which is the most common means of satisfying these expectations."

"You're talking about religion, aren't you?" asked Step.

"And the Mormon religion in particular, since yours is, as I understand, a somewhat, though not extremely, charismatic sect. As I have learned from Lee, there is considerable emotional display at your testimony meetings once each month, at which many people stand up and weep while they speak. This is clearly a hysterical phenomenon, and is not unhealthy—many churches throughout the South have long had a similar tradition and it has served them well as an emotional release. However, Stevie is one of those unfortunate enough not to be able to produce the appropriate hysteria, and he is also unwilling or unable to lie or pretend. Therefore, he produces hallucinations."

"Dr. Weeks, the only hallucinations Stevie has had

are his imaginary friends, dating from our arrival in Steuben."

"On the contrary," said Dr. Weeks. "Stevie has told me that he had several experiences in early childhood in which he sensed a very evil presence, threatening to destroy him. I immediately recognized this as the father-fear that is not unusual in boys of that age and which they usually outgrow. However, he says that he told you and your wife about these 'frightenings' and 'bad feelings,' as he called them, and you both informed him that these feelings were from the devil."

"We said they might be," said Step. He was trying to stay calm, but it made him feel invaded, to have her skeptical eye turned on those tender moments from Stevie's childhood, when he and DeAnne had tried so carefully *not* to impose their own interpretation on Stevie's dreams.

"To a child of his age at the time, of course, there was no meaningful distinction between 'might be' and 'is.' But I would not have expected you to know that, since you are also caught up in the same belief system. In any event, Stevie began to associate all spiritual phenomena, about which he heard much but of which he experienced nothing, with this oedipal anxiety from his earlier childhood—"

"When he felt afraid at night," said Step, "I would lie by his bed for an hour or two hours, until he fell asleep, singing or humming to him. It wasn't me he was afraid of."

"Of course he did not *know* it was you he was afraid of. He had displaced the fear and shifted it to a nameless imaginary entity which you conveniently named for him. From that point forward, then, his response to the pressures of your culture was to hallucinate, and in every case you labeled these hallucinations as spiritual experiences. Thus he was able to be part of the culture. He was brainwashed."

"I'm surprised that you allowed Lee to join our church if that's what you think we're about," said Step.

"I'm a scientist, Mr. Fletcher," she said. "I mean no offense by this. I simply feel that we would be doing Stevie a disservice if we did not recognize that he has long had hallucinations unconnected with the move to North Carolina, and therefore treating only the symptoms that arose since your move here would leave his basic underlying condition unresolved."

"*If* it turns out that this is the correct diagnosis," said Step.

"As I said, I only *lean* toward this interpretation. But you must understand that when he told me about his baptism, and how during that experience he saw a bright light in the water, which entered him and drove all the darkness out of his body, well, that shows me that he is hallucinating more than just imaginary friends."

Stevie had told no one about this experience, no one but Dr. Weeks, who thought of it as madness. "Do you *know* that it was a hallucination?" asked Step.

"You were there, Mr. Fletcher," said Dr. Weeks. "Did *you* see that light?"

"No," said Step.

"When one person in the midst of witnesses sees something that no one else sees, we are generally safe in identifying these experiences as hallucinations."

"Or maybe he has clearer sight than the others," said Step.

"Oh? You think there really was some underwater light source that no one else was able to see?"

"I think," said Step, "that it's possible for something to be both subjective and real at the same time. Just because only one person sees something doesn't necessarily mean that what he sees isn't there."

"But by that standard, Mr. Fletcher, I fail to understand why you have even brought Stevie to me. After all, what worried you and Mrs. Fletcher was the fact that

Stevie was seeing imaginary friends that no one else could see."

Step had never thought of the imaginary friends this way. It made him angry, her linking spiritual experiences with Stevie's delusions. But she *had* linked them, and if she was right, if they really were alike, then all of Stevie's extraordinary sensitivity to other people, his ability to perceive good and evil, his aliveness to the spiritual side of life—all of that was also imaginary, hallucinatory.

On the other hand, it might also mean the opposite. That just as Stevie's sensitivity to spiritual things was real, so also his ability to see imaginary friends was real. In which case Dr. Weeks was right, and they had made a colossal mistake bringing him to her. Just as he had been telling them the truth with his absurd-seeming story about Mrs. Jones's mistreatment of him, so also he was telling them the truth about these imaginary friends.

Which meant there really *were* invisible boys playing in their yard whenever Stevie went outside.

No, thought Step. No. The reason this is not true is that Dr. Weeks is wrong from the start. His imaginary friends are *not* the same thing as his spiritual sensitivity. The other thing she said—adjustment disorder with depressed mood and withdrawal—that was enough to account for all his symptoms, or at least all of them that Step and DeAnne *thought* were symptoms. Dr. Weeks simply hated religion, and so she was going to read psychological disorders into the cosmology of Mormonism.

Of course, if she hated religion, why was she driving Lee Weeks to church every week?

"Is there any other possible diagnosis?" asked Step.

She spoke briefly about residual-type schizophrenic disorder, but it was clear she didn't think much of the possibility. "But I can see that you would prefer almost any diagnosis to the one that casts doubt on your cherished belief system."

"I prefer whatever is best for Stevie," said Step. "I'm perfectly able to see how our religious beliefs appear to those who don't believe in them."

"Do you intend to let Stevie continue receiving treatment?"

"I don't make such decisions alone," said Step. "I'll have to confer with my wife."

"Bring her in," said Dr. Weeks. "I think it really *is* time for you to join in the treatment process. I think that if the constant insistence that Stevie demonstrate loyalty to your belief system were toned down—note that I do *not* say they should be stopped—he might be able to relax back into more normal strategies for dealing with these parental and societal expectations. We may be able to extinguish the hallucinations in a year or two, provided that the entire family cooperates."

"Thank you for your willingness to tell me all of this, Dr. Weeks," said Step. "I can see that you've been doing your best to understand our son's situation."

"Then there is hope that I can continue working with this very sweet boy?"

"I don't know what will happen," said Step. "As I told you from the first, money is a serious concern for us right now. But if we discontinue Stevie's treatments, it won't be because we think you've been doing less than your best with him as a doctor."

Dr. Weeks nodded graciously. She was too professional to allow herself a smile—but Step was reasonably sure that he had left her feeling good about him and about Stevie, and good enough about the Church that she would not stop bringing Lee. *Why* she was bringing Lee to church, given the attitudes she had toward religion, was difficult for Step to understand. But she was doing it, and he didn't want it to be his fault if she stopped.

At the receptionist's desk he even confirmed next week's appointment with Stevie. Then he walked out of the office, switched off the tape recorder, and headed home. DeAnne would listen to the tape with him tonight, and he seriously doubted that Stevie would ever go back to Dr. Weeks again.

DeAnne had a frustrating morning with the baby. He simply couldn't be roused enough to eat anything at all. A nurse helped her pump her breasts, something that she had never done with the other three kids, and stored the milk in the freezer to feed to little Jeremy later, but it did nothing to calm DeAnne's anxiety.

When she expressed her worries about the baby's excessive sleepiness to the neonate, he simply nodded patiently and then said, "Of course you know that you can hardly expect a baby who's taking seizure-control medication to be as responsive as your other children were. And until we know what is causing the seizure activity, we would be irresponsible to remove the medication. Seizures can lead to serious brain damage or even death."

"Can't too much phenobarbital cause problems, too?"

"It could if he were getting too much," said Dr. Torwaldson. "But he's not." And that was that.

But DeAnne couldn't get her worries out of her mind, and so when Dr. Greenwald, the pediatrician, came by, she explained it all over again. "He's losing weight, isn't he? More than the normal amount. Isn't that one of the things we're worried about? And if the pheno is making him so sleepy he won't eat . . ."

"Well, I'll tell you what," said Dr. Greenwald. "Let's just happen on down to the ICU and let me take a look at the dosage. It never hurts to doublecheck."

So DeAnne and Vette followed him to the ICU, where he stopped and looked at several of the babies before finally getting to Jeremy. "Hey, Zap," he said. He reached his hand into the built-in gloves in the side of the incubator and began probing a bit, touching the baby here and there, lifting his arms and legs, lifting an eyelid.

"Some of these babies here just break my heart," said Vette. "So tiny or so—wounded."

"Ah," said Dr. Greenwald. "But they don't break *my* heart, because on this particular day all my babies in here are doing quite well. I think we're going to keep them all. Especially Zap here. He looks downright husky."

DeAnne noticed with resignation that everyone was picking up the name *Zap*, despite her resolute use of *Jeremy*. But as long as he was telling her that her baby was doing well, DeAnne really didn't care all that much what Dr. Greenwald called him.

"He's pretty nonresponsive, isn't he?" said Dr. Greenwald.

"Like a rag doll," said DeAnne.

Dr. Greenwald looked at the chart. "Hmm," he said. "Quite a dose of pheno, too."

"Is it too much, do you think?"

"No," said Dr. Greenwald. "It's a normal dose."

"Oh," said DeAnne. "I just thought—it can't be right that he's so sleepy that he doesn't *eat*."

"No, it isn't right. In fact, I'd say he's got way to much pheno in his system right now."

"So it *isn't* a normal dose?"

"Phenobarbital's a funny kind of drug. Everybody's body uses it differently. I'd say that it looks like your little boy's system just isn't flushing that drug out of his body as fast as most people do, and so it's getting built up inside him. Normal dose going in, but then it's building up, you see."

"Can you do anything?"

"Well, it isn't very hard. We just cut way back on the dosage until we find it maintaining at the right level in his blood. It means a few more blood tests."

"Do they have to keep taking the blood out of his head like that?"

"Oh, don't you like his haircut? Kind of punkish, I'd say. You see, this is a newborn baby. It isn't like his veins are particularly big or easy to find. Heck, we've got needles bigger around than his finger."

"That's all right, I know it can't be helped, it just looks so awful. Dr. Greenwald, would you mind telling me what his current dosage is?"

"Would the numbers mean anything to you?" asked Dr. Greenwald.

"No," said DeAnne. "But if the number's not lower tomorrow, *that* will mean something to me."

He grinned. "You're pretty stubborn, aren't you?"

She didn't smile back. "This is my baby," she said.

"Dr. Greenwald," said Vette. She was over at one of the other incubators. "Is it right for this one to have liquid dripping from this needle?"

Greenwald immediately went to the incubator where Vette was standing. "Not one of my babies, but I'll say that it *doesn't* look right. Hasn't been going on long, though, the sheet's not even marked yet. Dana!" he called.

One of the nurses immediately came toward him.

"Have a look at this while I call Dr. Yont."

The nurse named Dana came and immediately shook her head. "Have you been a bad girl again, Marisha? Pulling out your needles. We're going to have to *staple* this next one on." She looked up at Vette. "Thank you for noticing this. We check every baby every five minutes, besides constantly checking the monitors, but every moment counts. This one is so small we have a *very* hard time finding a vein, don't we, Marisha? And when she makes some sudden movement, out it comes."

"She's so tiny," said Vette.

"Yes," said Dana. "We're probably going to lose her.

She's not getting any better, and sometimes she's a bit worse."

"Her poor parents," said DeAnne, thinking of the anguish she'd feel if someone had just said that about Jeremy.

"I don't know," said Dana. "If Marisha lives, she'll be severely brain damaged. Not much of a life. Sometimes God is merciful and lets them come home without going through this vale of tears."

It was at that moment that Step came into the ICU. "Oh, good," he said. "I hoped you'd still be here."

"Is Mary Anne still with the children?" DeAnne asked.

"When I got home, her husband was there and he offered to come up and help me give Zap a blessing."

She saw now that Harv Lowe was walking with awe among the incubators. "These must be some tough kids," said Harv, "if they had to stick 'em with all these needles just to keep 'em quiet."

Dana laughed. "Oh, they're the toughest."

Step asked the nurse, "Do we have to use these gloves with Zap? He's not got a contagious disease or anything, and he's a full-weight baby. We don't absolutely have to touch him with our hands, but it would be better."

"You'll have to clear this with Dr. Torwaldson if you're going to break open the box," said Dana.

At that moment Dr. Greenwald came back with, apparently, Dr. Yont, who immediately started giving orders and working on the baby whose needle had come loose. It seemed that more than a loose needle was going wrong, and all the medical people were quite intense about what they were doing. DeAnne was content to wait. There was no emergency for Jeremy, and that was good.

A few moments later, Dr. Torwaldson came in, and at that point Dr. Greenwald withdrew and came over to the Fletchers. "Not my baby," he said, "and I'm not a neonate, so I'm one pair of hands too many, now that Tor's here."

"Is she going to be all right?" asked Vette. "The little one?"

"Doesn't look like it to me," said Dr. Greenwald. "But sometimes they surprise you. Sometimes they really want to live."

"Do you think they really have desires? When they're so small?"

"It all depends," said Dr. Greenwald, "on whether you think of them as having a soul or not. I happen to think they do, and so I think that yes, that soul can have desires even if the body isn't yet ready to put them into words. I've seen babies hold on to life with all their might, and I've seen others just give up and slip away. They don't talk about it, but that's how it feels to me."

"And is that what Jeremy is doing? Slipping away?"

"Why don't we wait to answer that," said Dr. Greenwald, "until we see what he's like when he's conscious?"

"Dr. Greenwald," said Step. "I think you'll understand—we want to give a blessing to my son, and we'd like to be able to lay our hands directly on him. We also anoint him with a single drop of pure olive oil, on the brow or the crown of his head. Would that be all right?"

Greenwald glanced over at Torwaldson. "Oh, I can't see why not. Zap is really a husky little kid. Compared to these others, he's a regular Larry Holmes."

Dr. Greenwald opened the incubator, and Harv took the oil, anointed Jeremy's forehead with a drop of it, and then said the short prayer that went with it. DeAnne noticed that Dr. Greenwald watched, bowing his head respectfully. Then both Step and Harv touched the baby gently, and Step sealed the anointing, which was the longer prayer, the one that changed according to the needs of the person receiving the blessing, and according to what Step felt impressed to say.

Only a couple of months ago, thought DeAnne, Step was confirming Stevie, and now he's giving his newest son a different kind of blessing. It felt good to know that her husband was able to do this, was able to call on the powers of heaven on her children's behalf. I can give him milk from my body, I nurtured him inside me for nine months, and Step couldn't really share in any of that. But he can give *this* to our baby.

The blessing felt powerful to DeAnne as it was going on, and yet when it was done she realized that Step had said nothing about healing. He only blessed Jeremy that the doctors would recognize their own limitations and make no mistakes with him, and that he would soon be home with his mother and father and sister and brothers.

Dr. Greenwald shook Step's hand after he had sealed up the incubator. "Are you a minister?" he asked.

"No," said Step. "I'm a computer programmer. Harv's an accountant."

"Well," said Greenwald. "It still felt good, to see a father do that with his own child. Never seen that before."

From the other incubator, where the other doctors were gathered, they heard a voice, a soft one, but clear. "She's gone." And a moment later, the doctors started moving away. DeAnne heard Dr. Yont murmur, "I'll call the parents."

DeAnne put her arm around her mother, who seemed quite shaken by this. She noticed, too, that Dr. Greenwald took out a handkerchief and wiped his glasses, after which he also brushed at his eyes with the cloth. "I never get used to it," he said. "Even when they're not one of mine. Don't like to lose 'em." Then he visibly straightened himself. "Why don't we step on out of the ICU. We don't need to be part of what's going on in there now."

As he ushered them into the corridor, Dr. Greenwald reassured them. "Your little boy doesn't seem to be in any danger right now, and as for that lethargy, well, I'll have a talk with Tor this afternoon. You'll see some improvement, I promise, once we get the dosage right for his system. Nice to meet you, Mr. Fletcher. Mrs. . . ."

"Brown," said Vette.

"Nice to meet you," said Harv, shaking his hand. And Greenwald was gone.

"I feel good about Zap being in his care," said Step. "It has to help, that he really loves these babies. And that he . . . you know. That he takes us seriously."

"Thanks for coming," DeAnne said to Harv.

"I have an idea," said Vette. Her tone was suddenly bright, leaving behind the somberness of the ICU. It was a gift she had, to know the right moment to turn the mood of a group of people, to get them moving again. "I'll have Harv drive me back to the house and you two ride home together in the other car."

"Fine," said Harv.

"Thanks," said Step. "I need to talk to DeAnne anyway."

"One condition," said Vette. "I get the Renault. Air conditioning, you know."

"We'll open the windows on the Datsun," said Step. "We'll still be just as hot, but our sweat will help water the lawns on either side of the road."

Once they were alone in the Datsun, DeAnne asked first about the blessing. "Couldn't you have blessed him to be healed?"

"You think I didn't want to?" asked Step. "You think that wasn't what I *planned* to do?"

"You were so fatalistic about him the other day," said DeAnne. "Yesterday, I mean. Was that only yesterday? I thought maybe you'd given up on him."

"I tried to talk about Zap getting better and having a perfectly normal healthy body and I just couldn't say it. Maybe it's a lack of faith on my part, or maybe I was being told not to bless him that way. Either way, what

could I do? I said what I was able to say." Then he gave
one short, derisive laugh. "My atypical dissociative disorder apparently isn't as efficient at providing me with
appropriate hallucinations as Stevie's is."

"So," said DeAnne. "How did it go with Dr. Weeks?"

"First tell me how *you* are," said Step. "Pain still
bad?"

"I had a little bleeding, too. I need to lie down
more."

"So now I've got you in this rattly car, vibrating you
six ways from Tuesday."

"It's all the going back and forth to the hospital."

"So you're saying you should have stayed."

"I'm not dying, Step, I just hurt and I bleed a little.
Tell me about Dr. Weeks, Step. Did you quarrel?"

"Just listen to the tape," said Step. He pulled the
microcassette recorder out of his pocket and pressed
the *play* button.

For the first while, listening to the conversation
in Dr. Weeks's office, DeAnne wanted to shout at him
to stop it, he was doing it all wrong, he was deliberately provoking the doctor. But then she realized that
for Step, he was actually being quite controlled. And
Dr. Weeks really was resisting talking to him. So the
fact that he got her to tell her speculative diagnoses
was probably quite an accomplishment, as was the
way he sat still and listened, so that Dr. Weeks finally
did explain adjustment disorder. It sounded exactly
like what was going on with Stevie.

"I can do that," said DeAnne. "Write to friends in
Indiana. The school can give me the addresses of the
parents, or forward my letters to them, anyway."

Step pressed *stop*. "That's not the diagnosis she
believes in," he said. "And that's not the condition she
intends to treat." Then he pressed *play* again.

She listened to the rest of the tape without com-
ment, until it was over. "Well, Step," she said, "I can

hardly believe you didn't say *anything* snotty to her at all as you left."

"I didn't want to sour anything, in case you wanted to continue the treatment."

DeAnne was startled. "You mean you think we should?"

"I didn't know what *you'd* think," said Step.

"Yes you did," said DeAnne. "You knew perfectly well what I'd think. Here she is declaring that anybody who believes in a religion is marginally or totally insane—I mean, that's most of human society through most of history."

"Yes," said Step. "But maybe true sanity didn't exist until people like her emerged."

"From under a rock, you mean," said DeAnne. "We know a lot of Mormons, Step. But not many hysterical ones, and not many crazy ones, either."

"Well, there's Sister LeSueur."

"She's conniving, not crazy," said DeAnne. "The only really crazy Mormon I've known recently is Dr. Weeks's own son, and she can't blame that on *us*."

"Give her time," said Step.

"It makes me so mad that she would dismiss what we believe as if it wasn't even worthy of consideration."

"Well, she believes in a competing religion," said Step. "If ours is true, then hers is kind of silly."

"Well, ours *is* true, you know," she said.

"And hers is kind of silly."

"As you said all along."

Step shrugged. "This isn't about I-told-you-so. It's about Stevie. We can try another psychiatrist later. But I don't think he should continue going to a psychiatrist who firmly believes that the only way to help Stevie is to cure *us* of our religious delusions. Even if she could succeed, it certainly wouldn't help Stevie, since that's *not* his problem."

"I agree," said DeAnne.

"So Dr. Weeks is toast, right?"

"Right."

"Only for Lee's sake we tell her that we're going to hold off on continuing treatment for a few months, while we watch Stevie to see if he improves by himself."

"Excellent," said DeAnne.

The radio wasn't on very loud, but it happened to start playing "Every Breath You Take" during a momentary pause, and they both noticed it. "They're playing our song," said DeAnne.

"Weird stuff is happening to us all the time," said Step. "Makes me feel special."

"Jeremy's problems sure put things in perspective, though, don't they?" said DeAnne. "I mean, it's hard to get excited about Sister LeSueur's silliness when you've seen your baby in a glass box like that. And that anonymous record—"

"Still bothers me," said Step.

"Me, too," said DeAnne. Then she reached out and put her hand on Step's leg, feeling the muscles flex and move as he moved his foot from the brake to the accelerator. "Step," she said, "thanks for seeing Dr. Weeks. I don't know if I would have been able to get her to come forward with her diagnoses. It was obvious she was trying to keep us from finding out what exactly it was that she was doing to Stevie. If you hadn't kept pushing, we wouldn't have known."

"I only did it because I knew you were with me on it."

She squeezed his leg. "I love you, Step."

"I love you, too," he said. "I'd love you even more if you'd remember that I'm very ticklish on my leg and when you squeeze just above the knee like that I'm likely to have a fit and lose control of the car."

She squeezed his leg again, repeatedly, but even though he *was* very ticklish there, he had learned how to relax his stomach muscles and resist laughing—a technique that had allowed him to survive childhood with an older brother who was a merciless tickler. "You're no fun," she said.

"Try it again when you're in shape to do some *serious* tickling."

"I hope it's soon," she said.

"So do I."

When they got home, they found Stevie in the family room sitting on the couch, and told him the news right away: He wouldn't be going back to Dr. Weeks.

"Oh, OK," he said. "She was kind of stupid anyway."

"Oh?" asked DeAnne.

"She said that Jesus was just like Santa Claus," said Stevie. "Only everybody knows that Santa Claus is just a *story*."

"Well," said Step, "she believes that Jesus is just a story, too."

"That's only because she doesn't listen when he talks to her," said Stevie.

"I guess not," said Step. He glanced at DeAnne, caught her eye. "Clearly dissociative," he said, grinning.

She shook her head at him. He shouldn't try to joke like that around Stevie—he was likely to catch the drift of what he was saying.

"Does this mean I can still play with my friends?" asked Stevie.

DeAnne sighed. It was one thing to realize that Dr. Weeks was simply playing out her own prejudices, and quite another to suppose, just because Weeks was no help, that Stevie didn't still *need* help.

"I'd rather you played with your brother and sister," said DeAnne.

"But when I'm not playing with *them,* I can play with Jack and Scotty and those guys? 'Cause we got a new kid."

DeAnne wordlessly got to her feet and left the room. Stevie watched her go in silence.

"Do what you need to," said Step. "Do what you

think is right." Then he, too, left, following DeAnne into the bedroom, where she clung to him in silence for a long while.

They brought Zap home from the hospital after two weeks in intensive care, with a bill for more than eighteen thousand dollars and no diagnosis. It had finally come down to a day when Step and DeAnne were standing there listening to a doctor who had come in from Chapel Hill. He was describing several procedures and drugs they could try "in case" Zap's condition was caused by this or that, until Step said, "I don't think I want my son being treated for an undiagnosed condition." The Chapel Hill specialist looked at him in surprise; his whole demeanor changed; he was more respectful, almost apologetic for his early tone. "Oh, I didn't realize you were a doctor," he said. There was not a trace of irony in his tone, and so Step realized that this specialist really was proposing things that he might not have so confidently proposed if he had thought Step and DeAnne actually knew anything. That was enough for them.

The hospital was very good about things. They accepted two thousand dollars and a promise to pay at least half the balance as soon as Step got his option money from Agamemnon—or else the completion money for the 64 version of Hacker Snack, whichever came first.

Then they brought Zap home and began the slow process of discovering just exactly how much was wrong with him, and how little they could do about it.

The only really good thing that had come out of Zap's long hospital stay was that they realized how much they could depend on people in the 1st Ward who they had thought were merely acquaintances, and now discovered were true friends. Vette remarked on it, too.

You have a good ward, she said. They really care about you.

If only there were something about Stevie's condition that could evoke the same community response that Zap's had brought forth, thought DeAnne. If only they could rally around Stevie, and fast and pray for him. Maybe they should tell people about what Stevie was going through, and give them a chance to help him. But no. There was too great a chance that in the case of a mental illness and not a physical one they'd shy away, they'd shun the boy and make his isolation even worse, his descent into madness steeper and faster than ever.

And could we really blame them? thought DeAnne. If I were a mother of a normal child and I heard that a little boy of his age was seeing hallucinations of imaginary friends, would I really be willing to let them play together? Would I feel so much compassion for someone else's child that I would put my own child at risk of being hurt in some outburst of madness? No, the hurts of the mind were too strange, too invisible, too magical to hope for the same kind of tolerance and help from even the best of people.

It frightens *me*, thought DeAnne. Why should I expect others to be better than I am?

So Stevie's problem remained a matter for their family alone. Until a newspaper article forced them to see things another way.

12

·Friends·

This is the headline on the front page of the Steuben *Times-Journal* on the morning of Sunday, 21 August 1983: SERIAL KILLER IN STEUBEN? The headline brought fear to the hearts of parents all over the city, for this was not a tabloid, and the story was not irresponsible shock journalism. The chief of police had formed a task force that included the county sheriff's office and had close liaison with the North Carolina State Bureau of Investigation. They were also bringing in outside experts on serial killers, especially those who specialized in the kidnapping and murder of young boys.

For several months, the police had been deeply concerned about the number of unexplained disappearances of young boys in the Steuben area, cases in which no

body was ever found and no motive could be guessed at
for the child to have run away, even after the most heart-
less questioning of the distraught parents. And there was
also a rhythm to the disappearances. Not a definite pattern,
not a disappearance on a certain day of each month or
anything showy like that. Just a space of a couple of months
or maybe three between disappearances.

And for the first time anywhere, the names of all
the boys believed to be possible victims of the supposed
serial killer were listed together. Their pictures appeared
above the fold on the front page. There were seven of
them; all of them had disappeared since May of 1982;
and the disappearances were becoming steadily more
frequent, with less and less time between them.

This was the lead article; in fact, there were no
other articles on the front page except a sidebar on the
head of the investigation in Steuben, a detective named
Doug Douglas, who had been a rather colorful figure
during the civil rights disturbances of the sixties, when
he vowed that anyone violating city ordinances would be
arrested and taken to the Steuben city jail, but that by
God everyone who went into that jail would come out in
exactly the same condition they were in when they
entered it. Some in those days said that this would let
the niggers think they had free reign to do what they
wanted in Steuben, but in fact the most important result
was that the racial disturbances ended very quickly and
were replaced by talk and compromise. Douglas had
been chief of police then, the youngest one in Steuben's
history. Years later, the mayor who was elected in the
Reagan sweep of 1980 demoted him to chief of detectives, and some said it was a long-awaited payback for
Douglas's racial evenhandedness in the sixties. But
instead of resigning or even complaining, Douglas just
kept right on doing his job. The story was designed to
reassure the city that one of Steuben's finest was on the
case. It was also designed to reassure the black community

that even though all the victims were white boys, the investigation would not take on racial overtones, and blacks would not be singled out for harassment.

But the Fletchers didn't see this article on Sunday morning, because they didn't have time even to glance at the paper in the hurry of getting ready for church. This was the last Sunday before school started, and yesterday they had been so busy buying school clothes for Stevie *and* Robbie, who was starting kindergarten this year, that neither Step nor DeAnne had remembered to do a laundry and therefore the morning was spent fishing wearable clothing out of the laundry baskets in the kids' closets and pressing them so they'd look presentable at church.

The boys were dressed; DeAnne was taking snarls out of Betsy's hair; and Step had the assignment of changing Zap's diaper and getting him dressed for church.

About the only time Zap was any trouble was when he was being changed. He slept a lot, and even when he was awake, he didn't interfere with the process of dressing or feeding. Step almost wished he would, to show some vigor, some real awareness of the world. He rarely even cried. And as for moving his body, well, he seemed to have no muscle tone, no firmness to him. Now and then he'd move in a jerky kind of way, but most of the time his arms and legs were fairly loose and springy. As if he didn't much care where his limbs went. Zap's legs, though, always seemed to move back into a frog-like position, the knees widespread, the feet tucked up right under his buttocks. This meant that when his diaper was getting changed, his heels kept springing right into the midst of whatever was in his diaper. It made changing him a real challenge. Step would stretch Zap's legs out long and straight, and massage his thighs and calves, saying, "That's my long boy, see how tall you are when I stretch you out? Stretch out those legs, long boy." But it did little good. When the diaper came off, the heels

moved right back up into place, and it seemed as
though it took three hands to change him. Three hands
or an extra couple of baby wipes to clean his feet.

Still, Step was becoming rather adroit at the chal-
lenges of diapering a baby who thought he was a frog,
and he soon emerged from the bedroom with Zap lying
prone on his forearm, his head cradled in Step's hand,
his little legs dangling—froglike—as they straddled
Step's biceps. It was Step's favorite way to carry the
babies when they were very small. DeAnne had been
horrified at first, since it looked like a football carry, but
they both soon realized that when Step held a fussy
baby in that position, the fussiness usually subsided, at
least for a while.

Step could hear, from the screeching in the kitchen,
that Betsy was still getting her hair combed. So he stood
wordlessly in the door of the family room, watching
Robbie crash his Matchbox cars together and Stevie
play a computer game.

Not that it looked as though Stevie was actually
playing anything. From where he was, Step couldn't see
the screen, but he could see Stevie's hands on the con-
troller, and he just wasn't moving it. Oh, now and then a
sort of lean to the left or to the right, but most of the
time he was just watching the screen, his face trans-
fixed. "Do it, Sandy," he whispered. "Come on, now,
now, now. That's it!" And then, "No, Van, no, not like
that, he's going to get you, do you want him to get you?
You're too *quick* for him, if you just run." As usual,
Stevie was naming the characters in the computer game
after his imaginary friends. But what kind of game was
this, where apparently something engrossing was happening on the screen and yet the player of the game had
hardly anything to do? It couldn't be much fun, for the
player to have so little control that he hardly had to
move the joystick from minute to minute. Yet Stevie
was completely involved in it. Step had to see the screen.

He stepped into the room, walking behind Stevie and looking at the screen. It was that pirate ship game again, thought Step. I never did find that disk.

"Hey, Daddy, watch me crash these guys together!" said Robbie.

Step glanced down at Robbie and watched the two cars crash, as Robbie made an elaborate show of making the cars fly through the air and bash into the bookshelves and then rebound off of everything else in sight. "Enough, enough," said Step, "you make me want to never get in a car again!" Robbie laughed uproariously.

Step looked back at the computer screen, but it was blank. Stevie had switched off the game and was standing up from the chair. "Why'd you turn it off?" Step asked.

"Time for church, isn't it?"

"Yes it is!" called DeAnne from the other room. "It would be nice if we could arrive on time for once, instead of parading up the aisle like beauty contestants during the opening hymn."

Step helped the kids pile out to the car and strapped Zap into the carseat in front while DeAnne got Robbie and Betsy to share the middle seatbelt in back so that she and Stevie could cram themselves in and use the seatbelts by the doors. "No doubt about it," said DeAnne. "We ought to start taking both cars to church."

"This still works," said Step.

"Only because you don't have to sit in back," said DeAnne.

Step immediately got out of the car and walked around to her door and opened it.

"Oh, Step, don't make a scene just because I—"

"I'm not making a scene—you are, my love. What *I'm* doing is playing Sir Walter Raleigh and letting you tread upon my cape. Please, let me sit back here with the kidlets and you drive. Maybe it'll convert me to the idea of taking two cars to church."

"Step, I really don't feel up to driving yet," she said. "It hasn't even been a month."

"I thought you were better."

"Mostly," she said. "Drive. I shouldn't have complained, and now we're going to be late."

"Sorry," said Step. "I was just trying to be nice."

They weren't late, though, and they got a good bench on the side. Step was singing a solo with the choir, and Robbie had a talk in Primary, and so it was a busy Sunday for them. When they got home, the kids were starving and Step fixed dinner while DeAnne nursed the baby, which was a grueling experience for her, since Zap had a way of clamping his jaws down hard every now and then, nearly pinching her nipple off, or at least that's what she said it felt like.

"I think you ought to switch to formula," said Step. "The next kid's going to resent it if Zap succeeds in biting the nozzle off the firehose."

"I'm giving him formula sometimes, but this really is better for him, and he likes it better," said DeAnne. "I'll toughen up."

"Mm," said Step. "Calluses and scar tissue—very sexy."

"If he's still doing this when he gets teeth, Step, that's weaning day—cold turkey, I'll tell you."

If he's still doing it. If he learns. If he changes. If he starts sleeping on some reasonable schedule, instead of sleeping eighteen hours and then staying up twenty-four. If somebody figures out what all those scans and probes and measurements from the hospital mean. If somebody will just put a name on whatever it is that's wrong with Zap so we can start dealing with it—or not dealing with it. Whatever turns out to be appropriate.

The kids came in and ate the tuna patties that Step had made—a Depression-era recipe that his mother had raised him on. The kids seemed to like it well enough, provided that Robbie was allowed to pour six ounces of ketchup on his.

Then, finally, the kids went down for naps—or for lying in bed reading or staring at the ceiling, in Stevie's case—and DeAnne finally went out front and brought in the paper while Step sat down and idly looked among the disks lying loosely around by the Atari, trying to find something that might possibly be that pirate game. He got sidetracked, though, by the Lode Runner disk, which he booted up and began to play. It was a nifty little character-based game in which the eight-pixel player-figure has to run around collecting all the treasures on the screen while bad guys try to chase him. The way the treasures were arranged in the changing landscape made each level a new puzzle, and Step soon found himself addicted. This is a great game, even though it's so deceptively simple. No gimmicks like the ones I'm using in Hacker Snack. Just a fundamentally sound design that allows itself to unfold in new ways, over and over and over again. I need to learn from this.

He became aware that DeAnne was standing behind him. "Step," she said. "You need to come in and look at this story in the paper."

"In a minute," he said.

"Can't you pause the game or something?" she asked.

"If it's that urgent," said Step. He reached for the space bar to pause the game, but it took too long, and his player-figure died.

"Oh, I'm sorry," said DeAnne. "Did I make you lose?"

"I've still got eight lives left," said Step. "A real Christian game. Lots of chances for resurrection. But I'm bucking for the rapture at the end."

She didn't laugh, not even her courtesy laugh, the one that said I don't know why you thought that was funny but I love you. He followed her into the kitchen and sat down at the table. The headline at once caught his eye, and he read the whole story—quickly, but not missing anything. He hadn't pored over a hundred thousand

pages of Spanish-language newspapers while research-
ing his dissertation without learning how to distill the
essence from a newspaper story in a very short time.

"This is scary stuff," said Step. "I know you're
already careful with the kids, and so am I, but I really
think we shouldn't even let them in the back yard without being out there with them the whole time."

"Absolutely," said DeAnne. "But Step, didn't you notice?"

"Notice what?" he asked.

"You're going to think I'm crazy."

"Probably," he said. But his joking tone didn't fit
now; he realized that DeAnne had sounded genuinely
scared. She really thought that whatever she was about
to point out to him would make him think she was
crazy. "Show me," he said.

"I was hoping you'd just see it yourself. Look at the
pictures of the lost boys, Step. Look at their names."

He did. "Do we know any of their families or something?" That was absurd—if anyone they knew had had a
child disappear, they'd have known about it before now.

DeAnne laid a list of names on the table. It was
written in her handwriting. Step compared them to the
names under the pictures, since that seemed to be what
she intended. Most of the names under the pictures
were listed on the paper, or at least were similar. Scott
Wilson matched the name "Scotty" on the list. "David"
matched David Purdom. "Roddy" would be Rodd Harker.
"Jack" *could* be a nickname for Jonathan Lee.

"Does the story say anywhere that this Jonathan
Lee is nicknamed Jack?" asked Step.

"No," said DeAnne. "I hope he isn't."

"Well, then, what were you writing this list for?"

"Step, I didn't write this list today. I wrote this list
back in June."

Step waited for the other shoe to drop. Then he
made the connection. "That's a list of Stevie's imaginary
friends. I remember Jack and Scotty."

"It's more than that now," she said. "I've heard other names since then. I know I've heard him talking about a Van and a Peter, and look."

Step looked, and two of the boys were Van Rosewood and Peter Kemeny. "Good heavens," he murmured. "This is really weird."

"Is that all you can say?" she said. "That it's *weird?*"

"It scares the shit out of me," said Step. "But usually you prefer me not to talk like that. What does this serial killer thing have to do with our son?"

"I don't know," said DeAnne. "Nothing. It couldn't."

"Maybe Stevie's been reading the newspaper and picking up the names or something."

"But three of the boys disappeared before we moved here. We never would have seen articles about them. This article here is the first one ever to list all these names together. Think about it, Step. Stevie came up with almost the same list as these detectives did, and there's no way he could have done it. No way that makes any sense."

Step's hands were trembling as if it were cold. He *was* cold. "It's not just *almost* the same list," he said. "If Jonathan really is Jack, then this last one, Alexander Booth. . . ."

"He's never talked about an Al or an Alex," said DeAnne.

"But I watched him playing a computer game this morning and I heard him saying, like, Come on, Sandy. Sandy's a nickname for Alexander, too."

DeAnne pressed her face into her hands. "This article already scared me, Step. But then when I saw this— what can we do?"

"I don't know," said Step. "I don't even know what it means."

"Remember that record we got in the mail? The anonymous one?" asked DeAnne. "The song about I'll be watching you?"

424 • ORSON SCOTT CARD

He hadn't thought about it in a long time. It was still on the radio a lot, but all the things that had happened since the record came had put that old scare far into the background. Now, though, it took on truly sinister overtones. "Do you really think . . ."

"What if this . . . serial killer . . ."

"Watching us," said Step.

For a moment DeAnne seemed to go out of control, uttering some high whimpering cries while she hid her face in her hands. Step wasn't sure how to deal with this, or what was happening to her; he put his hand on her back, as if to steady her, as if she were tipping and he was going to put her back upright. "Oh, Step," she whispered. "Oh, Step, I'm so scared. Who could it be? What if the serial killer has . . . *talked* to Stevie?"

"Impossible," said Step. "You read the article. They say that this serial killer is extremely dangerous because he isn't leaving any evidence anywhere. They aren't even *sure* there's a serial killer anyway. Because they haven't found a single body. That's how these boys got on the list—their bodies haven't been found."

"But maybe he . . . No, Stevie would have told us."

"We could ask him. If anybody has ever talked to him."

"No," said DeAnne. "He's going to school tomorrow. There's going to be talk about this serial killer everywhere. They're going to be warning all the children about talking to strangers. He'll connect that with *us* asking him if somebody already talked to him. He's got trouble enough already without his own parents connecting him so personally to this."

"But he's already connected," said Step.

"Might be connected. This might just be a coincidence."

"Van and Sandy aren't such common names," said Step.

"Well, Sandy *isn't* Alexander and Jack *isn't* Jonathan."

"So what else do we do? Call the police? Oh, yes, Officer, we have a real lead for you in this serial killer thing. Our son, you see, has been hallucinating these imaginary friends, and they happen to have the same names as those lost boys. What? Oh, don't you have time to talk to us?"

"You're right," said DeAnne. "They'd think we were crazy." She fretted with the list, something she did when she was nervous, folding and tearing at paper until it was reduced to confetti. Step reached out his hand and put it over hers.

"Don't tear up that list," he said. "You wrote that *before* this article came out."

"Yes, but I don't have any witnesses of *that.*"

"You sent a copy of it to Dr. Weeks, didn't you?"

"Yes," she said. "Yes, that *would* prove that we had at least some of the names before. And we did get that record."

"I think you're saying that we *should* call the police."

"We should call somebody," said DeAnne. "We should do something. You don't find out that there's some weird kind of link between your son and a serial killer and then just fold your hands and say, How interesting."

Step looked again at the newspaper. "So, how accessible do you think this Doug Douglas is?"

They soon found out. DeAnne looked up the number of the police department and Step called. He asked the switchboard operator to connect him with Detective Douglas. "He isn't in on Sundays, but I'll try his line."

It rang once and a man picked it up. "Is this Mr. Douglas?" asked Step.

"No," said the man.

"Is he there? Can I speak to him?"

"Can I tell him what it's about?"

Step covered the receiver and whispered to DeAnne: "I think he's there." Then, into the receiver, he said, "It's probably about nothing. It's something that doesn't even make any sense to *us*. But maybe it'll mean something to him."

"Can you be more specific?" asked the man.

"About the story in the paper this morning."

"The serial killer story," said the man.

"Yes," said Step.

"I'm the one designated to take down all reports and information, so you've already reached the right place."

"But we don't have any report to make," said Step. "And what we have might not be information. And—look, can't I just talk to Mr. Douglas? It'll only take two minutes and then I'll be out of his hair."

"You've got to understand, sir, we've already received more than two hundred calls today about this story, and if Detective Douglas took all those calls personally . . ."

"Fine, then," said Step. "We don't want to bother him. Let me just leave you my name and number and he can call me back when he has time."

"Wouldn't it be easier just to tell me your information?"

Yes, it would, thought Step. But you're the guy whose job it is to take down all the crank calls and the sincere but irrelevant calls and filter them out, and you would think our call was one or the other of those and so you'd never mention us to anybody in a serious way and then we'd never know whether we were even right that the names matched—or, more important, we'd never know if we were wrong, so we could breathe more easily.

"No," said Step. "Here's my number. Take it down if you want."

The man took it down and read it back. Step said good-bye and hung up.

"Dead end, huh?" said DeAnne.

"I don't know," said Step. "The guy wanted me to tell *him*, but I didn't want to get put on their list of cranks. So I'm betting that the fact that I wouldn't talk to anybody but Douglas either puts me on their *serious* crank list or it gets Douglas to call me back. Either way, maybe somebody talks to us."

The phone rang.

DeAnne laughed nervously.

Step picked up the receiver.

"This Stephen Fletcher?" asked a man with a soft tidewater accent.

"Yes," said Step.

"This is Doug Douglas, Steuben Police Department. What's on your mind?"

Step mouthed to DeAnne: It's him. Then, to Douglas, he said, "Mr. Douglas, this is probably crazy and we're probably going to end up on your crank-call list, but we've got something here that if we don't tell you about it we're probably going to go out of our minds worrying about it, so if you've got two minutes I'll give it a try and then you can tell me I'm nuts and I'll go away."

"I got two minutes, son," said Douglas. "Go ahead."

"We've got a list here that has four names on it. Jack, Scotty, David, and Roddy."

"Mm-hm."

"That list was written early in June. Since then, and before we saw this article in the paper, we added three more names to it. Peter, Van, and Sandy."

"So you telling me you're a psychic?" asked Douglas. The weariness in his voice told Step what he thought of psychics.

"No," said Step. "Far from it. We got these names from somebody else, for a completely unrelated purpose. But you don't have to take just our word for it. That same list is also in the possession of a doctor here in town, who also collected it for a completely unrelated reason."

"Mm-hm."

"So then back in June we also got a forty-five rpm

record in the mail, anonymously, but it was postmarked Steuben. And the record was that one by the rock group The Police, the song called 'Every Breath You Take.' It has a part about how the singer of the song will be watching. We figured it was just somebody who wanted to scare us or punish us for something, and we didn't think the police would be interested or even if you were, what could you do? So we didn't report it. But now this article comes out, and we think—maybe the reason we had these names is somehow connected with the person who sent us that record. And maybe that person is somehow connected with the serial killer. And so maybe . . ."

"You're being a little cute with me, Mr. Fletcher. You keep not telling me why you have that list of names."

"I'm not trying to be cute, I'm just trying to tell you the parts that matter before I tell you the part that makes it all so hard for anybody to believe, including us. I mean, we want you to take this seriously."

"So far I'm listening serious, and I'm waiting for you to talk serious."

"Yes. Can you—first can you just tell me if our list really does correspond? I mean, was Jonathan Lee, was he ever called 'Jack.' Did Alexander Booth go by the nickname 'Sandy'?"

"Mr. Fletcher, I'm still on the phone with you. Doesn't that answer your question?"

"Yes, I guess so." Step took a deep breath. "Mr. Douglas, that list was written by my wife."

"She's the psychic?"

"No, she's the *mother.* I'm the father. The other person who assembled the same list is a psychiatrist. Our son's former psychiatrist. It's our son who came up with these names."

Douglas let out a stream of air into the phone. It occurred to Step that he was probably smoking. "Well now, that's interesting," he said. There was a pause on the line, as if Douglas was thinking. Then he spoke again. "Does your son live with you?"

"Of course," said Step.

"Does he have a job? I mean, is he working today, or is he home?"

"Mr. Douglas, our son doesn't have a job and of course he lives at home. For heaven's sake."

"Mr. Fletcher, how *old* is your son?"

"He turned eight in June."

There was a loud squealing sound over the phone. Step thought: He just sat bolt upright, and his chair squeaks. "Eight years old?"

"Yes sir," said Step.

"Jesus H. Christ," said Douglas.

"I suppose so," said Step.

"I mean, you said your son's psychiatrist, your son came up with the list—I thought you were telling me your boy might *be* the serial killer. Hell, I've been having my boys here check out your address and I've got three patrol cars heading for your house right now and you're telling me that your son is *eight?*"

"Yes!" said Step. He leapt to his feet, started pacing as he talked, urgently. "I'm only thirty-two myself, for pete's sake. Don't send a bunch of police cars here, we're not going anywhere! I was thinking about my son as a possible *victim,* that maybe this guy's been stalking *us,* stalking our son, trying to scare us or maybe even setting us up or something and you're sending police cars to *arrest* him?"

"Oh, Step!" cried DeAnne. "That's insane! Are they really—"

Douglas started talking again; Step held up a hand to make DeAnne be quiet so he could hear. ". . . already called them off, don't worry." Douglas chuckled. "See, we're a little excitable around here. The SBI wants to shove us aside on the investigation and so we kind of feel the tiger breathing down our necks, you know. But those cars are going back on patrol and so don't you folks worry. Still, I'd kind of like to come on over and talk to y'all. Think that's possible?"

"We'll be here all afternoon," said Step.

"Give me about thirty minutes, then."

DeAnne immediately began worrying about what might happen if the kids woke up and found a policeman in the house.

"He's a detective," said Step. "He'll be in a suit."

"And they'll be in the family room, and there's no way to shut this door so they can't hear."

"So we'll take him in the bedroom and close the door."

"With our room in the mess it's in?"

"So throw the bedspread up over the bed," said Step.

"You really don't care, do you!"

"I really don't think the appearance of our room amounts to a sparrow's fart in a hurricane compared to what he's coming over here to discuss, that's true."

"That's your philosophy. Mine is that I don't want him to think he's just found another lowlife family who don't care about their living conditions."

"But we *don't* care or our bedroom would already be cleaned up," said Step plaintively. But he followed her into the bedroom and joined her in a flurry of straightening. They were done, with a couple of folding chairs set up, when the doorbell rang. It had only been fifteen minutes.

"Maybe it's not him," said DeAnne.

It was Douglas, all right, standing on the porch, lighting up a cigarette. After the normal civilities, but before inviting him in, Step cleared his throat and said, "Excuse me, but we don't smoke."

It took Douglas a moment to realize that this actually meant that he was expected to respond in some way.

"You mean to tell me you don't ever have any visitors who smoke?"

"We don't even own an ashtray," said Step. "And we have a new baby, which means that we just can't have smoke in the house."

"Well don't that beat all. Antismokers in a tobacco town. My daddy worked in the tobacco factory all his life. What's North Carolina coming to?"

"As soon as that's out," said Step, "we'd be honored to have you come in."

Douglas hooted, then dropped the cigarette and ground it out with his shoe. "No offense intended," he said.

"None taken," said Step. "And vice versa, I hope."

This really wasn't the best beginning to their conversation, Step realized. And since the kids were still asleep, or at least quiet, DeAnne sat down across from Douglas in the living room while Step went back and quietly closed the kids' bedroom doors. When he got back, they had apparently got right down to business, because DeAnne was showing him the list.

"Well, you know, this could have been written anytime," said Douglas.

"It's not evidence anyway," said Step. "I mean, how could it be? But if you need corroboration, Stevie's psychiatrist at the time, Dr. Alice Weeks, has a copy of this list which DeAnne gave her back in early June. And she made her own list of the others."

"We deliberately kept the nicknames out of the papers," said Douglas. "We do that, among other things, so that we can tell the hoaxers from the real thing. Like they'll 'remember' seeing a man dragging a little boy along saying, Hurry up, Alex, only *we* know that Alexander Booth would have told anybody who asked him that his name was Sandy. So it's a fake."

"And so you took us seriously," said Step.

"Jack was the clincher," said Douglas. "Your wife

was telling me while you were down the hall there that these are the names your son gave to his imaginary friends."

"That's right."

"Pretty amazing," said Douglas. "And then this forty-five, this record. Comes in the mail. 'Every Breath You Take.'"

"We didn't think that much of it, after a while. Till the article."

"I'm not surprised."

"But, I mean, an anonymous package like that, it had to be meant to scare us."

"Oh, no doubt about it," said Douglas. "The trouble is, it doesn't help us much."

"No?"

"It almost certainly didn't come from the serial killer."

"Oh," said Step. "Well I guess that's a relief."

"But how do you *know* that," said DeAnne, "since you don't know who the serial killer is?"

"We've got psychological profiles. Some guys, they try to tease the cops. Son of Sam, you know. Taunting us. They want to get caught. But then there's the Ted Bundy types. Smart. Cool. All they care about is not getting caught. Bundy never sent letters to the papers. Bundy never tipped his hand to anybody. I mean, he had a girlfriend that he was sleeping with during half the time he was going out killing those women, and she never had a clue. She knew he did some shoplifting and stuff, but had no clue about the killings. This serial killer—*if* there is one, cause it's not like we can prove it yet—he's like Bundy. He's smart, and he doesn't want to get caught. He's *scared* of getting caught, and he doesn't like being scared. He isn't in this for the thrill. He's in this for—something else."

"What?" asked Step.

"I'm not here to tell you about serial killers," said

Douglas. "It'll ruin your sleep for a long while. It's sure as hell ruined mine. Begging your pardon for my language, ma'am."

"I just wonder how you know all this about him," said Step.

"We know it because we haven't found the bodies. Not a trace, not a clue. If he was a talker, after seven disappearances we'd've heard from him by now. Especially after the article. That's why we called in the press on this—we hoped we could flush him out. But he's the other kind. If he exists. He's the kind who can't stand the idea of public attention being focused on him. So now that the article's been run, I expect him to lay low for a while. He's been hitting every couple of months, but I imagine he won't hit again this year. All depends, though."

"On what?" asked Step.

"On how strong it is, whatever it is that's driving him to kill."

"I hate this," said DeAnne. "Because he has something to do with my son."

"Maybe not," said Douglas. "I'd like to meet your boy, if I could."

"I don't want him interrogated," said Step immediately.

"Oh, no, that's not my way. He's a boy, and he's a troubled boy. I've got children of my own. I just have to—make some sense out of him coming up with these names, don't you see. And if I meet him, get a feel for who he is, then that might help me understand what to make of this."

"I really don't want you to," said DeAnne. "We'd have to tell him you're a policeman, and then he'd—"

"So you wouldn't consider telling him I'm an uncle from out of town?"

"He knows all his uncles," said Step. "And he's not stupid."

"Why not trust me?" asked Douglas.

434 • ORSON SCOTT CARD

"Why can't you just—work from the envelope the record came in? We've still got it, and the record sleeve. You could take fingerprints or something."

"I'll tell you what," said Douglas. "Who do you think might have sent it?"

At once Step and DeAnne both became reluctant. "Well," said Step, "it would only be speculation. We don't want to get some innocent person in trouble."

"You see?" said Douglas. "You already have some people in mind who might have sent that record. You've got *enough* people you're thinking about that you know most of them are innocent, but one of them probably sent it. Right?"

"But the one who did—" said Step.

"The one who did is *not* the serial killer. That's just a plain fact. If there's one thing I've learned about serial killers, they don't change their pattern. Once they've got it set, they don't change. Even the ones who *think* they're changing it every time, they're only changing stupid meaningless details. The basic pattern remains absolutely the same because that's part of the ritual, you know? If they didn't do it the same, it wouldn't give them . . . what it gives them. But make a list of your acquaintances who might want to send you a threatening message. I won't go question them. I'll just hang on to the list. And then I'll compare it to other lists we've got, and if they show up on another list, *then* we'll go question them, and they'll think we're bothering them because of the other list, not yours. And if they don't show up on any other list, we leave them alone. Fair enough?"

"All right," said DeAnne.

"As for your record-sender, well, someday he might turn into a killer, but if he's still at the anonymous threat stage, he's got a ways to go. The evil is still creeping up inside him. Hasn't taken him over completely yet. In other words, he's still a basically civilized person. And he may keep that evil under control, too. May control it till the day he dies. Nobody'll ever know. And all he ever did, the worst thing he ever did was mail somebody a forty-five rpm record by the Police. Let's hope that's how it works out. That's how it usually does."

"Usually? There are a lot of forty-fives getting sent around?"

"A lot of anonymous messages. More than you could imagine. I'd say most people get a couple of them during their lives, and maybe most people *send* one or two. You get so filled with rage, you want to hurt somebody, only you don't have enough hate in you to poison them or burn their house down. So you send a letter. You throw trash on their lawn. You call them on the phone and then hang up—again, again, all night, until you start getting afraid that they might be having their phone traced so then you stop. You ever got strange calls like that?"

"Once," said DeAnne.

"Me, too," said Step.

"It's going on, all the time. There aren't enough policemen in the world to track down all of that. And most of the time it's just what you thought—somebody you know who's angry at you. Maybe even your best friend, only they can't bring themselves to confront you, so they send you a record and it gets it off their chest and nothing more ever happens."

"That's a relief," said DeAnne.

"Well, you *should* be relieved. But you should also find out who's at the door before you open it, and make sure you know who the next package is from before you open it. Because one time in ten thousand, the guy's not kidding."

"With one hand he giveth comfort," said Step, "and with the other he taketh it away."

"What can I say?" said Douglas. "I'm dying for a cigarette, and the thing I came out here for was to find out why you had all those names, and you aren't letting me meet your son."

"We thought you'd tell *us* why our son knew those names," said Step.

"Well, I'm not gonna subpoena him. But I'll tell you folks, every little boy in this town is in danger right now. This killer may lay low for a while, but he'll be back soon enough, and whatever he's doing, he's going to be damned hard to catch. How many more is he going to kill before he finally slips up? I hope not yours, but he'll kill somebody's."

"But Stevie couldn't possibly know—" Step began.

"What are you hoping to find out from him?" asked DeAnne.

"Not the name of the killer, so rest your minds about that," said Douglas. "Nothing concrete at all. I just want to get a feel for who he is. For the kind of person he is."

"He's a good kid," said Step.

"I'm sure he is," said Douglas.

Step laughed. "And I bet you hear that from the parents of drug pushers and rapists and embezzlers all the time."

"Either that or 'I always told him he'd end up in jail.'"

Step looked at DeAnne. DeAnne looked at him. "We've come this far," she said.

"We let him talk to that miserable shrink," said Step. "For two months. What can Mr. Douglas do worse than Dr. Weeks?"

"I'll get him," said DeAnne.

While she was gone, Step had to ask. "What *do* they get out of this? Guys like . . . the one you're looking for?"

Douglas raised an eyebrow. "Morbid curiosity?"

"Yes," said Step. "But I'm also a historian. I study human nature, and somehow this guy is human, right?"

"No," said Douglas. "Guys like that start out human, but there's an empty place inside them, a hungry place, and it starts sucking the humanity, the decency, the love, the goodness right out of them. And by the time they get to where this guy is, there's nothing left but that hole. And so the guy spends all his effort trying to fill that hole, to find something to satisfy that thirst, that hunger, that nothingness in him, only he never can. He just tries over and over and over again, and it's never enough. If the guy has any decency left, some scrap of humanity somewhere in the shadows, then he'll leave clues for us, he'll do like Son of Sam and taunt the cops, he'll cry for help. Free me from this hunger that's eating me alive. But the worst ones, there's *nothing* left. This guy, there's nothing."

"Well if it's all gone, his humanity, then wouldn't people around him know it?"

"They may know it. He may be a complete son-of-a-bitch who sics his dogs on anybody who comes near his property. But then he might also be the nicest, most normal-looking guy. You just never know. It could be your dentist. The bag boy at the grocery. A minister. He fools everybody."

"How?" asked Step. "Why can't people see through his lies?"

" 'Cause he doesn't lie," said Douglas. "It's like Bundy again. He really believes that he's innocent. Because it isn't *him* doing it, it's this evil thing inside him. He knows it's there, but it's not *him,* see, and so he doesn't even feel guilty, because he knows that *he'd* never do anything like those horrible things."

"So it could be anybody, and he wouldn't even know it himself?"

"Oh, he knows it," said Douglas. "Because all the time that he's telling himself that *he* would never do this bad stuff, in fact he's working as hard as he can to protect that other part of him. To keep anybody from catching him. No, he knows. If he didn't know what he was doing, if he was really crazy, we'd have found the bodies."

They heard DeAnne talking as she came down the hall. "It's nothing all that important," she was saying. "He just wants to talk to you."

Stevie came into the room, looking sleepy. So he finally *had* taken a nap, Step thought. Douglas didn't stand up, just stuck out his hand. Because he was sitting down, his head was at about the same level as Stevie's. "I'm Doug Douglas, son," he said. "Would you shake my hand?"

Stevie came forward and took Douglas's big hand and shook it, solemnly.

"I don't know how much your mama told you about me, but I'm a policeman."

Stevie glanced down at Douglas's suit.

"That's right, I don't wear a uniform. I'm a detective, so if your daddy ever drives faster than the speed limit, I'll let him go right by because traffic isn't my job."

Douglas paused, apparently waiting for Stevie to ask him what his job was. Of course Stevie didn't say a thing.

"The thing is," said Douglas, "there's a bad person in Steuben these days who's been kidnapping kids. Do you know what kidnapping is?"

Stevie nodded.

"Well, you're going to be hearing a lot about this guy at school tomorrow. What grade will you be in?"

"Third."

"Yeah, you'll hear a lot. Your teachers will tell you, cops like me will come to school and tell you—stay away from strangers. If somebody grabs you, scream your lungs out."

"We already taught him all this," said DeAnne. "He already follows these rules."

"Well, I'm glad to hear that," said Douglas. "Do you *always* follow those rules?"

Stevie nodded.

"And what if somebody wanted you to go off alone with him, and you said no, 'cause it was against the rules, but then he said, All right, but don't you ever tell anybody that I asked you. What would you do?"

"Tell Mom and Dad," said Stevie.

"What if he said that if you told, he'd hurt you."

"I'd still tell."

"This boy's been well trained," said Douglas. "Stevie, I hear you have some good friends."

DeAnne stiffened, and Step said, "Mr. Douglas."

"Now, now, Stevie doesn't mind talking about his friends. Do you, Stevie?"

Stevie shrugged. A little one-shoulder shrug.

"Well, I'm not going to ask anything hard. I just want you to tell me one thing. Who was it who told you their names?"

"Jack," said Stevie.

"Jack," said Douglas. "Now, is he *one* of those friends, or are you thinking about some other Jack?"

"He's one of them," said Stevie.

"So he told you his own name," said Douglas.

Stevie nodded.

"And everybody else's name."

Stevie nodded. "Except Sandy," he said.

"And who told you Sandy's name?"

"Sandy," said Stevie.

"Stevie, I bet you love your mom and dad, don't you?"

Stevie nodded, immediately, deeply.

"Well, I just want you to know that I've been talking to them for the last while and they really love you, too. More than you even know, and I'll bet you already think they love you a lot, don't you."

Again he nodded.

"They love you so much that they want you to be safe, all the time. Now can you do that for them? Can you keep yourself safe? Follow all those rules?"

Stevie nodded.

"Well that's it then," said Douglas. "I'm glad to meet you, Stevie. And if anybody ever gives you any trouble, you just tell them that Doug Douglas is your friend, and they better be nice to you, all right?"

Stevie nodded again. And then said, "Thanks."

"Can you go off to your room again now, Stevie?" said Step. "We just need to talk to Mr. Douglas here a little bit more, OK?"

Stevie headed back to the hall. DeAnne got up and followed him; when she came back a moment later, she said, "I just had to make sure he was back in his room."

"Well," said Step. "I don't know what you could possibly have learned from that."

"Oh, I learned what I needed to learn," said Douglas.

"And what was that?"

"Your son's honest," he said. "He's sweet. Deep into his heart, he's sweet. If God could taste him, that's what God would say: This boy is sweet, right through."

Step wasn't about to disagree with him, but he didn't see how Douglas could know *that* from the banal little conversation he had with Stevie.

"He reminds me of my late wife," Douglas said. "She'd have nightmares sometimes, terrible ones. She'd wake up in the middle of the night and make me hold her close and she'd tell me the nightmare. And then I'd get up in the morning and go to work, or sometimes I'd get a call that very night, and it would be a crime that had something to do with her dream." Douglas leaned back, remembering. "One time she dreamed of a blue dress, trying to put it on, only it kept slipping off of her, she couldn't wear it, and it frightened her, you know the way it is when you're dreaming, you get scared over silly things like that, not being able to put on a dress. And then I get to work and there's this woman and they're taking her statement and the story is that she was raped that night, the guy chased her, and three times she slipped out of his grasp because of the dress she was wearing, that blue dress."

"Oh," said DeAnne.

Step had studied folklore in college and he knew from the start how the story would end. They all ended that way. "That actually happened to your wife? Or didn't you hear it from a friend of a friend?"

Douglas laughed softly. "You're the man who called me up because you had that list, and you're asking me if this is just some fairy tale? Yeah, we're always skeptical about the other guy's story. But I don't really care whether you believe me because that's not what I'm trying to tell you anyway. What I'm telling you is, there's some people who do things so bad it tears at the fabric of the world, and then there's some people so sweet and good that they can feel it when the world gets torn. They see things, they know things, only they're so good and pure that they don't understand what it is that they're seeing. I think that's what's been happening to your boy. What's going on here in Steuben is so evil and he is so good and pure that he can't help but feel it. The minute he got to Steuben he must have felt it, and it made him sad. My wife was like that, always sad. The rest of us, we've got good and evil mixed up in us, and our own badness makes so much noise we can't hear the evil of the monster out there. But your Stevie, he can hear it. He can hear the names of the boys. Only, just like my wife made a dream out of it, a dream of trying to put on a dress, your Stevie takes those names and he makes friends out of them. And to him those friends are real because the evil that pushed those names into his mind, *that* is real."

"So you don't think Stevie is crazy," said Step.

"Hell, you *know* he ain't crazy. You got the list, don't you?"

"Is there something we should do?" asked DeAnne.

"I can't think of anything, except hold on to your children, hold them tight, keep them safe."

"Yes sir," said Step.

Douglas got up. "I need me a cigarette now, so I'll be on my way."

"I'm sorry we bothered you about something that turned out not to be helpful to you," said Step.

"Oh, this helped me a lot."

"It did?"

"Sure," said Douglas. He stood in the open doorway. Step and DeAnne stepped out onto the porch with him. "Before you called," said Douglas, lighting a cigarette, "we weren't a hundred percent sure that there even *was* a serial killer. But now—well, now I know. Because otherwise your son wouldn't have known those names, now, would he? They wouldn't have been all together in a list, would they, unless they all had something in common with each other and with no one else. There's a few kids disappear every year, and it's not evil, it just happens. It's part of the order of nature. Your son never noticed those. These he noticed. So now I know."

"You can't use this to prove it to anybody else," said Step.

"Don't have to prove it to anybody else," said Douglas. "*I* know it. So now I'll never rest till I find this guy and stop him."

"And then will Stevie stop having these—imaginary friends?"

"When the source of his affliction is gone, then there won't be any need for him to deal with it anymore, will there? My wife never dreamed the same dream twice."

He started to walk toward his car, when DeAnne called after him. "Do you still want us to give you a list of people we think might've sent that record?"

"Why not?" he said. "Might turn out to be useful."

"We'll phone you this afternoon, OK?"

"Fine," he said. "If I'm not there, tell it to whoever answers the phone, they'll be expecting it."

He got in his car and drove off. DeAnne and Step went back in the house, sat down at the kitchen table, and wrote down their list of names. People who had reason, or thought they had reason, to hate the Fletchers as of the time they got that record in the mail. Mrs. Jones, Dicky Northanger, Lee Weeks, Roland McIntyre. They debated back and forth about including Dolores LeSueur's name, but they finally did. It was ludicrous to think of Dolores LeSueur as a serial killer—it was ludicrous to think of a *woman* as a serial killer—but the list had to be complete or why make it?

They phoned it in. As Douglas had said, the man on the phone was expecting them, and he was thorough and businesslike. And then it was done.

Step and DeAnne faced each other across the table. "What a Sunday," said Step.

"This is going to sound awful," said DeAnne, "because that serial killer is still out there somewhere, but . . . I feel better now."

"Me, too," said Step. And then he laughed in relief. "Stevie isn't crazy. All that *shit* from Dr. Weeks—forgive me, but a spade's a spade—that's all back in the crock it came from. Whatever's going on in Stevie's life, it isn't made up and we didn't cause it and he isn't crazy. It's the real world that he's living in, only just as we thought, he sees it more deeply and truly than the rest of us. And when you think about it, it's kind of sweet, isn't it? I mean, whatever happened to these lost boys, they still live on in Stevie's mind. He imagines them and he's made playmates out of them, he's made *friends* out of them. And I'm not afraid of them anymore."

"I'm still afraid," said DeAnne. "I can't help that."

"Well, so am I—of the killer."

"I wish we lived somewhere else," said DeAnne. "I wish we could take Stevie away from this place."

"Me, too," said Step. "But this is the place where the doctors know about Zap. This is the ward that fasted and prayed for him. The rest of us can live anywhere, but Zap is already part of the life of this place. Those people in our ward, you think they're going to watch Zap grow up and think, What a strange-looking kid, why can't he hold his head up? No. They're going to say, we know that boy, he's one of us. We'll never find that anywhere else, DeAnne."

"I know," she said. "I know." But she was not yet comforted.

"The danger is still here," said Step, touching the newspaper article again. "But it's not pointed at us. I mean, it's like the article says, a child in Steuben is still far more likely to be killed in a traffic accident or a gunshot accident than to be a victim of this killer. Parents have to be less trusting of strangers for a while, that's all. And we were already nearly paranoid, so I think we'll be fine."

She nodded.

"And we can't afford to move, DeAnne. Unless you think it's worth abandoning everything and scurrying home to your parents' basement."

"I guess I'm just thinking, I don't want to be a grownup anymore. I want to go home and have mom and dad take care of me." She laughed at herself. "It's hard to *be* mom and dad. Isn't it? Because anything you decide might be wrong."

"Heck, everything we decide *will* be wrong," said Step, "because no matter what we do, something bad will happen later. So I refuse to regret any of it. I don't regret taking the job with Eight Bits and I don't regret quitting. I don't regret all those expensive tests they ran on Zap, because we had to know. I especially don't regret that day when I saw you talking on the phone and I thought I had never seen anything so beautiful as my wife being kind to someone else who was in need."

She leaned over to him and put her arms around

him and rested her head on his chest for a moment. "You make me feel so good."

"And think of this," said Step. "We not only got some assurance that nobody in our house is crazy, but we also got our bedroom cleaned for the first time since we moved in."

She pretended to bite him through his shirt, and then sat back up. "Well, no matter what I feel, it's time to feed Zap, *if* I can wake him up. I'm beginning to think if I didn't wake him up for meals he'd sleep the rest of his life away."

"I know the feeling," said Step. He carefully refrained from pointing out to her that she had just called the baby *Zap*. He did that the first time she called Elizabeth *Betsy*, and she had made it a point *never* to call her that again, so the poor kid was growing up thinking that she was one person to men and another person to women. Which might not be that far from reality, of course, given the way society worked. Pretty soon he'd probably give in and stop calling Betsy *Betsy*, so she'd have the same name to everybody. But he thought *Zap* was a great name, at least until he was old enough to complain about it, and if he could get DeAnne to slip into using it, too, that would be nice.

Step stayed in the kitchen and looked mindlessly at the newspaper for a moment. Then he realized that they had both lists out on the table—the list of Stevie's friends and the list of people who might hate him enough to send an anonymous threat. He got up and put them in a high cupboard. No matter what Douglas had said, Step wasn't really happy with either list. He'd much rather that everybody on both lists just leave his family alone.

Late that same Sunday night the phone rang. DeAnne woke up and sleepily answered it. She listened for a moment. "It's late," she said. "I think he's asleep. Oh, no, he isn't. He's right here." She held out the phone to Step. "'Sfor you," she said. She was back to sleep almost before he got the phone out of her hand.

"This is Step Fletcher," he said. "Who am I speaking to?"

"Hey, this is Glass, Step. Remember me? From Eight Bits Inc.?"

"Yeah, of course," said Step. "Isn't this a little late to be calling, though? I mean, it's almost midnight."

"Well, see, this isn't exactly a social call. They only let me make one phone call, and I thought about it for a minute, and you were kind of my best choice. Or at least I sure hope you are."

"Best choice for what?"

"I'm down at the police station. I need a ride home. Can I explain it to you later? I'm not arrested or anything, I just don't want to be driven home in a police car, you know? It looks bad, people ask questions."

"If you're not arrested, then how come you only get one phone call?"

"Oh, like, that was just theatre. You know? Just making it more dramatic than it is. It's really nothing. Except that I need a friend right now, you know? To pick me up and then not tell anybody *where* he picked me up."

"I won't lie for you," said Step.

"Oh, right, I knew that," said Glass. "But see, you don't work at Eight Bits Inc. anymore and you haven't exactly been keeping in touch so I figure, who's going to ask you? And you aren't going to go calling people up and telling them, right?"

"I don't know where the police station is," said Step.

"Well it's right downtown. Corner of Center and Church. Big city-county building, you can't miss it. I'll just meet you out front so you don't have to park and come in."

When Step hung up the phone, DeAnne roused enough to murmur, "Who was it?"

"Glass. Roland McIntyre. He's been picked up by the police for questioning and now he wants a ride home."

DeAnne's eyes opened now. "He was on our list."

"Yeah, well, I guess he was on another list, too, eh?"

Step made it to the city-county building in ten minutes, and, as he had promised, Glass was standing out in front. He looked forlorn in his plaid short-sleeve shirt and thick glasses.

"Nice car," said Glass as he slid in.

"It takes a lot of hard work to get the rust holes just right," said Step. "But hey, this one runs and the other one's always in the shop. Where to?"

"Home," said Glass. Then: "Oh, yeah, well, I live in the Oriole Apartments, out west on Shaker Parkway. Like you were going to the airport."

Step drove off.

"Nice of you to come get me," said Glass. "I didn't know who else to call."

"No problem," said Step. And at the moment he said it, that's how he felt. He hadn't felt that way *until* then, however.

"We miss you at Eight Bits Inc., man," said Glass.

"Glad to hear you remember me."

"Dicky's got his finger in everything now. He comes in and takes our working disks and fiddles with our code so we come to work in the morning and a program that ran fine the night before now crashes, and we ask him what he did, and he says, 'That was the most inefficient code I ever saw, so I started fixing it.' And when you say, 'Well it didn't crash before, and now it does,' he just looks at you and says, 'Do I have to do *everything?*' "

Step laughed grimly. Dicky. He didn't like remembering Dicky, even to know that he was still widely hated. Dicky was on his list. So Step changed the subject. "What was all this about tonight?"

Glass was silent for a minute, looking out the window. Then, finally, he settled back into his seat. "Well, it's not like you don't already know."

"If I knew, I wouldn't have asked," said Step, which wasn't true, but he didn't much care. Somehow being honest to Glass didn't seem to have the same kind of urgency as being honest to, say, his children or DeAnne or Mr. Douglas.

"I mean, you know about me." Glass sighed. "I've never actually done anything, you know? I don't even want to, really. But some parents complained because one of their older kids told them some cockamamy story, and so I got hauled in when I was sixteen, and that son-of-a-bitch lawyer my mom got for me told me that it was a real good idea to cop a plea as an adult in exchange for no time, instead of doing time as a juvenile and getting my record wiped. Because that's what the prosecutor really wanted all along—my new lawyer told me that I probably wouldn't have had to do time no matter what, the only evidence was some kid and he could have torn him to shreds in court and now here I am on their list of sex offenders." Step could feel Glass's eyes on him. "I'm on the pervert list. Anytime somebody anywhere near Steuben looks cross-eyed at a little girl, I get a phone call and they ask me where I was. Well, I'm almost always at Eight Bits Inc. with plenty of witnesses and so they don't actually bring me in very much."

"So why this time?" asked Step, feeling a little sick; he didn't know if he liked having Glass tell him this stuff, especially since he knew that Glass was probably *still* lying and in fact there was more than the one witness and he had in fact molested little girls, and a lot more than once or twice, too. But he let Glass tell his story without argument because why get him mad?

"It's that serial killer thing, if you can believe it. The SBI is doing a haul of every known sex offender in six counties, and this is when my name came up. It's completely stupid, it's complete bullshit to bring me in." There was real outrage in his voice now. "This serial killer's been doing little *boys*, for heaven's sake. What do they think I am, a *faggot*?"

Step said nothing, just drove, gripping the wheel.

After a minute or so of silence, Glass got back to talking about the gossip at Eight Bits Inc., and then they reached the apartment complex and Glass directed him to the building he lived in. Step let him off and then watched him get safely to the front door of the building. Watching him like that reminded Step of all the times he had walked babysitters safely to their parents' door, and then he thought of Glass babysitting for people, and he shivered. But I was a babysitter, too, Step thought. When I was twelve. And how did those people know that I wasn't like Glass? They had to trust me. You've got to trust people even though sometimes they'll betray your trust, because otherwise there's no life at all.

And then he had another thought. Glass had a mother and a father. A father who loathed him—did that start before or after Glass started messing with little girls? But that mother, she still loved him. She had carried him just like DeAnne carried Stevie and Robbie and Betsy and Zap, she had nursed him or given him bottles, she had gotten up in the night with him, she had dreamed of what he might be when he grew up. And he must have been a really bright kid. She must have been proud of him in school, and comforted him when the other kids made fun of him. And then this happened to her—this boy of hers turned out to have a thing for little girls. Something so dark and awful that even the worst criminals in prison find the presence of a child molester too loathsome to endure. And she has to live with that now—that her son is like this.

And Step thought of little Zap and he realized that there were worse things in the world than having a child whose body isn't working right. You can have a child whose soul is worthless. And Step thought of this serial killer loose in Steuben. If somebody forced Step to trade places, either with the father of one of those lost boys, knowing that somebody had taken him and used him and killed him, or with the father of the monster who had done the taking and the using and the killing, it wouldn't be hard to choose. The parents of those lost boys must feel the most terrible rage and hate and grief, and such a desperate sense of failure for not having protected their sons. But the parents of that serial killer would have most of that and one thing more: They would have the shame of having loosed a monster upon the world.

No matter what else happens, Step thought, all of my children are good. And even if something happened to them, if one of them was hit by a car like Rob Robles in fourth grade or got leukemia like Dr. Duhmer's little boy in Vigor, at least Step would know that every year of life that they lived was a gift to the people around them, their memory would be one of love and joy, not shame and despair.

I don't think it's you, Glass, thought Step. I don't think your monster has grown so large yet. But you were lying to me, you were trying to hide the monster from me, you aren't even the tiniest bit repentant about it, and that means that the monster has room to get bigger and more powerful inside you and you'll keep on plotting your little opportunities to possess the bodies of helpless children, and it might be kinder to everyone in the world if I went out tomorrow and bought a gun and came to Eight Bits Inc. and shot you dead, right in front of everybody. Could God call it murder if I did that, to protect all the children you might harm?

Yes, it would be murder. Because maybe the monster won't grow. Maybe somehow you'll get control of yourself. And if somebody killed you before that happened, you'd lose the chance to repent and be forgiven. If there *is* such a thing as forgiveness for the things you do, or want to do. God lets the guilty live right among the good, hurting them all they want; he lets the tares grow amid the corn. And all that the decent people can do is teach their children and try to be good to each other.

When Step got back into the house, he started to go to bed, but then he went to the kids' rooms and saw each one lying there asleep, and he kissed them, each one of them. Robbie, Stevie, Betsy, so familiar, he had seen them sleeping so often, he knew all the sweet beauties of their faces in repose. And little Zap, the helpless troubled stranger, his legs drawn up in frog position, his mouth open and his cheek always wet. All of you, Step said silently. I love all of you, I'm glad for all of you. I have so much hope for you. Even for you, Zap, with your reluctant body. Even for you, Stevie, though evil has sought you out. The world is better because you're in it, and though I want to hold you forever, I still know that even if I lost you, my life would always have joy in it because you were ever, ever mine.

13

·GOD·

This is how they finally found a name for Zap's condition: All through the autumn, every month they had a visit from Jerusha Gilbert, the nurse from the county high-risk baby clinic. Jerusha found on her first visit that everything she normally checked on, DeAnne and Step were already doing. She still stayed her full hour, however, and came back every month; as she told DeAnne, most of the kids she was tracking had fetal alcohol syndrome or prenatal care problems, so it wasn't hard to imagine that the homes Jerusha visited weren't usually the most pleasant places. And because she didn't have to do the usual remedial work, she began to research more advanced ideas that DeAnne and Step could be trying with Zap.

It was Jerusha who first said *cerebral palsy*. "It's not a diagnosis, of course," she said, "because it never is. Cerebral palsy isn't a medical term, it's a catchall basket in which we throw all the conditions that seem to be related to some kind of brain dysfunction. The rigid kids, the floppy kids, some retarded, some bright as can be. Some who walk, some who ride in motorized chairs, some who lie in bed emitting a continuous high-pitched whine the whole time they're conscious, if you can call it consciousness. At some point everybody sort of agrees that this particular condition is CP, and then a certain system takes over. So it's really your decision, you know. Start calling Zap's condition CP, and nobody's really going to argue with you."

"What if it's really something else?" asked Step.

"It's always really something else," said Jerusha. "The CP label just means that we all agree that we don't know what it is, but the kid needs help with a certain group of activities. And you're very lucky, if you decide that it's CP, because Steuben has one of the four or five best facilities for cerebral palsy in the United States."

"It does?" asked DeAnne.

"On the east side of town. The Open Doors Education Center. A really nice building, too. The city runs it now, but it was originally set up from contributions from the citizens. The parents of the kids with CP went around collecting until they had enough. And that's still the feeling there. The full range of everything—no matter what Zap turns out to need, they'll have it there. And also for preschoolers there's the Daggett Center. They charge, because their support is from foundations rather than government, but it's not that expensive. That kicks in when Zap is two. I mean, if you *have* to have a kid with neural problems, this is just about the best city in the U.S. for him to grow up in."

Cerebral palsy. Well, at least they had heard of it before. As soon as they had this name for Zap's problems, they talked about it with the kids in family home evening. Step told them about the kid he had known who had CP. "He was sixteen when I lived in Mesa," said Step. "I was about thirteen. He was in the same ward as me. I thought when I first saw him that he was retarded, because he walked funny and his head rolled back and forth when he walked, and when he talked you could hardly understand him. But then I remember standing there in the hall one time—I was reading the Doctrine and Covenants, I think, it was my project right then—and he comes out of one of the classrooms and just stands there near me, and I guess he was so mad that he just couldn't keep it in, he started talking to me. And it scared me, because he was strange, but I stood there and I listened and I realized that I really *could* understand him if I paid attention, and he was talking in complete sentences, and what he was doing was complaining about how the ward leadership wouldn't let him do anything and it made him so mad. I remember he said, 'They think I'm retarded but I'm not retarded, I get straight *A*'s, I'm smarter than they are, but they won't let me bless the sacrament! They didn't let me be baptized till I was twelve because they wouldn't believe I was smart enough to be accountable.' Of course he was saying all this really slowly, and he had a hard time forming the words, and I remember it was like a revelation to me. This guy wasn't dumb. He was a person. And his feelings were hurt, and I was one of the ones who might have hurt them sometime, because heaven knows *I* had been afraid of him, *I* had thought he was retarded. But when he was done with his rant about how they wouldn't give him a chance, I said, 'I think you should bless the sacrament.' And I guess that was all he needed to hear, just *somebody* agreeing with him, even a thirteen-year-old runt of a kid with a book in his hands, cause he said to me, 'Well someday I will.'"

"Did he?" demanded Robbie.

"Before I left there, I saw him lurch up those stairs to the sacrament table. Must have taken him five times as long as anybody else to say the prayer, but he said every word, and when he handed the trays to the deacons the trays shook and sometimes the water spilled a little but he did it. And at first people were embarrassed, but then later I heard them saying, That's one spunky kid, things like that. They were proud of him."

Then DeAnne said, "You kids are going to have a special responsibility as Zap's brothers and sister. You have to make sure that you treat him as naturally as you'd treat any other kid. That you never act ashamed of him in any way. Because if *you* act as if there's something awful or shameful about Zap, then others will, too."

"He's my little brother!" said Robbie.

"That's right," said DeAnne.

"It won't always be easy," said Step. "My Aunt Ella is retarded, which isn't the same thing, but she had a kind of look about her that made her seem strange and funny, and she was growing up in the 1920s, and people weren't very nice about things like that, especially the kids weren't. And my mom was her younger sister."

"That's Grandma Sal!" cried Robbie.

"Gammah!" shouted Betsy.

"That's right, your grandma Sal," said Step. "And when she was seven or eight years old, she was walking to school one day with Aunt Ella, and my mother tells how she was so embarrassed, she was really horrible to Aunt Ella, making her walk way behind her or on the other side of the street sometimes so that nobody would know they were together—but then, my mom was a little girl and nobody told her that she shouldn't be ashamed. And one time this bunch of kids came up and started throwing stuff at them and yelling ugly names at them, just because Aunt Ella was retarded, and my mom, just a little girl named Sally then, she sat down on the curb and cried and cried, with those kids still running around and yelling, and Aunt Ella sat down beside her and put her arm around my mom and said, 'Don't cry, Sally. They don't know. Don't cry, Sally. They're just mean.'"

DeAnne looked at Step rather oddly. "Why are you telling this story, Step?"

It occurred to him that the kids might get the idea that because Zap was their brother, they'd be teased or mistreated, and surely that wasn't why he started telling it. For a moment Step was confused and couldn't answer, so he did what any confused parent does, he pretended that he intended it to be a "teaching moment."

"Why do *you* think I told this story, Robbie?" asked Step.

"'Cause we don't *care* if they're mean to Zap, because we're going to walk to school with him anyway! And we're going to walk right with him and not cross the street without him because then he'd be scared!"

Robbie had found the right lesson in the story even if Step had forgotten what it was supposed to be.

Then Stevie, without even being called on, said, "I think Aunt Ella was the smartest one, even if she *was* retarded."

"Why?" asked Step, pleased that Stevie had come up with this on his own.

"'Cause all she cared about was that Grandma Sal was crying," said Stevie. "She didn't get mad at the bad kids, she just tried to make Grandma Sal feel better."

"OK, I think we've all got the point of the lesson, haven't we?" said Step.

"We have to tell Zap that he mustn't cry!" said Robbie.

"Zap can cry if he wants," said Step. "You know that's a rule in our family, that we can cry whenever we feel like it. Stevie, what's the main point of this lesson?"

"We've got to help Zap to be part of everything and not get left out and make sure people don't think he's retarded."

"That's very good, Stevie," said Step. "Now, it may turn out as years go by that we might find out that Zap really *does* have mental limitations, that he really *is* retarded, and that will be OK, too, because my Aunt Ella's been retarded all her life and she's a good person and she's made a lot of people happy. But chances are that Zap *won't* be retarded. And no matter what, we still treat him right and we're never ashamed of him."

"We're *proud* of him," said Robbie. "He's my very first *little* brother so I'm a *big* brother now!"

"Like me," said Stevie.

Step turned to DeAnne. "I think we've got this covered."

That ended the lesson. Robbie waved his arm around to lead the closing song and DeAnne helped Betsy say the closing prayer and then they had ice cream while DeAnne nursed Zap, shielding her modesty with a cloth diaper draped from her shoulder.

"Zap's getting his dessert, too!" cried Robbie.

"Bet it tastes an awful lot like his dinner," said Step. "And his salad, and his lunch."

"And his cornflakes!" shouted Robbie. "And his tuna fish!"

"Do I have to feed the baby in another room?" asked DeAnne. But she didn't really mind. None of their problems and worries had really gone away, but this was a good night. They were a happy family, for this hour, at least. That was enough for the day.

With only a few exceptions, that was how the autumn went. DeAnne drove Stevie and Robbie to their different schools every morning while Step stayed with Betsy and Zap. Even with two kids to take to school there was less stress in the mornings, because she didn't have to get Betsy dressed and fed, too.

Not that she could sleep in. She had to pull out of the driveway fifteen minutes earlier in the morning than last year, because so many other parents were driving their kids to school and picking them up afterward that traffic at the school was a nightmare. Fear of the serial killer had changed the lives of a lot of people in Steuben. The parents who couldn't pick their kids up met the schoolbus at the stop. Working parents formed co-ops, and a lot of local businesses let people take their lunch hours at the time school let out so that fewer and fewer kids had to let themselves into an empty house after school.

Being a mother was a full-time job for DeAnne now, so much so that she even let some of her church work slide now and then, giving a couple of lessons that weren't quite as well prepared as usual, though no one seemed to notice the difference. The focus of her life was now Zap—she had no choice, really. Whether it was lingering aftereffects of the phenobarbital or just Zap's native sleep pattern, he tended to sleep for eighteen or twenty-four hours straight and then wake up ravenous. This was very uncomfortable for DeAnne, of course—either she had to wake up and force him to eat at least every eight hours, or she had to pump her milk and freeze it for him. She had too much for the times he was sleeping and not enough for his first meal when he woke up.

Also, since he spent so little of his time awake, she couldn't bear the thought of him wasting any of that time lying alone in his bed. Because he didn't have the use of his arms and legs the way normal babies did, he couldn't experiment with rattles or even with his own body the way most kids did. Thus any time he spent awake and alone was completely empty, and DeAnne was afraid that he'd get bored and lose all interest in life and simply sleep himself to death. She was not about to let that happen. As far as she could manage it, there would be no empty hours. If he woke up at midnight, so did she, and stayed awake with him, talking and playing, moving his hands and feet for him, singing to him. She'd catch catnaps during the day when he was sleeping, and now and then she'd have a full night's sleep. But it was wearing her down and she didn't have much energy for the other kids. She couldn't help it—*they* were able to supply so much more for themselves that they just didn't need her the way Zap did. She still helped with homework and projects, as did Step, but Robbie and Betsy spent a lot of time entertaining each other— becoming quite good friends as Betsy began to catch on to some of the rules of civilized behavior. Stevie spent a lot of time alone.

Step tried to make up for DeAnne's preoccupation with Zap by playing games with the kids, but as often as not he was fixing meals or doing laundry while DeAnne napped, and so he wasn't actually involved in what the kids were doing. And whenever possible he closed himself off in his office, struggling with IBM PC assembly language until he finally realized that he could get similar results using the new Turbo C language, which amounted to throwing away all he had done so far and starting over. It was maddening work, in part because the computer was so annoyingly designed and he had to use so many kludges to make the graphics work halfway decently or to get the tiny PC speaker to produce sounds that didn't make you want to sledgehammer the machine into silence. When Step was finding a bug or puzzling out a solution to a particular problem, his concentration was so deep that he'd look up from his computer wondering if DeAnne needed him to help fix lunch, only to discover that it was dusk outside and she was already in the kitchen washing up after dinner. Back in Indiana they had already determined that their lives worked more smoothly if she didn't make it a point to call Step to dinner. If he was concentrating so heavily that he didn't notice her calling the kids, then he wouldn't want her to interrupt him anyway.

So they were both a bit hit-and-miss when it came to the three older children that fall, and when they noticed, as they often did, that Stevie was still involved with his invisible friends to the exclusion of almost everything else, it bothered them, but they were able to console themselves that it didn't mean he was losing his mind or that anybody was out to get him. It was just a trial he was passing through, and in the end it might even strengthen him. In the meantime there was Zap and Hacker Snack and not all that much time left over.

On the first of September CNN was full of the news of Korean Air Lines flight 007, which had gone down over Soviet airspace, probably shot down by the Russians. Step and DeAnne were complete news junkies—they ate dinner with the TV blaring away in the family room so they could hear it in the kitchen.

The phone rang. DeAnne was already up getting something from the fridge and she snagged the receiver off the hook, said a couple of words, and handed it to Step. "It's Lee."

"Hi, Lee," said Step. "You're really something, calling me on the first day of the month. You'll make me into a first-rate home teacher yet."

"Don't waste my time," said Lee.

"Sorry," said Step. What was *his* problem? "What did you call about?"

"I know all about it," said Lee. "I know what you did. You're the one who has to put everybody under the water yourself, aren't you?"

"What? I don't know what you're talking about."

"Don't act innocent with me," said Lee. "I can hear your TV on in the background. You're tuned to CNN just like Mother. You put them in the water, all of them."

"Lee, do you actually think I had something to do with that Korean Air Lines jet?"

"All I want to know from *you* is, are you prepared for the consequences of nuclear war? Because the Communists won't *let* you baptize them. They're not Christian, and they won't put up with it. They'll send the missiles. I've studied the effects of nuclear war. I know about nuclear winter. I know what it will be like for the common people. But you're too smart to be trapped. Nobody can trap *you*."

Whatever precipice Lee had been walking along all these months, Step realized, he was definitely over the edge now.

"Lee, there isn't going to be nuclear war."

Lee laughed. "Did you think you could just *lie* to me and I'd go away? No, I'm not going to forget you. I'm stuck to you like glue. When you get on that submarine, I'm going to be with you."

"Lee, are you at home right now?"

"God is in me now, Step. I'm not even using the phone, what do you think of that?"

"Well *I'm* using the phone," said Step.

"I don't need telephones when God is in me. I can see you right now. I can see your whole family."

"Where *are* you?"

"I'm everywhere. I'm in everything. I am love, Step. I am that I am." He giggled. "Moses never *did* understand what I meant by that."

"Lee, get ahold of yourself."

"All of those people under the water, like Pharaoh's army in the Red Sea. You want to be Moses? Parting the water, drowning people? Well, you can *be* my prophet if you want to. But you'd better pray first. You'd better offer a sacrifice."

Lee's words had long since gone from strange to disturbing. "Where *are* you, Lee?"

"You can't find me," said Lee. "Nobody can, because I'm invisible."

"Why did you call me?"

"Because you're the only one who has the power to say no to me."

"Not even your mother?"

"Shh." Suddenly he was whispering. "Don't tell her. Promise."

"I can't promise that, Lee. You need help."

"No, *you* need help!" Lee sounded very angry, now, but he was still speaking in a fairly low voice. "You need a *lot* of help, because I'm going to stop you before you put everybody under the water. I will not allow you to destroy the world again."

"Lee, I'm just a guy you go home teaching with."

"I know that," said Lee, derisively. "Do you think I don't know who you are? You must be crazy if you think you can hide from me."

"I'm hanging up now, Lee."

"Don't leave without me." Lee suddenly sounded frightened, desperate. "Let me have a place on the submarine! I won't eat much."

"Good-bye, Lee."

"Do you really have to go?"

"Yes."

"OK." Now he sounded cheerful. "Nice talking to you. Ta-ta for now!"

Step set the receiver back on the hook. "DeAnne, I need Dr. Weeks's number."

Before he finished saying it, she handed him a note card with the number written on it. "Her home phone?" he asked.

"I looked it up," said DeAnne. "I had a feeling you'd be using it."

When he got her on the phone, Dr. Weeks did not sound at all surprised to learn that Lee had called. "He said he was invisible," Step explained. "He said that he was talking to me without using a phone."

"Well, he *was* using the phone," said Dr. Weeks.

"Yes, I *know* that." He covered the receiver and

whispered to DeAnne, "She thinks *I'm* crazy." Then to Dr. Weeks he said, "Listen, something's wrong with Lee and I wanted you to know, that's all. He's really upset and he's talking about being God and he thinks I shot down flight 007."

"Apparently you've become a power figure to him," said Dr. Weeks. "These fixations never last and he means no harm."

"So you've got things under control?"

"He palms his pills, you see," said Dr. Weeks. "But eventually he has to sleep."

"He's on medication?"

"I don't discuss matters like this with nonprofessionals," said Dr. Weeks.

"Fine," said Step. "Just keep your son from *calling* nonprofessionals and you won't have to discuss it with them."

"Thank you for your concern," said Dr. Weeks. "I'll handle things now. Good-bye."

That was that.

"What did she say?" asked DeAnne.

"I guess she's handling it." But he thought of the delusions that Lee was creating about him and his family, and he wondered if Dr. Weeks really had anything under control at all.

Step was in the grocery store when an insistent voice started calling out, "Brother Fletcher! Brother Fletcher!" It startled him, to hear himself called *Brother* outside of church. Most Mormons were a bit more discreet than that. Then he saw it was Sister LeSueur, and he understood.

"How is that lovely family of yours doing, Brother Fletcher?" she asked.

"Just fine," he said.

"I've been praying for your family every day," she

said. "And I dedicated my Thursday fast to your little baby last week. I fast every Thursday, you know."

"Thanks for thinking of us," said Step, eager to get away from her. She was speaking so loudly. She must want something from him, but he couldn't guess what it might be.

"I received a witness that you are indeed special unto the Lord," she said.

"How kind of him to tell you that," said Step. He glanced past her down the aisle, to see if anyone had been attracted by the noise. No one was even there. Or behind him, either. They had the canned soup section all to themselves.

"But there must needs be a time of testing first," said Sister LeSueur. "That's what your dear little baby is all about."

Step felt anger well up inside. How dare she attempt to co-opt Zap's tenuous little life. "I think Zap's life is going to be about himself," said Step. "Just like any other child."

She reached out and touched his arm, beaming. "You are so right, Brother Fletcher. It must be wonderful, to be blessed with so much insight from the Spirit."

"I really have to get the shopping done and get home, so . . ."

At the end of the aisle, a woman was standing, watching them. Step knew her, but he couldn't place her. Was she somebody from Eight Bits?

"Don't you think it's time for you to bless your child?" asked Sister LeSueur.

"Don't you think that's a matter for me and DeAnne to decide?" No, the woman wasn't from Eight Bits. It was Mrs. Jones. He hadn't recognized her immediately last time, either, when they met in the drugstore back when Zap was still in the hospital. She was so nondescript.

"The Lord expects us to act boldly and with faith,

Brother Fletcher," Sister LeSueur said. "That's what I was told in my dream. The blessing is yours by right, if only you have faith enough to demand it. Like the time I was urgently needed to perform compassionate service. There had been an ice storm the night before, and yet I didn't have time to clear the ice off my car. So I told the Lord that if he wanted me to perform this service in his name, he would need to clear my windshield so I could drive. And when I came outside, mine was the only car that didn't have two inches of ice encasing it."

Mrs. Jones's gaze never wavered. She thinks I'm stalking her, thought Step. With a cart full of groceries and a list in my hand, she thinks I'm here just to pester her.

"The Spirit spake to me in a dream and told me that it's time for Brother Fletcher to claim a healing blessing from the Lord."

"We ask for blessings," said Step. "We don't demand them."

"'I the Lord am bound when ye do what I say,'" she quoted. "Bind the Lord, Brother Fletcher, bind him and heal your child. You are holding his sweet little soul hostage to your pride, saith the Lord."

Saith Dolores LeSueur, Step answered silently.

"You must bend yourself to the will of the Lord, and cease rejecting his word to you. Do you pay your tithing faithfully?"

Still Mrs. Jones stood there. If only I had the tape with me, I could throw it at her and make her stop watching every move I make. He smiled at Sister LeSueur, thinking: I'm faking a smile. Mrs. Jones is watching me like that song by The Police.

"Go unto your child, lay your hands on his head, and command him to rise up and walk!"

'That *would* be a miracle," he said. "He's barely two months old."

It was as if he had dashed cold water on her. "I

know that," she said. "I was sure you would understand
that I spoke figuratively."

I'm sure you'll understand that I speak figuratively
when I tell you to go sit on a broom handle and spin.
"Sister LeSueur, I appreciate your advice. Now I need
to finish my shopping." He swung his cart around to
head down the aisle away from Mrs. Jones. But Sister
LeSueur caught at his sleeve.

"Brother Fletcher, you cannot resist the Lord forever."

He turned to face her. "I have never resisted the
Lord in my life, Sister LeSueur, and I never will. But
I'm not so hungry for dialogue with him that I have to
make up *his* part as well as my own."

Her voice got a hard edge. "Beware of how the
Lord will chasten you for your pride."

This would be the perfect moment for Mrs. Jones
to pull a gun out of her purse and shoot me dead. Sister
LeSueur could live off that one event for the rest of her
life. But Mrs. Jones wasn't there anymore. She had
slipped away while his back was turned.

"'I will visit the sins of the fathers upon the children,'" said Sister LeSueur.

He pushed his cart away from her. In one moment
he had played out in his mind the whole scene of his
death at Mrs. Jones's hand. It had been so vivid that he
could now remember moments of it as if he had actually
seen them. The gun coming out of her purse, pointing
at his chest—he could have reached out and touched
the cold metal. Was that how Stevie's imaginary friends
were to him? How Sister LeSueur's visions were to her?
Never there in reality, and yet when they came back in
memory, so real-seeming.

"'Unto the third and fourth generation of them that
hate me,'" said Sister LeSueur.

He turned the corner at the end of the aisle, leaving
Sister LeSueur's vengeful doctrine behind him. He
quickly propelled the cart through the store, weaving

among the other shoppers as if on the freeway. It took a while before he realized that he was no longer running away from Sister LeSueur, he was looking for Mrs. Jones. Because she had been watching him. Because she had made him think of the song. He had to know.

She wasn't down any of the aisles. She wasn't in the checkout lines. Abandoning his cart, Step rushed out of the store and scanned the parking lot. There she was, walking briskly among the cars. He hurried after her.

Perhaps he should have called to her, but he was afraid that she would run away, since she already thought he was stalking her. As it was, when he caught up with her, just as she was putting her key in the door of the Pinto, she gave a little scream.

Step made sure to stay well away from her, his hands in plain sight.

"Mrs. Jones, I wasn't stalking you. I was grocery shopping."

She said nothing.

"But are you stalking *me?*" he asked.

Her lip curled in contempt.

"You sent me that record, didn't you?"

Her face went blank. "What record?"

"By The Police. That song about watching. Someone mailed it to our house."

"I don't even know where you live."

"We're in the book," said Step, "so don't be absurd. Just tell me if you sent it."

She smiled. "So," she said. "You don't like knowing that somebody's watching, is that it?"

"I never dealt with you anonymously, Mrs. Jones."

"I didn't mail you anything, Mr. Fletcher," she said, "so it must have been one of the other people you're blackmailing."

"Nobody else has persecuted any of my children," said Step.

"So you think it's me. You blame one more problem

in your family on a woman who isn't even your son's teacher anymore."

She's enjoying this, he thought. She loves knowing that I'm really bothered by that anonymous record. Just as with Stevie, she loves to make somebody else squirm.

"Your lawyer never called me about a restraining order," said Step.

She shrugged.

"But Captain Douglas of the Steuben police thinks that the fingerprints on the envelope the record came in should be enough to make a positive identification that will stand up in court."

"Don't be stupid," she said.

"Wore gloves, huh?" he asked. "But you didn't wear gloves when you licked the stamp and pressed it onto the envelope."

The stricken look on her face would have been answer enough. Her sudden relaxation a moment later confirmed it.

"That was a relief, I see," said Step.

"What do you mean?" she said.

"Remembering that you had the guy at the post office meter it."

Her face revealed her inner struggle. Had she really let him know that she sent it, or was he bluffing?

"You never thought I was stalking you," said Step. "You've known all along that you were the one watching *me*. So I'm telling you now, stop it. I've already given your name to the police as a possible sender of that record. They're watching *you*. So it's time for you to leave me and my family alone."

"Leave *you* alone!" She sounded defiant, but his mention of the police had clearly bothered her.

"We've done you no harm. I could have reported what you did to the school board and sued the school district and you personally for what you did to Stevie. Your name could have been in all the papers. Instead I

tried to be decent and handle it privately. Be grateful
for that and stop looking to get even."

"Grateful," she scoffed. "To *you*? You're so smart,
Mr. Fletcher. You and your *clever* little boy. You can
take away other people's careers. You can make them
work as temps and live with humiliation and fear every
day of their lives."

"Just as Stevie did," said Step.

She glared at him, opened the door of her car,
turned her back on him as she slipped inside.

"I keep almost feeling sorry for you," said Step.
"And then you prove to me all over again that you thrive
on hurting other people. That's what *evil* is, Mrs. Jones.
That's what *you* are."

She hesitated before closing the door of the car, as
if searching for some final, clinching retort. Then she
slammed the door and started the engine. Step watched
her pull out of the parking place and, with a squeal of
tires, race for the street.

At least now I know who sent the record, thought
Step. It wasn't from the killer, just as Douglas said. It
was from a bully. It was no worse than that.

When he got inside, someone had taken his shopping cart. No doubt a store employee was carefully
putting everything back on the shelves. He sighed,
pulled his list out of his pocket, and started over.

One night late in September, Step was going to be alone
with the children while DeAnne was making a presentation on journal-keeping at homemaking meeting. He
knew he should be helping to keep the children out of
her hair as she got ready to go, but he was in the middle
of a complicated algorithm that wouldn't seem to go
right, and he kept thinking, In a minute I'll go help.

Robbie was walking up and down the hall, bouncing
a ball as hard as he could, a relentless thump, thump,

thump that was about to drive Step crazy. Finally he couldn't stand it anymore. He got up and went into the hall to put a stop to the bouncing. At the same moment, DeAnne emerged from the bedroom in her slip, with the same mission in mind. Poor Robbie stood in the hall between them, looking in dread from one to the other. "Sorry," he said in a small voice.

They both burst out laughing. "Just stop bouncing the ball inside the house, Road Bug," said Step.

"OK," said Robbie. "It don't bounce good on the carpet anyway."

"It *doesn't* bounce *well*," said Step.

"I know," said Robbie, puzzled. "I told *you*."

Half an hour after DeAnne left for the church, the phone rang. It was DeAnne. "This is going to sound stupid, Junk Man, but would you mind asking Robbie where he got that ball?"

"He's had it for years," said Step.

"But it rolled down one of the yucky holes in front of the house the first week we lived here," she said. "I want to know how it got out again. *You* didn't rescue it, did you?"

"I didn't even know it was lost. Maybe I could put it back."

"Step, please find out or it'll drive me crazy for the rest of my life."

He agreed, hung up, and went in search of Robbie.

"The invisible guy got it for me," said Robbie. "He said it wasn't very far down in the drain, and it came when he called it."

Step might have rebuked him for making up such a weird story, but the mention of an invisible guy gave him pause. "Where did you meet this invisible guy, Road Bug?"

"In the yard today," said Robbie. "He was naked because if he wore clothes people would see him."

"But you could see him," said Step.

"I'm your son," said Robbie, as if that explained everything.

Lee Weeks, thought Step. "How long ago was this?" asked Step. "Before or after Stevie got home from school?"

"Before," said Robbie. "He's gone now. He had to fly to Raleigh."

Step went around the house, double-checking the locks. Then he made Robbie and Stevie go into Betsy's and Zap's bedroom while he went outside.

It was nearly dark, with scant moonlight, but Step saw him almost at once, a pale ghostlike figure standing up against the neighbor's high hedge in the front yard. Step locked the front door behind him and strode toward him.

"How did you get over here with no clothes on, Lee?" he asked.

Lee laughed in delight. "I *knew* you'd be able to see me. Just like your son."

"You're lucky it wasn't a cop who saw you, Lee. This is called 'indecent exposure' and you go to jail for it." In fact, though, Lee's naked body was more sad than anything, so pale, the hair making feeble shadows. "I don't appreciate you talking to my son in this condition."

"I can't help it if he has your power to see the invisible," said Lee.

"You've been palming your medicine again, I guess."

"Mother checks my hands," said Lee. "She checks my mouth. And she watches me so I don't throw it up."

"Do you hate it that much?"

"It makes me feel like I'm moving through the world in a fog," said Lee. "When I don't take it, everything gets so sharp and clear. I can see forever. And my thoughts—I can think the thoughts of God. I don't have to sleep. I haven't slept in five days."

"I can believe it," said Step, noticing that if Lee was God, then God chewed gum. "Why are you here?"

"If you're really going to be my spokesman, then you have to be tested."

"I'm not going to be your spokesman, Lee. Where are your clothes?"

"Those are the robes of my captivity," he said. "I never had clothing."

"Yeah, well, they don't fit your mother."

"My mother likes you," said Lee. "She thinks you're really smart."

"How nice."

"But she says you don't like woman psychiatrists."

"She's mistaken," said Step.

"Oh, you don't have to pretend. I don't like them either. They're so *bossy*. And they don't understand what it's like. They've got their drugs to turn you into a robot, when you're just *this* close to seeing it all. To getting the whole picture."

The picture I need right now, thought Step, is how to get you safely back into your mother's care without endangering my family and preferably without bringing in the police. "We never get the whole picture in this life, Lee."

"I do," said Lee. "I see that you're planning to call my mother."

"Of course I am," said Step. "You need your medicine."

"Never again. I'm going to go seven days without sleeping and on the seventh day I'll come into my full power. It's sleep that dulls our minds, you know. I almost made it once before. I was driving along in that jet-black Z and I knew that all I had to do was just lean back to the right angle in my seat and I could fly anywhere. It was God in me. I wish I'd done it, Step. But the police wouldn't listen to me. The guy from the car lot must have called them. He didn't understand that it was *my* car now. I drove exactly fifty-five, so the policemen wouldn't stop me. But they have no respect for the law. They knew they had to stop me before I began to fly. They cut me off, about five or six police cars, and I got out of the car when they told me but they made me lie down on the road and the gravel got into my face and it really hurt." His voice went high at the end. A kind of whimper, a childlike cry. It made Step think of Howie Mandel's little-kid voice, small and high. It was funny when Mandel did it.

"That was the time I was in the hospital. I told them, I can't stand to be confined. But they strapped me down anyway, it's this kind of straitjacket for when you're lying on the table. You can, like, lift one arm, but if you do, it tightens down the straps on all the others, including the one around your throat. So if you move your arms both at once you can choke yourself. And I kept thinking, what if I fall off the table? I'll strangle here and they won't do anything because they're jealous of me and they want me to die without ever coming into my power."

"I think they were trying to help you, Lee."

"It was killing me. So I started screaming, I don't like this, I don't like this, over and over but when the guy finally came in he just tightened it more so I couldn't even move one arm anymore and he said, We won't loosen this until you show us that you're in control of yourself, and I said How can I be in control of myself when you've tied me up? You've got to let me stand up, I won't go anywhere, I promise, and he says Yeah right. And then Mom got there and she had the medicine again but when she tried to give it to me I threw up right on her." He laughed uproariously. Then stopped. "She won't let me drive anymore. I had to walk all the way over here. Look. My feet are bleeding."

It was true. When he sat down in the grass and held up his feet for inspection, Step could see even by the light from the porch that they were badly lacerated, with bits of gravel and road dirt ground into the wounds.

"That must hurt," said Step.

"I'm above pain," said Lee. "That's how I know I'm on the verge of my power. Pain means nothing to me. I could break you in half and you couldn't hurt me. I could break you up into pieces."

Step thought of Lee talking to Robbie in this condition and shuddered with retroactive dread.

"It's time for your test," said Lee. "To see if you're worthy to be my servant and accompany me into immortality."

Step could think of several ways to enter immortality, and he didn't want any of them to happen right now, least of all with Lee Weeks. "I don't intend to take any tests," said Step.

"Fine," said Lee. "But I'll bet you can't guess how I faked Mom out about the medicine."

Step said the first thing that came to mind. "You hid the pill in your chewing gum."

Lee cackled with glee. "That was the test! You passed it!"

"One question? The whole test?"

"That's it. I'm going to take you with me now." Lee scrambled to the hedge on all fours, and started searching for something. A gun? Step didn't intend to wait to find out.

"Wait a minute," said Step. "What about *my* test for *you?*"

"You don't test *me,*" said Lee. "I'm God, you idiot."

"So you *say,*" said Step. "Anybody can *say* that."

"But I'm invisible."

"Not to me."

"What's your test, then?" asked Lee.

"Let me go in and get it."

"Get what?"

"The test. It's an object, and you have to tell me where I got it. If you're God, you'll know."

"I already know what it is," said Lee. "God already

knows what your whole test is. When I asked you, *that* was a joke."

"OK," said Step. "Wait there."

He unlocked the front door, went inside, and locked it behind him. He called Stevie's name as he headed for the phone. Dr. Weeks's number was ringing when Stevie got into the kitchen. "Go get me Robbie's ball. Tell Robbie I need it right now, and bring it to me."

Then Dr. Weeks answered.

"Are you looking for Lee?" asked Step.

"Is he there?"

"Naked and talking about taking me into immortality with him. He might have a gun."

"Lee isn't violent," she said.

"His feet are badly injured. I think you'll want an ambulance."

"We'll be right there. Don't let him leave." She hung up.

Stevie came back with the ball. Robbie had followed him. "Go back to Betsy's room, boys," said Step. "Stay there and don't leave."

Back outside, the door locked behind him, Step held out the ball. "Do you recognize this?"

"I called it, and it came to me," said Lee. "I have called it again, and you have brought it unto me."

"How did I get this ball, Lee? If you're God, you'll know."

"You got it from Robbie, of course," said Lee.

"No, Robbie got it from *me*. It was a present. So I ask you again, how did I get this ball?"

Lee tried several answers, but as soon as he spoke, he immediately refused to let Step tell him whether he was right or not. "This is very hard," said Lee. "You have great powers, Brother Fletcher. You are able to conceal this knowledge from me."

The guessing game lasted until the ambulance and Dr. Weeks arrived ten minutes later.

"You tricked me, you bastard," said Lee.

"That was the test," said Step. "To know that the ball wasn't the test."

Lee's fury turned to disappointment. "Then I failed."

"You aren't God, Lee. You're just a nice kid with a serious problem."

Lee stood impassively as the men from the ambulance took him by the arms. Dr. Weeks came up to him, baring the needle of a syringe.

"Please don't, Mom," said Lee. "You'll ruin everything. It'll all be wasted."

"You need to sleep," said Dr. Weeks.

"I need to sleep with *you*," said Lee, laughing. "Isn't that what your precious Freud said? I need to kill Dad and sleep with you."

"How did you get off your medicine this time?"

"Step knows," said Lee.

"He hid it inside his chewing gum," said Step.

Lee looked crestfallen. "You told."

Dr. Weeks pushed the plunger down and Lee watched, fascinated, as the fluid went into his arm. "Is this the fast stuff?"

"Yes," said Dr. Weeks.

It was true. By the time they got him to the ambulance, Lee wasn't walking under his own power. They strapped him down inside. "Take him right in," Dr. Weeks told them. "They're expecting him. I'll be there very soon."

They drove off. Dr. Weeks stood there on the lawn, facing Step. "Thank you," she said.

"It must be hard," said Step. "Being a psychiatrist, and having a manic-depressive child."

"Lee is the reason I became a psychiatrist. So I could understand him."

"And do you?"

"No," she said. "Not when he's like this. Not even when he's *not* like this. I think he likes his madness better.

I think he doesn't want to get well." She smiled wanly. "You don't like me, Mr. Fletcher."

"I think you should have warned us about Lee when he joined the Church."

"When one is alone and at wit's end," she said quietly, "one seizes upon even the tiniest hope."

"Did you think we could heal him?" asked Step, thinking of Sister LeSueur and wondering if she would think herself up to the job.

"No," she said. "But I thought, since you believed . . . as you believe . . . that God talks to human beings . . . I thought you might accept him."

"We did," said Step. "As best we could."

"And I, too," said Dr. Weeks. "As best I can."

After she left, he rummaged through the hedge, looking for whatever it was that Lee had been reaching for. It wasn't a weapon after all. It was the Book of Mormon that the missionaries had given him.

The autumn wore on, the routine changing but not in any important way. Jerusha brought along a physical therapist on her October visit, and he told Step that what he was doing, stretching out Zap's muscles and moving his limbs through their full range of motion, was not only good but essential. "It's like his brain doesn't have the normal connections to his muscles. When he shoots off a command, it does too much, which is why he kicks so hard, but then it disappears, just like that, and so he can't sustain anything. By himself he can't keep his limbs limber, so to speak. So you have to keep his tendons from tightening up on him. Same thing they do for coma patients."

"We'll have to do this for how long?" asked Step.

"Till he finds some alternate neural pathway to let him do it for himself. He will, you know. Just give him time."

It was encouraging, and now DeAnne and Step took turns twice a day, flexing and extending all of Zap's joints. Robbie and Stevie even picked up on it—Stevie silently, wordlessly doing exactly what he had seen Step and DeAnne do; Robbie far too rough and never quite correctly, so that they had to insist that he only do "Zap bending" when they were there.

DeAnne's hardest job with Zap was bathing him. Zap didn't cry much—only when he was in real pain, which happened mostly when she fed him formula and he didn't burp enough. However, bathtime was torment for him. For some reason the water terrified him. Maybe, Step speculated, because gravity was the one constant, the one thing that felt in control in his life, and in the water the gravity just wasn't there the same way. DeAnne only answered, Maybe, but who can know? What mattered was that bathtime was the only time that Zap ever got really upset, and then he was frantic, and his desperate cries just tore DeAnne apart, because she couldn't help him feel better and yet she couldn't give up bathing him, either. Finally what she evolved was a song that she called "Tubby Time for Jeremy." It was completely absurd and the first time she realized Step was listening to her she blushed and stopped, but he insisted she teach him the words and he sang along with her, so she wasn't embarrassed anymore.

> *Tubby time in the city.*
> *Tubby time in the town.*
> *Tubby time for Jeremy,*
> *It's tubby time right now.*
> *So rubby-dub and scrubby-dub,*
> *It's time for your nightgown.*
> *It's tubby time all over the world,*
> *So please don't frown.*

As she explained to Step, the song didn't really help Zap at all. But it helped *her;* it soothed her so she could endure his desperate sobbing and keep on bathing him without going to pieces inside.

Around the middle of October, Step and DeAnne both became aware that Stevie's behavior was changing just a little. He was no longer being quite as obedient as before. In fact, at times he seemed almost rebellious. The rule in the house now was that no kid could go outside without one of the parents, and Stevie knew that— in fact, he had several times caught Betsy going out and brought her back in. But one day DeAnne came into the family room from the back of the house just as Stevie was coming inside through the back door.

"Stevie, what were you doing outside?"

"Looking," said Stevie.

"Good heavens, young man, you're *filthy!* Where have you been?"

"Under the house," he said.

She remembered the latticework skirt around the base of the house and immediately flashed back to her imagined picture of what it was like under there, all the bugs and webs and mud and filth. Having crickets come up through the closet last winter hadn't done anything to change that image in her mind, either. "That's just incredible!" she said. "You know what the rule is about going outside, and to think you pried open the latticework and went under the house, that's just unspeakable! I'm going to have Bappy come over and nail it all down. Now get into the laundry room and strip off your clothes while I get a bath running."

Later that night DeAnne and Step discussed what had happened, and they realized that because of Stevie's hard adjustment and their worry about these invisible friends of his, they had been slack with him. They may not have held him to a firm enough standard of discipline.

"But when you think about it, when would we have disciplined him?" asked Step. "I mean, till now he hasn't done anything wrong."

"Well, now he has, and I don't know what to do about it. I can't start deadbolting the back door and taking the key out because what if there was a fire? I can just see the headline: FAMILY HAD PLENTY OF TIME TO ESCAPE BUT DEADBOLTS WERE ALL LOCKED AND KEYS COULD NOT BE FOUND IN TIME."

"They don't write headlines that long," said Step.

"Oh, good, so we'll die and no one will even know why."

"Less embarrassing that way."

"I think we need to show him that this is serious. I mean, there's a killer somewhere in Steuben, and Stevie's cutting out of the house without even telling us. Not to mention crawling under the *house,* I mean that's disgusting."

"Not really," said Step. "Not when you realize that my younger sister and my younger brothers used to eat dirt."

"Oh, gross!" cried DeAnne. "Did you have to tell me that?"

"They'd come into the house with flecks of mud all around their mouths and then try to act innocent when Mom said, 'Have you been eating dirt again?' And they'd open their mouths to say, 'No, Mom,' and the whole inside of their mouths was black with mud."

"I'm going to throw up, Step. I mean it."

"I'm just saying, kids like to mess in dirt. I always liked to dig in it, and maybe Stevie would like to, too, only there's just no place for it."

"It's a rental house. We can't just tear up a section of lawn for him."

"Oh," said Step. "That's what I was just about to suggest."

"And it's October, it's not going to get any warmer

out there. And most important, that has nothing to do with him going outside in the first place without permission. He has to know we're serious."

"OK, so we confine him to the house."

"Step, that's not a normal life, being confined to the house. Besides, I want him outside."

"So we cut off his computer privileges. Tomorrow, no Atari."

"Oh, that really *will* hurt. He's always playing that Lode Runner game."

"Oh, he is? I've never seen him play it. I thought *I* was the only one who ever played it—I thought it had turned out to be a real lousy birthday gift for him."

"No, he plays it all the time. In fact, a couple of times I've thought that I'd really like it if you'd teach *me* how to run it."

"It's not hard. You just make sure there aren't any cartridges in the computer, put the disk into the drive, close the door, and turn the machine on."

"Right, that's easy for *you* and *Stevie.*"

"Let's do it right now."

They went into the family room and Step showed her each thing to do and then he switched on the computer and the game came up and he said, "There it is. You just move the little guy with the joystick and try to get the treasures without the bad guys getting you."

"That's not Lode Runner," said DeAnne.

"Yes, it is," said Step.

"No, that's the little-man game that I saw *you* playing that time."

"Right, and the little-man game is called Lode Runner."

"No," she said.

Step popped open the disk drive and pulled out the disk and showed her. "Look! A miracle! The disk says Lode Runner, and yet what comes up is the little-man game!"

"No, I mean, of course you're right, I just thought that Lode Runner was a different game."

"What, then?"

"That one that Stevie always plays. The pirate ship game. It really looks beautiful sometimes, when they're just sailing along, the sails snapping in the wind. And the sailors climbing all over—I've never seen any other game like it. No offense, Step, but I kept thinking, If only Step could do a game that looked like that."

"Oh, no offense, right," said Step. He *was* a little miffed, but what mattered was that she, too, had seen the pirate ship game, only she saw it all the time, and she had watched it long enough to see different aspects of the game. "He must switch it off whenever I'm around," said Step. "I've never caught more than a glimpse of it."

"Oh, no, he plays it for hours," said DeAnne.

"In front of you?"

"Yes."

"Talking to his friends the whole time?"

"Well, yes," she said. "That's how I've picked up their names. Hearing what he says to them."

"Have you noticed what he does with the joystick when he's playing the game?"

"Oh, I think he moves it now and then, but it doesn't seem to be that kind of game."

"No, I'd say not," said Step. "Does he ever type anything? Ever use the keyboard? Or the paddle controllers?"

"Not that I remember," said DeAnne. "Why?"

"Only because if he's not doing anything with the joystick or the keyboard or anything, then how is it a game? What is *he* exactly *doing?*"

"Does he have to do anything?"

"DeAnne, if he causes things to happen onscreen, it's a game. If he doesn't, it's a movie."

"Well, people go to football games and watch them,

and they never throw the ball or anything and it's still a game."

"Because there are human beings down on the field playing. But what human being is playing this pirate ship game? Not Stevie."

DeAnne frowned. "You know that I don't know anything about computers, really, except how to boot up your Altos and get Wordstar so I can do things for church."

"Take my word for it. The reason I've never programmed a game that had all that wonderful animation is because it can't be done."

"Well it can," said DeAnne. "I've seen it."

"There's only 48K of RAM in that machine, and the disk doesn't even have a hundred kilobytes on it. Three seconds of that ship sailing along with the sailors climbing all over the rigging would chew up every scrap of that memory. And yet the ship moves all over the screen, right?"

"Two ships, sometimes three," said DeAnne.

"And sometimes they're bigger or smaller?"

"They get big when they move closer, I guess."

"It can't be done. It certainly can't be done fast enough to be smooth animation."

"Well, I've *seen* it, Step, so don't tell me it can't be done just because you don't know how!"

Step held his tongue.

"This whole discussion is about how to let Stevie know we're serious about him going outside, remember?"

"Right."

"So we'll tell him that tomorrow he can't use the computer at all, OK?"

"OK."

It was not that simple after all. When they told Stevie this the next morning at breakfast, before he went to school, he looked positively stricken. "You can't," he said.

"Actually," said Step, "we can."

"Please," said Stevie. "I'll be good."

"We know that you're a good boy," said DeAnne. "But we have to help you understand how serious it is that you not go outside without permission."

"Please don't make me not use the computer." He was in tears. It had been months since Stevie had cried about anything.

"It's not like we're taking it away permanently," said Step.

"It's just for a day," said DeAnne.

"You can't," said Stevie.

"Why not?" asked Step.

Stevie slid his cereal bowl away, laid his head down on the table, and sobbed.

Step looked at DeAnne in consternation.

"Stevie," said DeAnne. "This reaction of yours actually worries me as much as your having broken the rule and gone outside. I had no idea you were so dependent on using the computer. I don't think that's healthy. Maybe you need to stay away from the computer for a lot longer than a day."

At that, Stevie shoved his chair back and staggered into the corner of the kitchen near the window. He looked savagely, desperately angry. "You can't! That's the only thing they're staying for! If I can't play they'll go away!"

DeAnne and Step looked at each other, both reaching the same conclusion. Has it been that easy to get rid of the imaginary friends all along? Just turn off the computer?

"You've got no right!" Stevie screamed at them. "I've been trying so hard!"

Stevie's words were so strange that Step couldn't help but flash on his conversations with Lee during his madness. No, Step thought, rejecting the comparison. I just don't understand the context of what Stevie is saying. It'll be rational if I just understand the context.

"Calm down, Door Man," said Step. "Calm down, relax. Your mother didn't say that we were definitely going to take the computer away. But look at yourself. You're out of control. That's really pretty scary, and it makes us think maybe you've been spending way too much time on the Atari."

"Not as much as you spend on the IBM in there," said Stevie.

"That happens to be my work," said Step. "That happens to be what pays for our house and our food and for Zap's doctor bills."

"Are you the only one in the family who has work to do?" Stevie demanded.

The question took Step aback. "Why, do *you* have work to do?" he asked Stevie.

"Please don't make me stop playing the game. I'll never be bad again ever, please, please, please."

"Stevie, you weren't bad, you were just—"

"Then I'll never be whatever it was that I was, only don't make me stop playing with them, they'll go away and I'll never find them again. It was so hard to get them all together, it was so *hard*."

Suddenly a picture emerged in Step's mind. This game with the pirate ships had become, in Stevie's mind, the whole world of his imaginary friends. He used to play with them in the back yard, but it must have all moved indoors so that now he could only find them when he was playing with the computer. That meant that maybe Stevie wasn't hallucinating them anymore. Maybe the *only* time he could actually see them was when they were pixels moving on the screen, and he was afraid that if they slipped away any further, they'd be gone.

Well, wasn't that what Step and DeAnne wanted? They had thought that Stevie wasn't showing any progress, but without their even knowing it, he had stopped having hallucinations. It was gradually getting better by itself, and so they didn't need to push it, didn't

need to force the issue. He had made up these boys to
fit the names that were forced on him, to give them sub-
stance, and then he had built his whole life around
them. Let him outgrow them, as he was already starting
to do. Let him gradually wean himself back to reality.

"How about this?" said Step. "Instead of cutting
you off from the game, we put a time limit on it. If your
homework's done and you've had your dinner and your
bath and everything by seven-thirty, you can play until
eight-thirty, and then no matter what the computer's off
and you're in bed."

"Every day?" asked DeAnne. "That doesn't sound
like much of a restriction to me."

"Why don't we talk about it ourselves later," said
Step. "We'll start with an hour a day and go from there.
All right, Stevie?"

"Even today?" he asked.

"Today is still off-limits," said DeAnne.

"Why not say this," said Step. "No computer after
school for sure, and then your mom and I will talk it
over and decide about later tonight."

DeAnne looked at him, her face full of exasperation, but Step remained expressionless, insisting on
holding her to the bargain that they never play good-
parent, bad-parent in front of the children—though in
fact he had just violated the bargain himself.

Actually, the bargain included an unspoken agreement that if one parent felt very, very strongly, the parent who felt less strongly about it would go along. And
even though DeAnne clearly thought that she should
have been given precedence, the very fact that Step had
insisted anyway told her that maybe she should back off.

So she did.

In the meantime, Stevie had calmed down a lot,
though his eyes were still red-rimmed, his face white.

"Do you think you can still go to school today?"
asked Step.

He nodded.

"Stevie, have you made any friends at school this year?"

He shrugged.

"I mean, do the kids talk to you?"

He shrugged, then nodded.

"Stevie, do you ever have *fun?*"

Stevie just looked at him. "Sure," he finally said.

"I mean, besides with the computer?"

When Stevie didn't answer, DeAnne interrupted. "If we're going to get either of you boys to school on time, we've got to go now. And then your father and I are going to have a long discussion."

They had the discussion, but it wasn't rancorous. Step explained his thinking, DeAnne agreed with him, and they decided that limiting Stevie to an hour a day would help him taper off without giving him the stress of quitting the game and losing his friends all at once.

"The funniest thing," said DeAnne. "You know when he said, 'You're not the only one with work to do?' or whatever it was he said?"

"Yeah, I didn't know whether to be delighted to see him showing so much emotion or appalled that for the first time in his life he was yelling at his father."

"Do you know what went through my mind when he said that?" said DeAnne. "I thought, 'Wist ye not that I must be about my father's business?'"

Step just looked at her. And then said, "Do you know what *that* reminds *me* of?"

She shook her head.

"Lee Weeks," Step said. "First he thinks he's God, and then you think you're the virgin Mary."

"I wasn't joking."

"I was hoping you were," said Step.

"Maybe he's doing something really serious, Step. Maybe he's got a clearer vision of the world than we have. I mean, we already know that in some ways he *does* understand more than we do, and he always has."

"I know," said Step. "But we're talking about computer games here."

"We're talking about Stevie being aware of evil in the world. Have you forgotten that he knew the names?"

"The serial killer hasn't done anything since that article."

"But the boys he killed are still dead," said DeAnne. "And Stevie is still playing with imaginary friends that have their names. How do *we* know what is or is not important? When the boy Jesus stood there talking to the learned men in the temple, that was more important than Joseph's carpentry and more important than Mary's worry about him."

"Maybe you're right," said Step. "But nevertheless, Mary worried about him, and Joseph still kept doing his carpentry, because that was *their* job. And when they came and got Jesus from the temple, he went with them. He didn't stand there and cry and scream at them. I mean, I know we believe in likening the scriptures to ourselves, DeAnne, but it can be carried too far."

"You're right," she said. "I was just telling you what went through my mind."

The last phone call from Lee Weeks came on the twenty-sixth of October, a Wednesday night. It was the second day of the invasion of Grenada, and Step had stopped working the whole day, watching the news. At one in the morning Step was still up, sitting in the family room flipping the TV back and forth between news broadcasts and stupid old movies. When the phone rang Step thought either someone had died or someone in Utah was calling and had forgotten the time difference again.

"The war is on," said Lee.

"Hi, Lee," said Step.

"I saved the quarter you sent me. I picked it up from the sidewalk where you left it."

Please, thought Step. Please just don't call me again.

"They saw me pick something up on my walk, and they strip-searched me, but I swallowed it."

"You swallowed a quarter?"

"I knew I'd get it back, and when I did, I'd call you. I found it on the day they blew up the U.S. Marines. I knew that God was through with the world, and then you sent me the quarter and I thought, I am prepared. And now when war is raging over the face of the earth, I got the quarter back."

"Where are you calling me from?" asked Step.

"The payphone in the waiting area. I don't have long to talk, because the attendants will find out I'm not in bed pretty soon. That's why you'll have to act quickly. Is the submarine ready?"

"Lee, I don't have a submarine."

"No!" he shouted. "No! No!"

Step almost shushed him, but then he realized, if Lee is in an institution somewhere and he's hiding, having him yell into the phone will help them find him.

After a moment, though, Lee stopped shouting. "She put me here," he said. "But God is getting impatient. He is tired of the way I keep falling asleep, but I can't help it. I can't help it." He started to cry.

"Lee, it's all right, really. Everything's going to be all right."

"Step, you're my only friend. You're the only one who ever understood the glorious being inside my humble body."

"That's still true, Lee. You're trapped inside a body that isn't working right. It keeps giving you a distorted version of reality."

"I tried to see the truth," said Lee. "But I didn't see enough, did I? I didn't measure up. So you're going to leave without me, and I'll be here for the day after. But I'm not afraid. I'd rather die than live on, knowing that I didn't have what it took to be saved."

"Lee, you didn't fail a test. You just have to take the medication they give you."

"That's what you have to say to the ones who fail. I understand that, Step. You could have burned me up when you saw how weak I was. But I'm not as weak as they think. I got even with them. This is so beautiful, you're going to love this! You want to know what I did?"

"Sure," said Step.

"I didn't wash the quarter." Lee burst out laughing, long and hard. "I didn't . . . wash . . . the quarter!"

There was a flurry of noises. Lee stopped laughing and said, quite cheerily, "Ta-ta for now!"

The line went dead.

14

• CHRISTMAS EVE •

This is what Stevie bought with his Christmas money: For Robbie, a Go-Bot, since Robbie was called Robot sometimes and he liked vehicles and the Go-Bot turned from one into the other whenever you wanted. For Betsy, two blue ribbon bow clips for her hair, because she was so proud of how long it was but it always got into her eyes. For Zap, a cassette tape of songs for Mormon children, sold by Dolores LeSueur's daughter, Janet, the Bright Music distributor in Steuben, on the day when she came over to the house to make a combined sales call and visiting-teaching visit for the Relief Society.

For Jack, a Hot Wheels race car because he was so fast. For Scotty, a deck of cards because he bragged about what a good poker player he was. For David, a small fake-ceramic dog because he liked dogs. For Roddy, a harmonica because he liked songs. For Peter, a ball of string because he liked kites. For Van, a Star Wars button because it was his favorite movie. For Sandy, a squirt gun because he was such a good aim.

Stevie had saved his allowances and added it to the twenty dollars of Christmas money Step and DeAnne doled out to each of the kids, so he had enough—barely. DeAnne had Stevie with her, and Zap in a stroller, while Step had Betsy and Robbie, so that the two pairs of kids could buy presents for the others and for the parent they were not with; later, they would meet in the food court of the mall, have sweet rolls, and then redivide the kids so they could finish the shopping. So it was DeAnne who first realized who it was Stevie was shopping for. She made an attempt to deflect him from his purchases, but it came to nothing.

"Stevie," she said, "we don't allow our kids to buy presents for friends, just for family."

Stevie looked at her and said, "Nobody else is going to buy presents for them."

She didn't have the heart to forbid him then, even though she thought it was foolish of her to let him carry it this far. Well, she thought, at least he's never required us to set a place at table for his imaginary friends, the way some kids do. We'd have to rent a banquet hall every night if we did.

When the shopping was done and they were all walking out to the cars in the cold night air, Stevie spoke up. "Mom and Dad."

"Yes, Stevie."

"I didn't buy presents for the two of you, but that's OK, because I'm doing something else."

"That's fine, Stevie. We don't really need anything except for our family to be together and to be happy and kind," said DeAnne.

Stevie said no more about it.

But that night, alone in their room, DeAnne and Step talked about the problem of his presents for his imaginary friends. "What are we supposed to do with them?" asked Step. "Handle it like letters to Santa Claus or something? He leaves them under the tree and the next morning we have little faked-up presents supposedly from his friends?"

"We can't do that," said DeAnne. "We can't encourage him to believe even more than he does."

"I don't know," said Step. "Maybe he has his own way of giving things to them or something."

"All we can do is play it by ear."

Christmas was going to be on Sunday this year, which was always something of a pain because it meant that there'd be a conflict between the American custom of present-opening on Christmas morning and the Church requirement of going to sacrament meeting. It was a relief when they found out that the Steuben wards had a tradition of holding a single combined sacrament meeting at ten A.M. and then canceling Sunday school and all the other meetings so everybody was home well before noon. That way even if the present-opening had to be split in half, the kids would have all their stocking presents—the only ones from Santa under the tree— and a few of the family presents before they went to church. The edge would have been taken off their anxiousness.

But the special Christmas sacrament meeting meant a serious choir program. The choir leader of the 2nd Ward apparently regarded herself as the queen of music in the western hemisphere, and Mary Anne Lowe found herself quickly outmaneuvered as a combined choir was formed exclusively under the direction of the 2nd Ward choir leader. DeAnne toyed with the idea of boycotting the choir out of loyalty to Mary Anne, but Mary Anne just laughed at her. "It's Christmas," she said. "What do *I* care who's the boss of things? I just want to sing and have us sound great so that it really feels like Christmas to the rest of the ward." So the last few weeks in December were a flurry of ward and stake and Relief Society and quorum Christmas parties and socials and programs, with choir practices shoehorned in wherever possible. Step attended as many practices as he could, alternating with DeAnne so that they didn't have to take the kids outside very much. The weather was turning bitterly cold, and there was talk that a cold front would be coming through Christmas Eve that would make Steubenites think their town had been swapped with Duluth in the night.

In the meantime, Step was working at a frenzied pace to finish debugging the PC Hacker Snack, which was really shaping up as a terrific program. He had to get it done before New Year's, so that they'd get the completion check in time to cover the Christmas credit card bills, not to mention the final installment of Zap's hospital bills and the last of the back taxes owed to the IRS. Their collection officer had sworn faithfully to them that this year the IRS would not come in and strip their checking accounts while all the Christmas shopping checks were outstanding, the way the Indiana IRS office had done the year before. But Step and DeAnne kept what money they had out of the bank during Christmas anyway, paying for everything with cash or credit card; the IRS had never once kept a single promise in their sorry history of dealing with them over back taxes, and they didn't really expect anything different this year, either.

The Sunday before Christmas was a disaster at Church, because Dolores LeSueur found out that the two bishoprics had decided to do something new for the Christmas program this year. In past years, Dolores's husband, Jacob (*not* Jake, *not* Cubby, no matter how long you had known him before he married Dolores), had always read the entire text of "The Other Wise Man," which Dolores had been told in a dream was not fiction at all, but a true story which was originally in the Gospel of John but was removed by wicked scribes working for the sun-worshiping Emperor Constantine in the fourth century A.D. This year, the bishoprics had decided to have a short talk by Emil Houdon, who had visited the Holy Land in the summer despite the hot weather and the fighting in Lebanon. Emil had promised to tell a couple of inspirational anecdotes and quit talking after ten minutes, and everybody who knew what was being planned thought this would be the best Christmas Sunday in a long time. Sister LeSueur, however, knew that it was a sign that both wards were on the high road to apostasy, and she caused such a fuss that by the time the 1st Ward had wrapped up its meetings at noon on Sunday the eighteenth, it was decided that the entire program, including the choir numbers, would be replaced by the reading of "The Other Wise Man."

Then the 2nd Ward choir leader found out that she had been preempted, and *she* raised such a stink that by four P.M., when the 2nd Ward meetings were finished, the choir program had been restored and the special Christmas sacrament meeting would now run to about two hours, if all went smoothly. The bishopric members went home knowing they had been utterly defeated, but grateful that at least this brouhaha had been settled without Dolores calling one of the General Authorities in Salt Lake City.

Through all of this, Step and DeAnne watched with a mixture of disgust and despair. "And to think that when I was a child, I wondered how the true Church of Christ could ever have been lost from the earth," said DeAnne.

"Oh, this is small potatoes," said Step. "People have been killed over the question of what date they should celebrate Easter."

"Yes, but we're supposed to know better," said DeAnne.

"We do," said Step. "After all these years, no one has yet arranged for a public stoning of Dolores LeSueur. The Steuben wards are populated by true Saints."

DeAnne went to choir practice that evening and shared a music book with Dolores LeSueur. They got along fine with the singing, but at the end of the choir practice, after the closing prayer, as people were gathering their coats and purses and, in a few cases, children, Dolores put her hand on DeAnne's arm and said, "Sister Fletcher, I've been praying and praying about your little boy, and I want you to know that the Lord truly loves him."

"I know that," said DeAnne.

"I cannot share with you all the sacred things that I have seen in vision about your little boy, but I *can* say that it must surely be a blessing to you to know that his spirit is so righteous and perfect that he will be caught up into the celestial kingdom without having to taste of sin and temptation."

DeAnne realized that Sister LeSueur was assuming that Zap was retarded, and therefore had the same promise as children who died unbaptized before the age of accountability, that they would be exalted. It was really annoying to have her assume what even the doctors did not dare to predict—that Zap was going to be mentally impaired. And what made it downright infuriating was the sweet, beatific smile on Dolores's face when DeAnne knew perfectly well that this woman had browbeaten and backbitten her way through two bishoprics that morning and that because of her, she and her family were going to have to sit through a two-hour sacrament meeting on the coldest Christmas morning in Steuben's history.

So DeAnne placed her hand firmly on top of Dolores's, pinning her there, and moved her face in very close to Dolores's face. Then, in a quiet but extremely intense voice, DeAnne said, "My son Jeremy is a child of God like any other, and he will have to pass through the same trials and choices in this life as any other. If he gets to the celestial kingdom, it will be because he chose righteousness. Furthermore, Sister LeSueur, if you ever again speak to me or anyone else on this planet about any vision or inspiration you think you have had about my family, I promise you that when we are both dead and you are standing before the judgment bar of God, I will leap to my feet and tell the Lord all about your horrible, selfish behavior this morning as you bullied the bishoprics into letting your husband read that wretched story for the fifteenth year in a row, and I assure you that if God is just, he will send you straight to *hell*."

Through about the last half of this, Sister LeSueur had been trying to withdraw her hand from DeAnne's arm, but since DeAnne had her pinned, Sister LeSueur could only turn her head away like a child refusing to listen to a stern parent. When DeAnne finally released her, Sister LeSueur staggered a couple of steps away and then turned back and spat out the words, "I forgive you, Sister Fletcher! And I will pray for you!" The words themselves were, by habit, a blessing; but her tone was so loud and nasty and hateful that everyone still remaining in the chapel turned and looked at her. DeAnne couldn't have composed a better picture if she had choreographed it: DeAnne herself, standing calmly with a rather surprised look on her face, and Dolores LeSueur, leaning toward her, her face a mask of fury, her mouth open with her lip in a sneering curl, her eyes glaring, and her face so red that it actually showed pink through her makeup.

The vignette remained only for a moment. Then DeAnne said, "Thank you, Sister LeSueur." Dolores recovered her composure and turned to float out of the building, but from the way people averted their gaze,

DeAnne could see that if anyone in *this* group, at least, had any delusions about Sister LeSueur's sincerity and balanced temperament, those delusions were now destroyed. "I'll regard it as my Christmas present to the ward," DeAnne told Step later.

On Wednesday night, Step was pounding away at the vanity-board subroutine in Hacker Snack, which was causing the program to hang about a quarter of the time for no discernible reason. He was aware, in the back of his mind, that DeAnne was getting the kids to bed and having a little trouble doing it, partly because tomorrow was not a school day and Stevie and Robbie didn't seem to think that they should have any bedtime at all.

Finally, Step heard DeAnne telling Stevie, "I've asked you three times to turn off the computer and go to bed, Stevie, and you always say yes and then I come back a half-hour later and you haven't budged. Now just because there's no school tomorrow doesn't mean that our one-hour rule about computer games is over."

The tone of her voice was really agitated, and Step was already upset at the program because he couldn't seem to find an error anywhere, so he got up from his desk and rushed out into the hall to use the full power of the wrathful male voice to get some obedience. He and DeAnne had long since learned that while the children tuned out her voice quite easily, Step seemed to get the same results one would expect from the voice of God. He strode into the family room, stood behind Stevie's chair, and said, "Your mother shouldn't have to ask you three times to do anything, Stevie."

While he said this, though, Step could see that there was a new game on the screen, one he couldn't remember seeing before. A train was speeding along a track, with the scenery passing behind it very rapidly. The animation was every bit as fast, the graphics just as realistic as in the impossible pirate game, and, just as in the pirate game, there were characters swarming over the train. Now he remembered that between DeAnne's bedtime calls, he had heard Stevie calling out the names of his friends and saying things like, "You can do it. You've got to do it!" But the game itself didn't really look all that fun—the kids were just running along the top, jumping from car to car, with no enemies or obstacles or anything. Just each other. Beautiful graphics, but pointless.

Stevie was reaching his hand behind the machine to turn it off.

"Stop!" cried Step. "Don't move your hand. Don't turn off the machine. Just stand up, right now, and go to your bedroom. I'll shut everything down in here."

Stevie held his pose there for a moment. Step could see that he was deciding whether to obey or not. Step could have reached down and physically coerced him, but he did not. It had to be Stevie's choice, and after that moment of hesitation, Stevie left the room, leaving the computer on.

"I wish I could just borrow your voice at bedtime," said DeAnne. "I yell at them and bellow at them till I feel like some kind of fishwife, and you come in and say three sentences and they *go*."

Step was barely listening as he slid into Stevie's chair, trying to resume the play of the game. But somehow the people had all disappeared from the screen. There was just a train speeding along the track. As Step moved the joystick to see what would happen, the background stopped, too, so there was just a train and nothing else. And then the track disappeared, and the wheels stopped turning.

Then the screen turned blue. Blank.

"Step, why did you make him leave it on if *you* were just going to turn it off?"

Step reached for the keyboard, typed "list." He

pressed the return key, hoping that some part of this program's extraordinary code might remain in memory for him to examine. But nothing happened. Not even an error message. The cursor just went to the left margin of the next line. Step typed some more, hit the return key a lot of times. The screen started scrolling, but that was all. "There's no program," said Step.

"What do you mean?"

"The Atari's in memo-pad mode. It's dead."

"Well, you're typing."

"That's all it'll do. You can't run a program from memo-pad mode."

"Can't you boot it up again?" asked DeAnne.

Step popped open the disk drive. No disk. He popped open the cartridge bay. No cartridges. "There never was a program here."

"What are you talking about?" said DeAnne. "There are disks all over around here."

"Have you ever seen that train game before?"

"No," said DeAnne.

"Well, I haven't bought any games since Stevie's birthday. And we sure never saw that train game at Eight Bits Inc. before I left. I've been all through these disks looking for the pirate ship game, and I *sure* didn't see any train-game disks."

"Stevie's eight years old, Step. He didn't program it himself."

"DeAnne, nobody programmed it. Don't you understand? There *was* no program in this machine."

DeAnne stood there, staring at the blue screen. "I wish you hadn't turned it off," she said. "I wish I could have looked at them longer."

"Who?" asked Step.

"The boys. The lost boys. His friends."

They both looked at the screen for a while longer, and then Step sighed and stood up. "I don't know," he said.

"Don't know what?"

"What to do. What to think. Anything."

On Thursday, Zap got sick. It was the first time he had ever been ill, apart from his neural condition, and DeAnne and Step weren't quite sure how to handle it. For one thing, even at almost five months of age, Zap still couldn't consistently turn his head at will. If he was lying on his back when he threw up, there was a risk that he wouldn't be able to turn his head to empty his mouth, and he'd choke on it, drown in it. But if he was lying on his stomach, then his face would be in it and it would get in his nose and eyes and he still might end up breathing it in. He wasn't crying, though, and he didn't seem to have much fever, if any. DeAnne called the doctor anyway, and he told her over the phone to do exactly what she was already doing. So she just kept holding him and rocking him, waiting for him to throw up again, or not to throw up for long enough that she could feel safe in laying him back in bed. "No formula for a while," she told Step. "But maybe he can keep down my milk."

This began shortly after lunch, and continued through the afternoon. Step gave up on working, of course, and played with Robbie and Betsy between helping DeAnne and working on dinner and answering the phone and all the other things that kept coming up. Step couldn't understand how DeAnne could live with this, never able to concentrate on something, to follow through on it without interruption.

Stevie, of course, wasn't part of the little-kid games, but that was no surprise anymore. The surprise was when Step passed through the family room on the way to answer the doorbell and realized that Stevie wasn't playing computer games, either. Must still be in his room, wrapping presents, Step thought. He had borrowed the tape and scissors earlier in the day.

It was Bappy at the door. He had a kind of sheepish grin. "I don't mean to be a bother," he said, "but I'm just a sentimental old fool and I was driving by a couple nights ago and I saw y'all didn't have no Christmas lights up."

"We haven't had time," said Step.

"Well, time is all I got these days, and I still got the lights we put up on this house last year and the year before. I bet all the old nails and such are still right where I put 'em. Y'all won't mind if I haul my ladder out and tread your roof awhile? It doesn't add that much to the electric, specially seeing as how there's only a few days till Christmas."

"No, that's fine," said Step. "That'll be nice. Where will I plug them in?"

"There's an outlet out back, by the utility room door. I just run me a long extension cord up over the house. Brought the same one I used last year, so I know it works."

"That's great. Thanks," said Step.

Bappy nodded and waved, even though he was standing right there by the door, and then he was off for his pickup truck and Step closed the front door.

Just as Step was heading for the kitchen to check the meatloaf he had made, Zap started throwing up again, proving that DeAnne's milk wasn't going to stay down any better than the formula had. And now Zap was getting fussy instead of just being complacent after he vomited. DeAnne checked his temperature again with the plastic forehead strip, and it was over a hundred. "I've got to take him to the doctor," she said. "If he was a normal kid I'd wait, but he's so weak." So once they got Zap cleaned up again, Step found the phone number and called Dr. Greenwald's office and the answering service relayed the message and a couple of minutes later he called back. DeAnne talked to him and then said, "He's going to go back to the office just to see Zap. Isn't that sweet of him?"

"What if he throws up while you're driving him there?" asked Step.

"I didn't think of that," said DeAnne.

"Do you think Mary Anne would come over and watch the kids while I drove you down?"

"She will if she can," said DeAnne.

She could, and since she didn't live far away, she would be there in only a few minutes.

Step remembered the meatloaf. "I can't believe the timer hasn't rung yet," he said.

"Maybe it has something to do with the fact that the timer was never set."

"Oh, no, it must be burnt to a crisp by now," said Step.

"I don't think so," said DeAnne. "The oven isn't on."

"I didn't turn the oven on?"

Sure enough, the meatloaf was dead raw.

"Well, we can't eat *that*," said DeAnne.

"We can cook it now, can't we? Mary Anne can serve it to the kids when it comes out."

"No, Step," said DeAnne. "You can't serve meatloaf that's been sitting around this long at room temperature."

"You can't tell me the meat would go bad this fast."

"Not the meat," said DeAnne. "The eggs."

"I forgot the eggs," said Step.

"If I weren't here, Step, the kids would have salmonella all the time."

"Probably. So what about supper?"

"Throw some bowls and cold cereal on the table and call the kids in to eat," said DeAnne. "It's the last resort of the mother in a hurry but hey, that's me."

Robbie and Betsy came right in. "Stevie!" Step called again. "Come on in to supper *now!*" Knowing he would be obeyed, Step headed outside to open the car door for DeAnne. Just as DeAnne was settling in with Zap in her arms, Mary Anne pulled up into the driveway behind the Renault. Step waved her back, and she put her hands to the sides of her face to show her embarrassment. Then she put her car in reverse and parked out on the street just ahead of Bappy's pickup truck. It was getting dark, and it occurred to Step that if Bappy wasn't done with the lights, he probably ought to quit for the night. It wasn't safe to be wandering around on the roof in the dark.

Mary Anne came running up the driveway. "How's little Zap doing?" she asked.

"He's probably not even that sick," said DeAnne. "But we just have to be sure."

"If the doctor calls wondering where we are, tell him we're on the way," said Step. "The kids are in the middle of coating the inside of the kitchen with a layer of cornflakes, so enter at your own risk." As Mary Anne jogged up the two steps and into the house, Step called after her, "And lock the deadbolts!"

"I always do!" she called back.

Dr. Greenwald didn't seem to mind that they had taken so long getting to his office, and after poking and probing and listening, he reassured them that it was nothing all that serious. They apologized for wasting his time, but he assured them that they had been right to be concerned. "With a baby this fragile," he said, "everything is serious."

When they got back home, the house was completely rimmed with white lights. "It looks like gingerbread," said DeAnne.

"For an impressively ugly house, it lights up real nice," said Step.

When they got inside, however, chaos reigned. Betsy and Robbie were standing on chairs in the kitchen, and the second DeAnne and Step got in the door they started screaming, "Spiders! Daddy longlegs!"

There weren't any spiders in the kitchen that Step could see. He held the baby while DeAnne took off her coat. "Where's Mary Anne?" asked DeAnne.

"Is that you at the door?" shouted Mary Anne from back somewhere deep in the house.

"Yes it is!" called DeAnne. "Where are you?"

"In the land of the monster spiders!" shouted Mary Anne. "I could sure use some help and another roll of paper towels!"

"You take care of Zap and the kids," said Step to DeAnne, "and I'll see what's going on in the bathroom." He ducked into the laundry room to get another roll of paper towels.

"You don't suppose we're having another invasion of insects, do you?" asked DeAnne.

"Nope," said Step. "Spiders are arachnids."

In the bathroom, it looked as though someone had tried to resurface the entire room in wet paper towels, and then reconsidered and spattered ink on it. But the ink turned out to be daddy longlegs spiders, and the wet paper towels were Mary Anne's strategy for immobilizing as many spiders as possible while stomping the ones that weren't pinned down under the wet towels.

Apparently Mary Anne had kept her cool quite well while she was the only adult present. But as soon as Step came into the room and she tried to explain what was happening, she began to shudder and shiver, then screeched as a daddy longlegs crawled up onto her ankle. She stamped and stamped until it fell off; Step gripped her by the shoulders and guided her out the door into the hall. "You stand there and keep watch to make sure none of them get out. Remember to look up and check the ceilings."

Outside the bathroom, she was able to calm down as Step methodically slaughtered spiders. "They were coming up out of the drain in the bathtub," said Mary Anne. Step glanced into the tub and sure enough, it had been plugged with wet paper towels. "Betsy was on her little potty when she started yelling 'pido, pido,' and I finally realized that it wasn't some cute bathroom word like *peepee*, she was saying *spider*."

"You did great," said Step. "You kept it under control. You won't believe it, but this happens like about once a season. First crickets, then june bugs, then gnats on the night that Zap was born. I think we're going through the ten plagues of Egypt."

"Spiders are the horriblest things. I can't *stand* the way their little legs go up and down so *delicately*, like monster ballet dancers."

"Oh, keep talking, I can't wait to see what inhabits my dreams tonight."

"You're *looking* at them, my talking can hardly be any worse than that," said Mary Anne.

"Yeah, but now I'm not looking at spiders, I'm looking at monster ballet dancers. Disney missed a bet with *Fantasia*."

Finally the spiders were cleaned up and all the paper towels were clotted in the bottom of a garbage bag. When Step came back into the kitchen from taking the bag outside, Mary Anne was standing by the table talking to DeAnne.

"Well, you're a hero, Mary Anne."

"Any time," said Mary Anne. "Only next time we can skip the spider part." She started for the door into the laundry room, then stopped. "Oh, your mom called, DeAnne. Nothing's wrong, don't worry, she just wanted your pie crust recipe."

"My mother wants to make *pies?*"

"Oh, doesn't she ever?"

"My dad's the piemaker in my family," said DeAnne. "But miracles happen every day, right?" Step dialed the wall phone for her, then handed her the receiver so she didn't have to get up while nursing Zap.

They said their good-byes to Mary Anne. Then came the mess of getting Robbie and Betsy to bed. Stevie was already lying in his bed, and Step made Robbie get under the covers quietly so as not to waken his big brother.

Only after Step was already in bed beside DeAnne did he realize that the Christmas lights were still on outside.

"Oh, just leave them," said DeAnne.

"Just as you wouldn't allow your family to eat that meat loaf, I will not permit my family to sleep in a house that has some weird extension cord arrangement connected up outside."

He put on a bathrobe, and then, remembering how cold it was outside, a coat over that. Out back Step found the plug and pulled it, then walked around front to make sure the lights were off. By now he was quite cold, and he rushed back into the house, locked up, took off his coat, and then moved through the house checking that all the doors were locked and glancing in to make sure the kids were covered.

The routine was so set that it wasn't till he was already walking into his and DeAnne's room that he realized that he hadn't seen Stevie in his bed. Robbie was there, but Stevie's sheets were pulled back and the bed was empty. Was he up going to the bathroom? He hadn't been in the kids' bathroom or anywhere else in the house—could he, for some reason, be in the master bathroom?

Step walked around the bed and checked in the bathroom. No Stevie. This was impossible. Unless Stevie was playing a trick, hiding in the closet or something, there was nowhere that he could be. Step headed back to the boys' room to check the closet before he pushed the panic button, but then he had to stop cold in the doorway. There was Stevie. Right there on the top bunk. The covers were all the way down, as Step remembered, but Stevie was there. He was curled up and looked like he was completely asleep.

I am way too tired, thought Step. When I actually looked into the room I didn't see anything wrong, did I? It was only afterward that I *thought* I hadn't seen him, but of course he was there all along.

Step went back to bed, where DeAnne was already snoring, and soon he was asleep, too. If he had any spider dreams, he didn't remember in the morning.

The next couple of days were a flurry of activity, but that was to be expected. Everybody got up at different times and it seemed like half the ward was either coming by or calling up and insisting that DeAnne or Step or both needed to do this or that in preparation for Christmas. In the afternoon of Christmas Eve, as DeAnne was helping Elizabeth wrap a present in the living room, she thought of something and called out to Step, who was in the kitchen putting away the groceries. "It just occurred to me that I honestly can't remember seeing Stevie eat anything for the past few days."

"I haven't seen *anybody* eat anything for the past few days," Step called back. "I don't think anybody has eaten in the presence of anybody else since school let out for the holidays."

"No, I'm serious," said DeAnne. "And he hasn't been playing computer games or anything, he's mostly been in his room. Do you think he might be sick?"

"I'll check on him when I'm done with the groceries," said Step.

That took only a few more minutes, and then Step headed on down the hall and turned left into the boys' room. Robbie was on the floor, wrapping a present. "Get out get out!" he screamed at Step.

"Sorry," said Step. He immediately turned and stepped back into the hall, drawing the door almost closed behind him.

"You ruined the surprise!" Robbie shouted.

"No, I didn't," answered Step. "I didn't see anything. I was just coming back to see if Stevie was all right."

"I'm fine," answered Stevie.

"He's fine!" shouted Robbie.

"I can hear your brother quite well without your relay service, thanks just the same, Robbie," said Step.

"Stevie, your mother's worried that you haven't been eating much lately."

"I'm not hungry."

"You've got to eat *something*."

"Yes," said Stevie.

"Will you come to supper tonight?"

Stevie didn't say anything for a moment. "I guess," he said.

"Stevie, is something wrong?"

Another pause. "Nope."

Step went back to the living room, where DeAnne was still wrapping presents with Betsy, who periodically inserted a hand or a finger or, sometimes, her face into whatever DeAnne was doing. As a result, DeAnne had stuck about a dozen small pieces of tape all over Betsy's face, and they were protruding everywhere like a peeling sunburn. "Ooh, Betsy, you look so pretty."

"I heard you calling to Stevie," said DeAnne.

"Robbie wouldn't let me in the room. He was wrapping presents."

"He already wrapped yours."

"He's wrapping Zap's. But he didn't want to ruin the surprise."

"Didn't he buy it with you standing right there?"

"You know Robbie," said Step. "If you wreck one of his surprises, you might as well cut off your own head and save yourself a lot of suffering."

Step finally had a break about four o'clock and slipped into his office to catch a few minutes' work on the program. He was *this* close to finishing it, and if he could have it done, ready to fedex it to Agamemnon, then he would have so much more relaxed a Christmas. It was just ticky stuff now anyway, but it meant changing a line or two, then compiling it, then running it and seeing what it looked like, then tweaking it again and compiling it again. . . . It ate up the clock without making that much visible progress.

"Step, can't you come to supper on Christmas Eve?"

Step turned around to see DeAnne standing in the doorway of his office.

"And Stevie won't come either. I didn't prepare a banquet but even self-employed people are allowed to have Christmas Eve off."

"I'm so close, DeAnne."

"All right, suit yourself," she said, and she closed the door.

Step sighed and got up from the chair. When he reached the hall he heard her saying to Stevie, "Go ahead, apparently males in this family don't eat anymore."

"DeAnne," said Step. "It's bad enough when you sound like *your* mother, but now you're sounding like *mine*."

She looked annoyed for a moment, but then decided to take it as a joke. "That's fine with me," she said. "I like your mother. And she likes me. In fact, she likes me better than you."

"Better than I like *you?* Or better than she likes *me?*"

"Both," she said.

"Impossible." He was now at the end of the hall and he nuzzled her and held her close and whispered in her ear, "Let's forget *these* kids and go make us another baby."

"It's too soon," she said. "I haven't forgotten how much it hurts yet."

They both remembered Zap's troubles and her words took on a second meaning, and now when he kissed her it wasn't romantic, it was tender, consoling.

Then he opened the door to the boys' room. Stevie was lying on his back in bed, staring up at the ceiling. "Come on in to dinner, Stevie."

"I'm not hungry, Dad," he said.

"I didn't ask if you wanted to eat," said Step. "It's Christmas Eve and we need to be together."

"I think he's sick," said DeAnne. "Maybe he's got whatever Zap had a couple of days ago." She pushed past Step into the room, heading for Stevie. And then, to Step's amazement—and DeAnne's too, of course—Stevie sat bolt upright and shied away from the edge of the bunk, looking fearful. "Don't touch me!" he said.

"Well, I've *got* to touch you," said DeAnne. "I've got to see if you have a fever."

"I just want to be alone in here for another little while," he said.

"Stevie," said DeAnne. "Just let me see if your forehead's warm."

"I'm fine," he said.

"DeAnne," said Step. "Please, let's not make a quarrel of it on Christmas Eve."

"But if he's not well I can't just leave him in here . . ."

"He looks fine," said Step, ushering her out of the room.

"Suddenly you're the miracle doctor who can diagnose people across a room?"

As soon as they were out the door, Step pulled it shut and said, "DeAnne, didn't you see the look on his face? He was absolutely terrified."

"I know, Step. That's all the more reason to think he might have a fever. He didn't seem rational."

"His face wasn't white or flushed, and he always gets one or the other when he's sick. He's really upset, but listen to what he said. He wants to be *alone*."

"On Christmas Eve, and that's *sad*." Then she realized what Step was thinking. "You mean—without his imaginary friends."

"Have you seen him playing with the Atari in the last couple of days? At *all?*"

"You mean he might be going through some kind of withdrawal?"

"I don't know, but it's a sure thing he's really edgy right now, so let's go in and eat and then I'll come back in and talk to him, or you can, and we'll see if we can calm him down. He's not going to want to miss the ceremonies, right? He's the one who remembers things best, he always likes to tell the stories. He'll come around, if we don't make an issue of it right now."

DeAnne sighed. "Whenever you get so patient and understanding with the children it makes me feel like I must usually be a shrew."

"So what do you feel like when I yell at them?" asked Step.

"Vindicated."

After supper, Step brushed his teeth and then went to Stevie's room to try to persuade him to eat something. Stevie wasn't in his bed; DeAnne must have talked him into the kitchen.

Step meant to join the rest of the family, but he paused by his office door and thought, If Stevie's eating that'll take a while and so I've got a few minutes and that might be time enough to finish. He resumed where he had left off.

He didn't know how long he had been working when there came a knock on his door. He turned around. DeAnne was standing there, leaning on the doorknob. She looked a little wobbly, as if she might need to sit down. "What is it?" he asked, concerned.

"Step, Stevie has his friends at the door. He wants to invite them in for Christmas Eve."

Step's heart sank. Stevie wasn't coming out of it after all. He'd tried but then he couldn't let go of this fantasy world. Maybe because the evil hadn't gone out of Steuben yet. Maybe he couldn't let go until they caught the serial killer. Or until the family moved again.

"Maybe when I finish this program we *should* move," he said. "Get Stevie away from here for good."

"No, Step," DeAnne answered. "I mean his friends are *at the door*."

Now it sank in. Why she looked so weak.

Had the power of Stevie's imagination finally over-powered DeAnne? No, that couldn't be, she was far too strong.

He stood up, meaning to put an arm around her, steady her. But the moment she saw he was standing up, she moved away from the door, and when she walked he could see that she was steadier than he had thought.

He followed her. It wasn't the front door, appar-ently, because she didn't go to the living room, she went into the family room. The back door was standing half open, even though the air was bitterly cold and the room was getting very badly chilled. She stood well back from the door, looking through it. Step walked straight to the door and opened it wider.

There in the back yard stood Stevie. Grouped behind him were seven boys, ranging in age from per-haps five to ten or so. A couple of them were dressed for the cold, but the others were in T-shirts and shorts, and one of them was wearing a tank top.

"Dad," said Stevie. "Can they come in? I told them you'd let them have Christmas Eve with us. That's what they miss the most."

Step could feel DeAnne put her arm through his and take hold of his hand.

"Of course they can come in," said Step. "We've been wanting to meet them."

It was one thing to say it, another thing to watch them walk up the stairs, one by one, and come on into the house. DeAnne, who had a better memory for names and faces, was picking them out from the news-paper photos. "Van," she said.

One of the boys smiled at her.

"Roddy. Peter? David. Jack. Scotty."

One by one they grinned at her and then looked at each other as if to say, Hey, she knows us, she knows us.

"Sandy," she said.

Step closed the door.

"I wish," said Step. "I wish I could have seen you before."

"We tried, Dad," said Stevie. "I knew they could do it, I knew they *had* to show themselves to people or nobody'd ever believe me, but they just couldn't figure it out till I showed them how."

"We believed you, son," said Step. "We always knew you weren't lying to us."

"But you thought they were pretend, Dad," said Stevie. "And they're not pretend."

Then there was a moment's silence, and one of the boys, in a soft, faint voice, said, "Merry Christmas."

"Yes," said Step. "Yes, Merry Christmas. Please, come into the living room. That's where the tree is. We were just about to put out our presents and have our ceremonies, and we'd love to have you with us."

The boys smiled. And Stevie—ah, Stevie smiled! Step had almost forgotten what a glorious smile he had. It had been so long.

Stevie led the way into the living room, the other boys trooping silently after him.

DeAnne still held to his arm. He heard her murmur, "Showed them how?"

But he couldn't think about that. It was Christmas Eve, and Stevie had brought his friends home at last.

He and DeAnne followed the boys into the living room, and then she said, "I've got to get Robbie and Betsy and Zap," and she left him there.

"Sit down," he said. "Anywhere, except leave that soft rocking chair for Stevie's mom, she has to sit there and hold the baby." Then Step surveyed the room, seeing it now as if through their eyes. The Christmas tree, covered with a motley of decorations, most of them handmade: the tiny needlepoint pillows that DeAnne had made for that first Christmas, while she was pregnant with Stevie. The little puffball animals that she and

Step had glued together for the first Christmas tree that Stevie ever saw, though of course he was only a baby then and hardly knew what he was seeing. Decorations older than Stevie, thought Step. He's never had a tree without them.

And not just the tree. The whole room was decorated with red and green tassels and little wooden villages and a stuffed Santa hippo beside a wicker sleigh and a large chimney-sweep nutcracker and anything else that Step and DeAnne hadn't been able to resist buying or making over the years.

DeAnne led Robbie and Betsy into the room. Betsy was shy with strangers, and she hung back a little, but Robbie forthrightly took her hand and led her to sit in front of the couch at Step's feet. DeAnne sat down in the rocking chair and propped a sleepy Zap up enough for him to see what was happening, even though there was no sign yet that his eyes were able to focus on anything for even as long as a second.

They began with a song—"Away in a Manger"—and as Step sang out, keeping the tempo up, he remembered all the nights for months, for years, that he had lain beside Stevie's bed and sung that song so he could sleep, so the fear would go away and Stevie could rest.

Then it was time for the stories. Step started by asking Robbie to tell them about the angel coming to Mary. Then he asked Stevie to tell what Joseph did when he found out she was going to have a baby, and so on, Robbie and then Stevie, then DeAnne or Step taking a turn, telling a part of the Christmas story. The shepherds, the wise men, and then on to the Book of Mormon story about the day and night and day without darkness when Christ was born on the other side of the world. Then Step went on and told what Jesus lived for. About forgiveness for the bad things people do.

The boys had been listening, enthralled in the experience of being part of a Christmas Eve after all, their eyes sparkling in the treelight. Now, though, one of the boys spoke up. "Everything?"

Before Step could be sure what he was asking, Stevie answered, sharply, firmly. "No. Not killing."

DeAnne gave a tiny gasp and covered her mouth, blinking her eyes to keep from crying.

"Stevie's right," Step said. "In our church we believe that God doesn't forgive people who kill on purpose. And in the New Testament, Jesus said that if anybody ever hurt a child, it would be better for him to tie a huge rock around his neck and jump into the sea and drown."

"Well it did hurt, Daddy," said Stevie. "They never told me anything."

"It was a secret," said one of the boys.

"I told him I'd never never tell so he wouldn't . . ." The boy's voice trailed off, growing weak.

"Don't leave!" said Stevie. "You said if we did Christmas!"

"It's *hard*," said another of the boys.

Stevie turned to Step. "Dad, you got to call Mr. Douglas. If he sees them all, he'll have to believe it, won't he?"

"Yes," said Step.

"I knew he wouldn't believe just me telling him, because if you didn't believe me then why should he?"

"We believed you, Stevie," said DeAnne, struggling not to cry. "We really did."

"I mean you didn't believe in *them*," he said. "I thought you could see them like I could, but then you couldn't, and not even Robbie except once for a second."

Step thought: Robbie saw, but I couldn't, and DeAnne couldn't.

"And I tried to figure out how to show them. They told me they were all buried under the house and so I—"

Again a gasp from DeAnne, and Step felt a wrenching in his gut. It wasn't just some disturbance in the fabric of the universe that Stevie had felt, it wasn't just some nameless evil somewhere in the city. It was here. It was under the house. The place from which spiders and crickets had fled. The place where the bodies of seven little boys had been concealed, where no one could find them no matter how hard they searched.

But someone had been under the house since they moved there, yes, more than once, more than once. Bappy has been under this house. And Bappy lived here before us, before his son made him move out so he could rent the place to us. Bappy lived here when the first of the boys were taken, and Bappy has been here so often, ever since.

Stevie went on. "So I crawled under there and buried myself up but it didn't help, I still couldn't do it, and anyway you got mad at me for getting so dirty and going outside and so I didn't try that again."

My son was under there, Step thought. He wanted to scream the way he had screamed after the Fourth of July picnic. But he held it in.

"I didn't know what to do anymore," said Stevie, "and so I gave up, I thought nobody could ever see them. But I couldn't just let him go on doing it, could I, Dad? That wouldn't be right. They didn't like it, I knew that, even if they *didn't* tell me how much it hurt."

He looked at the other boys, and some of them looked away, perhaps ashamed.

"So I remembered what you said about how bad people hate the truth, it scares them, so I broke the rules and I went outside when he was doing the lights and I said, I know what you're doing, and he said, I don't know what you're talking about, and I said, They told me about you, and he said, Who told you? and I said, They told me about Boy, and I said, Mr. Douglas is a friend of mine, I met him, and he said so. And I said, You got to stop, and he said, I already did. He said, Boy don't do that no more. But I knew he was lying, because

I could see that Boy wasn't like they told me, Boy wasn't somebody else, *he* was Boy, Boy was his own self, and then I ran to get back in the house but I wasn't fast enough."

DeAnne was crying now, her face covered in her hands, and Step could feel tears on his own cheeks, because now he knew, beyond all doubt, beyond all hope, that there were eight lost boys, not seven, sharing Christmas in their house tonight. Eight lost boys, not seven, buried in the crawlspace.

"And I thought I wrecked everything," said Stevie. "But then I knew that I didn't at all. Because I *did* know how to make you see me. It was really hard the first night and I think a couple of times you didn't see me when you were supposed to, but I got better and better at it and then I really *could* show them how because I was *like* them now, and so Daddy, here we are, and you got to call Mr. Douglas because Boy is still there and he's got to stop."

"Yes," said Step. "Will you stay, boys? Till Mr. Douglas comes?"

They didn't answer; they looked at each other, some of them, and others looked at the floor.

"They're afraid of seeing *him* again," said Stevie. "The old guy."

"Boy," whispered one of Stevie's friends.

"Boy," echoed several others.

"*I* know what we should do," said DeAnne. She was trying to sound cheerful, despite her tears. "You've all sat here and seen what *our* family does for Christmas Eve. Why don't you each tell the rest of us what *your* family does. You don't have to if you don't want to, but I'd really like to know, because I don't think any two families in the world do Christmas *exactly* alike. What about you, Jack?"

DeAnne led them in sharing tales of Christmases past as Step went to the kitchen and called the police station. "Call Mr. Douglas and tell him that Step

Fletcher has to see him tonight. I know it's Christmas Eve, but tell him that the answers are all here but only if he comes now to see them with his own eyes."

Step worried for a moment that this policeman might be too fearful of offending someone, of losing his job or a promotion, to dare to call his boss on Christmas Eve.

"I promise you, my friend," said Step, "that if you make this call, you'll be giving Doug Douglas the best Christmas present he ever had."

"Easy for you to say," said the man. "But I'll give it a shot and see if he wants to talk to you."

It seemed less than a minute—yet such a long time—before the phone rang. Step picked it up so fast it barely had time to echo.

"What have you got on Christmas Eve, Mr. Fletcher?"

"I had the list before, Mr. Douglas, and that wasn't a fake, right? I told you the truth, right?"

"Right."

"Come now, come quickly. I have all the answers here. But no lights, no sirens. Because you'll frighten them and they might go."

"Them? Who?"

"The boys, Mr. Douglas." Step hung up, trusting that Douglas would have faith enough in him to come.

He got there before the boys had finished telling all their memories. He came in quietly, and when he saw them gathered there, Step could see the hope in his eyes, the wonderment that they were not dead after all. But then he saw Step's face, and Step knew that it was no secret that he had been grieving, and then Douglas began to understand. "Your boy really did see them," said Douglas.

"All along," said Step.

"But why is it that *we* can see them now?"

"Because Stevie showed them how. And he kept them here so you could see them."

Douglas walked slowly, carefully, to the center of the room. "Ah, boys. If only I could have found him sooner. If only I could have stopped him before . . . But I can stop him now. Just tell me who it is."

So Stevie told it all again, and this time with more details. The deep place under the house. How he didn't really understand what had happened to his friends until he saw that place and then he made them tell him, and he made them tell him who it was, too. "Bappy," he said.

"Boy," said a couple of the others.

"Baptize Waters," said Step. "Our landlord's father. He used to live here. I wrote down his address and phone number for you while you were on the way."

"Boys," said Douglas. "I'll tell you something. I don't think you should ever see that man again. I don't think *any* children should ever have to see him again."

They nodded.

"So I promise you that if you stay right here in this room for just a little while longer, you *won't* ever see him again. And if you wait, I'd like to call your parents. I'd like your parents to have a chance to see you."

"They'll be mad," said one of the boys. "I didn't stay where I was supposed to."

"No," said Douglas. "I've talked to all of them and I can promise you that not one of them will be mad. Not one. Can you stay just that much longer?"

"It's hard," said one of the boys.

"Then I'll hurry."

Douglas left the room, went into the kitchen. Step could hear him phoning, speaking quietly. Later he would learn how the phone calls went. We have found where the bodies are hidden, and your son is one of them. But there's also something else, a chance of something else, to say good-bye to your son, if you hurry. Tell no one. Come quickly. They didn't understand, of course, but they came. And soon they had spread out through the house, the grieving parents, the boys, shy at first, and softspoken, for none of them was as strong as Stevie.

And while they talked inside the house, the policemen worked beneath it and outside it, and the bodies were brought out one by one on pallets and were laid under the bright lights on the lawn. Bappy was brought to the house on Chinqua Penn, he and his son and his son's lawyer, furious at first about being dragged out here on Christmas Eve. But then they saw the bodies on the lawn, and the son turned to the father, and in a voice rising steadily to a shout, to a scream, he said, "You told me you stopped. You told me you were too old to want it anymore. But you *didn't* stop, you old son-of-a-bitch, you went on doing it only now you *killed* them!" Weeping in shame and rage and terrible memories of his own, the son shoved his father to the ground and then he kicked him until the police grabbed him and held him, and he stood there sobbing. "He said he stopped. I would have told you about him if I'd known he was still doing it, if I'd known he'd do *this,* I would have told you."

"So why didn't you tell us anyway?" asked Douglas.

For a moment he couldn't think of how to say it. And then he could. "He's my father."

"It wasn't me," said Bappy.

"Yes it was," said Douglas.

"It was Boy," said Bappy. "I never wanted to. What do you think I am, anyway? I'd never do anything like this. It's always that *Boy.*"

All of it was on videotape. The son. The father. The grim-faced lawyer urging them both, far too late now, to be quiet, to say no more. All on tape, and so there was no need for any of the men outside the house to see or even know about what was happening inside.

As Bappy was led away, as the bodies were brought out of their hidden graves and under the police lights of that bitter cold Christmas Eve, one by one the boys inside the house no longer had the strength or the need to keep trying anymore, and they said good-bye, and they were gone. One moment there, the next moment not there. Then their parents left, weeping, clinging to each other, with just a whispered word or two from Douglas. "Tell no one," he said. "You don't want your boy's name in the press. Just go home and thank God you had a chance to say good-bye. One small mercy in this whole cruel business." And the parents nodded and agreed and went home to the loneliest Christmas of their lives, the Christmas in which questions were answered at last, and love was remembered and wept for, and God was thanked and blamed for not having done more.

Inside the house, Stevie was the last to linger; he had been the strongest all along. Robbie and Betsy were both asleep, and Zap also was asleep in DeAnne's arms. So Stevie was alone with his parents at last, as he had been alone with them when their family was just beginning.

"Ah, Stevie," said Step. "Why did you face him by yourself? Why didn't you *make* us believe you? Why didn't you *explain?*"

"I was the one they came to," said Stevie. "It was my job. Isn't that why we moved here?"

"Not to lose you," said DeAnne.

"I just did what you taught me," said Stevie. "I didn't mean to die. But I didn't know how to *do* it until then. Did I do wrong?"

"Oh, Stevie," said DeAnne, "what you did was noble and good and brave. We knew that's the kind of man you would be, we knew it all along."

"We just thought we'd have a chance to know you longer," said Step. "We thought we'd die long before you. That's how the world is supposed to be."

"Nothing was how it was supposed to be," said Stevie. "Nothing was right, but now it's better, isn't it? I made it better, didn't I?"

"For all the mothers and fathers who won't have to grieve," said Step, "because you stopped that man before he found their sons, yes, you made it better."

"And you're not mad at me for breaking the rules?" asked Stevie.

"No, we're not," said DeAnne. "But we're sad."

"Stevie, will you forgive us?" said Step. "For not understanding? For not *knowing* that what you said to us was true?"

"Sure," he said. "I could see them and you couldn't. I was only mad at you until I figured that out." Then Stevie sighed. "It's so hard, staying here like this."

"I don't want you to go," said DeAnne.

"It's so hard," he said again.

"I love you, Stephen Bolivar Fletcher," said Step. "I love you more than life. I'll miss you so much."

"I'll miss you too, Daddy. I'll miss you too, Mommy. Tell Robbie and Betsy bye for me. And tell Zap about me when he's bigger, because I'm still his biggest brother."

"I love you," said DeAnne. She wanted to tell him what that meant. What *he* meant to her, how it felt to carry him for all those awful months of sickness and how it all was worth it when she held him in her arms, and more than worth it as she watched him grow and saw what a fine boy he was, so much better than she could have hoped for. She wanted to tell him of all her dreams for him, of all the children she wanted him to have, children lucky enough to have him for a father. She wanted to tell him how she had once dreamed of lying on her own deathbed, knowing that it would be all right to die because Stevie was sitting there beside her, holding her hand, and she dreamed that he said, Good-bye, Mother. And then: Be there waiting for me when I come.

"Good-bye, Mother," said Stevie. "Good-bye, Father."

"Good-bye, Door Man," whispered Step.

And DeAnne said, "Oh, Stevie, be there waiting for us when we come."

15

•NEW YEAR•

This is how the Fletchers found their way to the end of 1983: They called the Lowes, who only had to hear two sentences before they came rushing to the house on Chinqua Penn. Mary Anne helped them pack what they'd need for the next few days while Harv telephoned the bishop and Sister Bigelow, who also came. Long after the Fletchers had been taken to the Lowes' house to spend the rest of that long Christmas Eve, the bishop and Sister Bigelow remained, gathering up all the presents that Step had pointed out to them, wrapping those that were still unwrapped, filling the stockings with the candy and gifts that Step and DeAnne had prepared, and then carrying it all to the Lowes' house before any of the little ones awoke. Step

and DeAnne watched quietly as Harv and Mary Anne
made the Fletcher children's Christmas a bright and
happy time.

While they stayed home from church, the rest of
the two Steuben wards gathered, and the much-fought-
over Christmas program was scrapped on the spot.
Instead the bishop, sleepless as he was, told the story of
the innocents of Bethlehem, and then the story of Alma
and Amulek as they watched the deaths of other innocents. And he said, "Such children of God will soon forget
all pain and death, as they are greeted with rejoicing.
It's those who are left behind who need our help and
comfort now."

Help and comfort took many forms in the next few
days. A new but empty condominium was found, and
the landlord, hearing a little of their story, let the
Fletchers have it for the first month free. While the
police line still barred most people from the house on
Chinqua Penn, the elders quorum crossed the line to
carry all the Fletchers' worldly goods to a U-Haul truck,
which was shuttled back and forth until everything was
in place in the Fletchers' new home. They never had to
set foot again in the house where Stevie died.

Sister Bigelow stayed after all the others who
helped with the move had left. "I found something," she
said. "I thought you should be alone when you got it."
She set a brown paper sack on the table. "It was in the
back of the closet." Then she hugged DeAnne and left.

They opened the bag. Inside were two odd-shaped
Christmas presents, wrapped. DeAnne's was heavy. She
opened it to find two stones glued together and painted
to be a rabbit. One stone was the body, the little one was
the head, and there were two construction-paper ears
glued on. On a 3 x 5 card Stevie had written, "The Yard
Bunny." Step's present was much lighter, and harder to
figure out at a glance. Stevie had taken a Cool Whip tub,
glued a used-up plastic tape dispenser to the lid, and

painted the whole thing bright red. On the card was a careful diagram showing a watch dangling from the arm of the tape dispenser, several pens sticking through the hole in the dispenser, and loose change in the Cool Whip tub. There were fifteen pennies in the tub to help him get started. It was a dresser caddy to hold the stuff he kept in his pockets.

They held hands across the table for a long time, the presents framed by their arms.

None of the parents broke the silence about what happened on that Christmas Eve, and Doug Douglas made sure that the journalists heard only the story of Bappy and his son, and a family that had kept the dark secret of the old molester until it was far too late. So it was only pictures of Bappy and his son that ran on the evening news and on the front pages. Doug Douglas would keep in touch with all the families over the years, even after he retired from the Steuben Police Department, but he never brought up the subject of that night or of the year that led to it; they all knew the nature of the threads that bound them together. They shared with him the friendship of people who have been on a long journey together, a journey that is now behind them but can never be forgotten for a single hour.

Doug Douglas called the Fletchers only once. In going back over the records of the case, just for his own peace of mind, he had come up with a correlation between the times their house had been strangely infested by insects or spiders and the nights that boys had died. They confirmed the dates for him. Stevie hadn't been the only one to sense how the world was being torn.

Step and DeAnne buried their oldest boy in a cemetery on the western edge of Steuben, surrounded by thick woods full of birds and animals, a living place. They both knew as they stood beside the grave that their days of wandering were through. They had been anchored now in Steuben, both by the living and by the dead. Little Jeremy would enter Open Doors when the time came; flowers would be tended on this grave.

There were seven other funerals in Steuben during those few days between Christmas and the new year. The bodies of those seven children were accompanied to the grave by the small gifts that had been found with them: A Hot Wheels racer, a fake-ceramic dog, a harmonica, a ball of string, a Star Wars button, a squirt gun, a deck of cards.

Because life must go on and bills must be paid, Step finished the program he had been working on and sent it in, and Agamemnon would pay him and he would begin his next project for them because his family needed him to do it. Just as the family needed DeAnne to tend to Jeremy and Elizabeth and Robbie, the three who remained. It was their needs now that mattered, and she supplied them, and Step, too, as best they could.

On New Year's Day the family members who had flown from Utah to be with them all flew home. The ward members who had dropped all their regular concerns to help the Fletchers now picked them up again. Gradually life settled back to normal for all of them.

Even for the Fletchers, life settled. Not back to normal, for there was no going back for them. Rather their life settled into a new way, a new road. There was always in Step's mind a sense of someone watching, as if he could always turn at the moment of some triumph and say, See that? Pretty good, hey? And the one who watched would say, Neat. Neat, Dad.

In DeAnne's mind she saw him as a light in the distance, a beacon. If I always look toward that light, she thought, if I always walk straight toward it, then someday, even though it's very far away, I'll reach that goal.

They remembered Stevie on his birthday every year, and told stories about him until Robbie and

Elizabeth could almost recite them all from memory. Every now and then Robbie would refer to the Christmas when Stevie's friends came, though the family never actually talked about that night.

One other thing was lost, too, that Christmas Eve. Step no longer called Robbie "Robot" or "Road Bug"; Betsy became Elizabeth to him; and Jeremy was Jeremy. With Step not using them, the nicknames soon died out, except when Robbie now and then teased Elizabeth by saying, "We used to call you Betsy Wetsy, you know." As the children grew up they lost all memory of their parents calling each other Junk Man and Fish Lady. They wouldn't have believed it if you told them; no one told them.

It wasn't that Step or DeAnne actually decided that the nicknames ought to stop. It's just that those names were part of a set, and it didn't feel right to use any of them unless you could use them all. But someday they would use them, they knew. Someday they would use all those old names, when Door Man met them on the other side.

ORSON SCOTT CARD has won several Hugo and Nebula Awards for his works of speculative fiction, among them the *Ender* series, most recently *Xenocide*, and *The Tales of Alvin Maker*. He lives in Greensboro, North Carolina, with his wife and three children.

MORE THAN FRIENDS
Barbara Delinsky
The Maxwells and the Popes are two families whose lives are interwoven like the threads of a beautiful, yet ultimately delicate, tapestry. When their idyllic lives are unexpectedly shattered by one event, their faith in each other — and in themselves — is put to the supreme test.

"Intriguing women's fiction." — *Publishers Weekly*

CITY OF GOLD
Len Deighton
Amid the turmoil of World War II, Rommel's forces in Egypt relentlessly advance across the Sahara aided by ready access to Allied intelligence. Sent to Cairo on special assignment, Captain Bert Cutler's mission is formidable: whatever the risk, whatever the cost, he must catch Rommel's spy.

"Wonderful." — *Seattle Times/Post-Intelligencer*

DEATH PENALTY
William J. Coughlin
Former hot-shot attorney Charley Sloan gets a chance to resurrect his career with the case of a lifetime — an extortion scam that implicates his life-long mentor, a respected judge. Battling against inner demons and corrupt associates, Sloan's quest for the truth climaxes in one dramatic showdown of justice.

"Superb!"
— *The Detroit News*